For All

The

Wrong Reasons

Bill Robinet

Billville Press
Veneta, Oregon

Other books by Bill Robinet and Billville Press:

By The Skin Of My Teeth, A Cropduster's Story

By The Skin Of My Teeth, A Cropduster's Story is an exciting auto-biographical account of Bill Robinet's experiences cropdusting in the 1950's. Still available from Billville Press or from Border's or Barnes & Noble bookstores.

For All The Wrong Reasons

Bill Robinet

Billville Press
Veneta, Oregon

For All The Wrong Reasons
By: Bill Robinet

Published by:

    Billville Press
    87130 Muirland Dr.
    Veneta, OR 97487

All rights reserved. No part of this book may be reproduced or transmitted in any form or by any means, electronic or mechanical, including photocopying, recording or by any information storage and retrieval system without written permission from the author, except for the inclusion of brief quotations in a review.

    Copyright ©2002
    Printed in the United States of America

    Library of Congress Catalog Card Number:
    Cataloging in progress.

ISBN 0-9657473-2-8

All characters in this novel are fictitious. Any resemblance to living persons, present or past, is coincidental.

Dedicated to:
My Uncle Lenny
The last of an era.

Chapter 1

It is generally accepted in aviation circles that pilots get the girls. What is not admitted is that flight instructors get more girls, and anyone with a lower rating has to be satisfied with the leftovers. This is why Billy Cotton wanted to become a Flight Instructor. He just didn't feel he was getting his share. His appetite yearned for more than his wallet could handle and available time would permit. Flight instruction was the vehicle he was certain would fill his needs, no matter that he wasn't a very good pilot and would ultimately end up being a worse instructor.

These aspirations manifested themselves in 1948 during his senior year of high school at Phoenix's main institution of secondary education, Phoenix Union High School with an enrollment of approximately 5,000. It had the distinction of being the place of learning that could count among its graduates the likes of Senator Barry Goldwater, several Arizona Governors, including Paul Fannin, and the famed WWI fighter pilot, ace, balloon buster and Medal of Honor recipient Frank Luke Jr. To pay homage to the hero, the name Luke shows up at many locations around the Valley with the most prominent being Luke AFB.

Billy wasn't particularly attracted to flying. As a matter of fact he was afraid of airplanes, what they did, and what they could do to you. As far back as he could remember airplanes ultimately ended up in a heap of junk with a dead pilot as a result. Stories on radio and in the comic strips depicting aviation as it was in the Thirties with the associated fatalities, as well as factual reports of the disasters of WWII helped fuel the fires of his fears. He was downright petrified. He had never been in an airplane and up until that time had no intentions of changing his mind.

He was also afraid of dying. The nuns were to blame for that, especially Sister Olympus. The fear was instilled firmly in his psyche during his grammar school days, more particularly when it was opined that the good and Holy Sister was experiencing the trauma and discomfort of that time in her

For All The Wrong Reasons

life when her child bearing years were finally a thing of the past. His parents, wanting Billy to have a good Catholic education, thought it was worth the price of a thousand dollar per year tuition fee for the privilege, regardless that he would carry some internal scars that would affect his behavior for the rest of his life.

The nuns pounded the church dogma up his ass involving sins. They preached that there were basically two kinds. The more severe of the two was of the cardinal type commonly referred to as a mortal sin. This one damned the offender to an unbearable fiery inferno for eternity, with no consideration whatsoever for reprieve. An example of this sin would be the deliberate absence from Sunday Mass.

The other was a less offensive kind referred to as a venial sin. Simple lying or contemplating "dirty" thoughts of a sexual nature were examples falling under this category, warranting a limited term in an equally fiery hole called Purgatory. The term of incarceration was limited, with the length determined by the number of "sin" points accumulated since the last absolution. There were ways to wipe the slate clean or to shorten the term in Purgatory, but the details are not germane to this narration and are therefore left for others to explore.

The above mentioned indiscretions and other sins were something Billy did in the daily routine of his existence, so it was easy to see why he was in a constant state of nervousness during the most impressionable years of his life. The constant fear of dying and going to Hell or Purgatory didn't stop him from committing the transgressions, it only made him afraid to do so, knowing full well the consequences. As far as Billy Cotton was concerned it was best to stay alive as long as possible to avoid the inevitable curse of the hereafter.

So thanks to the Sisters of God, who didn't give a damn that they were ruining his life, and who as a by-product of his education beat the shit out of him every time they caught him at some naughty transgression. It was little wonder that he was afraid to meet his maker, and in turn was afraid of airplanes, because they represented a way of expediting his journey to the not so enticing existence of the hereafter.

All of these factors contributing to his odd outlook and behavior were fortified by the recent tragedy involving Frank Luke Jr. III, a distant nephew of the famed WWI ace and balloon buster. He ended his life a year or so

Chapter 1

earlier when he augered in while performing a first class buzz job in an Airknocker (Aeronca Champion). It was his last buzz job and the grand finale that provided him a one-way ticket to join his great uncle in the happy balloon-busting hunting grounds of the hereafter. He managed to stick the airplane in the side of Hole-In-The-Rock Mountain that is located within the boundaries of Phoenix's Papago Park.

The mountain, which is no more than two to three hundred feet high, is a solid rock formation with a large hole running through it near the top one-third. If he was trying to fly the airplane through the hole, he almost made it, evidence the large smudge that remained half-way into the aperture until the rains, that almost never come to the valley, washed it away. However some argued that it was the sandblasting from the more frequent duststorms that eventually removed the stigma from his survivors. But in the meantime it turned out to be a tourist attraction with more than frequent curiosity seekers, including Billy Cotton and his buddies.

Even with all of the horrors of flying firmly etched in his mind, Billy was going to fly airplanes in spite of himself. Actually his eventual affinity for this niche evolved for the most part from peer pressure. Normally one thinks of peer pressure and drugs or cigarettes in the same context. Drugs were not the in thing during that era, but flying in the "Valley of the Sun" was. Therefore if he was going to belong to the "group" he had to indulge. His five or six buddies that comprised the "group" finally obtained his interest and eventually talked him into joining the Phoenix Union High School Flying Club. He was launched on his new adventure.

The club, indeed it was more like an entire Phoenix Schools System's program, was unique. At the time the other participating institutions were the Phoenix Junior College, which was part of the Phoenix school systems and the central participant of the aviation program, Phoenix Union High School, Saint Mary's High School, and the only other high school in the city, North High.

The club's physical facilities were a large two-story building and an adjacent maintenance hanger, located on the north side of Sky Harbor Municipal Airport. The building more resembled a stately residence than an office building, with a second story balcony spanning its entire width. It was accessed from the pilot lounge and afforded a wide view of the airplane parking ramp and runway. Besides the spacious lounge, other areas included

For All The Wrong Reasons

offices for the flight instructors and the Director of Operations, two classrooms, and a Link Trainer room.

Unlike their counterparts who either free-lanced or instructed at other fixed based operations, the Director and flight instructors at this institution were certified high school teachers. As such they were on the school system's payroll with all the benefits and wage rates afforded other teachers at the high schools or junior college. This provided an additional benefit for the student, as there was no additional cost added to the airplane rental for dual instruction. At other flying schools the student was required to pay for the instructor separately.

The rental rate for the Airknocker (Aeronca Champion) was a big two dollars an hour with fuel included. During that period of time, Hobbs hour meters were not normally installed in rental airplanes. These came later and were used to record the actual time the engine operated and as such the instrument was used to provide the renter with an accurate means to charge the pilot. Nor were most of the airplanes equipped with recording tachometers, which was an alternate means for determining flying time.

The method of choice therefore was much like one uses when renting a horse, a time piece that is normally fastened to one's wrist, otherwise known as a wrist watch. This provided an additional benefit for the students at the school. When they scheduled the airplane for the usual period of an hour, they flew for something like an hour and a half, reporting an even hour for the purpose of the billing. It made for some very cheap flying time.

In the fleet of airplanes there were six or so Airknockers, a four place Stinson Voyager, and an Aeronca Chief. The Chief and the Stinson were the only two airplanes equipped with electrical systems and radios. Sky Harbor did have a control tower that used the old frequency of 3105 kc, but radios were not required to operate from the airport. Not being so equipped, the pilot of an Airknocker relied on light signals from the tower for operational control.

This presented no problem for the tower people as the no radio airplanes all entered the traffic pattern from the south side of the airport, with the air carriers and other more sophisticated flying machines with the ability to communicate approaching from the north. The main hard surfaced runway was located along the north edge of the airport providing some convenience for these airplanes. On the south side of and adjacent to the runway was a large gravel patch of ground that could land three airplanes abreast

Chapter 1

without interfering with the traffic on the runway. This is where the Airknockers and other no radio junk landed. All departures were from the hard surface.

To be sure, it was the graveled area that came to be referred to as the grass mat that Billy and his fellow students obtained all of their landing practice. The reference to grass was a gross stretch based entirely on wishful thinking. The only green substance that flourished there were immature bullhead sticker plants that eventually dried out producing small, hard and very sharp thorns that proved devastating to the tires.

The students would enter the traffic pattern from the south side of the airport, and when firmly set up on the downwind leg could expect a green light from the control tower. The first airplane in line for landing would establish a final approach to line up with the far north side of the patch; the second would take the center portion, and the third, if applicable would use the south edge. On the landing roll out the pilot would continue straight ahead to the far end, across a white line, stop and turn the airplane to face the tower, and when it was clear to cross the runway, would be given a steady green light, indicating clearance to cross and continue to the parking area. A red signal, of course, meant that there was activity on the runway and the student held his position until he received the appropriate clearance to proceed.

As an additional requirement for acceptance in the flying program, Billy, as well as the others at Phoenix Union, had to enroll in the aeronautics course, which was provided by the physics department. Appropriate high school credit was earned as a result. This was more than acceptable to Billy because it looked like the type of course he could coast through with no undue effort.

He wasn't a particularly disciplined student anyway. He didn't like school, and because of that he barely managed to squeak out a "C" average throughout his high school years. In defense of this less than stellar performance, he bragged to those who were concerned about his future that his substandard grade average was a result of not having to exercise the discipline of completing outside study or home assignments. No telling what his grade point average might have been if he had applied himself like most conscientious students did. After all he was no dummy. But there was no room in his life for distractions afforded by homework and extra curricular activities, as his

For All The Wrong Reasons

part-time job and play schedule took up most of his waking hours.

Since his parents had no money left after attending to the essential needs of providing for a large family, Billy had to work part-time to make the installment payments on his Cushman motor scooter and to support his flying habit. This he did by working several evenings a week for a local dairy, washing and servicing the delivery trucks when they returned from their routes. As an unofficial fringe benefit associated with the job, he was able to also service his motor scooter, which included a full tank of gas at the end of his shift. Every little bit helped.

Most of his remaining free time was taken up by hanging around the flying school's facilities at the airport, or drinking beer at the Rainbow Tavern with his buddies. At these sessions they would fantasize about the vast realm of possible benefits they could derive from the use of a pilot's license, if and when they were fortunate enough to earn one. The number one fantasy was that of a fighter pilot hired on by mercenaries or some foreign government to do battle with the enemy. It was rumored that the Jews were hiring pilots to shoot down all of the bad Arabs and in addition to the high pay, they were awarding big bonuses for every kill. The downside was that if you were captured by the enemy you were automatically executed. But how could that happen? Nobody flew airplanes better than American pilots. It had to be a sure thing that after a short tour of duty one would be financially fixed for life.

There was also the same opportunity in China. The Reds were in the process of running Chiang Kai-shek and company clear the hell out of the country and he needed fighter pilots. There were more than enough wars to go around. Cropdusting was another easy way to a sure quick route from rags to riches. And so as the beer flowed, the avenues blossomed, until the man behind the bar gave the familiar signal of blinking the lights indicating it was time to come back down to earth and go home.

There was still a long row to hoe before any of these prospects could become a reality. At this stage of the game, the prospect of even obtaining a license seemed remote. Flying airplanes was still foreign and unnatural to Billy. As far a he was concerned, if God wanted man to fly he would have issued the proper documentation at birth. Billy wouldn't have accepted the fact that these heavier than air, cloth covered pieces of shit could get off of the ground if he hadn't witnessed the fact on a daily basis by merely looking

Chapter 1

up at any time of the day. He was told in school that some wop named Bernoulli had worked it all out. Actually he was later informed that Bernoulli wasn't from Italy after all, but from one of those other foreign countries. What did those foreigners know anyway?

Move anything fast enough through the air and it will sustain flight; even a barn door, his teacher maintained. The fact that it was a foreigner and a pot-bellied, bald-headed physics teacher that arrived at these conclusions didn't do anything to fortify his faith in the system. If they knew so much, why hadn't they succeeded to higher goals in life? So throughout the aeronautics course he merely took the theories and other information for what he thought it was worth, a big "C", and plodded along staring at the clock on the classroom wall in anticipation of the end of the day when he could get out and do the bigger and better things on his agenda.

If the educators knew then what they have since found out, they would have concluded that Billy was in fact suffering from what is known as "Attention Deficit Disorder" and as a solution would have given him gratuitous "A's" instead of the hard earned "C's" on which he was skating by.

The rest of the gang had already started their flying lessons when Billy went out for his first flight. His instructor was an equally mindless, lazy but handsome Mexican, whose only ambition was to screw all of the female students he could corral, and drink all of the beer that his budget could tolerate. In the case of the female students, there were only two enrolled in the flying program. Of these, he managed to declare one for himself, yielding the other to the School's Director. So it was no surprise to Billy when his newly appointed instructor approached the new assignment with less than enthusiastic fervor.

His name was Jose (Joe) Mora. Like most of the other bums that flew airplanes, he was a pilot during the Big War. However, his military career was short and without distinction. He was relegated to flying P-39's; the worst fighter plane developed for WWII. Most of them were generously donated to Russia for their war effort under the lend-lease program. Others were converted to flying pinball machines to be shot at by our own for gunnery practice.

Through the miracle of American ingenuity they were electronically configured to activate an electrical enunciator when hit with a plastic bullet. A more detailed explanation was beyond Joe's mental capacity and communi-

For All The Wrong Reasons

cation skills to adequately explain the concept or the mechanics of the process. In any event the airplanes were literally used for target practice by the gunners in the bombers, and Joe flew one of them for that purpose.

This took place over the Gila Bend gunnery range located between Gila Bend, Arizona and the Mexican border. It was never intended that the airplanes be actually shot out of the sky but to merely register or record electrically when successfully hit. Supposedly, there was enough armor plating and other protective measures, that the bullets, other than recording hits were not to penetrate or otherwise harm the airplane or its contents, Joe Mora.

But as he related the war story, one of the bullets managed to penetrate the radiator or some other vital part of his cooling system. As one might expect, in due course the engine overheated and seized, and the airplane became a glider. Joe bailed out. He spent the rest of the day in the desert of the gunnery range in the sparse shade of a Palo Verde tree with the rattlesnakes, gila monsters and scorpions, until somebody could muster a jeep and venture out to fetch him.

Being shot at all of the time did nothing to bolster Joe's self esteem. Being a Mexican only made matters worse. This and his reduced mental capacity hampered whatever ambition he may have had to seek a position with the airlines, or as a corporate pilot for some other promising young firm. But Joe had at least one distinguishing attribute. He was very handsome, on the order of Anthony Quinn, the famous Mexican movie actor. If he would have only learned to keep his mouth shut, some of these higher paying opportunities might have come his way. Somehow when he opened his mouth to utter a phrase all that came out were heavily accented unintelligible, guttural sonifications that resembled speech. It made it difficult to hold a simple conversation with him.

His only other ticket to success was his Flight Instructor's rating. With the instructor's rating and belonging to a minority class, he applied for and was accepted into the Phoenix School Systems as a full-fledged teacher assigned to the flying program with all benefits and privileges accorded thereof. At the time, the Phoenix School Systems not only maintained jurisdiction over the high schools but the Phoenix Junior College as well. This is why the Aeronautical program was consolidated to include all of the schools.

For the flight instructors to obtain their State Teacher's Certificate, an essential piece of paper, it was necessary for them to receive additional

Chapter 1

schooling (or in the case of Joe, omit the word additional) in the evenings or during the summers over a two-year period. Judging by how most of the student generation of the time evolved, the topics of study must have centered around, "How to transform a well rounded, normally adjusted kid into a shiftless basket case."

In the meantime however, the flight instructors were allowed to exercise their teaching privileges based on a temporary certificate, provided they worked diligently toward the permanent one within a two-year period. This applied to all three instructors since none of them had the necessary degrees that would all but automatically qualify them. So as a remedy for their academic deficiencies, Joe and the other two instructors attended evening classes, while at the same time poisoned the minds of Billy Cotton and the rest of his cohorts during the day. This went on until they ultimately received the proper credentials, along with the respectability and other fringe benefits enjoyed by their peers, who had to struggle through four years of college, and sometimes graduate school, to earn the same license that these people were practically handed on a silver platter.

Chapter 2

Billy's first flying lesson was also his first airplane ride. From day one it was pounded up his ass that if an object went fast enough it was bound to fly. Take a rock for example. Throw it and it sails through the air, for a while anyway. That wasn't the part that had Billy worried. It was when the rock hit the ground that didn't seem to set well. With all this wisdom imparted by his loyal buddies, he embarked on the first flying lesson.

After all of the niceties of preparing the airplane for flight, which among other things consisted of listening to Joe ramble on in his Spanish-accented recitations on the necessities of a thorough preflight inspection, they embarked on his first adventure through the great wild blue. The advancing of the throttle all but took his breath away. The Airknocker rattled off down the runway with Joe adding to the ear-splitting noise in an attempt to belt out some song about getting it off in the wild blue yonder or some such place. His delivery turned out to be a cross between the Mexican-American country singer Freddie Fender and Louis Armstrong. The noise generated by the engine, the loose fittings on the airplane, and the air rushing past the airframe added to Joe's enthusiasm for song and only made him louder.

Initially it appeared to Billy that they were going fast enough along the ground accelerating to a respectable speed, but as soon as the Airknocker became airborne, it seemed to stop in midair. There was no sensation of speed at all. He was frightened and was beginning to think they were going to wind up rolled up in a ball the way the rock did, only worse. He would have screamed, only no one would have been able to hear him with all of the noise Joe and the airplane were making. So with eyes as big as saucers, he held on as the Airknocker made its way out to the practice area while being serenaded by the Mexican hillbilly in his rendition of WWII esprit de corps

For All The Wrong Reasons

songs.

The rest of the orientation ride was no better than the take-off. To alleviate his anxieties, Joe directed Billy's attention to the airspeed indicator that was registering 60 mph as soon as the airplane became airborne and increased to something on the order of 80 mph later. It was hard for him to believe that this piece of shit was actually mobiling through the air at 80 mph, but it must be true because they were putting distance between themselves and the airport.

The first lesson was forty-five minutes long. It went by very quickly. For the most part it amounted to Joe showing off his airmanship and demonstrating the effect of controls to his student. When Billy tried his hand at steering the airplane through the air, all he managed to exhibit was his lack of coordination. It was all very confusing and it took Joe's superb skills to sort out the discombobulations inflicted on the airplane by this unworthy neophyte. Joe was not at all bashful in pointing out his superiority with the handling of the airplane and if Billy Cotton applied himself and submitted himself completely to his mentor, some day he too might be able to fly as skillfully as the Master.

Before Billy realized it they were just a couple of miles south of the airport in the process of entering the traffic pattern for the landing. This was the entry leg and consisted of flying northbound perpendicular to the direction of the runway, and when less than a quarter of a mile from the landing apron a ninety degree turn to the west established the downwind leg for a landing to the east. This is where the control tower directed the light signal to the pilot for either a landing clearance or denial, whichever the case may be. In this instance it was a green light, which Joe made a particular effort to point out to his student.

The next turn was to the north to establish the base leg, and when almost lined up with the intended landing path, Joe started another right turn to the east to establish the final approach. They were lined up along the north edge of the gravel pit (grass mat) to make room for other airplanes that might be following in the pattern and who might want to land at the same time on the same surface. When Joe knew he had the runway made, he chopped the power; the cockpit got very quiet. With the one stroke of the throttle, from 2,000 rpm to idle, Joe converted the Airknocker from powered airplane to glider. They touched down in good fashion, rolled straight ahead to the

Chapter 2

other side of a prominently wide white line, then stopped and turned the airplane ninety degrees to the left, facing north in the direction of the control tower.

The tower was located in a second story room on top of the airport administrative offices. Although not very high, with glass on all four sides, it commanded a respectable view of all traffic in the area. After a few patient seconds the tower beamed a steady red light indicating that our heroes should hold their position. Joe explained that this happens when another no radio airplane is landing on the mat at the same time and they should wait as directed lest they tangle wings, or that another airplane was using the hard surfaced runway. In this case it was an airplane on approach to the runway since any other airplane on the mat would be behind them and as a result would be no factor. Before long they received their anticipated steady green light, and taxied north across the runway to the parking area.

They shut off the engine, secured the airplane with tie down ropes, and adjourned to the school's pilot lounge. Joe must have been exhausted after that forty-five minute ordeal, for he immediately plopped down on the couch, stretching out the full length, while shouting out commands for Billy to gather up the paperwork and bring it over to him, so he could properly terminate the lesson by completing all of the necessary entries. All of this took place while Joe was flat on his back, which was a position, that Billy Cotton and the rest of the students would be accustomed to seeing throughout the course of their flying activities.

Lesson number one was over, but not before Billy had to retrieve a Coke from the refrigerator for Joe's consumption. Flight instruction had to be a hard and trying affair. Already Billy was gaining respect for his flight instructor, if not for his insouciant behavior, then for his superb display of airmanship. Being a flight instructor may not be such a bad deal after all.

The back alley seminars with the gang helped clarify some of the elements of Billy's first flying lesson. On that first trip he was more pre-occupied with his nausea and perspectives than the control elements that embodied the lesson. He was flabbergasted by the view afforded from 2,000 feet. It was awesome! The buildings were but miniature models with tiny cars scurrying around like so many ants. Joe's contribution to his impressions was to present the whole affair with an air of superiority and arrogance; the con-

For All The Wrong Reasons

queror of the *GREAT MYSTERY OF FLIGHT*.

Actually, the back alley seminar was really a drinking bout in the dark corners of the Rainbow Tavern. But to some degree it amounted to a post flight critique adding more to Billy's understanding of the elements of the lesson than Joe was able or willing to contribute. Jack Monett and Don Schooner, two of Billy's closest friends who were primarily responsible for Billy getting involved in the first place, were the principle disseminators of information at that meeting. They were farther along in the process and understood the mechanics of flight. It was because of these two that Billy stayed with the program and derived his only interest, knowledge, and development.

During that era one was expected to solo the airplane after receiving only about six hours of dual instruction. Joe liked to cooperate along those lines, not necessarily because he believed in the practice, but because he was extremely lazy and would just as soon log "couch time" on the sofa in the lounge. The pay was the same whether he was in the airplane or screwing off. His other less-than-noble motive was to elevate his stature in the eyes of his peers and other students. He thought that the sooner he could get a student soloed the more it indicated his superiority as an instructor; never mind that some of them had not achieved the proficiency required to undertake the challenge. So between Joe and his pals, Billy was closing in nicely on the magic six-hour number. Still he was to be the last one in the group to fly it alone. The fact that the others mastered the art spurred him on.

Flying the airplane was becoming noticeably less difficult. He no longer became nauseated, and Joe's incessant attempts at song became tolerable. The two thousand foot separation between the airplane and terra firma was less intimidating, and his attempts at mastering the controls were improving. Successful takeoffs and landings were even within the realm of possibilities. So while he was grinding it out in the Airknocker with Joe in the back seat chewing in his ear, Jack and the others were soloing the airplanes, comparing war stories, and telling of the death defying close calls and other perilous feats that they experienced. Billy couldn't wait to get involved. In the meantime he would settle for another beer.

On the day of the first solo, there was no one less ready and less capable of flying the airplane than our hero. If there was to be any more time and

Chapter 2

effort expended on dual instruction necessary to tune the candidate to a point where safety, if not proficiency, was the consideration, then the magic six hour parameter would fall by the wayside. Joe couldn't have that. His reputation as a super instructor was at stake. Thus true to tradition, Joe terminated the touch and go (take-offs and landings) practice session early, got out of the airplane, instructed his student to go out and complete two touch and go's followed by a full stop landing, then adjourned to his favorite haven, the couch.

How could something be a disaster and a success at the same time? Well that's exactly what Billy's first solo was. The landings were interrupted by go-arounds. The successful ones were atrocious at best, but the airplane, through Divine providence, came out unscathed. For Joe it was all part of a day's work. Throughout the ordeal he remained in his favorite position on the couch sucking on a Coke, and fantasizing that more of his students should be of the opposite sex. Billy, the timid ignorant kid who had absolutely no aptitude for the adventures of the big sky, nor respect for the airplane, had managed to conquer the great mystery of flight. He was one of the boys now. He could now follow in the footsteps of his hero and mentor, Joe Mora. So as soon as the niceties such as backslapping, shirt cutting, and story telling ceremonies wound down, he slunk over to the couch to try it on for size. This is where he belonged, and to be sure it was where he was destined to spend most of the time during the rest of his life.

Chapter 3

With a lot of practice Billy got quite proficient with the Airknocker, in spite of the fact that he didn't know what he was doing, how he was doing it, or why it should be done. Since direct supervision was not high on the list of the instructor's priorities, some of the students would do what they could to push the envelope, to add a little spice or excitement to their lives. The events they indulged in made for good conversation later on in the dark corners of the Rainbow Tavern.

More often than not Jack and Billy would manage to schedule airplanes for the same period. During these anticipated and mischievous excursions to the practice area, they would take extra precautions to depart the airport separately. This was designed to avoid suspicion. After leaving the traffic pattern they would fly to an area east of Scottsdale, over the Indian reservation to form up for fun and games.

The reservation, which was mostly unpopulated open range, was inhabited by large herds of wild horses. These were thought to be mostly runaways from their Indian masters over a long period of time, propagating into large herds, rather than the romanticized version of being descendants from those of the conquistadors. In any case, the horses provided some of the more entertaining challenges for the group of would be fighter pilots.

The first order of business was to locate a herd. Then the neophyte pilots would dive down on the unsuspecting horses as though on a strafing run, scattering them until "hell wouldn't have it," pulling up and completing a low-level turn for another pass while flying some semblance of a formation. Any one of these maneuvers was enough for them to end up dead. For some reason God looks after most fools. As if one or two passes wasn't enough, they would run the horses for over an hour before going home. Total flying time was maybe an hour and a half. Time recorded on the time sheets for the purpose of billing, an even hour. It was all in a day's work. Back to the

For All The Wrong Reasons

Rainbow Tavern for debriefing.

Dog fighting was also a great sport. Forming up over the same area, Billy and three or four of his flying pals, would participate in an effort to kill themselves. John Wing, representing the Chinese contingent of the group, gave full meaning to the term "chicken." His bold and fearless tactics were too much for the others. They attributed his fearlessness to his agnosticism and genetic predisposition. He would come sliding in on his buddies for the kill, and if they did not yield to his challenge, at least two airplanes would have been seen fluttering to the ground in a tangled mess. It wasn't fair. This was supposed to be a game, but not a game of chicken. He played it that if the other airplane did not yield it was all over for both of them. Long conversations were held with John in an effort to get him to back off, but all he would do at the notion was to laugh and relish his position.

His conduct in an airplane was an extension of his philosophical behavior. He showed complete disregard for his own safety and that of anyone else's in his company. That included driving, hunting and now flying. Like the others he was blessed with only a student pilot's license and nine lives. Normally in the Phoenix area, the Chinese were a close-knit group, but because of his attitude and recklessness, his community all but abandoned him, leaving his flying buddies to fill the void. This was part of the reason he took up flying. In spite of his character flaws, or maybe because of them, the other fledgling pilots accepted him.

Ultimately John was kicked out of the program for screwing up on a cross-country. As part of the training, students were assigned a cross-country exercise as one of the requirements for a private license. The first cross-country was with the instructor and subsequent ones were solo. For John's solo cross-country he was to fly from Phoenix Sky Harbor west to Litchfield Park, on to Gila Bend, then east to Casa Grande where he was to land, take on fuel, and return to Phoenix. Ordinarily the trip from Phoenix to Casa Grande via Litchfield Park and Gila Bend was possible with ample fuel reserves, but not in John's case.

In the vicinity of Gila Bend he jumped a large flock of ducks heading off in the direction of Yuma. Being an avid duck hunter, he was naturally curious as to their destination so that he might invade their nesting grounds at some future date. In trail he flew-off in the direction of Yuma, a heading that took him in the opposite direction from Casa Grande.

Chapter 3

Tiring of the game he was playing with the ducks and realizing his fuel situation, he turned the corner and instead of stopping at Gila Bend to top off his tank, continued on to Casa Grande. He almost made it. In fact he came within ten miles of making it before his engine breathed its last. The only place to plop it down was the bale storage yard of a cotton gin not hardly big enough for an airplane even with a good pilot.

But this wasn't just any ol' pilot. This was John Wing the confident and fearless ace who was skilled far beyond his total flying time. His dead-stick landing was so good that Mr. Farraday (Boots Farraday to his good friends and lovers,) the school's director, paid him superlative compliments on the excellent job he did before giving him the ax.

Putting the airplane down successfully was only the beginning of John's adventure. His job wasn't over yet. The first thing he did was push the Airknocker over to a place close to the building for protection. Then he embarked on a search to procure enough fuel to get him to the airport. If he would have settled for car gas, which was available next door, the result would have been his complete undoing because the yard wasn't long enough for a successful take-off. But John felt that airplanes needed airplane fuel, so he was settling for nothing less than what was available at the Casa Grande airport.

By the time he got there it was all over for him. The CAA had already instituted a search and as procedure dictated they called the manager of the Casa Grande airport to see if John had made it that far. He had, but without an airplane. The manager couldn't believe it when this Chinese guy fitting the description walks up asking for a can and five gallons of gas. It was his day of good fortune. He was sure he was in for a reward or at least something on the order of a commendation.

As the drama unfolded, Bruce, John's instructor, arrived in the Stinson accompanied by the first string, Mr. Farraday, who immediately took charge of the whole fiasco. It was apparently the most exciting thing that had happened to him since the "Big War," and he was going to ride it for all of the mileage he could get. The first thing they did was to drive out to the gin to assess the situation there. Then they flew John back to Phoenix and told him to go home and not to come back until he was summoned.

Ultimately it was necessary to pull the wings off the airplane and truck it back home. Flying it out of the short field was out of the question. John,

For All The Wrong Reasons

however, maintained for as long as anyone would listen that he could have done it. There was no doubt in anyone's mind that given the chance and had he not been stopped at the Casa Grande airport, he would have tried it.

John and Billy had at least one thing in common. Neither one had any respect for the airplane. The big point stressed in the ground school class and other less formal lectures by the gurus at large was to have respect for the airplane. That puzzled Billy somewhat because all his life he was taught to show respect for his parents, elders, church officials, and other prominent members of society, but never a mention was made of airplanes. In fact he even respected Joe Mora even though he recognized him as a worthless piece of shit. As time wore on, he would come to emulate Joe more and more, which was no portent to a promising future. But how could he stretch the logic to equate that piece of junk of an Airknocker sitting out there on the ramp to these other cogs in the wheel of life. The fact that the airplane was called an "Airknocker," a bastardized version of Aeronca, was an indication that others must have shared his view.

It gnawed on him to the point of finally challenging the concept. It happened during a ground school class conducted by the almighty Mr. Farraday, the school's director. Outside of earshot he was disrespectfully referred to as Boots, but otherwise it was Mr. Farraday with a forced reverence. Instead of teaching, Mr. Farraday would lecture by talking down to his captive audience, recounting one war story after another, as "has-beens" habitually do. It was always in the vein that the peon students could learn from his great and vast experiences. Nothing much in the way of new knowledge was derived from his lectures. No one had the courage to object or to go over his head with a complaint.

When the subject of "having respect for your airplane" came up, it was embellished by a liberal splashing of personal encounters and other never ending bullshit stories. Boots never seemed to run out of them, and if he did, he would go over the same old ground again and again, oblivious to the fact that his audience had heard them before and couldn't have been less interested.

Billy saw his opportunity to air his misgivings. He brought up his concerns, professing his philosophical differences and his unwillingness to adulate a lifeless assemblage of tube and fabric. He let it all out, rambling on in a hangdog fashion much in the same way and delivery of one leaving his

Chapter 3

church or girl friend for another. It was difficult. Words would not flow smoothly. What started out as a simple question ended up as a confession. Throughout, Boots displayed the expression of someone who had a dog turd stuck to his mustache.

When Billy finally finished regurgitating his sense of values and priorities, Boots at first appeared shocked, then offended. Actually this was his piece of cake, his stage and he was the star, his opportunity to stand tall, to exert his uncompromising authority, and to be a bully without actually being accused of being one. Because who could argue against motherhood, apple pie, and respect for one's airplane? Billy had shit on the flag, desecrated the credo, and Boots was going to make him pay while the others looked on.

Before the hour was up Billy had less respect for both the venerated Mr. Farraday and the adulated piece-of-shit-of-an-airplane than he had before. Nothing Boots raved about changed Billy's mind. It only affirmed his beliefs that these people were self-indulgent, egotistical hypocrites and show-offs, using the airplane not as a vehicle for travel, but to thrust themselves into the category of super-humans to be adored by those naïve enough to buy it. Boots Farraday was the stereotype, the poster boy.

This adoration was made to order for those whose motives were to indulge in the sport of womanizing. There was no room in this macho club for the opposite sex. They were the prey.

The contingent of students did include two females. Both were enrolled at the Phoenix Junior College. Cathy, the older of the two, filled in on a part time basis as the school's secretary-typist, while Nancy just showed up to hang around, talk flying, and exert her prowess as the master of the airplane. Both came across as being uppity. They gave their male counterparts the impression that they were lowering themselves by having to occasionally converse with the other students.

There were only two things that Nancy and Billy had in common. They shared Joe Mora as their instructor and they both wanted to get screwed. Speculation by the back booth crew (reference to the Rainbow Tavern) had it that the stick time she was getting from Joe involved more than from the controls attached to the airplane. This scientific conclusion resulted from her obvious conduct, as she spent most of her time hovering over Joe as he lay prone on the couch, indulging in idle chatter, and at the same time trying

For All The Wrong Reasons

to make it appear that their discussions were professional, concerning the finer points of flying airplanes.

In the meantime Cathy seemed more than devoted to Mr. Farraday. She logged many an hour in his office behind closed doors, and most of the time when she emerged, the top page of her secretarial pad was as blank as when she went in. Who was she trying to kid anyway? They were both making it with Joe and Boots, and the thought made Billy horny as hell. He couldn't wait to get some of the action. He would work harder toward that rating.

Joe was inclined to accept Billy's indifference toward the airplane and the strange attitude he exhibited. He was becoming more attuned to agreeing with the maverick student's philosophy regarding the respect thing, and when they would fly together, the pre-flight inspection was accomplished in a more or less haphazard fashion. The other pilots, instructors included, would go over the airplane with a fine tooth comb, closely examining all of the controls, attach fittings, tires, brakes, oil and fuel quantity, Billy, when not watched, would ensure that the airplane had oil and fuel, and for good measure he would kick the tires, climb in and scream for a prop.

Although they never discussed it, Billy always suspected that Joe held the same views as he did, but after the ass-chewing by Boots in the classroom, Billy made sure that in front of all concerned, including his instructor, he would do whatever it took either verbally or in action to avert any suspicion about how he really felt. As far as Mr. Farraday was concerned, Billy's conversion was complete. He had transformed a wayward, disrespectful upstart into a promising young aviator with a future. He was very proud.

Joe was less than concerned with Billy's conduct or how he felt, as long as he didn't wreck the Airknocker. After all his reputation as an instructor was at stake and this was one job he didn't want to lose. Besides he had better things to do, one of which was to spend more time with Nancy. Suspicions by the others were really running high by now. Nancy wandered around the place like a mind-numbed robot, not talking to anyone, except of course Joe, and this, among other indications affirmed that Joe must have really been banging her.

Wrecking the airplane was certainly not on Billy's agenda. In fact it was the farthest thing from his mind. He was more concerned with not rocking the boat, which carried the same consequences as wrecking the airplane. He was beginning to like the program, the camaraderie and the fun and games

Chapter 3

he indulged in with Jack and company when they managed to sneak out in separate airplanes to dog fight and chase range horses.

As mentioned earlier, Billy didn't believe in preflight inspections. He always thought it was the job of the mechanic to keep the airplanes in airworthy condition. If nobody of importance was in the vicinity where they could observe him, he would do the minimum which included checking the oil and fuel, hang around the airplane long enough to have accomplished the exercise, then make noise about needing someone to prop the airplane to get it started. More often than not it required a hike to the office to commandeer a hot body for the chore. Joe could always be found in his favorite place, but he let it be known that he would accept the chore only as a last resort. It was beneath his dignity to step out into the elements for such a menial task.

Billy's reasoning concerning pre-flight was simple if not flawed. First he didn't feel that he was qualified to determine if any component was in such a condition as to render the airplane unsafe. Second, even if such a condition existed he wouldn't recognize the discrepancy anyway. And finally he had the distinct impression that these fun and games were ritualistic in nature, and had to be the product of the one and only Mr. Farraday who had nothing better to do but dream up policies and practices to secure his position in the scheme of things. He always maintained during his various discussions on the matter that if one really was interested in the welfare of the airplane, then he should walk over to the shop and ask Ernie the mechanic. If Ernie didn't know then Ernie should hike out to the line in the hot sun and inspect the airplane until he knew.

Further he opined that the major discrepancy in the airplane was the Airknocker itself. He didn't believe in the inherent safety of the machine and nobody should be allowed to invade the atmosphere in them, or any other airplane for that matter. So Billy fatalistically adopted the philosophy that ignorance is bliss and what he didn't know couldn't hurt him, and if he was going to continue on with this ridiculous charade of a hobby, then he should merely kick the tires, fire it up, hold his breath and go. But for the time being he would continue to preach respect for the piece of shit that passed for an airplane, for all who would listen, especially if his diatribes were within earshot of the exalted Mr. Farraday. As far as Mr. Farraday was concerned he reveled in Billy's complete conversion taking it as a personal

For All The Wrong Reasons

victory. It was evident that he was very proud of himself.

One time in private session, when the beer and the bullshit flowed between the boys in the bar, Billy offered his well thought out dissertation on the folly of "pre-flighting" airplanes. He asserted in his thesis that the exercise was pure folly and he intended to logically prove it. In his mind he assumed that there had to be something, no matter how insignificant, wrong with the airplane at all times. Has anybody ever owned a vehicle that was in perfect condition, or one that could be turned over to another without first schooling the individual on the idiosyncrasies of the machine? Well, he reasoned the same truism would also apply to the airplane. If a pre-flight inspection were performed on the airplane by a qualified mechanic, there was no doubt in Billy's mind that the result would uncover something that would merit the grounding of the airplane and aborting the flight. If this were the case, why should a pilot even show up to fly?

Extend this to all of the airplanes scheduled to fly and the result would be that none of them would progress to flight; they would all be down for maintenance. The skies that were touted to be overcrowded would then be safe and void of the evil machines because no one would be taking to the air. So, as his reasoning went, if one was hell bent on undertaking a mission in the skies, he should proceed on pure faith, waiving the ridiculous exercise of first going over the airplane with a fine tooth comb, subscribing to the maxim that ignorance is bliss. His pals all thought there was merit to his argument because, if for no other reason, they were all numbed by the booze.

Chapter 4

Mr. Boots Farraday acquired his cushy position as director of the flying school by bullshitting the higher-ups in the Phoenix School Systems. It was easy to understand how that was possible for two reasons. The people who were responsible for making the selection knew nothing about administering a flying school and Mr. Farraday exhibited a very striking impression, especially with the uninformed.

He was a suave looking individual in his mid-thirties who was more image than substance. He was of medium build, about five feet ten inches tall and was adorned with a thick shock of black wavy hair. His facial features were very French, with a long, slender, prominent nose and a thick black neatly trimmed mustache. He didn't merely walk but felt he had to swagger or strut to impress his audience.

When delivering a lecture, to buy time or to emphasize a point, he would stare off into space, as if looking for divine guidance, and as though in recognition of an inspiration, he would smack his lips. In fact, it was opined by the more realistic students that he smacked or puckered his lips and searched the upper half of the room when he needed to stall for time, because unless he was narrating a past personal experience, which he was more often than not, he lacked substantive communication skills and knowledge of the subject matter. The word was out that "Boots" was more than a first name; it was a suggestion as to the preferred footwear, seeing as how things got rather deep when Mr. Farraday got wound up.

After being exposed to this ridiculous man who passed himself off as an educator, Billy and company concluded that Mr. Farraday was a pompous "never was" as opposed to a "has been." He let everyone know whether they wanted to or not, on as many occasions as possible, never considering that the group he was bullshitting had heard it before, and that he was a fearless WWII glider pilot. It was obvious that his trip into this realm of adventure never took him out of the country, otherwise the student body, or

For All The Wrong Reasons

anyone else who got close enough would have been graced with the hair-raising tales of the innermost episodes of the war and his part in bringing Hitler to his knees and ultimate victory for the country.

As far as it could be determined, the only rating to his credit was a Private Pilot certificate, the lowest pilot rating possible. If he held advanced ratings he would have surely flaunted them. This led anyone who was brave enough to talk about him behind his back to wonder how he managed to obtain a position of such prominence and responsibility.

Boots considered Cathy his personal secretary. She was never willing to do secretarial chores for other members of the staff and he was equally unwilling to share her time with them. It was strongly suspected from the beginning that he had more interest in her than mere steno duties, evidenced by the fact that they were observed in his office more often than it was considered normal, deep in conversation when they both should have been more productive on behalf of the institution.

To her male counterparts she was overly snobbish and uppity. She was a student at the Junior College but her lack of interest in the academics were noticeable because she spent almost all of her time at the flying school either working, flying or sniffing after Mr. Farraday. Admittedly her only interest in the college was to maintain her eligibility to stay enrolled in the flying program, and to take advantage of the cheap flying rates. At first Billy openly lusted for her. After all he was an aviator, or so he thought, and it followed that Cathy should fall all over him because of it. It didn't take long for him to figure out that she was Boots' "private stock" and when Billy finally got the message he backed off.

Billy still thought she was gorgeous. She was tall and slender, slightly on the skinny side, but to offset her slenderness she was endowed with a nice set of firm boobs. Billy was a tit man. It was this attribute that attracted him and his buddies to her. Their off campus discussions turned into familiar fantasizing diatribe from how she would appear stretched out in the nude to how each one of them separately but exclusively would give anything to bang her.

Billy made sport in taking every opportunity to stare down her blouse. She made no attempt to discourage the move. It seemed to Billy that in fact she might be, in a perverse way, egging him on. But his friends let him know that this was only wishful thinking. Mr. Farraday had first and only dibbs on

Chapter 4

her. Still, she always wore low-cut, loose fitting blouses, and whenever he approached her desk, she would consciously bend over to retrieve something from either the desk top or one of the lower drawers letting the blouse fall away from her body thereby exposing the pristinely white bra. On more than one occasion he thought he was going to faint.

In the normal progression to a pilot's license, Billy discovered that night flying time was required. He wasn't particularly enamored with the idea of mobiling these tinker toy contraptions around the sky in the dark, not being able to see where he was going when it was hard enough to drive a car under the same circumstances and almost impossible to herd an airplane around the sky during the day. Other people were doing it, and it was a requirement, so he decided to bite the bullet and give it a try, if he could get Joe off of his ass long enough to show him how.

When the time came, Joe told him to schedule an airplane for the coveted night dual instruction. What Joe failed to impart was that any old Airknocker wouldn't do. It had to have lights so other people could see where not to go. So with his head down, already feeling like a failure, Billy once again approached Cathy apologetically, requesting that she change the schedule to reserve the Aeronca Chief instead of the Airknocker he had been using to charge through the atmosphere. He wasn't so humbled that he restrained himself from stealing a glance or two down her blouse at the same time fantasizing about blowing bubbles through her cleavage in a tub full of suds. The kid really had a problem, although he didn't seem to think so. With all of the niceties of the encounter with Cathy and the schedule accomplished, he reported back to Joe who reminded him of how stupid he was.

Besides the Stinson, the Aeronca Chief was the only airplane in the school's fleet that was equipped with an electrical system and as such was further equipped with position lights and a landing light. The Stinson would have been a much nicer airplane to use, but it was considered private stock by the higher-ups and used mostly for special occasions.

When he first approached the airplane, Billy was hard pressed to accept that the little bitty lights with the colored lenses on the wing tips were powerful enough to throw adequate lighting for him to see where he was going. The one on the tail was particularly interesting because it had a clear lens and he knew from experience that he wasn't going to back this sucker up. It

For All The Wrong Reasons

did, however, throw more light than those on the wing tips.

All this was cleared up when Joe showed him the landing light and explained the operation of the complete system. After this was put behind them, Joe already appeared to be exhausted. It would have been perfectly acceptable to Billy if he would have called off the whole thing and let Joe retreat back to his favorite berth.

But as it turned out, the lesson went extremely well; so well in fact that Joe accused Billy of putting him on with his supposed ignorance. The lesson was strictly touch and go landing practice. Billy virtually painted the first one on which gave rise to Joe's cynicism. The others were almost as good leaving Billy to firmly believe in the art of compensating errors. The entire episode lasted forty-five minutes; they logged in thirty.

Ernie, one of the two mechanics on staff had a typical five by five stature. He was about five feet tall and as wide as he was high. He worked the four to midnight shift. Pete, the exact opposite in build, was his counterpart who was on duty during the day to see that things ran well, service the airplanes and perform whatever maintenance was required. It was Ernie who dispatched the Aeronca Chief at night since there was no other staff available during those hours. He also picked up whatever squawks that were generated from the days activities that Pete couldn't handle, and made sure that the airplane was properly tucked in for the night after the students gave up. They were both licensed aircraft and engine (A&E) mechanics and well qualified for their tasks.

However, on one particular night that Jack and Billy were scheduled to solo the Chief at back-to-back hours, Ernie failed to show. This resulted in the event of the century which when witnessed by our altar boy aviators, answered forever all of the lingering questions and speculations concerning the exalted leader and his "private stock" of a secretary.

On the fateful evening in question, Billy and Jack arrived at the school parking lot in Jack's 1934 Chevy for some solo touch and go practice. It wasn't permissible for the students to fly together or to carry passengers so it was the plan for each to go out individually for an hour while the other would wait around shooting the bull with Ernie. Actually it was more like an hour and a half each and then log in an hour on the schedule sheet. It was more economical if done this way.

After the fun and games were over, it was off to the scheduled de-briefing at the Rainbow Tavern which was the place that had no qualms about

Chapter 4

serving the under age patrons providing that their strict rules were closely adhered to. These only amounted to the ability to pay, make no attention drawing conduct, and at least give the appearance of being close enough to the legal age.

As they strolled up from the parking lot, they noticed that the shop was dark but the lights were on in Boots' office. This was strange because Ernie was supposed to be there to help them get started. Maybe they could get Mr. Farraday's support, although that seemed unlikely because anything that required a modicum of effort was beneath his dignity. The main entrance of the building took them past the window to his office. The venetian blinds were drawn but not so tight as to prevent the curious, with minimal effort, to see through the cracks at the bottom and around the sides.

After a halfhearted attempt at trying the door and finding it locked, Billy approached the window with the idea of knocking on it to draw Boots' attention. But curiosity being what it was, he first peeked through the edge of the blinds. He remembered his mother's favorite quote "Curiosity killed the cat, but satisfaction brought it back." In this case the results of his curiosity could prove the converse to the saying. Boots' desk was at the near side of the room close to the window, oriented such that if Boots was seated at his desk, his back would be to the window. Across the desk at the far side of the room was a couch situated such that those seated on it would be facing the window. Needless to say Boots and his steno, Cathy, occupied the couch.

What Billy saw took his breath away. His gasp was loud enough to almost give away their position. He motioned to Jack to share in his discovery but as Jack nudged him, he was told to find his own peephole. This was too good to share even with his best friend. There stretched out on his back on the couch was the great Mr. Farraday clad only in his high ankle socks. These were still being duly supported by the in-vogue garters of the era. His left arm was draped across his eyes in a manner that suggested his unwillingness to witness his own pleasurable orgy. His mustache and the tip of his nose were the only protrusions visible beneath his forearm. His right arm was hanging loosely over the edge of the couch - his hand resting on the floor, palm up.

Straddling his body in an upright position across Boots' most significant area, her arms outstretched in front of her with her hands on his chest in a manner that indicated that she was holding him down, her back appropri-

For All The Wrong Reasons

ately arched as if to receive full penetration, was his prized student and part-time secretary. Needless to say she too was naked as a jaybird. They were both so engrossed in the project at hand that they were oblivious to the voyeurs who were taking it all in. This wasn't a flying lesson, it was a lesson in human relations. All of a sudden Billy's ambition suddenly came into focus. He wanted to become the director of a flying school, and as such he felt he needed to continue to study the scene in great detail, absorbing all he could for future reference.

As if this wasn't enough, there was more to come. One thing seemed to dominate the scene even more than the socks and garters, even more than the lifeless position of Boots' arms, and even more than the position of Cathy's hands as they dug into the hairy chest of the Adonis. It was the one highly significant feature on Cathy's chest (or lack thereof) that caused Billy to regret that he stole glances down her blouse, and vowed to never do it again. She was as flat chested as a billiard table. That is, all but the nipples that stuck out prominently in their hardness. No wonder Boots was reluctant to look.

Other than that, her body was lean and curvaceous. But what happened to her boobs? Well a further examination of the den of sin gave up the answer. There on the floor, among the articles of clothing, strewn about as if waiting to be fed to the washing machine, was her bra. It stood by itself in the same position taken by a pair of spectacles that would be carefully placed on a flat surface with the lenses on a vertical plain so as not to be damaged. The cups were full and continued to hold their form. It must have been a shock to Mr. Farraday when she peeled off the bra and threw it on the floor taking her boobs with it, foam rubber and all. No wonder he went into hiding.

That aspect of the scene was so disturbing to Billy that he was almost tempted to cover his eyes, but the quest and hunger for knowledge prevented him from such drastic action. Ever since entering the program, he had fantasized about rolling in the hay (or the back seat of a car) with her, and what had excited him most about her was the firmness and respectable size of her breasts. Every time she would stoop over in front of him for one reason or another, he would strain to gain visual access down her cleavage. Now he knew it was all for nothing.

Jack and Billy were speechless in their hypnotic fixation on the mating ritual taking place in front of them. It sure beat the hell out of flying air-

Chapter 4

planes. They watched for several minutes, motionless for fear of disrupting the scene, watching her contortions in slow motion. She was displaying a strained exertion, her fingers trying to grip Boots' chest, her head thrust back with her eyes closed. She was obviously savoring the ecstasy of the moment.

But the completion of the mating ritual was not to be. Without notice and succumbing to an irresistible urge, Billy gently tapped on the window. It wasn't a hard knock but it was sufficiently audible enough to break the trance. His motive for doing it was derived from deep down in his subconscious. He had learned way back in grammar school, from one of the back alley seminars, that if a couple in the act of copulation was shocked by the sudden interruption of an intruder, the female organ would clamp shut, resulting in the couple being hung up, similar to that which occurs between dogs. It was a highly controversial theory, first advanced by his boyhood friend. Other than the older boys of the community confirming the notion as fact, he had no way of knowing for sure. He certainly wasn't going to ask his parents about it. Therefore it was always in the back of his mind that the theory should be tested. Not only did he want to test the theory, but if it were true, more worthy candidates would be hard to find.

Billy's subconscious beliefs were finally verified. It was an old wives tale, or more appropriately, an older friend's tale. Yes, one of Billy's older friends from back in the Parochial school days was the culprit who perpetuated the myth. As he was about to find out, there was absolutely no truth to it, at least in this case. As soon as the sound waves penetrated the portion of her brain that called for the reaction that enhances survival, she came alive. Actually it was more than that, she was virtually panic stricken. Before Boots could react, she jumped off, exposing the rest of Boots' anatomy. Billy was in awe at the size of his appendage and immediately noted that if he were so endowed he would not want for anything again. The instant she extricated herself from her host, his member, as gross as it was, remained upright for a split second, then flopped back on his stomach, reposing like a beached whale.

In one leap she went from her perch high on top of Mr. Farraday, to the floor on her hands and knees collecting her things. Boots was apparently oblivious to the ruckus caused by the voyeurs. This was attributed to his partial deafness, a failing probably caused in part by the ear splitting noises generated by the gliders he flew during the big war. He lay there for a sec-

For All The Wrong Reasons

ond or two gazing at her in gross bewilderment until she screamed at him that there was someone out there knocking on the window. And on that cue he too joined the frenzy to cover his body, including his oversized appendage - oversized to the extent that made Billy wonder if there was enough fabric on the premises to adequately do the job.

The two love birds were scrambling around, alternately looking over at the window for some clue as to what was happening, while trying to sort out the puzzle that they had created with their tangled mess of clothing - all tangled except for the bra. It stood on edge all by itself, looking more like a crown or a Halloween mask than an undergarment. It was the passion of the moment that resulted in their hastiness to get into the fray that got the best of their normally tidy habits causing their garments to be scattered about the floor like some tornado had interfered instead of a mere tapping on the window.

The two perpetrators couldn't hang around any longer. They ran off to the parking lot as fast and as quietly as they could, climbed in the '34 Chevy sedan and rattled off in a cloud of smoke as hastily as the mechanical wonder would take them.

Now that '34 Chevy of Jack's was very noisy. Boots may not have heard it given his lack of hearing but Cathy certainly must have. The previous year Jack and a couple of his buddies decided that the perfectly good motor that went with the car needed to be overhauled, "to give it more torque." The severe knocking that emitted from the motor at all times except when the car sat dormant, which according to the more responsible element of those affected, should have been permanent, was caused by installing heavy cast iron pistons. Jack maintained that the noise was a result of a loud piston slap against the sides of the cylinders. He said that the heavy pistons afforded the car more torque than normal, making it possible for him to drive off in third gear from a dead stop if he wanted. Further, the hill climbing characteristics were supposed to be better, not that it was going to be of any benefit for them now.

Billy thought it was all a bunch of bull to rationalize a screw up on the overhaul. Nevertheless he was sure that they would be found out, if not because Cathy could identify the culprits by the noise, she certainly would wonder why the two never showed up to fly as the schedule indicated they should. What were they going to tell her if and when she asked?

The fat was in the fire, so to speak. There was no time to worry about it

Chapter 4

now. Getting the hell out of there, far away from the place was the first order of business. Driving in the direction of the Rainbow Tavern was the second order and the more instinctive. It was their refuge, a haven of safety, their mother's womb. It was a place where they could gather their thoughts, as dirty as they were, and a place where they could rehash the events, washing it all down with beer. More importantly it was a place where they could discuss the situation of Cathy's tits, or lack thereof. They would need drink for that one, plenty of it in fact.

Not much was discussed until the terrible two were settled in a dark booth with a brew in their hands. At first the discussion centered on how flat-chested Cathy was. Then it was on how Mr. Farraday was so generously endowed. What Cathy lacked in chest size Boots more than made up with his endowments. After that short review of the two segments, fright took over. What was going to happen when Boots became aware of who was responsible? "But how could he?" Billy wanted to know. "Simple" responded Jack. "First there was the noisy get-a-way, and then the flying schedule. By merely checking the schedule Boots would know who was expected and at what time." But Billy was still frantic. It was as though his whole future was at stake. He should have been the cool one; he was after all the instigator. But now Jack was taking over as the one in control. "But when he realizes that we were the ones involved what could he do about it?" With that, Jack took another swig on the bottle, stared at the label as though he was seeking out an inspiration, and finding one answered, "Nothing, but it's important not to look him in the eye anymore. As a matter of fact, stay the hell away from him as much as possible for as long as possible." It would be like a Mexican standoff. "The worst thing he could do to us would be to flunk us, or worse yet, throw us out of school, and he knows better than to do that. Why, we would blow the whistle on him and his girlfriend if push came to shove." No matter what events the future held they were both dead certain that things at the school would never be the same again.

As the beer flowed the nervousness wore off. The mood and thus the argument changed from being scared of the possible consequences to why Billy had to do a dumb thing like knocking on the window. On this there was disagreement. Billy maintained that it was more like a "tap-tap." Jack swore that it was more like a loud knocking on a door. Billy's excuse for

For All The Wrong Reasons

interrupting the orgy fell on deaf ears. Besides Jack was beginning to enjoy the show. It was just beginning to get good.

Jack said he knew that it was just a myth that lovers get hung up like dogs when startled during the act of making out and stressed that if Billy really wanted to know the truth about it, all he had to do was ask instead of getting them both in trouble. He confessed that he was an expert having been discovered in the act by his mother while making it with his girlfriend in his bedroom. So it was, with more consumption, the points became academic, but they felt that they had to rehash it over and over again until the familiar blinking of the house lights gave the signal that they should both give it up and go home.

Chapter 5

Things were touch and go for the rest of the semester. It was a real game of nerves between the lovers and the voyeurs. There was no doubt in Billy's mind that Cathy knew who the principle offenders were in the nefarious encounter on that fateful night. She was responsible for maintaining the flying schedule, so it followed that all she had to do to find out was to refer to it to identify the vultures. Another item that re-enforced Billy's conviction that they had been found out was her apparent disregard for the two missing their flying appointments. Under normal circumstances she would review the schedule the next day as part of her bookkeeping responsibilities and seeing the lack of entry that is normally completed at the end of each flight would have sought out an explanation from the two. But nothing was ever mentioned. Nor were the boys ever billed for having flown that night. It was getting very scary.

Following Jack's advice, Billy avoided all eye contact. Cathy's own guilty conscience came into play. She avoided speaking to either Billy or Jack, which was weird because normal conversation especially small talk was the order under normal circumstances. Now, not only were eye contact and cordial conversation avoided, but the usual attempts to fix on her cleavage when she bent over her desk as well. Not that he didn't want to look, he was still curious as to how a bunch of foam could transform her flat chest into something that approached voluptuousness. But he was more afraid than curious, so he left it alone. He could see that it was definitely going to be a strained relationship.

Boots on the other hand maintained his usual arrogance, strutting around like an oversized peacock, smacking his lips and twitching his mustache when he embarked on making a point. You would have thought that he took pride in getting caught with his pants down and his dong out. It was definitely more difficult for Billy to confront Boots on any given subject, than it

For All The Wrong Reasons

was for Boots to respond. Ground school was much the same, except Billy huddled over his desk virtually avoiding his share of class participation.

But the fun and games continued. These included dogfights, herding wild horses and speculating on whether Joe was getting his share by banging Nancy. It was inevitable that soon the student body of future aviators were well schooled on the events of the fateful night and were making book on Joe and Nancy. It wasn't too far down the road that Billy and Jack were able to confirm their suspicions. It took place at an inactive auxiliary airfield north of Phoenix, in fact north of Squaw Peak Mountain, a couple miles east of the small town of Cactus.

The town of Cactus, since swallowed up by the developing metropolis, was located about three miles northeast of Sunnyslope, where Cave Creek Road tops the rise before heading north to the town of Cave Creek. It consisted of a bar-restaurant, gas station, grocery store, a small dirt airport, and a few houses. Other than Cave Creek road, which provided access to the community from Sunnyslope, there were no paved roads in any direction from this location.

Just about a mile due east of Cactus along a single-lane dirt road, (later to become known as Cactus Boulevard, when the road was paved in multiple lanes to accommodate the swelling residential area,) was situated the large military auxiliary airfield, referred to as Thunderbird Auxiliary No.1 (Aux.1). It consisted of a large, smooth, dirt area one-half mile square with no vegetation. During the Big War the area was used by the military as a place where the students could practice their touch and go landings in the Stearman trainers that were based out of the Thunderbird Army Air Corps flying school located north of Scottsdale. The Thunderbird facility later became Scottsdale Municipal airport.

Along the north edge of the dirt field, an additional one-half mile was scraped out to the east, so that the total landing surface running east to west along that side was a full mile long. The width of the extension approximated two hundred feet. It was here under a Palo Verde tree on the south side of the extension that Joe and Nancy were caught doing their dirty thing with his and her dirty things.

The school's practice area was designated and limited to an area east of the city of Scottsdale over the Indian reservation. This was nice for the restless Centurions as it provided them with the necessary livestock to practice their horse-herding techniques. One would never know when this skill

Chapter 5

might come in handy. It was both expressed and implied that the novice aviators were to go directly to, and as directly, return from this area when indulging in solo practice. Touch and go practice was to take place at Sky Harbor. This wasn't good enough for the young and the restless. To spice things up even more, on the way home after practice, Billy and company would fly west across Scottsdale, about five miles to Aux.1, shoot several landings, then proceed south through the gap between Camelback Mountain and Squaw Peak, maneuvering to the east to avoid Sky Harbor, and setting up south of the airport for a normal pattern entry. Getting caught at this meant, of course, dismissal without recourse. But as normal developing teenagers, consequences never got in the way of their activities.

It was during one of these sojourns to Aux.1 that the speculation concerning Joe and Nancy's conduct was upgraded to fact. Jack was in the lead as they approached the field with Billy in trail by five hundred feet. The intention was to circle over the top at least once to survey the conditions on the ground, and then set up a normal left hand pattern for the landing practice. As they started the exercise they noticed the Airknocker parked off to the side. Not recognizing the airplane as belonging to the school, they both continued. But as both broke from the top and headed off to intercept the downwind leg, Joe and Nancy appeared from beneath a Palo Verde tree. Both were looking directly at the two Airknockers overhead. Unlike the two heroes, Joe knew exactly to whom the airplanes belonged. And probably at the same instant Billy and company identified the subjects on the ground. Without missing a beat, both airplanes broke off and headed as quickly as the Lord permitted, out of sight to the south, in the direction of home.

It would have been all over for the two, except for the fact that Joe and student were just as guilty. This probably wasn't the first time the two lovers chose Aux.1 to hold court under the shade of the Palo Verde tree. On many occasions they would be gone in the airplane for two hours only to log an hour. This by itself wasn't cause for suspicion, because everybody played with the flying time to minimize the expense of flying. But in their case even the mechanic commented that the lengthy trips didn't consume enough fuel to justify the extended flight.

Billy and Jack thought it was all over. Purgatory would be nothing compared to what was in store for them now. On returning to the airport, they

For All The Wrong Reasons

parked the airplanes, retired to the pilot's lounge, uncorked a Coke, and sat at the table and stared at each other. There was nothing they could say. They were both guilty as sin. On one hand they were tickled that their curiosity was satisfied, but on the other, they knew that this was to be their last drink at the facility. All they could do now was wait for Joe Mora to return with dirty Nancy, and lower the ax.

But it didn't exactly work out that way. To say that it developed into a Mexican standoff would not only be appropriate considering the nationality of the key player, but would be an understatement. All they got when the Latin Lover returned was the scariest eye piercing protracted stare that is only possible when two of the meanest heavy-weights square off in the ring listening to the meaningless last minute review of the rules prior to bashing each other's brains out. Joe tried to say something but nothing came out. His body English indicated the beginning of utterances on several occasions but no sound followed. He continued to pace and stare, not seeming to know how he should conduct his next move. The guys knew they were in a serious situation when Joe declined the services of the couch. Eventually he turned and walked out of the room leaving his worst nightmares sitting at the table drinking in silence from empty Coke bottles.

Nancy was nowhere to be seen. She disappeared completely for the next week before emerging as though nothing happened. Nobody had the guts to ask her where she had been. In fact nobody had the guts to even think about it. As things cooled down, notwithstanding the Mexican stand-off, Billy and his thug cohorts resumed their usual behavior, which included embellished accounts, over beer and pretzels, of how they were able to discern the actual fornication of the two under the tree while circling at five hundred feet. Billy's only regret was that there were only two members of the opposite sex enrolled in the program.

Chapter 6

Phoenix Junior College was called a high school equipped with ashtrays. To be sure, smoking was allowed in the classroom, or for that matter, anywhere else on the campus. Other than that peculiarity, classes, teaching techniques, and other organizational matters were conducted in the same fashion as the other high schools in the district. One was made to feel completely at home in this environment, and if the student felt comfortable during his or her high school years then it was a natural transition to the field of higher learning.

Discarding cigarette butts by grinding them out with the sole of a shoe on the classroom floor, or anywhere else on the campus, was discouraged, but because of the lack of ashtrays it was allowed. By the end of the day a typical floor was covered wall to wall with butts which was a real challenge for the janitor. Nothing could stink worse than showing up for class in the morning, when the janitor didn't show up for work the night before, and confronting a situation of stale tobacco droppings that fermented in a tightly enclosed environment for the previous fourteen or so hours. It happened all too often making you wonder about the benefits of indulging in the first place, and feeling somewhat compassionate for the non-smoking teachers especially those of the fairer sex. None of them seem to mind, at least to the extent of registering complaints.

The smoking privileges afforded Dave Staple a sure fire way to cheat on his tests by way of crib sheets. Crib sheets are small sheets of reference material on which information essential to excelling on an exam is crammed in a minute fashion so easy access is readily available to the candidate, while at the same time not discernible to the instructor. Hopefully the student knows enough about the material in question to be intelligently able to assemble enough of the pertinent information in the very small space to cover

For All The Wrong Reasons

the subject matter on which the test is based. Dave's method incorporating cigarettes was unique.

For those interested, he faithfully demonstrated his technique during a coffee break at the Student Union one afternoon. To execute the procedure, Dave always donned a baseball cap, which was an essential piece of equipment in the endeavor to beat the system. An additional item of equipment was a jumbo-sized book of paper matches otherwise known as gopher matches. The term "gopher" is derived from the exercise exerted when using book matches. Light one, then go for another. The size of the matchbook needed to be at least three times the size of a single book in order to record the essentials of the test. On the inside flap, before the test, he would inscribe in very small print, the salient facts essential to the success of passing with at least a respectable grade. Dave wasn't interested in setting the world on fire. He wasn't that arrogant. He merely wanted to get through the first time. Repeating courses wasn't in his scheme of things.

Every time the occasion reared its ugly head, when he needed to retrieve an essential piece of information, Dave would raise his ugly head and pull out his giant book of matches on the pretense of lighting a cigarette. He would then tear out one of the matches, strike it, and while holding the match up to the end of his cigarette, he would position the open book of matches at the end of the bill of his cap which in combination with everything else enabled him to review his notes that were inscribed in the area between the flaps. Then, after the necessary information was retrieved and the crisis of the moment had passed, he would gingerly close the cover and return the array back to its nesting place in his shirt pocket. It was a very effective method of cheating one's way through school, albeit hard on the lungs.

Because this afforded a foolproof opportunity for advancement, Billy took up the smoking habit. As far as he was concerned, a bad and expensive vice like cigarettes wasn't going to stand in the way of bigger and better things like obtaining a degree from an institution of higher learning.

When Billy enrolled at Phoenix College, he hadn't decided on a course of study. In fact he had continued on at the junior college after graduating from Phoenix Union High School only because of the continuation of the flying program. He was still under the influence of his high school cronies and their decision to proceed along the junior college route for the same

Chapter 6

reasons, settled it for him.

While perusing the school catalog, a necessary exercise before enrolling, he discovered that the institution actually offered a curriculum under the caption entitled "Commercial Flying." Well at least for the time being that suited him just fine. It was a legitimate reason for being there, a justification for fucking off, a badge he could carry with him through the foreseeable future to justify his existence to those who claimed to be interested in his future. So it was Commercial Flying that he entered in the appropriate space on the admissions form. And for the next two years this is what he would study, or more accurately go through the motions of doing so, in addition to washing trucks at the local dairy, smoking cigarettes, and drinking beer at the Rainbow Tavern.

Chapter 7

For a moment it's back to the final months of his senior year at Phoenix Union High. Things in general at the flying school during those months looked grim and a future at the place of higher learning was the farthest thing from his mind. This was mainly because of the tension generated after discovering Boots and Cathy screwing up a storm in Boots' office on that fateful night. Finding Joe and Nancy in a compromising position among the trees at the auxiliary strip north of town, when they should have been channeling their sweat in more productive academic ways in the Airknocker instead, didn't help either. But in spite of the stiffness surrounding the principals at the school, Billy drove on in pursuit of his immediate goals until mercifully during the final month of his last semester managed to earn his Private Pilot's License.

This accomplishment was more gratuitous than meritorious. It was Mr. Farraday's thinking that if Billy and company got their ticket (license) they would go away after graduation, never to be seen or heard of again. This would allow him to continue with his play toys (Cathy and anyone else of the opposite sex that wandered in looking for thrills) without constantly looking over his shoulder because of the potential sneers and giggles of the incorrigibles.

His biggest fear, and one that was to become a reality, was that they would continue on to bigger and better things through the attendance at the junior college. If that were the case, he faced an additional two-year sentence of the reminders of the event that would feed his paranoia. That was probably one of the motivating factors that caused him to forever lecture the students on the merits of the other institutions of higher learning such as the Spartan School of Aeronautics and Northrop Aviation. Both offered a two year course of instruction which when completed culminated with a

For All The Wrong Reasons

piece of paper that gained the candidate the admittance into nothing, but was touted as the sacred key to the door of most airlines. Unfortunately, all of the schools that he promoted required vast infusions of green stuff to get through the door, not to mention the cost of subsistence in the big cities.

Getting the Private license was a snap. For one thing, the school had Bruce Birran, a CAA approved examiner on staff. He danced to the tune of Boots Farraday. Talk about your conflict of interest. It was in Bruce's best interest to kiss Boots' ass because he had a wife and six kids to feed. As it was, it was more than obvious that he was barely scraping by. His continued appearance was of one who should be living under the nearby railroad overpass. One such manifestation was a need for a decent haircut instead of the neck shaves provided by the Mrs. His budget didn't allow for the professional niceties which distinguished a good haircut from a bad one by the neat taper at the fringes. Others claimed that the real difference between the two was two weeks. His appearance was a reminder to the guys not to overindulge in the reproductive scheme of things lest they be deprived of indulging in their other vices including but not limited to the lengthy excursions to the Rainbow Tavern.

By modern methods a check ride, otherwise referred to as a Private Pilot examination, comprises a written test, an oral quiz and a flight test. The written part is administered during the instructional part of the syllabus and is valid for two years. The practical part, which includes the oral quiz as well as the flight test, has to be completed within two years after the written part. During the era that Billy was operating, all that was required to obtain the ticket was a flight test. The written requirement wasn't instituted until a year or so later and the oral was sort of glossed over at the discretion of the examiner. If he turned out to be a "Santa Claus" or in the case of Bruce, a whore, all that was required was the visible evidence of a twenty-dollar bill.

So at the time this was taking place, when one's instructor thought his student was ready, he endorsed the student application, corralled Bruce, and both Bruce and the candidate took off in an Airknocker to show that he was sufficiently proficient in handling the airplane to be bestowed the coveted license. This license to kill, be killed or learn, allowed the individual the unrestricted privileges of charging off into the atmosphere with first his mother, other members of the family, and then on to impress the girls; but

Chapter 7

not with the school's airplanes.

These were off limits to everything except so-called training flights. After all, this was supposed to be serious business. In fact, unless the student pursued additional ratings, he or she was out of the program. Under those circumstances, two options needed to be considered. The most important was to declare the intentions for continuing on in pursuit of a commercial rating, and the other was to find another operator in the area that would rent their airplanes at an affordable rate. Even when satisfying the first option, and since the school's equipment were not considered play toys, it was still necessary to affiliate with another operator to exercise Billy's extra curricular activities.

Immediately upon successfully completing the check ride, and being congratulated by all those present, including Mr. Farraday, Billy so declared, observing Mr. Farraday's facial transformation in both color and expression, and his less than gracious retreat from the ceremony to his office while smacking his lips in complete disdain. It was almost an expectation by at least one in the group to hear the unfamiliar report of a handgun erupting from Mr. Farraday's office but no such luck. His recuperative powers were remarkable. He immediately settled back and accepted his fate.

The check ride was by no means a shoe-in. Billy had trouble executing most of the maneuvers including forced landings. This of all parts he didn't expect to fail because he had practiced engine out procedures and spot landings since the time he was allowed to go out on his own. He fixed on these because they were fun not because they were necessary. He attributed the piss-poor performance to his nervousness and not lack of ability. When he hashed out the event with another instructor from another Fixed Base Operator (FBO) on the airport who seemed to be well acquainted with Bruce, he was told that he should have rolled up a twenty dollar bill, tucking it behind his ear so Bruce could see it throughout the ride from his perch in the back seat. That would have been a clear motivating factor for Bruce to rubber stamp the ride, but just as compelling was his knowledge that Boots wanted Billy gone and he let Bruce know it.

So after the ride, on the long walk from the airplane to the office building, Bruce embarked on a lengthy diatribe in the guise of advice which when boiled down to something discernible could have been summed up in one sentence, "Take your license, frame it, hang it in a prominent location

For All The Wrong Reasons

for all to see and get the hell out of flying." Normally the post check ride discussion included a critique on the various elements of the ride. But in this case Bruce faced a real dilemma. If he forced himself to completely review all of the exercises of the ride, he would probably have flunked Billy. He was torn instead between integrity, lust for the twenty dollars, and fear of Boots Farraday. The latter two prevailed and Billy got his ticket.

Instead of joining the others in the back-slapping routine and other congratulatory gestures, Bruce walked right past the group to his office to complete the paper work, and to offer a small prayer of contrition for the compromising act in which he had just participated. Was it a mortal sin or a venial sin that he just committed? After all he rationalized, he had a wife and all of those kids to feed and it was the Lord and the Catholic Church who admonished him not to indulge in birth control methods. So it was really the Church's fault that this had to be done, and if his actions resulted in Billy Cotton killing himself or others, then the Church must share the responsibility. This thought indulging rationale improved his state of mind sufficiently, but only enough to approach the group to quickly present Billy with his temporary certificate. Then as quickly as he appeared he retreated back to his cubbyhole for more meditation and repentance.

After a while and some small talk, Boots emerged from his hole with a revelation; that high school students could not pursue a commercial license or other advanced ratings. These options were reserved for those enrolled at Phoenix College. And since the equipment could only be flown for the purpose of obtaining a pilot's certificate, this meant Billy was through. The rule was possible only because Boots was allowed to make them up as he went along, and coincidentally enough, there were no high school students presently pursuing advanced ratings. So with great delight, feeling very proud of himself and showing it in his familiar fashion, in one fell swoop he rid the school of Billy Cotton and his other high school buddies who had either recently acquired, or were about to acquire a license of their very own. But no matter, it was Billy's final semester at Phoenix Union, and as a final measure of defiance, he let it be known that he would be back as a freshman at Phoenix College.

Chapter 8

The problem facing the group now was where they could rent airplanes for the same good deal they were getting at the flying school. At the next meeting that was held in the dark corner of the Rainbow Tavern, Jack announced that he found just the place, not too far down the line from the school offices. It was a real hole-in-the-wall ram-shackle joint made up of a clap board military surplus one story building, dragged in to the north side of the airport and set up as a flying school, only because it was the cheapest and most expedient thing to do. If the facilities furnished by the Phoenix School System could be considered first class then the rating deserved by this institution fell off the chart on the low end. The place was called Maddux Flying Service. Their specialty was in training WWII GI bill students who had nothing better on which to spend their GI benefits. If these prospects didn't use the funds in pursuit of academic achievement within a certain time period, the benefits would go away. In most cases the benefits would have evaporated anyway if someone had not pointed out to these bozos that they could use the government subsidies to learn how to fly and have fun in the process. All of this for merely throwing one's life on the line dodging bullets or whatever else the Krauts or Japs could throw at them.

The people at Maddux did not lack for students. One of the partners was well connected at the local Veterans Administration office (VA.) So in addition to lists of potential candidates who were duly solicited by phone, the solicitor who just happened to be a VA counselor, was unabashed in recommending that the GI spend his money on airplane rental in lieu of worthwhile endeavors in line with more mentally challenging academic pursuits. The black community in particular was targeted with a great deal of success. For the first couple of years in business, the clapboard facility rendered the appearance of a Harlem community. Then as the funds and black

For All The Wrong Reasons

candidates began to dry up, more ethnic diversity became apparent.

It was because of the initial success of the operation that Maddux was able to equip their line with a wide assortment of models of airplanes at reasonable rental rates. The reasonable rate which was, in reality, a discounted rate, applied only to those who graced the threshold with cash in hand. The GI students paid the higher prices since the ultimate provider was the Federal Government, and Lord knows that anybody who deals with Uncle Sam tries to screw him for all they can. Maddux not only wanted to, but did jump on the bandwagon in great fashion, milking the system for all it could.

The Maddux fleet was not only equipped with Airknockers, one of the more popular trainers of the time, but Cessna 140's, 170's, and a couple of Stinsons. To rent the Airknockers and the Cessna 140's they charged six dollars an hour wet. "Wet" means that the cost of fuel and oil is included in the rental rate. This wasn't as bad as it first appeared when compared with the hourly rate of two dollars that the Phoenix School System charged, because in Maddux's case they didn't care if you took a passenger along provided you were in legal possession of a pilot certificate. When sharing the cost of the rental with the passenger, the end result was only a dollar more than Billy and friends were accustomed to paying. Furthermore, the time flown was kept by the renter, the honor system, just like it was at the school. Billy also found the place to be more fun as a hang out. The people there didn't seem to care if you came in smelling of the remnants of the Rainbow Tavern.

The facilities at Maddux's weren't as elaborate as those at the school but in their own rustic way were just as comfortable. When the two partners decided to embark on the government fleecing operation, they needed a place to hang their hat. Out of the blue came this notice of a government auction that included several single story military office buildings of maybe 1,500 square feet each. It took an eight hundred dollar bid to buy one of them and another five hundred to move it and install it on concrete piers. The frame and plaster construction made it all possible. At the front end of the building closest to the flight line was the office. It was situated so that Mr. Maddux himself could view the activity on the flight line through the window from his desk. In the same space was one additional desk for the other partner of the firm. Both desks were purchased from the same auction

Chapter 8

at a token price, because not only were they beat up but were components of two badly broken Link Flight Simulators.

The other rooms were laid out in tandem down the remaining length of the building. Beyond the office was the lounge area. It was amply furnished with broken-down soft-backed easy chairs, a sofa in relatively the same condition, a Coke machine, refrigerator and the necessary table and chairs. This is where the instructors completed their paper work and critiqued their students favorably or otherwise for all to hear. The next in the chain of rooms, off to one side was the toilet room and broom closet. Down the short corridor on the other side of the toilet taking up the remainder of the building was the classroom.

The mood around the place was always very relaxed. The four flight instructors were WWII jocks who were marking time until they died. They were real has-beens. They had no regard for the decorum that necessarily existed at the other place. Therefore the dirty language and equally dirty jokes were rampant. Unlike the instructors at the Phoenix Flying School, they got paid by the hour. It was three dollars for every hour of flight instruction, but as an incentive they received an additional dollar for every hour their student flew by themselves. This little act of mercy on the part of management provided enough incentive for them to want to sit on their asses in an air-conditioned lounge in lieu of hustling the students in a hot airplane on an equally hot afternoon. It was barely starvation wages. Not having other skills to fall back on, and liking to fly airplanes more than eating or screwing, this line of work was the only option. There were more pilots out there than there were corporate or airline flying jobs. In that era the world was over saturated with pilots with more entering the system every day through the GI bill and other educational opportunities, the likes of which was provided for by the Phoenix School Systems.

And so it was that Maddux Flying Service became the hang out for Billy Cotton and his corrupting cronies during the last semester of high school, the following summer and finally the following two years of Junior College. The gang of youthful delinquents was a delightful diversion for the staff at Maddux, as the staff were a welcome reprieve from the boredom of their droll existence at the other place. The instructors became their idols, capturing the souls of the gang with their war stories and dirty jokes. It was such a bizarre relationship that it could be claimed that the term "airport bum" originated in that hole of existence. Now Billy's spare time was equally

For All The Wrong Reasons

divided between the Rainbow Tavern and Maddux. To his way of thinking, as expressed in his profoundest way of expression one hot afternoon in the dark corner of the meeting place, "it was a good time to be alive".

Maddux or the others on his staff never questioned the motives or the conduct of Billy and his friends. Flying the Airknockers and Cessna 140's became more of an adventure than they had at the Phoenix Flying School. Games of the same kind were played as before, except that each airplane carried two people instead of one. In addition to chasing wild horses on the Indian reservation, forced landing contests were held on a regular basis. Also short field landing contests and closed course races were added to spice up the activity. These took place at Aux.1, east of the town of Cactus. Billy learned more about the finer points of flying from these activities and from his buddies than he did from his flight instructors. The only trick was to live long enough to gain sufficient skills and experience to survive. He was reminded over and over again by the so-called elite of the trade that there are many old pilots, and many bold pilots, but there are but a few pilots who are both old and bold.

One of the games that he and Jack played with the Airknocker was a forced landing contest. At any time when one or the other would be flying the airplane, the one whose turn it was would chop the power and declare a forced landing. The other would pick what he thought was an appropriate spot on the ground, more likely a field, and try without the benefit of the engine to squeeze the airplane within the confines of the space. The rules allowed the pilot to clear the engine once by applying a little power to ensure in fact that the engine had not loaded up and quit for real, changing from airplane to glider. They would generally glide the airplane to within a few feet of the ground without making contact before adding full throttle and climbing out.

If a success was declared by the instigator, as evidenced by the relative position of the airplane to the target field, then the one who declared the emergency landing by chopping the throttle would likewise feed in full power, initiating the go-around. A successful forced landing was one score for the recipient. However, if a failure resulted, the airplane was flown back over the spot, at the same altitude and heading where the forced landing was declared in the first place, and the other contestant had to attempt and succeed where his buddy failed, before he could chalk up a point for himself.

Chapter 8

Making the instigator prove that he could complete the forced landing when the other failed, kept them both from putting the other in an impossible situation. The rules also called for them to alternate initiating the exercise.

It was during one of these exercises that the two got their signals crossed to the point of narrowly diverting a disastrous situation. At five hundred feet, northbound over the farm fields east of Scottsdale, Jack who was in the front seat, pulled the power back to idle, declaring a forced landing situation. At this point Billy was to takeover and execute the landing in one of the fields. It was more like a low approach to the field, or until Jack in his fair and infinite wisdom declared that if allowed to continue, the complete landing would have terminated in a successful one. Rising to the occasion, Billy assessed that he was on the downwind leg for a field on his left side. As he turned base, Jack advanced the throttle slightly to clear it, ensuring that he still had a functional engine, and in determining that he did, pulled the power off again. Billy rounded final and seeing that he couldn't get over the power lines that bordered the north edge of the field, and wishing that Jack had applied more power when he cleared the engine on base, he decided that to earn his point he would have to scoot under the wires.

Now when it was obvious that he could make the field by going under the wires, the two dauntless daredevils were too low to the ground and too close to the pole line to do anything but continue on with the exercise by going under them. But unnoticed before this moment of truth was a fence along the edge of the field and directly below the power lines. This meant what is commonly referred to in the industry as "threading the needle." And there wasn't all that much room between the two obstacles to take the maneuver for granted. At least that was the perspective from the pilot's point of view.

It's one thing to fly along clipping the tops of the vegetation, knowing that if you concentrated on holding that position, scooting under the wires would be a snap and the pilot wouldn't even have to concern himself with the clearance. But in this case the pilot has to divide his attention between the top of the fence and the wires and try to split the difference. If the airplane wasn't positioned exactly right, too low meant hooking the wheels on the top strand of the fence, and rolling it up in a ball. If that wasn't enough, getting chewed out by Maddux and company was nothing to look forward to for being less than prudent. Equal consequences lay in wait if the power lines were encountered. To add to the difficulty, Billy was flying

For All The Wrong Reasons

from the back seat, doing all of this with limited visibility, having to look over Jack's shoulder to see through the windshield.

While on final, close to the moment of truth, there was absolutely no conversation between the two. The airspeed was up to about ten mph above normal glide speed which was a plus, but the power lines appeared to be ten times their actual size and the fence took on the size of a billboard. Within fifty feet of the edge of the field, Billy thought there might be a chance for success, the quiet was interrupted by a gulping sound originating from deep down in his throat. He wanted to quit and brace himself for the imminent onslaught, but instead, mustering up a latent desire for survival, he overcame his weakness and stared straight ahead, still expecting the worst.

The wires flashed by over the top of the airplane, he felt that he was uncomfortably close to a power pole that passed by on his right, and until now hadn't been accounted for. It loomed large, as large as the Washington Monument. He didn't see the fence, but must have missed it, because there was no jolt as he slipped over the top. Almost too late, he added power just before hitting the ground and wondered why Jack hadn't done so since the rules called for him to feed in the throttle when he concluded that the forced landing had been successfully completed.

On another occasion, they seemed to get mixed up as to who was supposed to fly the airplane coming out of the field. Thankfully on this occasion the Airknocker was trimmed just right, because when Jack succeeded in his attempt and the airplane was just a few feet off the ground in a flaring position, he started to wonder when Billy was going to declare a success by feeding in the throttle. The airplane was beginning to slow down in the flare, Billy obviously had his head up his ass, and Jack was setting up for the touch down when Billy finally went to full power.

During the debriefing which took place at the Rainbow Tavern, Billy swore that after adding full power, he handed the airplane back to Jack to fly them out of there. Jack's position was different. He said it didn't happen, so he did not assume control of the airplane, and the fact that the Airknocker was climbing out nicely confirmed to him that somebody else was doing the job.

Nevertheless the airplane continued to climb out at a very shallow angle in an equally shallow turn to the left. Billy, his chin propped in the palm of his hand, elbow resting on the window frame, stared out the left window in deep thought about the ass he failed to get the night before. As the turn

Chapter 8

continued the bank gradually steepened, the rate of turn increased accordingly, and the pitch decreased. Within limited parameters, as the pitch goes so goeth the climbing rate, until in a short period of time the airplane was in a level turn. This went on until a ninety-degree turn was completed.

At that point Billy still staring out the side window wondering why she wouldn't put out, became aware that the Airknocker was standing on edge, not climbing, and passing perilously close over the top of a transformer pole. It flashed within twenty feet off the left wing tip. He swore that he could make out the sparks emitting from the gaps caused by loose connections of the transformer terminals. He sat up straight and congratulated Jack on the neat buzz job, whereas Jack responded that he was not on the controls and that Billy was supposed to be flying the machine. Now both were in a panic, and now both were doing the flying. It all concluded in the resolve that better communications and less day-dreaming was in order.

Other diversionary indulgences that appealed to the group of young aviators, but were short lived because of the severe ass-hole puckering risks involved, were closed course racing and short field landings. Both of these events were held at Aux.1. As mentioned before, Aux.1 was a small dirt field one-half mile square with an appendage along the north edge extending one-half mile to the east, making the total usable east-west distance along this north side to be one mile. The extended part which when considered in context with the entire facility, resembled a panhandle. The strip was about 200 feet wide. In summary, the closed course race involved three airplanes departing wing tip to wing tip from the far east end of the extended part of the field, west bound, around the perimeter of aux.1, and landing back from where they started. The gory details of the masochistic contest is delved into in more detail later.

The object of the short-field landing contest was to see who could land in the shortest distance from the east end over a 25 foot high Palo Verde tree. The measurement being the distance from the trunk of the tree to the spot where the airplane ceased to roll. The airplane of choice was the Airknocker. As this contest heated up, Billy ended up flying through the upper part of the tree. No sweat, the limbs were small and flexible. On Billy's final try, he not only took out part of the tree, but locked up the brakes on the way down. He was in a stall from the time the airplane clobbered the tree's upper limbs until it hit unceremoniously on all three wheels.

For All The Wrong Reasons

With the brakes hung up, the tail started to get light, preliminary to nosing over. At the moment of truth, Billy added full power keeping the stick firmly in the back position. This maneuver brought the tail back down firmly on the ground. But with the brakes still hung up, the airplane continued to slide. It was a sight to behold. The airplane was sliding down the dirt strip to an abrupt stop with the engine turning at near full power. This turned out to be the undisputedly shortest landing yet, not to be surpassed by anyone after that date. With all of the back slapping over, the crew concentrated their efforts to cleaning up the various parts of the airplane of the minor mess caused by the green foliage of the tree. The tiny leaves stuck to the oily surfaces of the oleo strut and other areas. The method of restoring the Airknocker to its former appearance is described more vividly in a later section of these chronicles.

Chapter 9

Mr. Farraday wasn't very happy to see Billy and his friends return to school in the fall, but there was nothing he could do about it. If his stamina proved formidable, and he managed to survive his worst nightmares, he would have to put up with their conduct for two more years. He should have been grateful that the Junior College was only a two year institution and not a full blown university, otherwise his misery would have been prolonged for an additional two years. Boots Farraday was even more forlorn when he found out that his delinquent charges were spending their spare time hanging out at Maddux Flying Service, renting beat up airplanes, and doing what was definitely against the rules at the Phoenix Flying School.

Even though the boys were enrolled at the Junior College, nothing at the flying school arm of the Phoenix School System had changed. Boots Farraday and Joe Mora were still screwing the same two girls. Bruce Birran was still trying to stay straight and earn enough to support his brood. Billy and his delinquent friends were trying their best to stay drunk and kill themselves. It was a good time to be a teenager.

Two new young reprobates entered the scene to add spice to the activities. One was Dave Staple, the other was a flashy Air Force dropout named Jim Pierce. Dave was the one who showed Billy how to get through the tests at Phoenix College. He was more afraid of airplanes than Billy. Dave would go out to the airport to hang out, and would even fly with the gang. But learn how to fly, he flatly refused.

Dave pursued a pre-architectural major. He did his best to convince Billy to find himself by doing more serious thinking and settling on a major course of study other than the worthless curriculum of Commercial Flying he was pursuing. Coming from a family of half-assed architects, the field was in his genes, so with prompting from his father, who specialized in designing ware-

For All The Wrong Reasons

houses with plain facades, Dave was hot to trot with a goal of designing a warehouse packaged like the Taj Mahal.

Dave was all for pushing Billy into architecture, but if he couldn't get Billy interested, then some other worthwhile profession like engineering would be better for the long haul than the dumb mindless activity he was moving toward. Even though Billy wasn't sold on the idea, in subsequent semesters he did take many of the same courses as Dave. His purpose was not necessarily for constructive reasons, but because he liked to hang out with the guy. Being with him, studying with him, and sitting next to him during the tests, simplified his life considerably.

Billy first met Jim Pierce, the other newcomer to the scene, while standing in line at the Registrar's office on the first day of registration. Since being drummed out of the Air Force, Jim wandered around in a rudderless fashion until, like a bird looking for a place to build his nest, he ended up on the doorstep at Phoenix College. At that juncture he wasn't aware of a Flying Club as it was sometimes called, and was only vaguely familiar with the opportunity of earning a degree of sorts in Commercial Flying. To him, a school with airplanes was inconceivable. That part of his ignorance was due to him and his parents having just relocated from Tucson to the Phoenix area.

Hanging around the house wasn't exactly in his mother's scheme of things. So she kicked him out the door with enough money to pay his tuition and he ended up on the doorstep at Phoenix College looking for some direction and maybe a few friends to boot. The one thing that Jim had in common with Billy was that they both lived with their parents. It was understood that as long as you were in school, living at home was not considered abnormal.

Because of a promotion, Jim's father, who worked for the railroad was transferred to Phoenix the year before. After Jim was mustered out of the Air Force for less than honorable circumstances, he dropped in on his parents, who up until then, thought they could live out their remaining years as a twosome with only an occasional visit from their son.

Resigned to the fact that Jim's stay was indefinite, his father had to do something to mitigate the drain on their income, such as get Jim a job. As the political system with the railroad goes, so goeth nepotism. Due solely to that, Mr. Pierce was able to get Jim a job during the off-hours as a fireman on a switch engine. This job was less than part time because with no seniority, he was relegated to the "extra board." As such he was required to sit

Chapter 9

back and wait until his name wicked up to the top of the list before being called out to work, and because of his so-called schooling, he could only accept assignments after normal working hours. However meager his income turned out to be, it at least provided some pocket change.

It amused him to no end when asked what a fireman on a train did. He would respond in a giggly, devious sort of way, almost exhibiting shame that he became a party to such a ridiculous bureaucratic operation that used firemen to oversee the potential fire hazards associated with the operation of a diesel engine and an electric motor. According to Jim, the position was a throwback from the good old days of coal-fired boilers that required some grunt to shovel the coal into the firebox. But since there were no steam engines anymore, except maybe in a few museums, the need for shoveling coal vanished and the position should have been retired. No chance, not as long as there was a union. No new-fangled machines were going to eliminate jobs. So what Jim and the other firemen did was to sit on their asses, stare into space and pay their union dues.

Jim had been away from home for about six months. He went away to join the Air Force, signing up for the Flying Cadet program. There was only one problem with this. He wasn't old enough. For Jim Pierce this was a minor obstacle. With the right contacts he managed to forge the necessary documents to show that he was twenty years old instead of the eighteen-odd years of his existence.

Initially, he managed to pull it off. He succeeded in completing basic training and half of his primary flight training before getting caught. From the outset he figured that it was just a matter of time before they caught up with him, and the length of time he managed to elude the truth was exactly the same amount it takes the FBI to run a background check on the applicants. His discharge was swift; his reprimand to the point. He was let go under less than honorable conditions, but no disciplinary action was taken. His papers carried the phrase, "utterance of false statement." So, off to Phoenix he went, back to Mom and Dad, and into Phoenix College.

If nothing else, the Air Force taught him two things. One was never to tell a lie; a lesson he quickly rationalized into "unless you think you can get away with it," and the other was how to fly an airplane. As a result of his flight training, all in North American AT-6's, in a limited sort of way, he was quite good at it. He had even progressed as far as basic aerobatics and was

For All The Wrong Reasons

reasonably proficient in the execution of the basic maneuvers, such as loops, rolls and other variations of those two that took on fancier titles such as Cuban Eights, Clover Leafs, and Immelmanns.

In short order Jim became one of the gang, a member of the flying club, a hanger-on at Maddux's and a devotee to the Rainbow Tavern - not necessarily in that order. In spite of knowing how to fly, and since all of his time was in Air Force equipment, he did not have a pilot's license, and had to start from scratch. Joe Mora turned out to be his instructor. Joe was lazy, and since whatever his efforts were, the pay was always the same. So, it was on that basis that Joe found a star, soloing Jim in the Airknocker in record time, leaving him more time to play with Nancy, and logging more couch time in the process. While Joe was indulging in his games, Jim too, was soon indulging in all of the games the other hotshots were playing, attempting to show off his self-proclaimed superior flying skills.

After morning classes one particularly hot day, Jim and Billy decided to drink their lunch at the Rainbow Tavern. Instead of draft beer, Jim, exhibiting his self-induced maturity, got Billy to drinking a heavy-bodied ale that was much stronger and faster acting than he was used to. Not being a connoisseur of anything other than the cheap stuff out of the tap, and being ignorant of the potency and potential results on which he was about to embark, but wanting to be a good sport and try anything at least once, he went along.

When they downed six bottles apiece and several cigarettes later, Jim suggested they wander out to the Maddux facility and rent an Airknocker so Jim could show Billy some aerobatics. It sounded like a good idea to Billy until they stepped out of the bar and into the hot sun. There the world seemed to spin and close in at the same time. He knew immediately that the script outlined by Jim was not going to be, but instead of protesting he concentrated all his efforts in negotiating his way to Jim's air-conditioned car where he thought that things would take on a better perspective. But time has a way of compressing itself when the spirits have dug that deep into one's system, and before he could object, they were both staggering around Maddux's trying to sign up for an airplane.

Under normal circumstances, considering the condition they were in, they would have been noticed, reprimanded, and ejected from the premises. On that particular day, events were taking place that were anything but normal. It just so happened that a Lockheed Constellation (Connie) had just

Chapter 9

made an unceremonious gear-up arrival on the main east-west runway. Everybody was too pre-occupied with the happenings at the crippled airplane to pay attention to the two potential suicide victims. Other than being completely ignored, the inebriates were directed to a Cessna 140, with the understanding that the Airknockers were scheduled up and therefore not available.

Two significant things germane to the scenario happened before the fearless aviators took off. Jim being unfamiliar with the Cessna, failed to secure the oil cap in a locked position after checking the oil. And Billy, who was supposed to be overseeing the operation, since he was the only one with a pilot's license, and thus the pilot-in-command, burned his hand trying to light one last cigarette before embarking on the mission. When he struck the gopher match, he failed to first close the cover as the print on the matchbook very clearly stated. The one nearly imperceptible spark sent the whole apparatus with most of the matches still attached and unused up in flames as he was firmly holding the entire package "en flambe" in his left hand.

At the time his attention was diverted to the Constellation, and his senses were so far gone due to his severe intoxication, that instead of dropping the flaming mass immediately, as he should have instinctively done, he held on to them in wonderment, until his sensory nerves sent the message to his brain, and then back to his fingers with instructions to "let go." Jim, anxious to get out of there lest they be discovered, was oblivious to the fireworks, and in a nagging sort of way kept shouting to Billy that he was ready to go. Billy was astonished that with all the charred and discolored skin on his left hand, he hardly felt any pain.

As he licked his wounded hand, still trying to take in the action surrounding the Constellation sitting helplessly in the middle of the runway, and at the same time trying to respond to the nagging directives from Jim, somehow stuffed himself in the left seat of the Cessna 140. Jim had already entered and was holding the control wheel firmly with both hands, wondering how he could adapt from the familiar use of stick controlled airplanes that he had been flying to a control-wheeled airplane with which he had absolutely no experience. This was the guy that Billy was putting his trust in to demonstrate an aerobatic routine in an airplane that was not even stressed for it, not to mention the oil cap and the burnt hand of the pilot in command.

The airplane engine started right up, a clear demonstration of compensating errors. Billy called the tower for taxi instructions, added power to

For All The Wrong Reasons

start the airplane rolling, and wondered why it only wanted to move in a clockwise circle. Somebody forgot to untie the right wing chain. Since Jim was in the right seat, he got blamed for it, and being as drunk as Billy, he thought he deserved the dressing down besides the ass-chewing made him feel right at home, as back in Cadet training. All he did in return was mumble unintelligibly while maintaining his death grip on the control wheel.

Billy shut the engine down, climbed out, rocked the right wing to relieve the tension on the chain, unfastened the chain and with an exasperated grunt, sandwiched himself back in the left seat. All this time Jim continued to hold fast to the wheel, staring straight ahead as if they were actually flying.

This time they were not so lucky starting the engine. In the short time that it had run, the spark plugs managed to foul, and the subsequent cranking flooded it smartly. It was strictly a credit to the curiosity of the events centering on the Constellation that those on the ramp, some of whom were responsible employees of the firm, that the ensuing machinations were not discovered. But before the battery ground down to a halt the engine fired, first a weak hit on one cylinder, then a couple more, and finally all four indicated their readiness to go out and get killed along with the boys.

The tower, responding to the radio call, directed the dynamically drunken duo to the diagonal runway that joined the main east-west runway at the northeast end of the airport, right behind the wounded Constellation. It was runway 21 and as the number indicates heads out to the southwest. The taxi-way to the east end of the airport paralleled the main east-west runway and took the boys very close to the action, affording them a ring-side seat of the happenings around the accident.

As Billy taxied out he observed that the crew attending the Constellation, was in the process of inflating large air cells that were squeezed under the airliner at various strategic locations. These air bags when inflated would raise the Constellation high enough to enable the crew to manually wrestle the gear down, locking it in place by whatever means the situation allowed. This could range anywhere from welding the thing in place to installing oversized "C" clamps. Once the airplane was restored on its wheels, the air bags would then be deflated, removed, folded, and put in storage to await the next "arrival."

With all of the excitement on the runway, his injured hand, and his state of inebriation, it was all Billy could do to concentrate on the problem at hand, maneuvering the airplane out to the run-up area, located at the ap-

Chapter 9

proach end of 21, the diagonal runway he was instructed to use.

Another factor that added to his distractions was Jim who was still grasping the control wheel very firmly with both hands. If not for the noise of the engine, Billy would have perceived a "brrrr" sound from Jim's pursed lips accompanied by the fine spray of beer-saturated saliva. The spray was there all right, but barely noticeable. It was enough to make Billy retract his hand from the throttle that was in the line of fire, but not enough to cause the inside of the windshield to be splattered. This manifestation on Jim's part would have been grounds under normal circumstances to abort the mission in favor of more drink at the watering hole. But these were not normal circumstances.

The run-up was uneventful, only because if it had been necessary to abort the flight due to a mechanical malfunction, Billy would not have noticed anyway. So with the proper clearance from the control tower, they taxied onto runway 21, Jim still maintaining his death grip on the control wheel, poured on the coal, all 85 horses, and went screaming down the runway, hell bent for victory.

A left downwind departure took them on a heading toward Scottsdale. In their drunken state before they realized it, were on the north side of Camelback Mountain at 3,000 feet. At this point, Jim declared in his slurred and indistinct voice, that he had it all figured out. But Billy couldn't figure out what Jim had said he figured out. It was all very confusing to him until he finally realized that Jim was completely unfamiliar with a wheel control on an airplane. But when Billy, in his equally slurred speech tried to question him about it, Jim loudly professed that there was "no problem" and "the show must go on."

With that declaration, he pointed the nose of the airplane down to a negative pitch angle of about 20 degrees, quickly building up what he thought should be sufficient entry speed for a loop. Achieving that phase of the maneuver, Jim horsed back on the wheel bringing the nose up through the horizon, to the inverted position. Billy virtually floated in his seat belt, and Jim continued pulling on the wheel through the backside of the loop to where the next thing Billy realized, they were pointed straight down toward "terra firma." It was on the backside of the maneuver that Jim pulled the power off, and tugged reasonably hard on the wheel, sufficient to impose "G" forces that Billy had never experienced before.

For All The Wrong Reasons

Another thing that rattled Billy was the rapid build-up of airspeed experienced on the backside of the loop. The rushing sound of the wind and the severe buffeting made Billy wonder if it would all hold together, or if the wings would decide to go their own way.

Jim continued to pull hard, adding full power while bringing the nose up past the horizon to a positive pitch attitude of about 20 degrees, whereupon with maximum left wheel input, he rolled the airplane through a positive "G" aileron roll and declared in a loud shrilled expression that it was "all duck soup," ending what he considered an "obviously magnificent and successfully simple maneuver." Oddly enough they ended up back at 3,000 feet, and as Billy noted, that except for that short period of time on top of the loop, there where no negative "G's" in the process.

Now it was time that the guru of aerobatics show Billy how to do it. This proved to be no easy feat. On the first attempt, the airplane got uncomfortably light on the topside of the loop. It actually went negative for a short time, falling through the top on its back, and starving the engine of life sustaining fuel. The engine momentarily quit. The follow through was inadequate. There was not enough backpressure through the backside of the maneuver, therefore the airspeed built up past the red line. It would have been worse if Jim had not taken over at the appropriately critical time. The roll phase was quickly canceled in lieu of a hasty discourse by Jim on the merits of a well-executed loop, and the consequences of one not so well executed. To wit, they could both end up on the wrong end of a post-mortem critique.

Nausea and fear on Billy's part brought the lesson to a halt, probably saving their lives. He shuddered when the reality of the airspeed over red line, and the noise and buffeting occasionally reoccurred to him. It wasn't until on the return trip that oil on the windshield became apparent. That added to his despair. In addition to his nausea and fright he became deeply depressed.

Thankfully the Constellation was still sitting on the runway in a compromising position, continuing to distract those who would normally be interested in the adventures of Billy, Jim and the Cessna 140.

As the two fearless flyers parked the airplane on the Maddux ramp, in the process of tying it down, they noticed a copious amount of oil all over the front portion of the airplane. Further inspection revealed a very wet,

Chapter 9

black streak of the same stuff along the entire length of the belly. Tracing the origin of the streaks led them back to the oil cap, which when rotated slightly to the right, popped into the detent. This feature was specifically designed into the cap to indicate that it was not only tight against the gasket but securely in place.

Discretion and deviousness overtaking honesty and integrity, they decided to immediately take a hasty retreat from the area to their car without going into the office to log in and pay. This minor detail could be taken care of at a later date. At this time it seemed wise not to indulge anyone, other than themselves, in conversation for any reason.

On the way to the car, they both looked over their respective shoulders for any indication that they had been discovered. Thankfully to their good fortune, the entire crew from the flying service was still gawking at the activities on the runway, which had progressed to the stage of lowering the landing gear of the disabled airliner. Feeling slightly cocky as they drove out of the lot, Jim suggested another meeting at the Rainbow Tavern for the constructive purpose of a thorough debriefing. This was not to be, Billy was becoming dreadfully ill. The pain in his hand and his head were unbearable, an indication that the booze was wearing off.

It wasn't more than a few blocks down the road that he ordered Jim to stop the car. As soon as the car came to a screeching halt, he opened the door, leaned over the side and vomited his guts out. There would be no more nefarious activities that day. From there it was a trip home and to bed, in contemplation of when this whole episode would come back to haunt them.

The next day, so as not to prolong the agony, they decided to wander over to Maddux's to settle the account, settle their anxieties, and to face the music, if that was the case. Billy's worst fears became a reality. Both of the firm's partners suspected that the previous day's flight occurred while the two were under the influence. Maddux himself had to concede that they had no direct knowledge of the occurrence, neither one of them having been present because of the excitement surrounding the Constellation. But they had been told by a reliable source, whose identity could not be revealed for the sake of his well being, that the culprits were staggering around in less than a sober manner.

To defend themselves, Jim put on the ultimate con job, better than the one that got him into the Air Force, assuring Maddux that no harm would

For All The Wrong Reasons

come to the accuser if he would only divulge his identity for curiosity's sake alone. All the time Jim was conning Maddux, Billy was shouting over him that if he ever found out who in the hell it was that made such an outrageous charge, he would beat the shit out of him.

Then there was the oil on both the inside of the cowling and over a large percentage of the outside to consider. Why did they so hastily depart the premises without first paying for the flying time or reporting the oil problem? According to Maddux, the engine had thrown out all but the last quart; one last quart and our heroes would have been history, if not from the crash then by the hands of Mr. Maddux himself.

Billy was adamant in his response. At the insinuation of less than stellar conduct, he took on the role of the injured party. The explanation was reasonable. They did try to check in after flying the airplane, but there was no one around tending the office, and they were running late for school. Those who should have helped them were out by the runway reveling in the miseries of others, namely the two pilots of the Constellation, instead of minding their own business and providing a service to their good and conscientious customers. As for the oil leak and paying the tab, that was the very reason they returned the next day, as soon as they could.

Before the bullshit session was over, it still remained a mystery as to how all of that oil got tossed overboard, but nevertheless Maddux and his partner ended up apologizing for the inconvenience and the close call suffered by Billy and Jim. It didn't take long during the discussion before Jim realized that there was probably less than 15 minutes of operating time left on the engine before it would have seized for lack of lubrication, and turned the airplane into a glider.

Maddux's mechanic could find no tangible reason for the oil phenomenon. He could only wildly speculate on far fetched theories he pulled out of his ass to explain why the problem could not be duplicated and the engine subsequently ran as well as could be expected containing all of the oil in its proper place, the crankcase. A stuck ring that later became unstuck was accepted as the most popular explanation.

Even at the impassioned insistence of the two delinquents, Maddux refused to squeal on the source of his information, but to appease Jim and Billy, who by this time had taken the offensive, he agreed to waive the rental charge in exchange for forgetting the entire incident. With sadness over

Chapter 9

being questioned unfavorably about his conduct, Billy agreed.

The episode of the drinking, flying recklessly while drunk, and escaping being called to account spurred Jim on to bigger and better things. He attacked his program at the college with more vigor and enthusiasm. Merely flying the Airknocker wasn't enough, nor did he think that the antics of Billy and the rest of the boys were noteworthy. No, he was hell bent on wringing out the Airknocker, and this he did with a series of loops, each followed immediately by an aileron roll was something that the rest of them were too chicken to attempt, especially in an Aeronca Champion.

One fine and sunny day, while Jim was out in the practice area over the cotton and alfalfa fields, he met the challenge. On the very top of a loop Jim and the airplane got awfully light. For some reason, either he was distracted, lost concentration, or merely wanted to feel the sensation of negative "G's," he didn't pull hard enough on the stick to maintain a positive, or at least a zero "G" force, enough to feed life sustaining fuel to the engine. The small 65 horse Continental that had up to that instant been the dependable workhorse all could reasonably count on to bring the troops home to the familiar pilot lounge, and the other lounge of less repute, gave up the ghost for lack of 80 octane in the carburetor. No problem thought Jim as he took up the slack by applying more backpressure on the stick in effort to pull the "G's" back into the scenario. It was too late and too little. All he was successful in doing was allowing the flimsy machine to fall toward the ground in slightly less than a true inverted configuration. Little Jim was in big trouble.

The small, 65 horsepower Continental engine selected for that model airplane normally provides good and dependable service. It is actually lauded as an excellent power plant, able to continue to function almost maintenance free for the 1,500 some-odd hours between recommended overhauls. But being a good engine also had its downside which was excellent compression. So good that when the rpm slowed because of fuel starvation, the propeller came to a sudden halt at the same time Jim was on his back struggling to save his ass.

He spent his time concentrating on how to right the airplane without pulling the wings off, giving little regard to the other problem of no power, thinking that engine stoppage was normal under the circumstances of slow airspeed. His thinking was once the "G" forces were restored, on the backside of the loop the airspeed would increase to the point that the rushing air

For All The Wrong Reasons

over the blades would cause the propeller to windmill, reestablishing the engine to its normal role of pulling the Airknocker through the air.

It's like pushing your car to get it started, something that all starving students who couldn't afford replacement batteries had to do on occasion. Either a group of people, or another car, would push to the extent that the vehicle would go fast enough to kick the motor over after the driver, when he thought the time was right, would disengage the clutch. After a few jumps and bucks, hopefully the motor would catch and it would be off to the races so to speak. This is what was going on in Jim's mind while he wrestled with one problem at a time.

The same principle was being applied in Jim's case, but instead of a herd of people or another airplane doing the pushing to jump-start the engine, he was counting on potential energy afforded by altitude, or what was left of it to do the job. At the bottom of his loop, with a dead engine and a stationary prop that was all but sticking in his face, he had only 1,000 feet left.

Having recovered from the worst of it, he diverted his attention to the next critical problem of restarting the engine. He pointed the nose of the airplane down below the horizon to build up more speed, exceeding the red line on the airspeed indicator; a line that should have told him that wiser designers and test pilots thought advisable not to encroach. This provided a very slight movement of the propeller, but not enough to rotate it through a compression stroke; therefore, not enough to get it started. However, it did manage to move the blade over enough to get it out of his face. He dared not go faster, not because the airplane couldn't take it, because after all, according to what he had been taught, there is always a built in safety factor in virtually all designs, but because of the unbearable noise and shaking in which he was being subjected. He was too chicken to push the limits any farther than he already had.

With only a meager 500 feet left, and still a dead engine, Jim decided that he would rather become a better glider pilot than he was an aerobatic pilot. Straining the landscape to find a suitable landing site, and almost giving up in despair, he finally discovered a lush alfalfa field directly beneath him that was one-half mile long and just as wide. There appeared to be no obstructions, such as trees or wires, on either end. Wind wasn't a factor, as it was still too early in the morning for the sun to have generated enough wind or gusts to cause him problems. It was to be his first experience at a "for real"

Chapter 9

dead stick landing, and bona fide emergency. The question was, would he rise to the occasion, or fail miserably as the odds indicated he should?

Everything considered it was a stellar performance. He had the presence of mind to set up a regular traffic pattern. A quick turn to the left and Jim was on downwind for a landing to the west out of the sun. It was a move he was to later claim was calculated, but the others in the discussion maintained that it was just dumb luck. His base leg was perfect, though a little low, so he was forced to quickly turn final close to the near side of the field. As it turned out it was another stroke of dumb luck because it put him on the same side of the field that the farmhouse was located. The touch down was perfect, in the first third of the length, with a reasonable three point landing.

The field as it turned out was dry, hard and smooth. The alfalfa was mature and as such was long enough to be Jim's downfall with Boots Farraday. On the roll out, it slapped the shit out of the wheels, the lower part of the landing gear structure, and possibly the tail feathers, to the point where the noise, sounding worse than it was, played hell with Jim's nerves. But he kept his head and let the airplane roll to a stop without the need for brakes. There was still plenty of room. At this point it wouldn't be prudent to stand on the brakes and end up sliding to a stop on his back.

Alfalfa fields in that area are normally graded with six or eight-inch high irrigation humps about thirty feet apart, in parallel, running the entire length. Protruding from the sides of these small banks, at an angle in the direction of the flow of irrigation water, are additional humps of the same size, about four or five feet in length. These are constructed to ensure that the crop is evenly irrigated, and could pose a problem if the airplane rolled across the humps. Not to Jim; his concentration was directed to steering his airplane straight between and parallel to the humps, right down the center, lest any direction contrary to the intended might have the same result as standing on the brakes; inverted flight along the ground.

After what seemed to be a small eternity, the Airknocker rolled to a safe and complete stop under the watchful eye of the farmer. He had observed the airshow from the very beginning. Having substantial experience with airplanes he thought Jim was a complete nut for over-stressing the machine with the aerobatic maneuver, and wasn't surprised when the results were as happened especially since the Airknocker wasn't equipped with an inverted

For All The Wrong Reasons

fuel and oil system.

The farmer just happened to be out preparing the field for irrigation and thought that Jim's timing was fortunate because at that time the ground was dry and very hard. If Jim had tried his foolishness a few hours later when the ground was wet and soggy he would surely have ended up on his back. It was this fact that he kept repeating when he constantly reminded Jim of how lucky he was which was a premise Jim completely disregarded in lieu of his perception that the whole exercise was a demonstration of excellent airmanship.

The next step was to get the hell out of there. No, the farmer didn't know how to prop the airplane. Yes, he had the sense and know-how to sit in the seat and hold the brakes while Jim cranked on it, and no, he wouldn't call the school for the purpose of blowing the whistle on the perilous pilot. With all those assurances and still feeling quite cocky, Jim stuffed the farmer into the back seat, and under Jim's guidance held the stick back and placed his heels on the brake pedals pushing as hard as he could.

After a few twists of the prop, the engine willingly gave in, running like a Swiss watch. Both participants were equally impressed with the little effort it was taking to get the show on the road. Jim then slid into the front seat, relieved the farmer of his duties, and cautioned him against unwarranted collision with the rotating prop after exiting the airplane. He continued to ramble on with his admonishment, letting the farmer know that after all he had been through he didn't need his blood and guts splattered all over the airplane. The farmer, feeling insulted by the insinuations that he was stupid, slammed the door, stepped back and threw Jim the finger.

Jim didn't even taxi to the end of the field for his departure run. He merely turned the airplane around with copious power and the added assistance of the farmer who pushed on the appropriate wing strut, lined up with the rows, and without the benefit of a pre-takeoff magneto check, hauled-ass charging through the atmosphere.

His trip home was direct and uneventful. He would have been successful in pulling off the caper undetected, except for two things; one, there was alfalfa stuck in every crack and crevice of the main gear and tail section. This was discovered when he returned. And the fact that Bruce Birran was flying overhead at 4,000 feet witnessing the whole thing, except the loop, didn't help him a bit.

Chapter 9

Bruce beat him back with ten minutes to spare. Like Paul Revere when he discovered the English were on their doorstep, Bruce for lack of a horse, ran up to the office, and announced Jim's unusual circumstance and impending arrival, for all to hear, including the mechanic, Boots Farraday, and other students who were just hanging around.

Thinking that he pulled off a successful caper, it was a surprise to Jim when he taxied to the parking area to discover the small gathering waiting to greet him. Even before he exited the airplane, Boots and company were surrounding it, pulling alfalfa from the various parts, while displaying strained facial expressions of those who might be handling dog shit instead of wholesome plant life.

The upshot was a torture session, one-on-one, with Boots in the privacy of his office. These confrontations represented some of Boots' finest hours. Being the bully he was, he relished them, virtually lived for them, and took full advantage of the opportunity to display all of the quirks of his theatrical conduct, like twitching his mustache, smacking his lips, staring off in space, and mustering all of his experiences in related matters.

But Jim was not to be denied either. He had been up against the very best; the Air Force. He was much faster on his feet than Boots. In Jim, Boots had met his match. Jim was very smooth. His story was ironclad. Every argument Boots had for terminating him, Jim had a counter argument and a more persuasive one. After all, Jim in his own mind, had done nothing wrong.

Boots maintained that engines don't just fail. Jim must have done something to hurt the engine for it to quit on him. Jim, on the other hand, had a reasonable explanation as to why it failed for no apparent reason. He had been in the process of practicing very steep power off stalls, when, with the nose of the airplane "way up in the air," the engine idled down to a very slow speed, and probably due to fuel starvation, breathed its last.

The explanation had merit, but Boots' mind was made up. Jim must go. Without calling him a liar, he really didn't believe a word of what Jim was selling. Besides, Boots hadn't kicked anyone out of the school since axing John Wing for his dead stick landing at the cotton gin near Casa Grande, and his appetite needed satiating.

The final verdict according to Mr. Farraday's best judgment: Maybe the explanation for losing the engine had merit but Jim should have left the airplane in the field and called the school for help. He should not, as a

For All The Wrong Reasons

student pilot, risk having an accident by attempting to bring the airplane home. Therefore he was to be tossed out on his ass, but not before he was to be held up before the entire class as an example of what to do in similar situations and conversely what not to do.

In playing out the final act, Boots had to make a simple matter complicated by sprinkling the lecture with a half dozen stories, based on his own experience, of people getting killed doing the same or similar things etc. etc. etc., all the while staring off in space, smacking his lips, twitching his mustache, and strutting around the room like an eighteenth century actor. Jim was history.

Chapter 10

The antics of Boots Farraday didn't impress the delinquents one bit. It only reinforced their conviction of why he was called "Boots." In any case they were tiring of the usual games of chasing horses and dog fighting in the school's Airknockers, so it was only a coincidence that they quit abusing the school's equipment around the time of Jim's demise and not because of any action taken by Mr. Farraday. They resorted instead to a different method of boredom relief, that by its nature, required the use of Maddux's airplanes. This new adventure took on the characteristic of a poor man's Cleveland Air Race, to be held at the site of Aux.1 north of Phoenix, the same place that Joe was caught diddling Nancy. Now they were really getting serious about killing themselves.

On the day of reckoning, six of the group showed up in three of Maddux's rentals, two Airknockers and the fateful Cessna 140. The latter, but for the grace of God, should have bitten the dust when Jim and Billy were practicing for future airshows. It was incredible to them that nobody at Maddux's appeared suspicious that six of the biggest trouble makers on the airport were all departing in three separate airplanes at the same time in the same direction. But suspicious or not, it was not Billy's concern. After the lack of an adequate pre-flight inspection, the three airplanes departed for an uneventful flight from Sky Harbor, headed north in loose formation, landed at Aux.1, parked and grouped up for the essential meeting to establish the rules of the contest.

The race was to be conducted as follows; the airplanes were to line up on the extension strip, three abreast, facing west. This part of Aux.1 was barely wide enough to accommodate them, but except for the uncomfortably tight squeeze, they managed. At some god-awful signal which nobody understood anyway, they were to go like hell, flying straight out for the mile

For All The Wrong Reasons

it took to get to the west edge of the field, then complete a pattern to the left, staying outside the boundary of the one-half mile square that comprised the main part of the field. After establishing a downwind leg outside of the southern border of the field, it was balls out to see who could get on the ground at the starting point first.

Since there were only three licensed pilots in the group, the others would act as an additional pair of eyes as a safety precaution against the possibility of tangling wings. The term "safety precaution" seemed ludicrous in this context, in light of everything these people routinely did, or believed. In fact, they were all crazy and this exercise could only end up in a first class disaster.

But notwithstanding that possibility, they all fired-up and lined up on the strip, all three wingtip to wingtip, to await the signal. Their relative position was established by a coin toss which in itself was unfair seeing as how Jack owned the two headed coin, tossed it, and then called it in the air. When he won the toss, he selected the left or inside position. He thought this would give him an advantage seeing as how the inside route would be shorter. Being on the inside also made him the official starter or signal giver which was thought to be an additional advantage. He could jump start the process. For a partner he brought along his girlfriend. It would all make for good reading when the news coverage revealed that an innocent female was involved in the conflagrative disaster.

Billy and Jim Pierce were positioned on the far right side in the Cessna 140, with Don Schooner and John Wing in the precarious middle. Billy and Jim called "heads" when Jack threw the coin again, and selected the outside because as they reasoned, their airplane had more horse-power than the two Airknockers, and would supposedly accelerate faster, and drive around the circuit in a shorter time. Therefore the others agreed that his selection of the outside was a fair handicap considering the faster speed, but what Billy was more interested in was the ability to swing out of the way of the others in case things got too sticky for him. Jim had his own ideas as to the merits of the outside position, and the safety aspect was not one of them. He had it in his mind that his team would pull out in front immediately and do the first turn ahead and below the other two. After all, he was an almost bona-fide fighter pilot, and self proclaimed aerobatics expert, so he should know.

Holding fast to their positions by standing on the brakes, all three spooled up their engines to full power, creating a huge dust cloud. They just sat

Chapter 10

there with their brakes locked waiting for Jack's signal to start. It seemed like an eternity, making Billy wonder if Jack wasn't having second thoughts about the whole deal. Billy never did see his signal to roll. The first indication he got that the race was on, was Jack moving out in the lead, followed by Schooner in the middle. Billy immediately released his brakes, rolling ever so slowly behind the others. His immediate thought, as he started eating their dust, was that they had conned him when they put out that shit about the Cessna and its superior acceleration.

Before Billy and Jim broke ground the other two were a hundred feet in front and twenty feet in the air. It's even a wonder that they were able to get off without stacking the airplane, because the dust generated by the other two airplanes was so severe that Billy had no forward visibility at all, and managed to keep the airplane straight only by reference to the right edge of the runway. As soon as he became airborne, he slid sideways to the right side for a cleaner, more visible path.

Jim reminded Billy to hold it low, with the idea that they could make their first turn underneath their competitors instead of on the outside. Being very close to the ground made the Cessna fly more efficiently. It wasn't too far down the dirt field that Billy found himself catching up in a respectable fashion. By the time they reached the west end (a mile from where they started) the other two were in tight formation, about one hundred feet high, starting their first turn. Jim grabbed the wheel away from his partner. He was determined to turn underneath his competitors, even though they were very low and it didn't look like there was enough room. It was a tight squeeze but it worked. The show would have been more spectacular and entertaining if watched from a shady spot on the ground instead of the left seat of the piece of shit airplane. There it was, five fools and an innocent girl in three airplanes grouped tighter than sardines in a can, fighting for position in the first turn. The lower Cessna barely clearing the sage-brush and greasewood, with the other airplanes dueling with each other slightly higher and to the right of Billy and Jim. Thank God nobody burped. It would have been all over.

Schooner and Jack had no idea where the Cessna was. The last time they saw it was at the beginning of the take-off roll. They were too preoccupied in the exercise of self-preservation to be concerned with the position of Billy and Jim. These guys were supposed to be on the outside of the group anyway since that was the position where they started. Everything was

For All The Wrong Reasons

happening too fast for the good of Maddux's airplanes, the five degenerates and the innocent victim.

Screaming along on the second leg heading south on the outside of the west boundary, the fools in the three airplanes were almost neck 'n' neck, with the two Airknockers faithfully holding their position about 100 feet off of the deck. Billy and Jim in the Cessna, were below and slightly behind, but slowly catching up. The second turn to the east was no better than the first but it might even have been scarier. Jim laid the Cessna on its side with no consideration for the stark fear that was plain on Billy's face. It appeared to Billy that the left wing was going to drag the ground, and when he glanced over at Jim for some sign of reassurance, all he got in return was the toothy grin of a madman who was hell-bent on destroying them all.

The first time Schooner and Jack became aware of their competitor was on the downwind, outside the south border of the field. The run would be over a mile long considering allowances for a reasonable but short final approach. When the lead airplane was about half way along the south boundary, the Cessna finally overtook them, appearing to virtually squirt out beneath and in front of them. In a later discussion, Jack stated that he couldn't believe that there was enough room between him and the ground for an airplane to pass beneath. He said that at the time it appeared as though the Cessna was dragging its wheels through the brush. In fact, at one point when Jim became distracted, that's exactly what happened. Billy horsed back on the controls just in time to avoid what he thought would be a collision with a sagebrush. In retrospect the others remembered the incident when it happened, because the Cessna popped up abruptly in front of them. Jim, not ready to admit a potentially dreadful screw up, minimized the event by accusing the others of gross exaggeration. He maintained that he always had complete control of the situation.

From that point on, it was duck soup for the two in the Cessna. They were well out in front when they turned what Billy considered a dangerously close in base leg. Jim strained to look out the right window to the rear for a glimpse of the progress of their two competitors. What he saw shocked him into realization, and he began to wonder if they had not overextended their ability and luck. Monett and Schooner were virtually glued together in a low turn from downwind to base at an uncomfortably low altitude. He expected them both to go cartwheeling in unison across the desert.

Chapter 10

When he returned his gaze to the matters at hand, he found himself in no better position. Being disoriented from the backward glance out the right window during the turn to the left, the airplane got away from him. It was at that point that Billy started flying it again. Billy for sure thought he was going to die, because the airplane was headed for the ground in a steep left turn to final. Billy had long ago surrendered to the fear of dying, and now he finally knew how it felt to look death in the face. The back pressure to correct the problem was so severe that the airplane shuddered at the onset of a high speed stall.

Everything considered, it was a miracle that in spite of the gross screw-ups, it all ended well, probably due to compensating errors. They rounded out of the turn and shallow dive at the same time just above the Palo Verde tree that on a better day Billy would be destined to trim with the wheels of the Airknocker during a short field landing contest. Again because of compensating errors, they were lined up on the strip along the north edge, exactly where they were supposed to be.

A half-assed landing, a controlled stop after rolling straight ahead far enough to reduce the risk of being clobbered by their ass-hole buddies, and a 180 degree turn was completed in that order. There they paused long enough to assess the progress of Jack and Schooner. Jack came in a close second, with Schooner winning in a protestation contest, arguing that he was cheated throughout the entire contest. Billy, for a moment while unwinding, wondered what had taken place, and when he collected himself, vociferously declared that if he was going to do that again, it was going to be with bicycles. Jack's girlfriend thought the whole thing was great and wanted to have another race. She said it made her horny.

Chapter 11

That was the first, only and last of the closed course racing in airplanes. They had to come up with another plan. This called for unending deliberations at the Rainbow Tavern. Even this place became boring, but they were stuck with it because there was no other place in town that would take an under-aged group of that size. They needed another unique and challenging game to play and one not as dangerous as the last or they would find themselves spending too much time in the dark and beer-stinking corner of their meeting place.

Ultimately a unique form of short field landings took shape into something that had possibilities. In this event, each would take his turn in the Airknocker, to determine who could land in the shortest distance. The competition would take place at the popular Aux.1, on the one-half mile extended dirt strip on the north side. The approach would be from the east over a Palo Verde tree. When one of them was in the act of trying to destroy the Airknocker, the others while waiting their turn, would hang around, waiting in anticipation for the other guy to roll the airplane up in a ball in a fantastic spectacle. In addition to this morbid pastime, the spectators would mark the spot where the airplane ceased to roll - or more like sliding to a screeching stop. The exercise was slightly more challenging considering the Palo Verde tree was located very close to the threshold of the runway. It was tall enough to create a reasonable hazard standing at 25 feet high.

Two of the contestants would check out and ferry the Airknocker from the Maddux facility, while the others mobiled to the site. When it was all over, the plan called for those participating to share equally in the rental charge of the airplane but not before deducting the usual thirty percent of the flying time from the total to mitigate the expense. In all, the activity was

For All The Wrong Reasons

designed to provide a fun-filled afternoon for a very modest cost, probably less than that expended at the Rainbow Tavern in the same time frame.

Throughout these episodes, the landing distances became shorter in proportion to the added skills, better techniques, and more courage. They were all challenging the limits to get those few extra feet it took to be declared the winner. When it became apparent that the shortest landing was a thing of the past, only to be dabbled with around the edges, Billy devised a theory he jealously kept to himself. If he were to land with the brakes locked up, instead of applying them during the roll out, the result should produce the ultimate short field landing, bringing him glory forever among his peers. However, there was one big concern, the fear of flipping the airplane over on its back in the process.

In a round-about way, and in a fashion not to give away the reason for his inquiry, he consulted with one of Maddux's flight instructors about the chances of that ever happening. The guy was a WWII fighter pilot with "beau coup" experience, mostly in P-47's. Mark Trimble was his name. Although he was a shiftless airport bum and a "has been," he was still the best one with whom Billy could discuss the matter. He had more tail-wheel time than anyone else Billy knew, and could half way trust. The P-47 was, after all, a tail dragger, and Mark with all his war time exploits claimed to have operated off of a short PSP runway during the fighting without scuttling his airplane. This was a feat, according to him, that most of his comrades could not claim.

Mark's technique under the circumstances described by Billy, was simply to feed in and maintain a copious amount of power to hold the tail down. Even with full power and the brakes hung up, the airplane could slide along the ground in that mode and actually slow down. The forces generated by the prop-wash under the added power plays the part of holding the tail down, thus preventing it from going over the top resulting in an upside down embarrassment. It was very important according to Mark, that the pilot hold the stick all the way back in his lap during the entire exercise. He went on to explain that many times when he was in the precarious process of overshooting the runway, he would apply the technique when he felt the tail getting light because of heavy braking. Inevitably the down forces caused by the prop blast on the up elevator, stick all the way back, would hold the

Chapter 11

tail down, all while the net result was the slowing down of the airplane.

He expressed his surprise and delight that Billy was interested in the procedure, because of the safety aspect of keeping one out of trouble in case a situation called for landing on a very short strip. He wished that all young pilots were as conscientious and interested as Billy.

From that point on, Mark had found a protégé and would go out of his way to inform his new found friend on the intricacies of flying as he knew them. On the other hand Billy felt that he had created a monster. He wasn't interested and wished that Mark would leave him alone, but being basically a considerate individual, he tolerated Mark's interest when he had to, soaking up all his available knowledge. He didn't, however, go as far as to invite Mark to tip a brew with him and the others.

Billy couldn't wait to try the theory out. So without procrastinating, having lost the last encounter, and with his new found wealth of knowledge, he campaigned the others for a rematch. He couldn't wait to engage the combatants. He felt he had a sure fire method and was a shoe-in for victory.

It turned out to be a hot and gusty day by the time they all gathered at Aux.1 for the fun and games. Each took several attempts in their quest to close the distance from the spot where the airplane quit rolling to the threshold of the runway. So far Jack's landings were the shortest. Jim was there and complained that they wouldn't let him fly, for lack of a bona fide license, or he would show them all how it was done. It was a good thing, because it was the consensus that if he were allowed to participate, the airplane would most likely be returned to its rightful owner in the back of a flat-bed truck. With all his determination and the application of his new found knowledge, Billy was still coming up short of the mark. Even though he was doing sliding stops, a maneuver the others thought was gutsy, he was still too hot (fast) over the tree to enable a touch down close enough to the end to put him in contention with Jack.

On his last try of the day, He was determined to drag it in on the edge of a stall, just above the tree, chopping the power as soon it was directly below him, then dumping the nose down, and within three to five feet above the ground, horsing back on the stick, while at the same time applying full brakes. This sounded real good when he went over the sequence in his mind. He couldn't wait to try it, firmly resolving not to fake himself out into adding power, thus airspeed, over the top of the tree. The secret, he was

For All The Wrong Reasons

convinced, was in a partial stall approach.

Off he went, mentally rehearsing the routine as he charged around the pattern. To ensure the slow attitude over the tree, he made a very low, slow and long final approach. It was so slow that he was already in a partial stall well short of the end, and so low he was below the top of the tree as he approached. This was turning out to be a comedy of errors. Raising the nose to clear the top slowed the airplane even more, very close to a disastrous end. The answer was more power. He was reluctant to add very much more for fear of overshooting Jack's winning mark. Already, because of the prevailing gusts, jockeying the power more than he would have liked to, and constantly nibbling at the controls became necessary as the gusts were influencing the airplane's performance. He was being bounced around considerably. What started out to be a simple game of "who could land the shortest" had developed into a very scary situation.

However, there he was, sitting over the tree hanging by his fingernails, and if he was going to do it, he needed to pull the throttle now. He did! It was at exactly the right spot, at the right height, and the correct airspeed. At that instant, nature wanting to help in his quest to conquer his competition, contributed in the form of a downdraft, sending him, in a full stall with a nose high attitude, through the top branches of the tree. All of a sudden he found himself in a position that he was unable to escape by applying power and dumping the nose. He poked the throttle to it anyway, holding the nose up to avoid the inevitable. The Airknocker continued to shudder in a stall, as it settled through the top of the tree, chopping small branches on its way to the runway.

Up came the ground. Just in time, Billy once again pulled the power and at the same time horsed back on the stick to keep from hitting on the mains. Just as classic as it should have been, the Airknocker unceremoniously dropped in on all three wheels at the same time, on the very end, within ten feet of the tree. Billy subconsciously had both feet firmly planted on the brakes. The wheels slid. The tail got light, but Billy was ready. He goosed the engine with power, holding the stick all the way back in his lap. The Airknocker slid to a complete stop. Billy shut down, and trying to appear nonchalant, emerged from the airplane to both gloat over his feat and assess the damage that most certainly should have occurred when he drove the

Chapter 11

poor Airknocker through the upper part of the tree.

Without a doubt, it was an award winning stellar performance, beating the next best ever by over a hundred feet. He was virtually sitting within thirty feet from the end of the runway. He was very lucky that the stuff he plowed through was nothing more than small branches the size of twigs, and tiny leaves typical of the Palo Verde tree. Even the larger branches on these trees were no larger than three inches in diameter. The trunk on this one was less than six inches across. The stuff at the top where Billy blazed his trail was smaller than one-half inch with a lot of it more like one-quarter of an inch in diameter. He tried to point these facts out to his colleagues who appeared visibly shaken by the display of irresponsibility. It was no big deal. Other than the green stain that covered parts of the airplane, mostly the landing gear, and the tiny leaves pasted on the surface of the oily parts such as the bottom of the cowling and the landing gear oleo shocks, everything was in great shape.

Now that he was the victor, his next move was to concentrate on two more items. One was his compulsion to gloat over his tremendous feat while at the same time hiding the tremors in his hands, and the other was to receive honors and adulations worthy of the feat. A third item momentarily forgotten because of the first two, was the chore of restoring the finish of the aircraft components to their previous state. This turned out to be no easy task, but it was doable. Pitching sand on the oily parts of the cowling and oleo strut, then removing the mess with an equally dirty rag retrieved from the trunk of the car proved adequate to the non-critical eye. The same rag was put to good use on the green stains. The oil and sand mixture on the cloth acted as a rubbing compound and except for screwing up the finish to some minor degree, did the job at least to the extent of keeping them out of trouble. All that was left was to remove the twigs from the crevices and joints. This done it was home with the airplane, then on to the Rainbow Tavern to rehash the harrowing adventure, embellishing the details each time the event was retold.

Chapter 12

Billy Cotton's two year stint at Phoenix Junior College was mostly fun and games and studying was not included in his agenda. Otherwise it involved flying those small junky airplanes, washing trucks to pay his way, drinking all the beer that he could afford, and getting laid as often as possible. As for the latter, he used the airplane as the vehicle to achieve that end. Now he could see why Joe Mora liked to fly. There was something exciting about flying that made the opposite sex horny. The most difficult part of the sexual experience was not in getting it done but finding a romantic and comfortable place to do it. Most of the time even a car was adequate, but Billy owned a motor scooter. If he told stories about how he got laid across the seat of his scooter, he was just lying to impress the others. He drove the shit out of the motor scooter until it flat wore out, sold it for fifty dollars, and bought a Harley-45 for two hundred.

During the early part of his two year educational adventure, his friend Dave Staple thought that Billy should find direction in his life instead of floundering around, doing nothing more than chasing pussy and majoring in the worthless course of study entitled Commercial Flying. He should instead channel his efforts in a more substantive curriculum like engineering or architecture. Dave's interest was in architecture, so during his stay at the Junior College he took as many courses as he could along that line. Likewise, Billy could see the possibilities in the profession, envisioning himself designing award winning skyscrapers and making the big bucks in the process. So when Billy had an opening in the Commercial Flying syllabus that could only be filled by some worthless liberal arts elective, he would instead opt to follow his new buddy through some of his courses, arranging to sit next to him. This way he could cheat his way through the tests with relative

For All The Wrong Reasons

ease. He felt for the first time in his life that he really had it made, or as he would often declare, "Life was getting to look more like a bowl of cherries every day".

The only course of study that came close to architecture was pre-engineering, so Dave took as many of those courses as he could in hopes that they would be transferable to a University toward a full- fledged degree. One such course was drafting. Taking this course with Dave produced one of the more significant events that helped shape Billy's future. He was assured that taking the course was a sure fire way to find out if a career in architecture was in the cards. And he was right.

Billy took to the subject like a fish takes to water. Cranking out drawings was the most constructive and satisfying thing he had undertaken thus far; that is with the possible exception of getting his pilot's license. But in this instance, he was not putting his life on the line, or so he reasoned. After all, who ever heard of getting killed by a drafting pencil. That was his reasoning until one day a fight broke out in the hall during a normal break in the routine. In this altercation, one of the instigators was ironically stabbed with a drafting pencil.

In this class, he could take his work product home to show-off to his parents. Already they were immensely proud of him, but in this case they were sure that their boy was certain to become a successful architect. Where they failed to make a success out of their lives, they would live through his.

Billy had another subconscious reason for his affinity to the subject. Around the airplane he was always nervous and afraid. Before each flight, the anticipation sent his adrenaline skyrocketing. It was after getting back down and putting away the airplane that he mostly enjoyed the experience. It always held him on a high even though his hands shook for a while afterward, making the completion of the paper work difficult, including his log book entry. When doing this drafting thing, his hand was steady as a rock, and when through with an assignment, he would save the completed work product to be admired and shown off for anyone he thought should be interested. In this respect it was a gratifying challenge. So in the back of his mind, he felt that maybe Dave's calling was also his calling.

As time progressed through the two years at Phoenix College, he took as many basic engineering courses as were offered, including and most importantly, advanced drafting. And by all means, he worked on his commer-

Chapter 12

cial ticket, still with the lingering thought of becoming a flight instructor. After all, he was still the horniest bastard around. He was convinced from his association with the experienced WWII jocks, Joe and Boots included, that the only ticket to an orgy was an instructor's license.

Obtaining the commercial license was easy. It merely involved building time (two hundred hours) in the airplane, becoming proficient in advanced maneuvers such as lazy eights, chandelles, and spins, and passing a check ride, which included these and less complicated maneuvers designed to demonstrate one's proficiency. A token amount of what was called "heavy time" had to show in your log book. The Stinson Station Wagon served that purpose. The check ride could all take place in the Airknocker, if that's what the candidate preferred. Because the above maneuvers were considered aerobatic, parachutes had to be worn. The only chutes the school made available for this purpose were the heavy, bulky and unwieldy seat pack types. Both the candidate and check pilot wearing these in an Airknocker made for an interesting sight to behold by the casual observer when they taxied out or returned. The ride was equally unusual inasmuch as the seats were not adjustable, and if the pilots were larger than what the CAA thought should be the average, it made for one's head encroaching against the top of the cockpit, humping the stick and rudder pedals, and flying an airplane that over-grossed the weight envelope.

The written part of the testing was unique compared to later requirements. During that era, four separate tests were administered. These were categorized as Navigation, Aircraft and Engines, Civil Air Regulations, and Meteorology. Mostly, the different categories were studied separately, and taken one at a time on different days. Busting any of the four meant a retake on that part only, not the whole series.

It was near the end of his second year at Phoenix College that Billy completed the requirements for the commercial flight test. Boots was looking forward to the completion of Billy's work, because Billy and his cronies were still a thorn in his side, maybe even more-so, because as the end got closer the boys grew bolder and pushed Boots quite hard. They made him more of a laughing-stock than he was already, sometimes mocking his mannerisms directly in front of him. They would tell dirty jokes without regard to offending those within earshot, even loud enough to be heard by Boots himself in his office, behind his closed door. One time when Cathy walked

For All The Wrong Reasons

by, Billy winked at Boots, and out of the corner of his mouth, in a sly subdued way asked Boots, "wouldn't you just like to get in her pants." This was almost too much and Billy realized right away that he pushed the headmaster a little too hard. But Boots knew what they knew, and as long as their little secret was safe, so were the boys.

As the date of his check ride approached, he and his cohorts openly joked as to how Billy was a shoe-in to pass if he would just roll up a twenty dollar bill and tuck it behind his ear for Bruce to drool over during the ride. This joke had its significance because of the way the examiners were paid at the time. They didn't get their fee until the candidate passed, even if it took two or three tries to do it, and he couldn't charge extra for re-takes. But the twenty dollar fee belonged to Bruce, and only Bruce, and not the school. So this was windfall money as far as Bruce was concerned. A real bona fide bonus, not much, but every little bit helped when it came to feeding a house full of kids. So displaying the fee in the manner that was joked about, was to be the incentive for Bruce, or any other hungry check pilot, to get the show on the road and issue the ticket, safety be damned.

The day of reckoning was eventually at hand, and as Billy put it, he was as nervous "as a whore in church." He didn't, as he had bragged, roll up the twenty dollar bill and tuck it behind his ear to entice Bruce to expedite the ride. He really wasn't that crude. Billy was all business now, and he would take it one step at a time. If only he could remember to pre-flight the airplane. As it turned out Bruce was just as eager to get rid of Billy as Billy was to get out of "that chicken outfit."

Neither one of them was as anxious as Boots Farraday. He could actually see the end of the hoodlums and the time when he could reclaim his empire. The antics over the past two years or more were too much for him to bear. The stories were told and retold to anyone who would listen, that is anyone except the principle parties. They were becoming legend, as were Billy as his friends. Bad examples and disrespect were being passed on to new students. Some even joined the parties at the watering hole.

It wasn't a question of enticing Bruce with the visual display of his fee, he would have been lynched if he flunked Billy. Besides, anything but a passing grade on this ride meant they would have to do it over and over again until he passed. There was no percentage in that, especially since Bruce was on a fixed fee with no additional compensation for re-takes.

Chapter 12

It was a good thing that neither Bruce nor Billy were large, because as it was, stuffing the two into the Airknocker on top of the army surplus seat pack parachutes was like putting five pounds of shit in a three pound sack. At least three of the maneuvers were considered aerobatic, requiring the use of the chutes. But that didn't help our heroes in their quest to qualify Billy for his commercial ticket. Lighter and more compact backpack chutes had not been developed yet and what was mostly available at a reasonable price, were the war surplus heavy seat packs on which fighter pilots sat during their glory seeking days of the war.

Later, seeing a desperate need for relief and common sense, the Feds (CAA, FAA) amended the rule to exempt the necessity for parachutes while performing any aerobatic maneuver required toward a rating. During a similar revision to the regulations, spin training was dropped from the commercial syllabus because there was a consensus, also by the higher-ups, that the maneuver was too dangerous with the exception of flight instructor candidates. These people did not have to demonstrate their proficiency in executing spins, but instead had to show proof by a logbook endorsement from another flight instructor, that in fact they had completed the training. After spins were eliminated from the training, fatalities by stall-spin accidents increased dramatically. So much for the wisdom of Big Brother.

The ride was no piece of cake. Bruce was all business, which made Billy more nervous than he was initially. In addition to the fundamental maneuvers like "S" turns across some stupid road, and stalls, there were spins of two or more turns to a predetermined heading, chandelles, lazy eights, eights on and around some equally stupid pylons, and seven forced landings.

Forced landings, which were later called emergency landings, culminated at a point within the boundaries of the selected field and at the start of the flare to a landing. The examiner maintained control of the throttle during the procedure. If the student or candidate missed his intended touchdown point, or for other reasons concerning the safety of the flight, the examiner had the option of adding power to abort the exercise. During the simulation, slips were not allowed; the thinking being that if the pilot could successfully dead stick the airplane for practice, then he should really be able to succeed during a bona fide forced landing with the added benefit of slips.

Of all the maneuvers covered in the flight test, a forced landing was not the one that caused Billy concern. This was because of the intense practice

For All The Wrong Reasons

involving the exercise that resulted from contests he and Jack played during their fun and games. Billy missed only one of the seven given on the test, and this was due to a Bruce screw up. During the third attempt when Billy was contemplating his turn to the base leg, which in his good judgment would have resulted in a successful landing within the first third of the length of his target field, Bruce nagged him into turning early, because according to Bruce's judgment, a delayed turn to base would have them come up short of the field. Being naturally nervous, and afraid of failure, Billy turned immediately which resulted in a high final approach. However during a real engine failure, under this circumstance, slips would have fixed it. But these were not allowed on this day, therefore continuing on to culmination would have put them in a ditch at the far end. Billy tried to blame Bruce for the screw-up. Bruce's reply was that the responsibility for the poor decision was with the pilot and not him, and Billy should have continued on to a point he thought was appropriate before turning, no matter what Bruce said or did. The other four were completed in silence and were successful. Billy passed his ride, and was destined to soon become a commercial pilot with all rights and privileges barring mistakes on the final paper work.

Back at the office were more festivities. When Boots, in his patronizing way, asked Billy what he had in mind for his next accomplishment, he responded that he would like to work on an instructor's rating. Boots, in his condescending mannerism, immediately declared that no such program was offered at the school. This meant that Billy would not be flying the school's equipment any more which was a real cause for celebration as far as Boots was concerned. Actually, to the others present, it meant that Billy was being drummed out of the flying school, not unlike the John Wing and Jim Pierce demise, but in a slightly more honorable and face-saving way. He was figuratively being pushed through the top. Joe Mora, Bruce Birran and Boots Farraday could not have been more elated. The prospect of the troublemaker disappearing from the scene was more than they could bear.

But were they ever surprised when before too many days had passed, Billy started showing up again, hanging out in the pilot lounge. He added insult to injury by taking up space on the couch, especially when he knew Joe was about to show up in anticipation of his favorite spot. Much to Boots' chagrin he would be a fixture around the place until the end of the school year when he graduated and the flying school closed its doors for the

Chapter 12

summer. The only difference was that he could not fly the school's airplanes. That didn't stop him from flying. He continued to fly at Maddux's establishment making his passengers pick up the tab for the rental. That was of course, unless there was a piece of ass involved, in which case he considered the expense an investment. So everything considered, flying at Maddux's was a better deal than the school offered.

On the academic front, he continued his close friendship with Dave Staple. He considered Dave his mentor, and with his help and counsel Billy was to accumulate a sizable sum of technical credit hours that were transferable to the University of Arizona (U of A) toward a degree in architecture. He and Dave would end up graduating together, and continue their relationship as professional associates.

Chapter 13

The graduation ceremonies at Phoenix College brought proud tears to Billy's parents' eyes. He was the first of the clan to graduate from high school let alone earn a bona fide college degree, even though the degree was an Associate of Arts type that might get one a job digging ditches if the opportunity existed. Actually this didn't matter at all to his mother and father, partly because they didn't know the difference. As far as they were concerned, he was now on par with one who held a doctorate. Part of their ignorance could be attributed to their humble beginnings, reaching back to the "old country." But with the graduation of the oldest of their three children now firmly established within the group of successful people, they felt they had arrived with their son to a new and higher plane in their lives.

Cotton wasn't their given name, unless of course one considers a name change by a judge to be a gift. No, their unbasterdized name, originating in the old country was Cottonouski. In Poland the name represented a large clan of hard working semi-literate farmers. When Billy's father Jacob was barely past his eighteenth birthday, he married Marie, the daughter of their close neighbor. It wasn't exactly a marriage made in heaven. It was more like it happened on the grassy bank of a small stream that bordered the families' properties.

When they were caught in the act by her father who just happened to be passing by, they claimed that it was their first time, and that Jacob's intentions were honorable. What they didn't tell him, but what he should have known, as evidenced the grass in the area being permanently matted down, was that they had been making fierce and passionate love since the weather and temperature allowed and the birds and bees started doing it.

They intended to marry anyway. Now it was going to be sooner rather than later if her father had anything to do with it. It would have been ugly

For All The Wrong Reasons

but for the fact that his family was more formidable than hers. But the parents got together, made big plans which included keeping them separated or closely chaperoned, and set the date for the festive wedding without regard for the wishes of the principals, Jacob and Marie.

One of the newly weds' lofty ambition was to escape the bondage of poverty and their parents who still resented the circumstances of the hasty marriage. There wasn't enough time in their short lives to have accumulated enough wealth and other assets necessary for their independence. It is for this reason and their elders' panic for a quick solution that made it necessary for them to start their lives together living with his parents. Due to their rough start together, except for their strong religious ties, their marriage would surely have failed, but they were both ambitious, in love, and determined to do something to improve their lot and that of their future offspring.

It was an article in a travel magazine left behind by some tourist that stimulated events that would ultimately change their lives forever. Jacob picked it up from a park bench during one of his mandatory trips to the city for supplies. The text was in English, but the pictures were universal. They depicted such beautiful landscape and living environment that it stimulated Jacob's interest. He just knew that this was their escape. Off he went with both the magazine and the supplies to share his enthusiasm with Marie. She was just as interested as he, suggesting they take the magazine to the university for advice or a possible translation.

The journey through the halls of the institution finally ended at the office of Professor Horvath, the university's main English teacher. Initially he was impatient with them, but as he accommodated their request, his interest in them and their yearning to better their circumstances was contagious. He could identify. He too would like to get out of the hell hole that trapped him.

It was a pictorial article on Canada, in particular, that focused their interest. The article's main theme was how the Canadian government was encouraging immigration, provided the immigrants could contribute to the economy instead of being a drag on it. A sponsor already living in Canada would be a tremendous help toward qualifying. Momentarily they were stymied. The problem was that neither of them had a trade, other than farming, nor acquaintances living there. Dejected and pessimistic, they went

Chapter 13

home to ponder their plight.

At first Professor Horvath and the Cottonouskis pushed the subject to the back of their minds, but it kept preying on the professor's mind. Out of the blue, he placed an impromptu call to the Canadian embassy. Ordinarily he would have been rebuffed, given the bureaucratic attitude of the Vice-Consular, but after throwing out his title and affiliation, he was granted an interview. You see, the professor had a relative residing in Montreal, but he didn't want to impose on them without first exploring all of the ramifications involved. The more they talked, the more excited he became. He couldn't wait to get back to the Cottonouskis with the information and inviting prospects. Would his relative be willing to help? That was the question, and until he received the answer, he didn't want to discuss it with Jacob and Marie for fear of getting their hopes up.

Before too long the answer came back in the affirmative. With this information and his enthusiasm he searched out the Cottonouskis with the good news and a plan of attack. Implementing the plan, complying with all of the bureaucratic procedures, and scraping together what little money they had, and adding to it contributions from their people, they were on a freighter to Montreal, Canada, to start a new and fruitful life.

Their stay in Montreal proved the happiest and most fulfilling time of their lives. They found that with hard work on both their parts, they could earn more than they spent. In fact it was enough to pay off the folks back home, and to buy a car to boot. The people in the "old country" already referred to them, among themselves, as the rich relatives from across the ocean.

By attending evening classes, they learned to read, speak and write both French and English. They were determined and surprisingly intelligent people. When it came time to receive their citizenship papers, Jacob was not satisfied living in Canada. It was his opinion that the country was subservient to the United States, and if that was the case, he was going to live in the number one country.

His ambitious and inquiring mind lured him to the public library where he researched the literature for various locations in the U.S. that suited his fancy. If he thought the scenery in Canada was beautiful, it was nothing compared to what Arizona had to offer. If it was anything close to what the movies depicted then it was his kind of place. Marie was in complete agree-

For All The Wrong Reasons

ment. So before long, they liquidated their assets with the exception of their car, obtained a visa, and after a long and arduous drive, ended up in the cow town of Phoenix, Arizona.

They immediately knew that Phoenix was the place for them, in spite of the slight disappointment that the area was not overrun with cowboys wearing guns on their hips, Indians in full regalia, and the architectural decor of the nineteenth century. After all, this is how the area was portrayed in the movies.

Immediately after hitting town, they rented a one room apartment on the west side, and set out to find work. Both were successful on the very first day. Marie went to work at the Westward Ho Hotel on north Central Avenue as a maid. Jacob secured his job at a cotton gin located on the west side of Phoenix. From where they lived, Marie could commute to her job by streetcar, while Jacob used their car to go to work. Marie's job was short lived, as no sooner had they settled down, she discovered she was pregnant with their first offspring who, after much research and haggling, would be named William Joseph Cottonouski, or Billy for short. It was early 1931. The rest of the country was in a depression, but for them things couldn't have been better.

Jacob was very proud of his status, so much so that he worked his ass off and was soon promoted to a supervisory position. From the first he learned that the American way was a racist way, and he was by nature on the receiving end. The main thing that hurt his feelings was the banter he received by being Polish, and as such he was perpetually on the brunt end of all "Polock" jokes. In addition to the bad jokes and constant ribbing, his co-workers constantly bastardized his name until it evolved in the form that eventually stuck, Jake Cotton. It was appropriate, because he did work in a cotton gin, and at the rate he was going, might someday own it. So there it was, the name Jake and Marie Cotton used on their citizenship application that was granted just weeks before Billy Cotton was born. The date of birth was September 13, 1931.

Chapter 14

Whereas Phoenix College was considered a high school with ash trays, the University of Arizona (U of A) was a country club that didn't allow smoking in the classroom. So much for Dave Staple's sure fire method of cheating on the tests. Not only was smoking disallowed in the classrooms but in the corridors as well. It was an unusual sight to behold, when the bell rang indicating the end of a lecture, to see the whole building empty in something short of panic in the quest for a nicotine fix. It was sort of a fire drill in reverse, ordinarily performed to escape a fire generated smoke-filled building. In this case students were fleeing a smoke-free building for the purpose of inhaling a smoke-filled outdoors. Because of these handicaps, Billy would not have survived these and other drastic changes and the hectic pace that prevailed on campus, had it not been for this loyal and faithful friend. Because of Dave's encouragement, more like nagging, he not only ended up at this elite university, but was majoring in architecture and excelling in spite of himself.

Approximately one-half the credit hours accumulated at Phoenix College were transferable toward their anticipated degree. Taking this into account meant that Billy and Dave could finish up in three years instead of the usual four, with their summers off. During the first year, flying was put on the back burner in lieu of devoting his energies and channeling his intellect toward his studies. He was beginning to like the prospect of becoming an architect, not only because he felt he had the acumen for the profession, but because the courses were easy and the work load was small. Over and over again during the meetings with the aspiring students at coffee breaks or study sessions, he was reminded that after obtaining the coveted degree, one only had to sit back, supervise the peon draftsmen and collect big fees. He naturally inquired if this scope of activity included dickin' the female clients as well.

For All The Wrong Reasons

Most of the pain-in-the-ass courses such as English and the necessary Mathematics were taken at the junior college level. The most difficult challenge facing him in the curriculum were Strength of Materials, Statics, and Structures. These subjects took some work and discipline on Billy's part just to squeak by, but with the help of Dave and a new technique for cheating, which precluded the use of tobacco and gopher matches, the challenge became doable. The mandatory subject " History of Architecture" was nothing more than a fact-based bunch of horse-shit that did nothing more than adulate the European contingent of Architects as far as he was concerned. It was probably this attitude toward the subject that resulted in his having to take that segment of the professional exam three times before successfully passing.

It was somewhat of a challenge to persuade his parents to underwrite the expenses for the additional degree. What they didn't understand was the need for more schooling. His father's education in the old country wasn't as advanced as Billy's, and he was already a supervisor down at the cotton gin. As far as they were concerned, Billy had already received his college degree at Phoenix College, and with that piece of paper should be qualified to run the more sizable architectural firms. But after some persuasion, with the help of Dave and Dave's father who was a practicing architect in his own right, even though a piss-poor one, they agreed. It would be a strain on their budget, but what the hell, they would manage somehow even if it meant that Marie go back to work as a maid at the Westward Ho.

Their prediction was right. It did turn out to be a strain on their budget. Billy wasn't the only child, and the expenses for that first year were much more than they had anticipated. Billy was willing to help by working part-time, but there wasn't anything available within the parameters of his capabilities. After all, where was the demand for beer drinkers, and if there was one, how much could a job like that possibly pay? Besides he was homesick for his "Mommy," being the first time away from home, some 120 miles, and a job in Tucson would prevent him from spending most weekends at home in Phoenix. So it was, almost every weekend he would jump on his Harley and drive off to Phoenix for some first-class home-cooking, maternal loving, and spoiling. But the financial situation wasn't hopeless. Marie went back to work as a maid at the Westward Ho hotel to supplement their income, and everybody was happy, except of course Marie, who wasn't

Chapter 14

used to working outside the home, but took solace in the thought that her sacrifice was for a good and worthy cause, her baby's future.

Billy resolved to eliminate the hardship he was putting his parents through by earnestly pursuing his flight instructors rating the following summer. Working part time in that capacity would help a lot toward reducing the financial load incurred by his parents. Along that line of thought, during the first semester at the U of A, when not getting drunk, spending his time in some bar/house of ill repute on Canal street in Nogales, Mexico, or at home on weekends with his parents, he would hang out at the local FBO at Gilpin Field, paddling around the sky with some ignorant student with a subconscious death wish, willing to pay the rental charge for the airplane. Depending on how ignorant the individual was, or how well-heeled, he would add a little to the bill for pocket change.

He wasn't particularly interested in wooing the female counterpart in the airplane for the privilege of screwing her. There was no profit in that. He was getting all the ass he wanted in the Mexican brothels of Nogales. Whereas the tourists frequented the Main Street shops, buying all the worthless Mexican trinkets their budget allowed, the students and others in the know traveled a few blocks farther over narrow dirt roads to the fringes of town, where the bars offered cheaper drinks along with cheaper senioritas.

Nogales provided easy access to the restless and horny students. It was only sixty miles due south along a straight narrow two lane highway. Getting there was the easy part; getting back was more challenging, by the high incidence of fatal accidents along the way. It was one thing to drink and drive. It was exponentially more consequential to put in a full day at school or work, drive sixty miles to a place of sin, stay up half the night drinking, playing and screwing your brains out, and then drive back along a dark, straight and lonely road. The scenario made for a much needed "forty winks" with the fortunate ones waking up in the hospital.

If one was nervous about the prospects of contracting one of those social diseases of sorts, there was the "nurse" on duty to allay their fears. She provided, free of charge, "short arm" inspections before the client embarked on his amorous act, and for an equal sum, administered a military surplus "pro-kit" after the completion of the vulgar exercise. If she wasn't a bona fide nurse in the literal sense, she was still dressed in the appropriate white uniform, which was enough in the opinion of the management to lend cred-

For All The Wrong Reasons

itably, respectability, and above all, safety to the proceedings. As an added gesture of good faith, it was declared to all who were still nervous about possible exposure to the dreaded disease, that the girls were inspected on a weekly basis by a genuine Medical Doctor. Billy only hoped that these inspections were more thorough and taken more seriously than he did with his pre-flight routines. Billy was more afraid of airplanes than he was of contracting a venereal disease, so he indulged as often as the pocket book allowed, and as transportation was available from anyone of his ass-hole buddies.

Mark Trimble, Maddux's guru on short field landings in tail-draggers, would prove his worth afterall. He was the one who coached Billy in the short field landing techniques that resulted in his winning the contest at aux.1, but not before mowing his way through the top of the Palo Verde tree at the approach end of the runway in a full stall. Whereas Mark turned out to be a pain in the ass on the previous occasion, Billy needed his services now for the flight instructors rating. So, on one of the weekends, while at home in Phoenix, and with nothing better to do than hang out with the boys at the Maddux facility, he presented his problem to Mark, who yearned to be needed and loved almost as much as the urge to show off his superior skills with the airplane. Mark took on the challenge of getting Billy the additional rating. To keep things synched up, this time Billy invited him to indulge at the Rainbow Tavern with the ravaged remnants of the old gang.

The first order of business was to pass a written, 100 question, multiple choice test on the psychology of teaching techniques, and the theory of flight maneuvers. The first part of the exam concerning the teaching methods was ageless and could survive the test of a hundred years, but the part about testing one's knowledge on flying the airplane and executing the maneuvers was by no stretch of the imagination, obsolete. As just one example, it included a question on the proper method for taxiing a UC-78 "Bamboo Bomber" in a cross wind. At the time Billy took the test, all that was left of this type airplane were over-bloated termites.

Getting the written part out of the way before the next summer would be a big step in expediting the requirements for the coveted ticket. At that time, an instrument rating was not a requirement to hold an instructor's rating. Mark was really helpful in selecting suitable study guides, strongly

Chapter 14

recommending those published by "Ross." The whole exercise was easier than Billy had anticipated. After two weeks of intense study, he took the test. Seven days later, as a result of furnishing the CAA examiner a seven cent air-mail stamp for the return postage of the results, he was pleasantly surprised that he passed with scores in the mid-seventies. The minimum passing grade allowed was 70%. But he was satisfied, because as Mark told him to boost his morale, 70 was just as good as 98. It produced the same results.

As soon as school let out for the summer, he took off on his motorcycle and headed back to Phoenix to seek refuge in the warmth and comfort of home, mother's bosom and his worthless flying buddies, or what was left of them. Jack Monett and Don Schooner had gone off to the Air Force, Jim Pierce was still putting out non-fires on a diesel locomotive (reference his job as a fireman on a switch engine for Southern Pacific Railroad), and John Wing was managing his father's grocery store. Billy got his job back washing delivery trucks in the evenings, so his days were free to do anything he wanted, including working on his rating. The effort leading to satisfactory results were easier than expected. Thirty days after starting the program, Mark had him tuned and ready for the check ride.

Unlike other check rides that are farmed out to designated examiners, the one for the flight instructor's rating was strictly reserved for the CAA safety inspectors to conduct. It was set up that way under the guise of ensuring the standardization of flight instruction. In reality it was to short circuit the "whores" and "Santa Clauses" who might release just anybody who had the means of paying the fee. The CAA examiner, a government employee, was already being paid by the tax-payer, and as such could not accept money for the service, so there was supposed to be no incentive for compromising his/her integrity. On the other hand, Federal employees were thought to be inherently lazy with bad attitudes, or they would otherwise be out in the private sector making "real money." Because of this, the rides turned out to be easier on the candidate than they would have been if completed by a civilian designee. All of this reasoning was imparted to Billy by his mentor to bolster his confidence. This and the fact that the ride would not cost him made him feel better about the forthcoming ordeal. With thirty days of intense training behind him, a potentially lazy and worthless check pilot, and a free ride, Billy was beginning to think that he had it made.

To hear him tell it, in retrospect, he passed with flying colors, especially

For All The Wrong Reasons

the short field, soft field, and emergency landing part. There was a 20 mph cross-wind at the airport at the time, and his finesse in coping with it impressed the examiner to the extent that he overlooked two potential failings.

One happened during the oral phase of the test. It was Billy's reluctance more than his inability to complete a "cook-book" method of solving an aircraft weight and balance exercise that almost did him in. It wasn't that he couldn't figure it out, but was more like he couldn't do it in a timely manner. He instead used a method he was more familiar with that was taught in his "Static's" course at the U of A.

The theory involved taking moments around the a known datum on the airplane, setting them to zero and solving for the resultant moment arm. Billy's method may have had merit, but it wasn't the one that the examiner was familiar with, no matter that the answer came out the same. These numerical gymnastics were way over the head of the CAA man, who kept repeating some stupid rule involving "Man over Woman" (M/W—Moment divided by Weight). He won the argument by asserting that if Billy wanted to be a flight instructor he was going to teach the conventional way. It came down to: "The CAA way or the highway." Billy got the message. He all of a sudden started to do some serious ass-kissing, promising to thereafter preach the gospel according to Big Brother, and immediately set upon demonstrating that he could in fact teach the same exercise using the "dumb" math as outlined in the study guide; especially the "man over woman" part. That part was right up his alley.

The other faux pas happened during the pre-flight, or lack thereof. Old habits almost came back to haunt and bite him. When asked why he was getting in the airplane before performing a proper preflight inspection, Billy, always fast on his feet, responded that he had already satisfied that requirement before going into the office for the oral phase of the exam. Not good enough for two reasons. For one thing, something could have happened to the airplane while Billy was inside making a fool of himself over some X-rated weight and balance problem. He was lectured that every airplane should be gone over thoroughly prior to each time it flies. Billy mustered all of his willpower to resist expounding on his pet theory about the folly of pre-flight inspection, and if they are to be performed, it should be at the end of the flight not at the beginning. But instead, he bit his tongue and hung his head in hopes the problem would go away.

Chapter 14

The other thing the examiner needed was for Billy to demonstrate his ability to properly pre-flight the airplane, but more importantly to show that he could instruct in the procedure, explaining every detail and the probable consequences of a defect in each instance. This in itself made our hero very nervous. It would have been all over for him at that stage of the exercise except that the examiner had blocked out the entire afternoon to devote to the flight test. If he terminated early, it would leave him with nothing to do for the rest of the day except some nasty paper work the chief was liable to thrust in his direction. Like all other airplane junkies, he would rather fly than screw, and since he was going to flunk Billy anyway, he might as well fly with him, enjoy himself in the process, and then flunk him on some aerial maneuver. It was inconceivable that the subsequent parts would be any better than those which were completed. So on they continued.

What really and truly almost got him was the cardinal sin Billy committed immediately after he and the CAA man were firmly strapped in the airplane. All of his mistakes to that point were bad, but this one was unforgivable. He failed to holler "CLEAR" for God and everybody within miles to hear before he pulled the lever to start the Cessna 140. The engine fired right up at exactly the same instance he realized his mistake. It was also at the same instance the examiner caught it, evidence his spooky, icy, eye-piercing stare at a very nervous, perspiring pilot. Oh, how he wished that he could back the time just 10 or 15 seconds and make it go away. Instead, always fast on his feet, he merely looked his examiner in the eye, and as casually as he could said, "Is it too late to say clear." Seeing then that it was all over for him, a relaxed calm swept through his body, and realizing the inevitable decided he would finish the flight just for the fun of it. As fate would have it, he was so much at peace with himself, his performance during the rest of the ride was stellar. Nobody could have flown it better.

At the end of the session, during the critique, Billy could almost see the examiner flipping a coin in his mind. One side of the coin was an image of a confused scrawny kid being tossed out the door on his ass in complete disgrace, with the other side showing a ceremoniously celebrated genius with cap and gown, a diploma firmly gripped in his left hand, and shaking the hand of a smiling CAA official with the other. The more the examiner discussed the various elements of the test, the more he was convincing himself that maybe, just maybe, the kid was all right, especially when he mulled the flying portion around in his mind.

For All The Wrong Reasons

Then came the part where Billy was lectured on how a flight instructor was really an extension of the CAA, and continued on with an explanation of the duties and responsibilities associated with the position, especially the "trust" part that was being thrust on poor Billy, that came with the rating to develop future aviators. Actually what he was doing was talking himself into awarding Billy the certificate. He seemed to detect in Billy, a sincere interest in what he had to say, and Lord knows it is human nature to be taken in by a reaction such that Billy was displaying even though it was artificially generated. But this supposed sincerity is what tipped the scales. It was far more impressive to the examiner than previous candidates exhibited during their debriefing. He was more accustomed to witnessing self-assured cockiness and boredom during his closing dissertations. In Billy he detected a future apostle, an officer and representative of the agency. They were both proud. What started out as a disaster ended in victory. Billy was a CAA certified flight instructor, no matter that he had no respect for the agency, the airplane, or the aspiring students who were to depend on him.

Chapter 15

Keeping in mind the heavy burden of responsibility thrust upon him by the inconsiderate bastard at the CAA, Billy set out to find a worthy candidate for him to practice on. Back at the U of A the following October, he found the perfect specimen. One which, if he had to write a specification for, would fit the bill to a tee. Her name was Dolores Rodriguez, a senior, also in the College of Architecture. As her name and physical features indicated, she was of Mexican descent. He had known her on a casual basis for a year, meeting mostly at school functions and small parties. Billy didn't think he stood a chance with her. She was always with or surrounded by other Mexican students who were obviously in heat, and showed it. Billy thought the display was disgusting.

After he got to know her better, in more intimate encounters where idle conversation took on the appearance of importance, she admitted that her darker than normal features were due to her Yaqui Indian heritage. But unlike the stereotype Yaqui, she was tall and slender with a set of thirty-six C's and a twenty-eight inch waistline. Her hair was black and shining, flowing almost to the small of her back. Her very presence excited the shit out of Billy, causing him to squirm noticeably in her presence. When they parted company he fantasized, producing images of her naked body, with him being equally naked, entwined together in various erotic positions.

To produce a specimen of such beauty and proportions, it was Billy's theory that several hundred years ago a tall slender Spanish Conquistador bedded down with one of the locals during their occupation of Mexico, in an effort to do his part to dilute the pagan population with the more aristocratic genes of a European species. She may have been part Yaqui Indian, but her tall slender frame, firm well proportioned boobs and creamy brown complexion, contrasting her shiny long black hair, was evidence that she

For All The Wrong Reasons

inherited the finer features of her descendants on both sides of the Atlantic.

Dolores was three years older than Billy, but was only one year ahead of him in school. She was in her last year, with him having two more to go. She carried a 3.5 grade point average, which surprised Billy because she didn't seem that sharp during their encounters. After he found out that her father was Barney M. Rodriguez, the famous architect from Phoenix, it explained her higher than expected grade point average and architecture as her course of study. Dolores, he discovered, was an only child, the son Barney never had. She was being groomed to eventually take over his architectural practice.

Barney M. Rodriguez was second in reputation only to the world renowned Frank Lloyd Wright, whose pioneer work in earthquake-proof buildings is the main reason Tokyo, Japan doesn't resemble Hiroshima just after the "bomb" was dropped. Later when Billy, in his dumbstruck way, reminded him of that piece of trivia, Barney was insulted. He made it known under no uncertain terms that he was second to no one, especially Frank Lloyd Wright. Being a Mexican prima donna had definite advantages, especially when it came to receiving awards, and getting laid. Every organization that had access to a printing press hounded him to speak to their group in exchange for and under the guise of receiving an award. It had to be already framed or he wasn't interested. The corridor leading to his office, which was at least fifteen feet long, was literally covered with these acknowledgments, achievements and other documents of recognition. And with all that, he bragged that he was turning down offers on a daily basis. Also because of his popularity, his firm commanded more design work than they could possibly handle. It was with relish that he took pleasure in treating the prospective clients the same as those who were bent on thrusting their awards on him.

Barney M. Rodriguez was considered a matinee idol by those around him. Of all the forms of recognition, it was this one that he was most proud. He was a tall, medium-built, dark-complected Mexican with black wavy hair, and a firm square jaw with a prominent nose to match. His dark piercing eyes compelled people in close conversation to look away. His voice was slightly on the high-pitched side with a meter that came across as a whining, "sing-song" delivery. Very much like the sadistic Mexican cowboy is portrayed in the western movies, especially at the time when he is about to relieve his victim of his possessions before dispatching him. On the wall

Chapter 15

of the Rodriguez office reception area hung a framed three by five foot, black and white bust size portrait of him. He was more proud of that than he was of the many awards that conspicuously lined the corridor.

Dolores was well aware of her dad's female encounters, however, both father and daughter did their best to shield Mrs. Rodriguez from his cavorting ways. He had so "much" available to him, that he was no longer interested in the Mrs., nor was he interested in divorcing her. Barney liked the comfort of his home, as well as the protection afforded a married man against his more aggressive lovers. To demonstrate his prowess, he liked to tell the story of a time on the way to his office when he just didn't feel like going in, and returning home was strictly out of the question. Instead he stopped at a convenience store to buy some hors d'oeuvres and wine. Then proceeded on to a motel where he checked in. After getting situated in the room, he took out his little black book and made calls until he found a live one, who like he, was equally bored with the routine of the day, and would spend the day with him in the room eating, drinking, watching TV, and making love, not necessarily in that order.

The prospect of a relationship with Dolores enticed the hell out of Billy. It was more than he could bear, that is, until he bedded down with her the first time. Then she was old hat to be used until a better deal came along. Billy thought it was ironic that since Joe Mora was screwing one of the Anglos, it was only fitting that he reciprocate by doing the same thing to his people. At least that's the way his racist mind rationalized. Another reason for his enthusiasm was her advancement in school. She was a senior with excellent grades and standing, and if he played his cards right, she could pull him along in a better fashion than his buddy Dave was doing. In fact, she eventually took them both on as her protégés; but only in the academic sense. There was only room for one of them in her sack. These other intimacies were reserved only for her prospective flight instructor.

Daddy was rich and influential not only in the industry but with the educators at the university, which explained why daughter's skids through the college of architecture were well greased. Another benefit bestowed on Dolores that Billy was to take full advantage of in the future, was the place where she lived. The great Barney Rodriguez was not going to have his only daughter and future associate living in a dormitory with a bunch of other lowly, raucous, sweaty, drunken students, who for the most part were merely putting in their time to party and land a well-to-do victim for marital prospects. No, she was too good for that. She was an aristocrat and had her own pad, a luxurious 1100 square foot, two bedroom kind, on the second floor of one of the better apartment houses. The extra bedroom was for Papa when he stayed over to stroke a client or two. A lot of his work involved projects in the Tucson and Nogales area.

It all started for real when Billy invited her to fly with him. They made a date for the following Sunday morning. They drove out to Gilpen Field in her Mercedes, checked out a Cessna 140 and took off for Nogales, some sixty miles south on Route 89. She thoroughly enjoyed the flight down. The idea was to spend the day strolling along the main downtown section perusing the shops and doing lunch with a few drinks before returning. Staying the hell away from Canal Street was foremost in his mind. He wasn't familiar with anything in the tourist section, and when she noticed his ignorance, she expressed surprise, assuming that he had not visited Nogales before. She was proud that she was introducing him to her culture for the first time. He did nothing to dispel the notion, and never let on how wrong she was. He was thinking, while taking in her guided tour, that if he wanted to, he could show her a few things about the town that would shock the hell out of her.

They toured the shops for a short time, then she guided him down a dirt street a short block off the main drag. For a moment he began to panic, thinking that she was taking him too close to his den of inequity for comfort. But before he panicked he was steered into a large high walled courtyard to a building and a large colorful sign that bore the name "Juan's." He observed that the courtyard was actually a parking lot and the building was a restaurant or club of sorts. He didn't resist or even ask when she casually led him through the main entrance where a waiter greeted and seated them. He was impressed. It was one of the finer places he had ever been, especially since it was located in a town that he considered to be trashy. There they dined, drank, talked, and generally had a good time. It was the first time he genuinely believed they were compatible. While they were having a good time, oblivious to them, things were happening with the weather that would almost ruin their day, if not take their lives.

Not only did Billy habitually forego his pre-flight inspections, he never felt the need to check the weather forecasts with the appropriate flight ser-

Chapter 15

vice station. This is because when he did talk to them, they always suggested that he file a flight plan. The last time he complied and filed one he forgot to close it. If a flight plan was not closed within thirty minutes from the most recent estimated time of arrival, a search was initiated. Then when they found you and your airplane in good condition, a violation was issued. At the time the offender had a choice of paying a $35.00 fine or face a hearing. A guilty verdict could result in a fine equivalent to the expenses incurred to find the pilot. So the $35.00 fine he paid along with a resolve to have as little to do with those bastards at the CAA as possible. This included calling them for weather forecasts.

If he had talked to them, they would have told him of a system moving in from the Gulf of California. It was due to arrive in south and central Arizona by mid-afternoon. Their predictions were right on track. Another chink in Billy's armor was his propensity to drink of the fermented fruits before he flew. He liked to do it because it numbed his senses, including his nervousness, and in turn his fear. That Sunday was no exception. He consumed his share of Margaritas. Dolores didn't give it a thought, an indication of her ignorance of the consequences of booze and airplanes. Besides they were too consumed in conversation, dirty jokes, and loud laughter to be concerned with the trivialities of getting back to Tucson.

When they were ready to leave, she picked up the check, added a generous tip to the bottom, and signed it. As much as he tried, there was no wresting it from her. It would have been one more way that he had to impress her, but then it was a few more bucks in his pocket by letting her do it. It was then he realized that this was one of her father's hang-outs, and explained the reason they had been pampered all afternoon by both management and waiters.

As they stepped outside, he was confronted by low ceilings that obscured the top of the surrounding hills, equally low visibility, a steady drizzle, and an empty feeling in the pit of his stomach. Needless to say, Billy was less than a good conversationalist during their seven mile taxi ride to the airport. All he could think about was getting the hell out of there before things got worse; as if that were possible. He was also pre-occupied with the prospect of scud running down the highway to Tucson, and tried to remember if the road contained any sharp turns, high obstructions, or even worse, tunnels. Maybe the charts could verify it. But hell, he didn't have

For All The Wrong Reasons

one. He would have to splurge thirty-five cents and buy one at the airport.

The airport was seven miles northeast of Nogales, along the road to Patagonia. This road and Route 89 to Tucson were surrounded by hills and mountains. The tops of which were sticking up in the clouds. So he surmised that the smart thing to do was to fly the airplane right on the deck down the road back to town, where he could pick up 89, flying by the same technique all the way back to Tucson. This made better sense than to try to intercept 89 by flying due west through the hills. It would be a little farther but they would live to screw-up another day. It never occurred to him to scrap the flight, check into a hotel, and try again the next day. No, that would be admitting defeat.

The dry feeling in his mouth reminded him that maybe he shouldn't have indulged in so many Margaritas. Being sober would give him the added edge needed for survival. He glanced over at Dolores for assurance, or at least some sign of concern, but what he detected was a look of peaceful gratification for a nice Sunday afternoon outing. So if he was going to continue to impress her, it would be non-serving to show his failings. From that point on he put on an air of nonchalant arrogance, letting her think that this sort of thing happened all the time.

Paying off the cabby they sauntered over to the airplane, and as casually as they could, untied the mooring ropes, and got in the Cessna. This was all done under the curious stares of a dozen spectators seeking refuge from the rain under the office overhang. Some of these people had airplanes sitting on the ramp, but unlike our potential victims/future lovers were waiting for the weather to improve so they too could fly out. For them, departing under existing conditions was out of the question. It wasn't a matter of courage, but more like good sense.

He started the engine, all 85 horsepower, taxied to the end of the runway in the drizzle, completed the run-up for what it was worth, and without so much as a glance at his passenger for some small hint of approval, took off in the drizzle, low ceilings, and piss-poor visibility. It was at this point that it occurred to him that he forgot to invest the thirty-five cents for a chart. So what, he didn't need one anyway.

Not only didn't he need a chart, he didn't need Dolores either for what he was about to do. What he needed most were his old friends from Phoenix. He needed the security they offered, the confidence they instilled, the

Chapter 15

cheap counseling on how this was going to be a piece of cake, and the flippancy in which they treated events involving airplanes; events such as the one in which he was about to become a statistic.

He wasn't drunk, but was certainly under the influence. He wasn't only insecure, but nervous and frightened. He was all alone. This was his challenge, and only his. The girl next to him was immaterial, a non-entity. If he lived, she lived. He refused to think of the converse to the postulate. He shuddered at the thought of slamming into the side of a mountain. Would it hurt?

As soon as he broke ground, he held the airplane down, as close to the runway as possible. He wanted to build up speed before attempting his first turn. As soon as he thought the time was right, he started a very shallow 180 degree turn to the left to line up with the road in the direction of Nogales. To stay out of the clouds, it was necessary to fly below 200 feet. Because of the rain, forward visibility through the windshield was zero. His only visual reference to the terrain was through the side windows. Dolores thought it was marvelous that Billy could fly the airplane without being able to see where he was going. On one hand things were hectic, but on the other, her comment gave him the confidence he needed and settled him down some.

Then there were a couple of other things that gave him a better outlook. The air was smooth, much to his surprise, and the visibility below the clouds was sufficient to get the job done; if only he could see through the windshield. During all this, Billy maintained his focus, his undivided attention to complete the low turn and become established on the road. Once there he concentrated on two other things: to stay out of the clouds and to keep the road directly underneath him. If he wanted to see what was directly in front, all he had to do was to cross the controls slightly to slip the airplane sideways. This would obtain the forward visibility through his side window. He wasn't concerned with colliding with another airplane, because who in his right mind would be flying on a day like this, especially at this altitude?

He followed the road along its southwesterly direction toward Nogales, and when the town came into view, began to anxiously search out the road northbound to Tucson. He almost screamed with delight when he first spotted his target, Route 89. Being cautious not to over or under-shoot his turn, he rounded the corner establishing a northbound heading along the road, and settled back for the sixty mile trip home. Billy was now feeling pretty

For All The Wrong Reasons

good about himself.

When under pressure, such as he was during this event, time has a way of dragging out. Without a chart he didn't know where he was other than the fact that eventually the road underneath him would take him home. Besides even if he had the chart, it wouldn't have done him any good because he dared not take his eyes off the road and surrounding terrain. Having Dolores perform the function of a navigator was also out of the question. She didn't even know what a chart was all about. She was having a good time just being out on a Sunday drive.

What seemed like a god-awfully long time, they flew over a small community. He thought he recognized it as Tubac, and worried that there might be an antenna or two sticking up in front of him. Because of that awareness he reminded himself to stay directly over the road. Who in his right mind would plant an antenna in the middle of a roadway? The only thing he should be concerned about were high-lines and tunnels. And then after a long straight stretch, the road took a slight dog-leg to the right at what he recognized as Arivaca Junction. This was confirmed by the presence of a small 3500 foot strip that he knew from previous experience to be the Kinsley Ranch. He was home free.

All he had to do was to avoid the Sahuarita Bombing and Gunnery Range that bordered the right side of the road. He wasn't particularly worried about interfering with supposed activities within its bounds, but didn't want to be observed by some Air Force official encroaching on the airspace. He knew this to be an unforgivable sin.

Then the buildings of Tucson came into view in spite of the drizzle and premature darkness of the late afternoon. His pre-occupation with the welcome sight of home, caused him to fly right along the edge of Tucson International Airport at 200 feet, and because the control tower was located on the west side of the airport, Billy's path took him perilously close to it. So close that he claimed in one of his bullshit sessions with his buddies, that he could see the whites of their eyes, referring to the controllers. It happened so fast and the visibility was so poor that it was doubtful that anyone in the tower became aware of his presence. Leaving the airport behind, and having the city in view, he headed directly for Gilpin Field. He was on his own turf, and felt more comfortable. He was also beginning to sober up. What he needed now was another drink.

Chapter 15

He flew directly over the top of the airport to check the wind sock, made a quick turn to a close-in pattern, glanced over at Dolores with a gratifying grin, and greased the airplane on as if it was all routine. She was duly impressed and wondered if he was as good in bed as he was in the airplane. As they taxied to the ramp, he noticed that there were no lights on in the office, indicating that they had all gone home because of the weather. So they parked the airplane, tied it down, tried the office door and found it locked, and headed for the car. It was raining quite hard now, and since there was nobody at the airport to take his money, he would settle with them tomorrow. They had been in the air slightly less than an hour; it seemed like a century.

They were in her Mercedes. He leaned over and kissed her on the neck. A celebration was in order, so he suggested the Stone Avenue Inn, a place of beverage where he and Dave frequented with their mutual friend Bill Daniel. Sid the owner was a regular guy and he would probably like to hear the story. She instead suggested her place, where she could and would "build" a meaner Margarita than they had that afternoon. She would serve it up with tortilla chips and Mexican salsa. Besides it would be cozier. They could change into something dry and more comfortable. Her father left his bathrobe and some of his clothes in the closet. Billy was all for it.

Up until that time he had never made a pass at her, discounting the light kiss on her neck back in her car. Every time they met at mixed gatherings, she was always in a group. Usually her escort was a handsome Mexican. He always assumed that he never stood a chance with her, so it amazed him that he was alone with her in her cozy apartment, draped in her father's robe, eating and drinking Margaritas that were free. It blew his mind. If the nuns could see him now. They would think that he had died and gone to heaven.

As he perused the apartment taking in all of the expensive layout, he fantasized about the prospect of getting intimate with her. At the same time her thoughts centered on what a cool character he was, maneuvering that airplane through all that bad weather, when other pilots stayed on the ground watching them go. To her he was smooth and fearless. If only she knew. She wasn't sophisticated enough to realize that in the process of getting back he broke several CAA regulations, including busting altitude restriction, flying VFR in IFR conditions and unauthorized incursions into controlled airspace,

For All The Wrong Reasons

Tucson International Airport. Up until this day she was unaffected by him, going along for the airplane ride because she had nothing better to do, and she liked airplanes. Now she was definitely attracted to him and looked favorably at the prospect of flying with him again.

The apartment was warm, dry and cozy. It didn't take too many Margaritas before they became tipsy which led to silly and then giggly as they embarked on jokes that became more risqué as the evening wore on. Then all of a sudden they were embracing, then kissing, and before he had a chance to get his hands beneath her bra, they were in bed together "au natural." She was a passive lover. He attributed that to her inexperience. For now he would be patient, but in time he would show her new ways that would drive her out of her mind.

The love making went on, fast and furious, most of the night. It was as though he was making up for lost time. He didn't want to let go, because if he did he might lose her to one of her Mexican suitors. So he was determined to make it last as long as possible. For her it was different. She had never been made love to like this before. The others just seemed to want to get it over with and go home. She was going to savor the feelings for as long as he let her. She laid back in what seemed to be a trance and let him do anything to her he wanted.

The prospect of attending classes became remote. Instead they slept in, made love one more time, as though it was going to be their last, showered together, dressed and went out for an omelet. This time he paid. Then they drove out to the airport to settle the tab and to discuss her forthcoming flying lessons. The FBO welcomed her onboard as a future student, and since he noticed the car they drove up in, started blowing smoke up her ass. He expressed surprise that Billy and company made it back the day before. He said that the weather was so bad, and not expecting their return, closed up shop and went home early. He didn't ask, nor was any explanation given for their unexpected return the day before.

Billy was in love. They screwed at least three times a week. He saw his parents less frequently and they began to wonder if there was something wrong. So, each time the subject came up at home, they ended up sending him more money. Dolores was becoming such a predictable habit, and he was spending so much time at her place that Billy suggested he move in. She wouldn't have it; her father would have a fit. In spite of all Barney's

Chapter 15

vices and extra marital affairs, he thought that his little girl was still a virgin. He would kill the son-of-a-bitch that would take that from her before the proper time of marriage.

Barney's visits to her place, more often overnight stays, were always unannounced, and even though on several occasions he encountered Billy and Dolores in the living room watching TV, or going over school material, he never suspected that the relationship went any further. On one occasion, when Barney showed up late in the evening and the amorous couple were in the "act," she had to scurry around to get proper before going out to greet him. Afterward, she thought that her flustered and nervous conduct had been a sure give-a-way. Did Papa see Billy's motorcycle parked outside? He never let on that he did, but how could he have missed noticing it? What were they going to do about her lover's presence in the bedroom? The answer in that particular close call was that Billy hid out in her closet with all of his clothes until Barney went to bed, then sneaked out the front door, and pushed his bike down the street before starting it, lest the noise draw Barney's attention to it. Exiting from the bedroom window was out of the question. They were on the second floor.

It was a real game of "Russian Roulette" as far as Billy was concerned, and was only a matter of time before her father would walk in on them, performing the holy ritual of mass reproduction. The experience was a serious close call, requiring some modifications to their already flawed behavior. So as a precaution they devised a few rules. In the first place, Billy would park his Harley around the corner out of sight. Then, unlike previous times when they made love on the floor in the living room while watching TV, there would be none of that except in the bedroom behind locked doors. At least if Barney were to show, from the time he jiggled the key in the lock until the time he called out her name, Billy would have time to drag himself and his clothing into the closet as he did on this last close call. She would still have the problem of putting on an act to avoid suspicion. The prospect of spending a large part of the night hiding out in the closet trying not to stir wasn't very appealing. Most of the time when her father arrived he liked to visit for a long time before retiring.

So the plan to end all other options was for Dolores to place a phone call to father in Phoenix under the pretense of satisfying a lonesome urge. If her dad was already in Tucson or on his way, her mother would certainly know.

For All The Wrong Reasons

If not, and she got him on the phone, then she could bullshit him with small talk for a while, before returning to her lover and the serious business of fornication. Barney was thrilled that his daughter was all of a sudden calling him more often than was her previous habit. He was also pleased that she was seeing Billy, a prospective architect, and that he was teaching her to fly. What he didn't know, and she hoped he never would, was that Billy was really teaching her a horde of new positions and ways to achieve sexual gratification, every way he knew except the one where they would try it standing up in the bathtub with roller skates on. They had no ready access to roller skates.

Dolores insisted that she pay for the rental of the airplane, and for his time as instructor as well. He was embarrassed to take her money until her father insisted on it, explaining that it wasn't her money after all, but his. He was becoming quite fond of Billy, and took them both out to dinner whenever he was in town. At one time he asked her if Billy was becoming too aggressive toward her body. She insisted that he was a perfect gentleman and never so much as laid a hand on her. Barney responded in a pleased sort of way, that he was happy to hear that because if he ever caught that "boy" desecrating his little girl's body, Billy would end up dead by one of the Mexican Mafia fresh out of Culiacan. This was as scary to Billy as the airplanes.

She soloed in seven and a half hours. Joe Mora would have been proud. They spent the rest of her senior year flying the Cessna 140, dining at Juan's in Nogales at Daddy's expense, and otherwise screwing up a storm. Before graduating and returning to Phoenix to work in the Rodriguez firm, she received her private pilot's license; a proud time for Billy and his first. During the time he spent teaching her to fly and doing other nasty things to her, he dared not take on other female students, lest he raise the ire of his Mexican lover and suffer the consequences. Of all the time he spent in the various schools during his life, the past two semesters were by far the most enjoyable. When he returned in the fall, he would have only one more year to go. And then he would be a bona fide architect, with all of the rights and privileges to cheat the client.

As soon as school let out for the summer, he moved back to Phoenix and back to the womb. He had a lot of explaining to do for not staying in better touch with his parents during the year. He owed them. His mother worked

Chapter 15

her fingers to the bone so he could better himself. And what does he do in return? He ignores them. He had a lot of making up to do, and he promised them he would. Like most parents they were gullible and with that, everything was all right again.

His relationship with Dolores dried up that summer. She became more interested in another young architect working at her father's firm. The new stud started screwing her, got caught by the old man, and was run off. At least he wasn't killed. Billy thought it was all very funny. He didn't seem to care about their separation or that she was getting serviced by another. For the last few weeks of their affair, she was getting to be "old stuff" anyway, and he, bordering on male nymphomania, needed new challenges, which to say the least, were plentiful for the challenging new flight instructor.

For summer work, instead of laboring over dirty trucks as he had been doing, he hired on at Maddux Flying Service. This came about after a discussion with the Maddux's flight instructors, who by nature of their laziness, would let him do all of the flying he could handle as long as they profited as well. In the final analysis, they agreed he would take on students from the individuals willing to give them up, and they would reap a dollar an hour for every hour the student flew, dual or solo. He would get the rest. The one exception to the deal involved the female prospects. He was being deprived the honor of instructing them because he couldn't be trusted. The regulars reserved that privilege for themselves for the same obvious reason he wanted them.

Each student he flew with was taught all of the bad habits he had accrued throughout the short but illustrious start of his career, including disrespect for the CAA. He taught them how to be "street smart." This is where a deliberate infraction of the regulations is incurred without the resulting consequences. Buzzing a friend's or relative's house was a case in point. He explained that you should make only one pass, then get the hell out of there before witnesses on the ground could get the numbers off the airplane. Those who get caught are always the ones who circled back for an encore. He taught them where to find the range horses and how to play havoc with them. He would have shown them how to dog fight but they were never in the presence of another airplane. He felt that his students were getting more than their money's worth by extending the scope of their education from just merely how to fly or "herd" the airplane to beating the system as well.

For All The Wrong Reasons

Their extended education took them to his favorite place for fun and games - Aux.1. There they would practice their touch and go's, and in particular short field landings. While messing around Aux.1, he would park and shut down the airplane using the excuse that he needed a piss break, but in reality he wanted to savor the situation, to reminisce from his past, to relate to his spongy-minded students all of the things he and his flying buddies did during those days. In particular Billy would show them where he managed to get the airplane stopped when he won the short field landing contest. Billy would also point out the spot where he pruned the upper ten percent of the Palo Verde tree. If they worked at it, they too could aspire to the ranks of the proficient fearless aviator such as he. Then the lesson got down to the nitty gritty. Did they have a sister, or an otherwise female acquaintance that they could introduce to him?

He flew hard that summer logging in over forty hours a week. His students were very pleased with him. His flying wasn't all instruction, since Maddux gave him a share of the charter work, which included hauling a case of blood to the Cottonwood hospital on occasion. His income was more than he or his parents expected. His mother even talked about quitting her job. Billy told her not to make any hasty decisions.

In September, Billy went back to school to finish up. The last year turned out to be a snap. The professors treated the seniors as equals. They were all on a first name basis. Graduation at that stage was all but automatic. If Billy busted a test or quiz, it was assumed to be a fluke, and the results reflected the assumption. At that stage of the game classroom sizes were small and informal. Tests were mostly open book. A lot of talk between teacher and student centered on the opportunities that existed on the outside. It was a pleasure to be enrolled.

Billy flew only occasionally during his last two semesters, mostly for pleasure. The heavy flying load of the last summer sort of burned him out, and he was happy just to be goofing off. He would get the occasional female on board, bang her and go on to somebody else. It wasn't like the last year with Dolores where they had her plush apartment to do their dirty thing. Now he had to rent a motel, and that cost money. There was no doing it in the back seat of a car. All he had was a motorcycle.

The least expensive way to get "his ashes hauled" was at the clubs (actually brothels) on Canal Street in Nogales. There he could get laid, drink, and

Chapter 15

eat on three separate occasions for the price of a one time airplane rental and a motel. But every time he crossed the border on the way to his playthings, he would think of Dolores and the good times they had at Juan's. It almost ruined his mood. Once he settled in at the bar, had a drink, and the senorita stroked his sensitive area, Dolores became a thing of the distant past.

Every once in a while, he and a friend would stop off at Juan's for good Mexican food and Margaritas. It was always a pleasure to eat there because the help recognized him from the year before, thought he was a personal friend of Barney Rodriguez, and treated him like a celebrity. They wondered why he didn't just sign the check like Dolores did.

His bigger thrill was when Barney came to town. Occasionally he would have Billy located through the Dean's office, pick him up and take him out to lunch or dinner. The people at the college didn't mind the inconvenience Barney was putting them through, because as a famous architect he was a very big man on campus. By association, this gave Billy celebrity status. At one time the Dean sought Billy's help to secure Barney as a guest speaker at one of their functions. It was an impossible task. Barney would never expose himself or his ignorance by complying. He was just not capable of performing in front of an audience, and he was the first one to know his limitations in this regard. It would take just one time to bring him down, and show him for what he truly was - a phony. On the other hand, they interpreted his refusal to just playing hard to get, which made them try over and over again, lending sort of an aura of mystery and sophistication to his being.

Once in a while Barney would drive them to Juan's for Mexican food and drink. On one occasion when the Margaritas loosened them up, the discussion centered on Dolores. It was then that Billy discovered that she was screwing one of Barney's junior architects. Barney let the whole sordid affair out, even the part about booting him out. He needed reassurance that Billy wasn't doing it to her when he was teaching her to fly. When the denials came, and Billy professed that the relationship was strictly platonic, Barney wanted Billy's help to straighten her out, to which Billy responded that he would cooperate to the fullest of his ability. However what Barney had in mind was for Billy to hire on with his firm. The picture he had painted in his mind included Billy and his daughter in wedded bliss, taking over the

For All The Wrong Reasons

firm for his own selfish reasons. There was no way this was going to happen as far as Billy was concerned. It was one thing going to school with her, banging her once in a while, it was another living with each other on a daily basis. Billy would not go to work for the great Barney M. Rodriguez.

Chapter 16

Billy had made up his mind. As much as Barney Rodriguez wanted his body, Billy firmly rejected his very attractive offer. As for other offers during his last semester at the university, it became evident that there must have been a shortage of architects on the outside, because recruiters came from all over the place. He signed up for many interviews, not necessarily because he was shopping for the best opportunity, but mainly to help the recruiters spend their expense allowances, and to take advantage of free trips to far-off home offices for further scrutiny and more wining and dining.

There was one basic reason the large firms from the big cities went to the schools to recruit fresh architectural graduates. Until the new architect put in his four years as an understudy or apprentice to a registered professional, he was considered nothing more than a glorified draftsman, at an hourly rate of little more than minimum wage. It was more cost effective for these firms to hire as many new graduates as they could absorb, even though they knew they would lose them after four years when these glorified draftsmen became registered and demanded more recognition and salary commensurate with their standing.

An experienced designer with no formal education and only "on the job training" would command a salary up to three or four times that which an individual with a degree could expect. The skilled designers did find their place with the smaller firms, because the new graduates felt the larger more prominent companies offered valuable experience in designing high-rise buildings and other more complicated facilities. Also, the principals of the smaller firms didn't feel it was worth the savings to baby sit or bring along a fledgling when a self-motivated seasoned designer was available.

So when the recruiters notified the school's placement office of their intentions to visit the campus for the purpose of interviewing prospects, Billy signed up for all of the ones he thought might be interesting. It in-

For All The Wrong Reasons

volved meeting with the prospect on a one on one basis in a room furnished by the placement office, for the purpose of seeking out some indication of compatibility.

If the initial meeting went well, the student was invited along with the others that interested the prospective employer, to dine and drink with him at an appropriate meeting place, generally a meeting room at his hotel, for the purpose of being sold on the company through a canned presentation. After that, the recruiter returned to his company with résumés and his personal impressions of the potential candidates for his bosses' considerations. If they were impressed, the candidate was invited out to visit the company facilities and to indulge in further talks with higher management.

Billy took full advantage of the five offers he received. These took him for interviews to Dallas, Houston, Detroit, New Orleans, and New York City. It was a real ball, being wined and dined by these important people of very large and successful firms, who knew how to spend money to impress someone. In the final analysis, he turned them all down opting to locate in Phoenix, the place he loved, to his family, whom he knew he would miss if he relocated to a far away place, and to people he considered his friends.

On the recommendation from Dave's father, he sought out a loner by the name of Jack Long. Jack's offer was surprisingly higher than that which was offered by the larger firms, but less than Jack would have to pay an experienced designer. Because of his increasing workload, Jack found that he desperately needed to take on some help, and so it was under those circumstances that Billy went to work for Jack Long and Associates, Architects of Phoenix.

Dave Staple also ended up in Phoenix. As expected, he went to work for his father, who turned out to be not in the best of health. All along family friends and professional associates of the senior Staple felt that it was Dave's destiny to eventually take over his father's practice, and it was in that vein that Dave's presence in the firm was greeted with fervor by all concerned. The practice wasn't very lucrative but it was active enough to support two working architects nicely.

Architects, unlike lawyers, have to work under the direct supervision of a licensed architect for a minimum of four years after receiving their degree, before becoming eligible to take the extensive two day test leading to the privilege of legally practicing under their own stamp (name).

Chapter 16

It isn't as simple as putting in your time, showing up at the designated place, taking the exam, and receiving the necessary document, which ends up to be impressive enough to hang on the wall for all to see. No, the culmination of the four hard years of internship is followed by an elaborate application which by comparison, makes the most difficult income tax return look like a kindergarten exercise. It includes among other intimate personal details and complete historical experience data of the individual, the request for recommendations by six individuals, three of whom have to be licensed professionals familiar with the candidates work.

Then the test is no push over. Most of the applicants fail various parts on the first try. Lucky for them that on retake they only have to repeat the failed portion and not the entire test. It is for these reasons that most of the newly graduated architects hire on with the larger and more elaborate firms who are geared to cultivate the neophytes in preparations for the grueling exams, and who have the professional staff in sufficient numbers to properly endorse the individual. And it follows that the motivating factors are also reasons that the pay is next to starvation wages compared to the experienced non-graduate designer. But if these fresh young architects aspire to eventually become registered (licensed) they have to tolerate the abuses of their mentors and the low wages for the four years of the beginning phase of their career.

At first Billy lived at the home of his parents. His mother quit her job at the Westward Ho in lieu of becoming a full time wife and mother. Billy contributed all that he could from his meager wages to pay his parents back for all the sacrifices and support they gave to him during his arduous struggle of the past several years, and just as important, his contributions went to help defray the educational expenses of his up and coming siblings. It was all very noble, but it was very hard on his love life, on par with the trials and tribulations of living in the college dorm. Billy thought he was becoming a slave of his own creation.

Dave's firm not only still cranked out warehouses and small manufacturing plants with less than plain facades, but started to venture out for one and two story office buildings as well. Dave's father had absolutely no imagination, skills, or aspirations to create grand or obtuse buildings that spoke of the visions of grandeur inherent with most other architects.

On the other hand, Jack Long and Associates specialized in small to

For All The Wrong Reasons

medium sized office buildings with the occasional residence thrown in. By the nature of the projects, it was important that the facilities Long designed made so-called statements on behalf of the clients in terms of appearance. This objective took precedence over practicality, lower first costs, and functionality. In a lot of the cases, to outdo previous designs, they cranked out shit under the guise of innovation, convincing their clients that they were first, on the cutting edge.

No matter what either firm did or how well they did it, they were both swamped with work, mainly because of the growing economy of the Phoenix area and the shortage of architects to meet the demand.

Flying airplanes seemed to have eluded Billy during his first two years in the business. This was due mainly to the long hours over a drafting table. Deadlines had to be met, and because of the increasing business, could only be met by working overtime, sometimes around the clock. More often than not, Billy would put in 14-hour days, with his average for a typical week being on the order of 60 to 70 hours. These long hours fattened his coffers. Everything over forty hours was paid at the rate of "time and a half."

The upside of these trying times was that it meant more money for the Cotton family to recoup their investment in the education of their number one son. The downside was the accompanying burnout associated with long arduous hours. In addition, it allowed Billy no time to pursue his favorite pastimes of flying and women.

Besides, he didn't like architecture all that much. Many times Billy would ponder his situation and wonder how it was that he evolved to the status in which he found himself. The longer he worked in architecture, the more flying became attractive to him.

He had enough flying time and experience that the anxieties he experienced before setting out in an airplane were less frequent and at least were not as severe as he remembered. The nature of the anxiety attacks was more associated with how often he flew. If he laid off for more than two weeks, he would be very nervous during the initial phase of the endeavor. But after breaking ground, all anxieties and fear would evaporate, giving way to intense concentration in the execution of the business at hand i.e. survival.

He heard that racecar drivers and others experienced the same phenomenon in similar situations. They too would be nervous, fearful and anxious until, in the case of the racecar drivers, the car rolled away from the starting

Chapter 16

line. After that it was all business.

When it became apparent that the workload would not let up, the long hours were there to stay. To save money on overtime and wear and tear on his architect, Jack Long hired two additional draftsmen/designers. This brought Billy back to forty hours a week, leaving him with evenings and weekends to play. Maddux and company once again saw a lot of him. He even took on a student, a female no less.

She was the secretary to one of Long's competing firms. Her name was Pauline Morse. He met her at one of the architectural trade shows that frequented the area from time to time. She was in her mid-thirties and plenty shapely. Just what he wanted - blonde, big tits and small ass with her mental capacity being inversely proportional to her good body. She was also very married which was another plus. He could break it off whenever he felt like it. The fact was that Pauline was more interested in screwing Billy than she was in flying. So they did both. And she got her private pilot's license in spite of herself, allowing Billy to stop screwing her and flying with her at the same time. After receiving the coveted license she quit flying as well.

For the six months it took to get her rated, it was a jolly good time while it lasted. It was a good thing that she was married to an affluent member of society because what it cost her after picking up all of the expenses for the airplane rental, Billy's fee, the room rental and other necessary expenses to support the tryst, she could hardly afford on a secretarial wage. He made it worth her while though, and when it was all over she agreed that it was the best six months of her life.

The first time it happened was after the initial flying lesson. He thought it fitting that they should do the debriefing part of the exercise at the Rainbow Tavern in the dark corner booth where some of the best bullshit sessions of his youth took place. This time he felt like he should imbibe on something a little classier than the customary beer that he and his cronies could barely afford. She suggested Drambuie. He agreed. The first one went down too easy, so it led to another and another until the atmosphere became hazy.

In the meantime he filled her with stories of the daring exploits that he and his friends pulled off, and how they always ended up unwinding and comparing their versions of each harrowing experience in the very same booth that he was now sharing with her. If he was trying to impress her, he

For All The Wrong Reasons

was succeeding. If he was trying to make her horny, he was wasting his time. She was and had been in that state since getting out of the airplane.

After a while, Pauline thought that if she was going to get laid it was getting on time for her to make a move. In fact, it was almost too late. If she let him drink anymore she was afraid he might end up in the same condition her husband was after over-consuming which was flat on his back in a drunken stupor, unable to perform. So when he called the waiter over for a fifth refill, she suggested a better place, one where they could both stretch out. He was already too drunk to get the message. What the hell, in his condition he would go along with anything.

To her it was a long drive from the Rainbow Tavern to the Western Village Motel on Grand Avenue. To him the trip took no time at all, especially because he occupied his time in the prone position on the front seat with his head on her lap nibbling on her stomach. It drove her crazy. But she had a mission and she knew exactly what to do. She pulled up to the front office of the motel literally coming to a screeching halt, left Billy laid out in the car, hurried to the counter, rented a room, and got him into the rack as quickly as she could.

Contrary to what she expected, booze had the opposite effect on him than on her husband. Usually the more inebriated he became the longer he could make the sexual experience last. In this case he worked her over for five hours before falling back in a deep sleep. It was almost dawn when she returned him to the airport to retrieve his car. When she asked him about the next flying lesson, he almost didn't know what she was talking about. Needless to say he wasn't worth a damn the next day.

The mating/flying ritual involved making love at the end or before each flying lesson, depending on whether she could wait or not. Fortunately for Billy, they flew no more than twice a week. No matter what day the lesson was scheduled during the week, Saturday morning was a must, and each lesson included the rental of a motel unit at Pauline's expense.

The sessions during the week started shortly after work. Usually they got right down to the business of flying. After the lesson was over, it was a trip to a place of beverage, sometimes the Rainbow Tavern, although that was not her first choice. There they indulged in drink and hors d'oevres, then on to the room at the Western Village for a quickie, a shower, and dinner and back to the room for more serious lovemaking.

Chapter 16

The preliminary quickie before the lesson was much preferred by Pauline. It sort of settled her down some, otherwise it was hard to keep her attention, or to keep her focused on the subject at hand. It was as though she had something else on her mind.

The routine on Saturday mornings varied somewhat. Sometimes they would meet in the coffee shop at the Flamingo Motel located on East Van Buren and 24th Street which was a stone's throw from Sky Harbor where Maddux Flying Service was located. There she would check in while he was finishing his coffee, then off to the room for a short one before embarking on the flying lesson. It seemed to him that the lesson went especially well when she got serviced first.

He always insisted on Pauline doing the room negotiations. There were still things that embarrassed him, among them were buying condoms, and another was renting motel rooms when it was obvious to the desk clerk the purpose for the rental. If she wanted his body, then she was going to provide the place. From her standpoint the arrangement was perfectly acceptable, although she failed to understand his position. From the standpoint of underwriting the expenses, she let him know that the money pit was all but bottomless.

After the flying lesson, it was lunch and cocktails, then back to the motel for a leisurely afternoon of the usual fare, which included swimming in the establishment's pool, weather permitting. On these extended orgies, they brought their own bottle. Both of them were happy with Scotch whiskey. She diluted hers with water; he drank his straight over ice cubes. This arrangement helped curb expenses somewhat since they were able to mix their drinks in the room.

Toward the latter part of the afternoon, when her cup runneth over, she usually made noise about going home to fix dinner for her husband. This made Billy wonder what her old man did on those days during the week. Anticipating this anomaly, she allowed that Saturday evenings were reserved for him.

The entire affair became old stuff after six months of humping the same woman, and he was thankful when she obtained her license. It was fun at first, but during the latter phase, the affair was beginning to cramp his style. He had met other women that he would have liked to fit into the program but because of Pauline and his job, he was hard pressed to find the time.

For All The Wrong Reasons

The other thing that bothered him tremendously, concerned the time that he was introduced to her husband. The man happened to show up one day at the Maddux facility. Billy knew that he must have suspected something if for no other reason the demeanor Billy exhibited in behavior and expression. By contrast, he was amazed at Pauline's cool demeanor. It was almost as though she and her husband had an arrangement and that Billy was part of it. He wasn't very happy with the thought, and it was an additional reason he didn't miss the affair when it eventually evaporated.

It was during this period of time that Dave Staple's father unexpectedly passed away from a heart attack. It was no secret that his health had been failing for the past few years but the condition was merely attributed to obesity, old age, and lack of exercise. He had lately complained that climbing a single flight of stairs winded him, but oddly enough no one associated his difficulties to an ailing heart.

Dave was immediately thrust out in front as not only the prime breadwinner of the family but the principle architect. He was hardly qualified for the task, not only because he lacked the practical experience, but also because he was not licensed by the State to head the practice. The business he was now in charge of not only included the tangible assets, which were small as a percentage of the total worth, but the clients, receivables, and work in progress.

There was no way he could continue on his own. There was more work than he could possibly handle, and he could not stamp the work. He still had two years out of his four to go before he would become eligible to take the test and become a certified architect.

The answer lay in his firm being absorbed into another with the capability and capacity of completing the work in progress and certifying the finished product. It was also important that he could trust these people to be fair and treat him right. The solution to the problem resulted from a very sympathetic Jack Long as a result of a three way meeting between Billy and the others, Jack and Dave.

In the final analysis what transpired was a legitimate merger between Dave Staple's firm and Jack Long, incorporating all of the legal documents that two opposing money grubbing lawyers could conjure up. It was the widow Staple who insisted that the lawyers become involved, mostly to protect her interest and those of her family.

Chapter 16

The lawyer thing was good for Dave because he ended up with half interest in the resulting company. Included in the scheme was a long-range side deal he made with his mother to satisfy her equity in the enterprise. Not being registered, the law did not allow Dave's name to appear in the company title. This contingency was also covered in the final document. That small detail would materialize later.

As a bonus for Jack Long, Dave came on board with an innovative concept that he and his father had been working on over the previous year. Because of their study, they contended that as a practical matter the exterior walls in high-use buildings could successfully be entirely constructed of glass. They had implemented the design on two occasions. One was a single story building and the other two stories. It was enough to gather data on both first cost and operating cost. They found that with double pane insulated reflective glass, the entire exterior walls could be so constructed with minimal additional first cost. They also found that there was little difference, if any, in the heating and air-conditioning operating costs. The real advantage was in the attractiveness of the building and the pleasant work environment. Still, human nature being what it was, other architects with the tendency to resist change would not venture out in what they considered a radical approach.

It wasn't until after Dave and Billy became registered that things with the glass buildings came into focus. A firm in the Minneapolis area was seeking proposals from architects for the design of a twelve-story office building on north Central Avenue, just outside of the Phoenix downtown area. The boys went after it with gusto. Jack Long wasn't so sure. He hadn't attempted anything of this magnitude before, and didn't think they stood the chance of a snowball in hell of being honored with a contract. And everything being equal, they didn't think they measured up against their competition. But in this case, things wouldn't be equal because they decided to go in with an all glass exterior design using the double pane insulated reflective glass approach.

To strengthen their position, they decided to go all the way and invest their time in preparing preliminary drawings. These drawings were given to an artist who specialized in architectural renderings and for a few hundred bucks developed a large colorized depiction of what the client could expect the finished product to look like. It turned out to be awesome looking. But

For All The Wrong Reasons

even with the stellar presentation, a radical approach and a lower design fee, the clients were still skeptical.

In spite of their apprehensions, the selection team was sufficiently impressed to short list the team of Jack Long and Associates, taking their presentation along with that of two of their competitors, including Barney Rodriguez, back to Minneapolis for a final evaluation and selection by the senior members of the firm.

Ultimately they were awarded the contract, but not before going through several more presentations with their mechanical, electrical and structural consultants to prove that in fact their concept was not only viable in all areas of construction and operating expense, but when completed, would be followed by copycat designs which was the highest form of a compliment.

The structural engineer who was brought on board had to present the selection committee with preliminary calculations to show that a facility of such a design was at least as formidably safe as a counterpart design constructed the more conventional way. Mechanical and electrical engineers provided extensive and detailed cost estimates of not only the installed first cost of the mechanical (heating. ventilating and air- conditioning) and electrical equipment, but a ten year owning and operating cost comparison with conventional buildings. Their presentations and resulting numbers bore fruit. To demonstrate good faith and as an added incentive for their prospective clients to honor them with a contract, Jack Long agreed to lease 5,000 square feet of office space in the building for five years.

When it was all over, they were awarded the contract, much to the chagrin of their closest rival, Barney M. Rodriguez and Associates. The project was to be their biggest challenge yet. When the final version of the contract documents arrived for Jack's signature, surprisingly it included a lease document for the 5,000 square feet in the appendix.

It was the celebration at Durant's on North Central Avenue that became the real turning point in the lives of the three architects. After much libation, the discussion faded from the back-slapping recounting of the past few weeks of shrewd maneuvering and hard negotiations to the future of the firm. It was Dave who cunningly steered the focus in that direction - the future. After all, on paper he owned part of the firm. It was time to put his name up in lights. As far as he was concerned, Billy was to be cut in on the action as well.

Chapter 16

This was a subject Jack Long would have just as soon avoided. A promise was one thing but follow-through was altogether different. But now Dave had enough drink and courage to push Jack through the rhetoric and pointless discourse, to the hint of a break-up and a fierce fight over the contract with the Minneapolis developers.

Jack Long cowered. "How would Dave envision the structure of the company?" "Easy - three ways, right down the middle, with all of the principles' names in lights." Only to save face, Jack argued that his name should rightfully be first in the title since he was the founding partner, older than the other two, and came with the most experience. Jack also suggested that Dave Staple's name be second in the sequence of names since he was already a junior partner with tangible equity in the firm. That suggestion was logical and indisputable. It was obviously only offered as a face saving gesture on the senior partner's behalf. But in the spirit of cooperation it was lauded by the other two as not only acceptable but original.

And so it was established in the plush, dimly lighted booth of Durant's, in the stupor of courage fortifying gin and olives, the firm of Long, Staple, Cotton Associated Architects was founded. It was a catching name appropriate to the vast long staple cotton-growing region of central Arizona. If for no other reason, it would attract the attention of the local cotton farmers. They too needed the services of architectural firms from time to time.

Chapter 17

Paradise Airport was North Phoenix' answer to the small operator as well as the airport bum who didn't particularly want to indulge in the worthless discourse required by the self-adulating group in the control tower, and as dictated by the terms for usage at Sky Harbor. Among others, there were two cropdusting companies operating out of there.

It was a small general aviation airport with a dirt mat about one-half mile square that for the most part facilitated operations in any direction. It was also liberally sprinkled with the growth of ground hugging bullhead plants that produced the small, hard, spiny seeds, which played hell on airplane tires.

Its exact location was on the west side of North 19th Avenue between Peoria along the north edge and the Arizona irrigation canal bordering the south side. The main terminal building was a very small facility constructed of cinder block, housing only a couple of offices, a waiting lounge area and a conference room. There was no restaurant. A restaurant was always considered a required element to maintain a relationship with the general aviation bum.

In the late 1950's, the facility was considered all but dead. Its fate being sealed by the lack of a hang-out in which to conduct the mandatory bullshit sessions before and after each death-defying trip through the atmosphere, as well as the tire-eating bullheads that seemed to thrive on the otherwise dry, barren ground.

Toward the end of its existence there was only one Fixed Based Operator who specialized in selling and renting junk, a row of dilapidated "T" hangars, and a cropdusting outfit run by a known alcoholic who tore up more airplanes in one year than most of his competitors did during their

For All The Wrong Reasons

entire existence. He let it be known to anyone who would buy, while listening to his stories, that he was able to survive the more serious pile-ups because his body was always in a relaxed state, induced by his perpetually inebriated existence.

It was also the place where Jack Coyner, one of the more respected crop dusting operators met his maker on a hot dusty afternoon in 1952. He was returning from a job carrying his two teenage loaders in the hopper of his dusting machine when he collided head-on with a departing duster owned by Marsh Aviation. Because of a third departing airplane there was a huge cloud of dust hovering over the area. Coyner chose to land in spite of the fact that he had no forward visibility. The pilot for Marsh decided to take off with a full load of dust even though he too couldn't see in front of him. The Marsh pilot accelerated in the dust cloud and was about to fly at the same place and the same instance Coyner touched down traveling in the opposite direction. They collided engine to engine. The loaders died in the ensuing inferno. Coyner survived for five days with burns over 95% of his body. The Marsh pilot came out of the wreck unscathed.

In the entrepreneurial sense, the property was deemed more valuable as a residential or industrial development site than as an airport. So it came as no surprise to anyone when the airport was closed and the land was sold off to make way for the fast exploding "Valley of the Sun." So it came to pass that Paradise Airport, which turned out to be anything but a paradise, yielded its existence to a new plot of land much farther north in the open desert where land was cheap. The place was called Deer Valley. It was a place where no self-respecting deer would live and no valley existed. The facility was appropriately called Deer Valley Airport.

The new airport opened for business in 1959. It was a grass roots development whose principal investor was the Hollywood celebrity, Art Linkletter. The main runway was paved running generally east and west. It was about 12,000 feet long. Just south of the runway at the west end of the airport was a relatively attractive terminal building with an observation deck on the roof. Happily for most pilots there was no control tower. The real estate east of the terminal along the south side of the runway was dedicated for hangars, tie downs, and Fixed Based Operators.

The airport's exact location was slightly east of the Black Canyon Highway, seventeen miles northwest of Phoenix Sky Harbor. Like the Deer and

Chapter 17

the Valley implication, there was no canyon and if one did exist in the area it would have been some color other than black. Maybe the implications went unchallenged because the place was so far out in the boondocks that no one cared enough to venture out to the so-called valley to feed the deer and explore the canyon. In fact it was so far out of town that the roads leading to the place from any direction were unpaved and it was inconceivable that Phoenix' appetite for expansion would ever lend itself to overtaking the area.

If not for the loyalty he owed the people at Maddux and the lack of a hang out in the form of a greasy spoon restaurant, Billy would probably have used Paradise Airport for his place of activity. It was a different matter when Deer Valley Airport came along. He was immediately attracted to it. Loyalty had its limits. From that point on most of Billy Cotton's activities would emanate from his new playground way north in the desert where the rattlesnakes and scorpions were referred to as deer.

From the onset, the place became a beehive of activity. Prominently located on the runway side of the terminal was a cozy cholesterol-building hash house that the owners passed off as a restaurant. It was the ideal place to hold court with his friends - old and new - over strong coffee and burnt toast. The view through the glass wall of the west end of the runway from any table in the joint, added to the entertainment and sometimes excitement. Every landing was critiqued. Some were very bad, with the occasional one ending up in a heap in front of God, man and sometimes Billy Cotton. He had no sympathy for the dumb-shits who couldn't control their airplanes. It was a good place to observe and because of these observations it was an excellent way to determine what not to do when executing the arrival in an airplane.

If Billy could glean something from these controlled crashes, he felt that they would provide valuable insight for his students. So before he would let them solo the airplane, they had to put in time in the restaurant swilling the goop the owner proudly passed off as coffee, or if that was too much to endure, they could park their asses on the observation deck on the roof and watch the endless array of pilots shooting touch and go's in their quest for a perfect landing. Ultimately he required them to critique some of the landings to him in a way that convinced him the student was learning from the experience. The technique proved valuable to both Billy, the instructor, and

For All The Wrong Reasons

the stupid student. It shortened the pre-solo time he had to put in the cockpit.

Since his specialty was in teaching the opposite sex, he would rather conduct his instructional activities at a location that provided beds. He often bragged that because of his technique, he regularly soloed his students in four to six hours, notwithstanding the extra time he had to log in the sack with the more amorous of the female wanna-be pilots.

Billy fit right in at the new airport. Besides the restaurant, what attracted him most was that the place was a magnet for the other airport bums and flaky operators in the area. It soon became a beehive of activity of junk airplanes and their owners. He could rent a Cessna 140 or a couple of years later a Cessna 150 cheaper than any of the other more legitimate operators in the Valley could offer, including his favorite standby, Maddux Flying Service. In fact it may have been a coincidence but Maddux went out of business shortly after Deer Valley opened.

The era of the early 60's was a good time for Billy. The architectural business was extremely good. The firm had been designing glass-walled buildings since their success with the first one. He hung out at the airport, often referring to it as his second home, during most of his spare time, not letting his hobby of flying, chasing women, and imbibing in the evil fermented fruit juices interfere with his professional responsibilities. He even talked his partners into buying an "F" model Beechcraft Bonanza, and later a 1961 "N" model.

Billy's one main drawback was that he mixed his booze and airplanes too thoroughly. It was an era when the consumption of alcohol and flying when taken together were not monitored by anyone of authority or concern. In fact the practice was considered cute in some circles.

It was a usual practice for Billy to be consuming a can of beer while taxiing out to the departure end of the runway. He did it for show more than anything else. He was actually far from being addicted and it would have been a stretch to consider him an alcoholic. As long as his buddies thought it was cute, his arrogance and ego compelled him to continue with this practice, and far worse endeavors in the future.

The bad habit would start with him sauntering out to the airplane while sucking on a can for all to see, untying it, and climbing in while balancing the can so as not to spill a drop, all without the benefit of his usual non-

Chapter 17

preflight check which included not checking the fuel. He would start the engine, and move out with his right hand on the throttle and his left hand firmly clutching the can, carefully so as not to spill a drop.

His run-up and pre-takeoff check was as typically quick and incomplete, mostly because he didn't want to know if there was anything wrong with the airplane, but it did include finishing off the beer, taxiing over to the edge of the ramp and throwing the can out the window onto the desert. Of all his practices, this was the most important. His instinct for survival told him that the worst thing that could happen was to survive a take-off accident only to have an open beer can discovered in the wreck by some FAA inspector.

It wasn't long before the desert adjacent to the run-up pad was littered with empty cans. He was proud that he caused it, and when others including his partners accompanied him on a flight, he made a special effort to call their attention to the display. His partners, Jack Long and Dave Staple, not only didn't concern themselves with Billy's conduct, but in their true ignorance in the ways of the aviation community, thought it was common practice. They had seen evidence of this sort of thing in literature describing the experiences of WWII pilots who supposedly arrived at the flightline for a mission so hung over that they had to inhale pure oxygen from their airplane's supply in order to clear their head enough to proceed. It was the order of the times.

Crazy Ed's place was located immediately off the west end of the airport. It was a western style bar and grill that featured barbecue fare, beer, hard liquor, and scantily clad waitresses. No telling how the floor was constructed because it was liberally covered with sawdust and peanut shells. The existence of both was deliberate, adding to the rustic decor. The shells were a result of a never-ending supply of peanuts that adorned every table and every few feet on the bar for the patrons to nibble on. The salt only increased their thirst for more beer, wine, or hard stuff. It wasn't the messiness of the patron that resulted in the shells ending up on the floor, the management insisted on it for effect, to add to the atmosphere.

For additional effect, draft beer was served in Mason jars. Regular mugs would have been simpler and probably less expensive, but the customers liked it and it was an added element to Crazy Ed's effort to be unique.

Billy had one student (not a female) who could virtually drink anybody under the table. His name was Dean Mooney. They called him Mean Dean

For All The Wrong Reasons

for short. Dean was actually a consulting engineer who worked for the firm on occasion. Thinking that an airplane would increase his operating base to remote locations in the state such as the Indian reservation, he went out and purchased a Cessna 182 from another consulting engineer who in due course found out that the airplane didn't do a damn thing to expand his business, but instead was a constant drain on his company's reserves. So after buying the thing, Mean Dean, as a tribute to his ability to think ahead, realized that the owner's manual wasn't complete enough in the instructions to further his ambition as master of the elements. It was at this point that he requested the aid of Billy Cotton.

Now Dean passed himself off as a super intelligent individual. But as Billy found out when he attempted to pass on the necessary aeronautical knowledge to fulfill the requirements to be master of the air, Dean was nothing more than a high-strung, over-compensated super-inflated bullshitter. Legend had it, perpetuated by his friends and colleagues, that as a college student he was so confident in his ability and knowledge, he took his tests with a fountain pen. That might not seem like an extra-ordinary feat for the regular essay types or multiple-choice tests as offered to the Liberal Arts majors but these were engineering problem types including Calculus and Differential Equations. His method left no room for errors or corrections. Initially Billy was impressed, but as time went on he concluded that the legend was myth, if not total bullshit.

At first Billy declined Dean's generous offer to be honored with the privilege of being his instructor, mainly because Dean was of the wrong sex. But after getting to know him better, he figured that it might be fun after all.

After each lesson, which took place in the Cessna 182, they would adjourn to Crazy Ed's for the debriefing. It was never a debriefing by ordinary standards. At Dean's insistence boilermakers became the order of the day. For the benefit of the uninitiated, a boilermaker consists of a shot of cheap bourbon whiskey slammed down and followed by the Mason jar of very cold draft beer. Chasing the bourbon with draft beer made the beer taste very mild by comparison. After several of these, Billy was wiped out and not good for anything else for the rest of the day.

The very first flight they made in Dean's airplane was a combination orientation lesson and fuck-off trip to acquaint Dean with the finer aspects of owning and flying his own airplane. It was a sojourn to Francisco Grande.

Chapter 17

Billy had often talked it up as a place to visit in an airplane. He hadn't been there in a while, and figured this was as good a time as any to re-savor the facility, especially since it was in somebody else's airplane at their expense.

They invited their newfound friend and business associate, Bill Simon, to join them on the trip. Simon was a freshly graduated attorney from the University of Arizona, who was handling some of the legal work for the firm. He was their kind of guy because he willingly agreed to meet with Billy or whoever at Crazy Ed's to ponder over legal issues or papers, while drinking with them.

Francisco Grande was a resort type of hotel, located in the desert ten miles west of Casa Grande on the highway from Casa Grande to Gila Bend. It was developed and owned by the San Francisco Giants baseball franchise for their spring training program. This was by any stretch of the imagination, a first class facility consisting of a high-rise hotel where the room balconies overlooked a cluster of baseball diamonds, an eighteen-hole championship golf course, large swimming pool, and a one-half mile dirt airstrip. A smaller single story motel was located just east of the swimming pool. It was in the motel that the baseball players called home for the duration of spring training.

Food, drink, and service at Francisco Grande were exquisite, plentiful, and reasonably priced. Green fees were also attractively low. This was all by design to attract the locals on a regular basis, tourists and conventions on occasion, during spring training as well as the off season periods. Most of the time the place bustled with activity. The top floor of the hotel was a penthouse party room where every Saturday night the management hosted a bash for the registered guests.

The airstrip was just west of the hotel, but because of a fence and the road from the hotel to the strip being circuitous, walking to the hotel was not an option. The strip was oriented in an east-west direction. At the east end was the airplane parking area, fuel dispensers, and a weather-proof phone with a direct line to the front desk. The management prided itself in being able to provide a ride within five minutes after a call was placed.

It was after work and getting late when Dean, Bill Simon, and Billy decided to venture out to try Dean's new airplane. Naturally, they were in Crazy Ed's, saucing it up over some legal matter. Billy was more interested in expounding on the merits of Francisco Grande, one of them being the

For All The Wrong Reasons

opportunity of shacking up without Dean's wife finding out, when in the middle of an ice cold beer, Dean in his animated exuberance jumped up and declared that they were wasting time. They should be on their way. With Dean's less than subtle declaration, Billy allowed that satisfying an impromptu urge such as the one they were contemplating was one of the benefits of Dean owning his own airplane. Bill Simon agreed wholeheartedly.

The fifty-mile trip south was uneventful. It was still light outside but getting late. Billy let Dean play with the controls from the left seat while Bill Simon fretted in the back seat. Simon was actually a white knuckled flyer, making it known to anyone who would listen that he was afraid of airplanes. Billy thought that was the one thing they both had in common.

As far as Dean was concerned, he was flying an airliner. He actually thought he was controlling the airplane, and further assumed he was in complete command of the safe operation of the flight, when in fact it was Billy who was subtly applying pressure to the proper rudder pedal, making the necessary adjustments to the trim wheel, and applying equally subtle pressure with his thumb to the control wheel when necessary to keep things from going to shit.

The sun was low on the horizon when they landed. True to their reputation, the management through the desk clerk hustled a car out to get them within the prescribed five minutes. It was driven by one of their more colorful bellhops named Clarence. Dean's inflated ego over his recent feat was carried over to his generosity evidenced by his greasing Clarence's palm with a five-dollar bill. Clarence responding in kind emphasized that the three should insist on using him for their return trip to the airplane. Two five-dollar bills back to back would certainly make his day.

Clarence was a real caricature of himself. He was a huge, black, gentle, and friendly individual who bell-hopped at the hotel since it was first opened. He gabbed insensitively from the time he picked the threesome up until he dropped them off at the front door. He made it known that bell hopping was a means of supporting his true avocation which was serving in the ministry. His church was small, tending to a poor congregation in a black neighborhood of Casa Grande. Working at the hotel was a necessary means of supporting his wife and four kids. His story may have been one of the reasons Dean was so liberal with this tip.

Settling down in the dining room, Dean, Bill Simon and Billy feasted on

Chapter 17

steak, martinis, and small talk. Billy was the client/flight instructor so Dean picked up the tab, as was the customary thing to do in the business arena as well as the flying community. It was 10 o'clock when they decided they had enough and should get back to Phoenix. As requested, they insisted that Clarence be the driver of choice to return them to their airplane. The desk clerk noting their condition and afraid to sway them otherwise made the necessary arrangements. Clarence, the happy camper that he was, immediately showed up on the scene. It was as though he had been hiding out in the dark corners waiting with bated breath for just the moment. They all took off in the car for the airstrip, Clarence at the wheel.

They arrived at the airplane, disembarked and prepared to untie the airplane, while Clarence continued to narrate the elements of his life's story, going over parts that he covered earlier, because he either forgot or he figured it needed repeating for his captive audience.

Billy noted that it was a very dark and moonless night. He looked down the runway to the west and observed that there were absolutely no lights in the distance on which he could take aim during his take-off roll, nor was the runway equipped with the necessary lights for night flying. The entire area was very black, so much so that Billy could not distinguish the outline of the runway from the surrounding terrain. He figured he would need a target at the far end of the strip to sight in on during the take-of roll. This is where Clarence came in.

At first Clarence didn't know what Billy was talking about when he was given his instructions. But after a lengthy explanation, Billy having to go over the scenario several times, Clarence finally realized that he was to drive the car to the far end of the runway, turn it around and aim the headlights back toward the airplane. In simple terms Billy attempted to drive home the fundamental truth that Clarence was to be the target. The realization that he was to situate himself on the receiving end of a hurtling hunk of metal with two drunks at the controls, and a wanna-be attorney in the back seat, gave new meaning to the word spook. Another five dollars and the assurance that the two brave and capable aviators would be well over the top of his car when they got to the west end seemed to push Clarence over the top.

Although reluctant, Clarence finally agreed. He must have understood everything except the part that required him to go to the far end. Instead he

For All The Wrong Reasons

drove about halfway down, turned the car around, and situated it in the middle of the runway in accordance with the rest of the instructions, as he understood them.

Billy had just about as much trouble convincing Dean to take up his seat on the right side of the cockpit as he did with Clarence and his role in the imminent disaster. Dean alleged that he was more than capable having done a superb job on the way down and furthermore it was his airplane and his left seat, the position of distinction. Billy eventually prevailed grumbling that it was a good thing Clarence was already on his way to his station and couldn't hear the argument, otherwise he probably would have packed up and gone back to the hotel. By this time, the illustrious attorney, Bill Simon, was getting nervous.

The booze must have affected Billy's depth perception. As far as he could tell, Clarence had followed his instructions and drove to the far end instead of merely a quarter of a mile away. Strapping in, starting the engine and positioning the airplane in the center of the strip in the direction of Clarence, he turned on his landing light and poured on all 235 horsepower, hurtling the drunken conglomeration hell bent for victory toward the good-natured preacher who was praying his heart out for the success of his new found lost souls.

Before Billy was halfway there, he realized that a car-airplane collision was in the making. Billy immediately eased the airplane over to the right side of the strip, the right wing hanging over the bordering fence, at the same time groping for the "Johnson Bar" flap handle. He tried to coax it off, but there was no way the airplane was going to fly before arriving at the car and the impending scene of the accident. It got light but not light enough. It would only skip along the ground. There was just not enough airspeed to sustain flight.

The avenue available to them, between the car and the fence, was only wide enough to accommodate the fuselage and possibly the wing struts. Billy wondered if there was enough room between the bottom of the left wing panel and the top of the car. There was nothing else to do but to try to thread the needle. He winced in anticipation of the inevitable wreck as the left wing approached and then passed over the top of the car - the right wing clearing the fence by not much more. But it flew, so did the conquering heroes, off to Crazy Ed's for the much needed sustenance and beer. As

Chapter 17

far as Dean was concerned, what they had just gone through was routine. Before too long he would also be able to do that.

On a subsequent trip to Francisco Grande, rehashing the events of that night with Clarence and his role in the fiasco, all Clarence could say was "I knowed you guys had jist one too many trips to the bar." As for Bill Simon, it turned him off of airplanes forever.

The two of them, instructor and student, would occasionally combine a business trip with an instructional session, especially when they were jointly working on an out of town project. One such job was located in Tucson. On the day that the construction was due for inspection, the two warriors deciding to use Dean's airplane for the task showed up at Deer Valley for a reasonably early departure. In the true spirit of an eager student, Dean proceeded to undertake a thorough pre-flight inspection. In an equally true spirit of his perpetual philosophy concerning pre-flight inspections, Billy tried to hurry Dean along wondering why he had to get up so early just to waste his time watching Dean waste his, when he could have been spending more productive time in the sack snuggled up to his latest squeeze.

In his ceremonious quest to find fault with the airplane, Dean called Billy over from his perch, which took the form of draping the upper part of his body across the rear of the fuselage, to inform him of a major discovery. Grumbling at the fact that he was jolted into awareness from the fantasies of what could be taken place if he would have stayed in bed instead of jousting the windmills of the real world, he sauntered over, grumbling all the way, to see what Mean Dean had discovered. Billy noticed that Dean was pointing to the front face of the right tire at what appeared to be an oblong spot.

On closer inspection, he could see that what his student was concerned about was the chord of the tire showing at the surface in an area of about three inches long by at least one inch wide. It was no big deal, Billy thought. He explained to Dean that the tire was still good for another dozen landings, and that he should not concern himself with such a trivial matter until he could see air through the worn spot instead of chord, "So cut the horseshit, get in the airplane, and get on with the show."

They took-off and headed out toward Sky Harbor Airport on the way to Tucson. Billy took up his usual position, which was sliding his seat all the way back and resting his head on the right side window. It made no difference to him that Dean busted Sky Harbor's airspace, because there was no

For All The Wrong Reasons

way of getting caught short of sending an airplane up to intercept the violator and retrieving the airplane's number. If there was such a thing as radar or something like a transponder at the time, the Feds could track the airplane to its destination where somebody on the ground could ID it.

Even though Dean hadn't soloed yet, he was far enough along that Billy let him make all of the take-offs and landings, no matter how atrocious the landings were. The controlled crashes that were Dean's trademark, accounted for the most part, the condition of the right tire. Billy wasn't concerned; after all it wasn't his airplane.

In true style, Billy let Dean make the approach and landing at Tucson's Freeway Airport, and as expected, it was a crash landing. They continued the roll out to the far south end, exited the runway to the right side, pulled up to a tie-down spot in front of the terminal building, and while Dean fucked around with the airplane, doing things that pilots are supposed to do when they complete a mission, like tying it down, he immediately went inside and plopped down on the couch, a la Joe Mora. Dean joined him after a short time, bitching once more about the tire.

The rest of the morning was routine. The contractor picked them up at the airport and drove them to the job site. After a couple of hours touring the project and developing a sizable punch list, they decided that it was time for martinis and lunch, all on the contractor's expense account, after which he returned them back to the airport for what was supposed to be an uneventful flight home. This time Dean didn't bitch about the tire. He didn't even pre-flight the airplane, which goes to show what a little libation will do to an individual's attitude. Billy was teaching him well.

The prevailing wind and the airplane that was shooting touch and go's indicated that it would be prudent to use runway 13. All of the activity on the airport, such as administration and tie-downs, occurred at the southeast end of the airport, all on the west side of the runway. There was no physical demarcation between the runway, taxiway, and tie-down area. It was all one solid asphalt mat that extended about half way down the runway. So when one taxied from the terminal building to the approach end of 13, the narrow part of the ramp between the parked airplanes and the runway was used for about half way to the end, then back taxiing was necessary to complete the journey. This is significant for what was about to happen.

The two fearless flyers piled themselves into the airplane, Dean adjust-

Chapter 17

ing his seat, sitting erect and pouring over the vitals while fantasizing he was flying a DC-7 instead of a piece of shit Cessna 182, while Billy slouching in his seat, ran it back to the rear stops. He only fastened his seat belt at Dean's insistence. In spite of Dean's clumsiness, the engine came alive with a roar, in fact too much so. Billy had to reach for the throttle and pull it back to a more reasonable speed. In due course, they ended up at the approach end of the runway, where Dean proceeded to complete his DC-7 run up, lingering to a point where the airplane that was shooting touch and go's found it necessary to go around.

Still slouching in his seat with his head resting against the right side window, with nothing better to do but stare down at the right wheel pant and the runway around it, he watched as the ground started to move under the wheel pant as the airplane gathered speed. His main concern was his student keeping the airplane straight, and if not, at least keeping it on the runway, because there was no room for error, especially on the right side where the airplanes were parked uncomfortably close to the runway.

Then the unthinkable happened. As his gaze was fixed on the action on the outside and down to his right, he heard a loud bang, witnessed the right gear leg drop and heard the god-awful grinding noise as the runway tried to eat up the right wheel and its associated wheel pant. The airplane immediately jerked to the right. Dean started to pull the power to abort the take-off. As Billy envisioned the entire conglomeration wiping out the row of airplanes bordering the right side of the runway, he yelled his objections to Dean's action thinking that the airplane and its occupants were better off in the air than on the ground tangled up with a bunch of other airplanes.

Because his seat was so far back, to grab the wheel he not only had to lean forward but his arms were outstretched as well. But grab it he did. With full power and the horrified grinding taking place out the right side, it was a good thing that Dean was feeding in enough rudder to keep it straight, because there was no way Billy could manage the rudder pedals from his position. His legs were just not long enough. But what he did was to crank in full left aileron by twisting the control wheel to the full left, and for just a moment the grinding stopped as the right wheel assembly left the ground, but just as quickly it fell back down to resume the hellish destruction. The cycle repeated itself a couple more times until the airplane gained enough speed to keep the wheel off the ground and soon after it started flying.

For All The Wrong Reasons

Billy sobered up real quick. As soon as he determined that everything was stabilized, he adjusted his seat to the forward position to do some serious flying. He reasoned that they should fly the airplane back to Deer Valley Airport to be in friendly territory where repairs might be less costly. Also how would they get home if they grounded the airplane in Tucson? Then there was the question of getting hurt in the landing. A hospital stay in Tucson would be more inconvenient than in Phoenix insofar as the relatives were concerned. It was these and other considerations that prompted Billy to decide to take the airplane back to Deer Valley for what he perceived as a disastrous arrival.

About twenty miles southeast of Phoenix Sky Harbor, Billy recalled incidences of wheels up landings at Sky Harbor where fire fighting foam was sprayed over the landing area, lubricating the surface in effort to minimize damage to the underside of the distressed airplane and to prevent a nose over.

This idea appealed to him. He immediately got on the radio and contacted Phoenix Radio. After describing the problem with them, covering all of the essentials as best as he could, the discussion progressed to the possibility of foaming the runway at Sky Harbor for them. The man at the other end didn't think it would be a problem and he would be more than willing to order it up from the city. Billy knew it was an expensive proposition and somebody had to absorb the cost, so he asked the man if he could kind of check that part out for him first, and if Billy and/or Dean had to bear the cost, how much might that be?

The man was beside himself. Here was a pilot in what was supposed to be in a life or death situation and he was asking him what he thought it was worth. So after expressing his concern, he agreed to inquire and would get back to them shortly. Within five minutes the answer of about $500 came back. Well, in those days that was a lot of money to Billy, so he declared for all on the frequency to hear that he was going to take his chances on the dirt sailplane strip at Deer Valley. Dirt had to be almost as slippery as foam he reasoned. And with that he changed to the Unicom frequency to enlist whatever help he could get at his destination.

The dirt strip was immediately north of and parallel to the main east-west runway. The wind was out of the southeast at 10 mph. Billy circled over the top contemplating the best attack. The people on the ground were

Chapter 17

using binoculars and reporting over the radio their assessment of the damage. According to them, it didn't look good. And besides, for a successful landing the wind was too strong, out of the wrong direction. The landing would require that he land with his left wing down for as long as possible throughout the landing roll and with a south wind component landing to the east into the wind would require that he hold the wrong wing down. To provide a wind component from the left side as required for the proper wing to be down, would mean a landing to the west, or in a strong tailwind.

Somebody on the ground suggested Turf Airport. Turf was a new airport about three miles south with a dirt runway that was oriented northeast to southwest. It was located very close and parallel to the backstretch of the newly constructed Turf Paradise racetrack. The runway orientation was perfect. It would provide a moderately strong ninety degree cross-wind from the left, allowing our hero to hold the left wing down for a very long time. In fact, Billy thought he could hold it down until they came close to a complete stop.

Dean was very nervous. He thought he was going to die. As Billy lined up for a long final approach with a touch of power, he yelled at his student to quit his sniveling, shut his fucking mouth and to stay away from the controls.

The touch down was perfect on the left wheel. As the airplane slowed, Billy continued to feed in more and more left aileron as required to hold the right wheel off the ground. It surprised him that he was still going fast when he ran out of aileron deflection and the airplane fell over on the damaged wheel. But the result wasn't as severe as he thought it might be. When the wheel hit, it dug into the soft river bottom soil and the airplane spun around in a bucking fashion for a turn of 270 degrees.

They shut the engine off, climbed out and waited for the anticipated help to arrive. It did, and a discussion ensued as to how best to deal with the problem. The answer was to set the right wheel, if it could now be called that, on a pallet, and drag the whole conglomeration down the runway to the tie-down area. This they did without difficulty and in the deal managed a ride back to their cars. All that was left now was a debriefing session at Crazy Ed's.

At Crazy Ed's, Dean did two things. He called his wife to tell her how close he came to dying, and then he ordered a boilermaker. The call was no problem. Consuming the boilermaker was insurmountable, because he was

For All The Wrong Reasons

shaking uncontrollably. He couldn't lift the shot glass to his lips without spilling it. Several suggestions came from the jovial crowd who were having a great time over the two's misfortune. One of them suggested a bottle with a nipple.

The bartender came up with a scheme that was brilliant. He tied the end of a towel around Dean's right wrist, ran the length around the back of his neck down to his left hand. Then he instructed Dean to grab the free end with his left hand while clutching the shot glass with his right hand, and slowly pull on the towel raising the drink to his lips in the process. Dean actually let him do it, and a laugh and good time was had by all, until after a while Dean forgot his problems and it was time to go home.

The whole lower right gear assembly on Dean's Cessna 182 was trashed. It required major work to the wheel pant and brake assembly, a new wheel, and by all means a new tire. Dean wasn't very happy about the deal. He blamed everything on Billy, maintaining that if they had only grounded the airplane when the worn spot in the tire was first noticed, the incident wouldn't have happened. He fired Billy as his instructor, took up with Dan Amousse, and was ripped off as Billy suspected he would be.

Chapter 18

Billy had many theories concerning the instructional techniques for teaching his neophytes on how to fly these mysterious pieces of shit called airplanes. Of course most of his practices were non-traditional and would probably have been highly frowned upon by the authorities who oversaw these activities. In fact, if they were even remotely aware of his activities, they would have more likely jerked his instructor's rating, as well as his other tickets. One of his ideas concerned the student's first solo. He let it be known to any one who would listen that his target was to launch each of his students in six hours or less. Other instructors would camp out in the airplane with their charges for 15 or 20 hours before gaining enough confidence to let them fly solo.

One day while holding court in a dark corner at Crazy Ed's, drinking draft beer out of a nonsensical Mason jar and nibbling on salted peanuts, Billy was expounding to those around him on one aspect of his many pet theories regarding the first solo. He told those who seemed interested, that if a pilot would treat each and every one of their landings as though it was their first, landing accidents would be non-existent. He pointed out that a student scuttling the airplane on the very first try was non-existent. He knew, because he had made it a point to do the necessary research on the subject.

Crazy Ed himself, overhearing the dissertation, immediately became an interested and active participant in the discussion. After Billy climbed out on the limb as far as he could, Ed pointed to a mangled propeller on display in the corner of the very room in which the discussion was taking place. This he pointed out was a perfectly good propeller until he embarked on his first solo. Then before the exercise of completing his landing, the elements suddenly took over, becoming the driver, while he just as suddenly became the passenger. As bad as the propeller looked, he said it was pristine compared to the rest of the airplane. This was just one of the crackpot ideas Billy had that someone else shot full of holes.

Another of his pet theories that originated elsewhere, but that he embraced wholeheartedly, contrary to the dictates of the FAA, was the application of pitch and throttle. Billy subscribed to the technique that the throttle was primarily the climb control and the stick (wheel or yoke) was the speed control. At the seminars conducted by the FAA for Instructor's rating renewal program, they emphasized, contrary to the way Billy was taught, that if one wanted to make the airplane go faster or slower the pilot should use the throttle, and conversely, if it was up or down that was desired, then the pilot should adjust the pitch of the airplane by applying forward or back pressure on the stick or wheel. They decreed that it was heresy to believe otherwise.

Billy refused to subscribe to their notion, exclaiming that his way was safer and that as long as he was the one doing the teaching, it would be his way. Of course he didn't let the exalted members of the agency know how he felt, and would continue to kiss their collective asses as necessary to maintain his good standing.

It was while pickling his brain at Crazy Ed's that he met and became good friends with Walter Marty. They hit it right off. Their personalities seemed to dovetail. Walter lived in Las Vegas when he wasn't out building roads. At the time they met, he was the superintendent on a road building project to pave Black Canyon Road that when completed would shorten the time it took to drive from Phoenix to Prescott from four hours to an hour and a half. Later the road would be divided and become Interstate17.

Walter appeared to be unusually young for such a responsible position and Billy told him so. This gesture among others, such as their mutually carefree nature, is what cemented their friendship.

Walter owned a Cessna 180. Other than being equipped with a tail wheel instead of a nose wheel, it was the same as Mean Dean's Cessna 182. He used it to commute from the job-site to his home in Las Vegas each weekend, presumably to get his "ashes hauled."

If Billy accompanied him home on one of his trips, he would ensure that everyone would have a jolly good time. Better yet, Billy should bring along his own play toy, as there was plenty of space in the form of a guest room for additional fun and games.

Chapter 18

The offer was too good to pass up. So with a relatively new acquaintance in tow, who answered to the call of Nancy, they took off one Friday in the early evening for what Billy anticipated to be a weekend of engrossing carefree activity completely removed from the pressures of his normal activities of trying to satisfy disgruntled clients. This weekend was designed to be the ultimate rejuvenator. He would return to the rigors of his architectural endeavors with his batteries completely charged. He couldn't wait.

The idea of the ultimate weekend was to get a head start on the event. First, they were to meet at Crazy Ed's for the mandatory attitude adjustment, where the sauce flowed freely from Mason jars and the peanut shells piled conspicuously at their feet. As the sun started to set and all parties developed the giggles, someone declared that it must be time to move on but not before procuring a couple of six-packs for the road.

Walter was pretty much shit-faced by this time. Billy later concluded that Walter was in fact a bona fide alcoholic in the early stages. Years later the addiction would progress to the point where he couldn't start the day without first jump-starting his heart with a shot of Bourbon.

They left Crazy Ed's, staggered over to Billy's car, noting how it was still hot outside for that time of day, drove the short distance to the airport, and with overnight bags in hand, made their way to the airplane. In his condition, Walter saw no need for the conventional preflight inspection. This suited Billy to a tee, because it was against his nature to perform the exercise anyway. He always maintained that it was a waste of time and didn't prove anything, except maybe to put on a show for the uppity pilots who might be looking on, and of course the exalted members of the FAA.

As a result, the tie-down chain on the right wing remained fastened. Walter took care of the one securing the left wing, his side of the airplane, and the tail. But he falsely assumed that since Billy was standing under the right wing kicking rocks and sucking on a can of beer, he would take care of the chain for that wing - not so.

They all clambered aboard, Nancy in back. Walter fired it up, released the brakes, added power, and other than the left side, the airplane went nowhere. The answer was to add more power. The chain became more taut under the strain of the anxious airplane, and the airplane still would not advance on the right side. By then they had rotated about 30 degrees to the right in the tie-down space.

For All The Wrong Reasons

It was only a matter time before Billy and company took notice of the seriously strained chain stretched out from between the underside of the right wing panel and the anchor point on the ground. Billy insisted that Walter shut down before he would disembark to release the airplane from its mooring, because he argued, the prop blast would muss up his hair.

With that last hurdle taken care of, and the sun dropping below the horizon, off they finally went toward the run-up area, where the first order of business was to toss the empty beer cans out of the airplane onto the desert adjacent to the pavement. Then, Walter went through some exercise learned a long time before, to prove that the airplane engine was sound enough to complete another mission. It was ceremoniously academic because no matter how the engine checked out during the so-called run-up, they were hell bent and determined to proceed on their adventure of sex, drink and gambling.

Surprisingly, the take-off, climb to altitude, and establishing the cruising mode, went off without a hitch, considering the other events leading up to that point. It was getting dark, and with the onset of nightfall, Billy on this cue, in addition to being tipsy, was getting horny.

A glance over his shoulder to the back seat revealed Nancy. It was as though he discovered her for the first time. He had trouble containing himself. She was in a relaxed position, sitting comfortably back in the seat, seemingly enjoying herself, the expression on her face indicating that she was ignorantly fascinated by the whole adventure.

Without any hesitation and zero invitation, Billy made a move to unfasten his seat belt, only to discover that he failed to fasten it in the first place, and scrambled over the back of his seat to take up a position next to his target.

Other than wondering why Billy was scrambling to take up a seat next to her, she thought nothing of the fact that he was vacating a position of responsibility for one of lesser importance. Sex was the farthest thing in her mind. She just couldn't fathom that they could indulge in such a confined place under what she considered impossible conditions. He intended to show her otherwise.

While Billy was involved in the machinations of extricating himself from the front seat to the position of glory, the airplane took on a life of its own. It bobbled through the sky, sometimes producing a negative "g" load, which

Chapter 18

pitched Billy to the roof, as the center of gravity changed, and as he continuously bumped the control wheel with his leg or foot. Walter not knowing better thought there was something wrong with the airplane. He screamed for help. Billy told him to shut up and fly the airplane. When he settled in back, everything stabilized back to normal. Walter thought it had something to do with his superb airmanship.

Billy got right down to business. He groped her body and unfastened her bra so he could explore her thirty-six plus breasts, all the time explaining how he was going to introduce her to the "Mile High" Club, a uniquely elite association. He assured her that Walter would not look. He was too busy flying the airplane. Besides, it was too dark for him to see anything if he wanted to.

It wasn't enough to merely complete the act; Billy had to insist that she disrobe completely. She consented only on the condition that he do the same. It wasn't that she was going along only to please him, but more because she was getting excited at the prospect of getting laid in an airplane no less. With all of the contortions it took to complete the disrobing, it turned out to be a mess of fabric throughout the cabin. Some of the garments ended up on the right front seat, her panties on Walter's lap, others beneath the rear seat while most of it ended up over the back seat in the baggage compartment. In the process, her foot hit Walter on the side of the head, which caused the airplane to momentarily go negative raising the two lovers off their seat. Walter grabbed the panties, took a sniff, and immediately threw them over his shoulder. That action in itself caused the airplane to bobble.

Billy grabbed a can of beer, which thankfully for Nancy was by that time getting warm. He proceeded to pour the contents a little at a time over the front of her body, licking it off as he went along. This made Nancy scream, which made Walter turn around, and which in turn caused the airplane to once again go negative, spilling some of the beer over Nancy and the back seat. The lover boy had to double-time it to lick the surplus off her body, which made the screaming more intense as she immersed in ecstasy. The cycle repeated itself throughout the trip as Walter strained to absorb the beauty of Nancy's naked body and the action taking place in the desecration of the same.

It was in this starkly naked fashion that they copulated for the entire remainder of the trip including the approach and landing. Their clothes were

For All The Wrong Reasons

scattered all over the interior of the airplane. It was dark, except for minimal lighting in the tie-down area, so it seemed prudent that they disembark in the state of nakedness, and sort it all out later.

It was this way that Walter's wife, Monique, found them as she drove up to the parked airplane to complete the unloading of the loaded occupants and their respective baggage. Like the nurse she was, and knowing her husband for what he was, she proceeded with the task at hand like a true professional, and even helped retrieve the loose garments from their hiding places.

The only person embarrassed by the state of things was Nancy. Walter was too drunk and acted as though everything was normal. Monique expected no less from her husband based on his past antics. It was probably why she left the children home with a sitter. When introduced, she even shook hands with the two lovers, and handed them the various pieces of attire as she retrieved them from the airplane.

It struck her as odd that Nancy had two pairs of discarded panties that didn't match. But being the lady she was she didn't ask. She would take the matter up with Walter at a later time. By the expression on Walter's face, Billy also knew that the matter was far from closed, but he couldn't be concerned, he was after all a member in good standing of the Mile High Club and as such he considered his nakedness as a badge of honor and a right of passage. He wanted another beer.

The real reason Monique left the children at home was so that the foursome could go directly from the airport to one of the casinos for dinner and other things grown-ups do when visiting Las Vegas. However, once they got in the car, she regretted the suggestion. To her the stench coming from the back seat was more than she could stand. It was a blend of stale beer, sweat, bad breath, and "eau d'after sex." Walter was oblivious to it all, which was no surprise to Monique considering the condition he was in.

In spite of the minor setback, to which over time she grew accustomed, it was a jolly good time for all. It was especially good for Billy who had never experienced the lights and good times that the city had to offer. He was duly impressed.

One would have thought that after all of the fun and games of the evening, the occasion would have been topped off by Walter getting caught up with his sexual matters from the week of being away on the job. Maybe Walt and Monique were too pre-occupied with the noisemaker that Billy had bedded

Chapter 18

down with in the spare bedroom. By the sound of things coming from the orgy, it appeared that Billy was killing her instead of merely using her body. Monique wondered if the kids were taking it all in, what they thought about it, and how they were reacting? This went through her mind as she lay on her back and stared at the ceiling, not saying a word to her husband but thinking that she ought to remind him, for her sake, not to invite those two for a stay at their place again. Finally the screaming stopped, but no sooner that she felt grateful for it, the loud snoring started. Was there no end to this?

The program that Walter planned for them the following day made Billy suspicious that Walter wasn't getting taken care of at home, and counted on his out of town work assignments to provide relief for his sexual needs. The agenda unfolded during idle conversation around the breakfast table among screaming kids and stares from Monique that made Billy unduly nervous. The plan which was a real shocker to both women, and which made Billy even more nervous, provided for the girls and the kids to go on a shopping spree while the two boys go off to do their own thing. Walter explained that he wanted Billy to meet an old friend of his, and the exercise would be nothing but boring to the others. This was as good a rationalization as any and coupled with the inherent female urge to spend money on worthless things at equally worthless shopping centers was the ticket that allowed Walter to pull off the charade.

Immediately after breakfast, without Billy knowing what was going on and caring less, the boisterous boys took off in Walter's pick-up for parts unknown to Billy but with a definite mission in mind for his buddy. The first stop was a liquor store for a pint of the finest. Then it was off to the airport for an airplane ride to a place that Walter guaranteed would blow Billy's mind as well as another part of his anatomy.

The destination was Ash Meadows, Walter's favorite fly-in resort and house of ill repute. In spite of the high alcohol content that continuously took charge of his body, Walter did a pretty good job of flying his Cessna 180. As long as he didn't try to kill him, Billy was content to let him fly the airplane and pull on the bottle at the same time. After reaching his cruising altitude and leveling off, Walter reached in the "glove box", retrieved the bottle of Old Crow, removed the cap, while bobbling the airplane in the process, took a long swig, and handed it to his friend and passenger who

For All The Wrong Reasons

quickly followed suit. This happened several times until the contents were almost gone.

It was about a ninety-mile ride, Billy was numb, tipsy, and he had to pee, but he could make it. What followed impressed him. Walter dove down on the facility completing a first class buzz job that made Billy proud, made a short approach, greased the airplane on, parked it and shut it down. They adjourned to the drinking part of the establishment, patting each other on the back all the way into the bar.

Besides the bartender, the only other patron snuggled up to the bar was a young man who was nursing a mixed drink while in serious conversation with the bartender. He was on a cross-country from Reno to Las Vegas. That explained the Cessna 150 that was parked next to Walter's airplane. The kid was trying to persuade a reluctant bartender to endorse his logbook to the effect that he was in Las Vegas and not Ash Meadows. Such endorsements for student pilots on cross-countries were a common requirement to ensure that the candidate actually arrived at the intended destination and not someplace else like, as in the situation that was unfolding.

Seeing the futility in the student pilot's efforts, Walter quickly obliged and signed the book, relieving the tension that was obviously generating, and just as quickly reminded the kid that he owed him and his friend a drink for his effort. For a short time the three drank, joked, and told harrowing flying stories, until looking at his watch, the kid downed the remainder of his glass, picked up his logbook, clambered down from the stool, and with gratuitous handshakes all around, he headed for the door.

The boys later ran into him as he exited the bawdy house on his way to his airplane for the flight back to Reno. What a great way for a student pilot to complete his cross-country requirements while at the same time becoming indoctrinated into the system, Billy reasoned.

They had a few drinks and more idle conversation with the bartender. It mostly centered on the young man with the logbook. The bartender was used to it. These guys were coming into his place wanting him to sign off on their cross-countries all the time. He was getting tired of turning them down. Word must have been spreading around Reno about what a good deal it was to fly into Ash Meadows instead of Las Vegas on their cross-countries. If he wasn't signing them off, who was? He said he did what he was about to do when Walter intervened, send them off to see the whores. It was a two for

Chapter 18

one deal, a piece of ass and a sign off for the price of one.

Then he really got wound up expounding on the morality and legality in doing what the students where doing. He was considering very seriously about reporting these infractions to the FAA. That was all Walter could stand. He told Billy to drink up so they could go over to where the whores hung out and talk to them about the situation. He would convince them of the errors of their ways.

No, Walter didn't need directions from the bartender; he had been there before. Without so much as a nod of approval from his buddy, which would have been automatic anyway, he extricated himself from his perch and started for the door with Billy in close formation.

The sex mill was located in a separate building a few hundred feet from the bar. It was a large two-story building that resembled a sorority house. Inside a fenced area was a covered patio and swimming pool. Billy thought that the pool must be there to rinse off the clients after their ordeal inside. It was on the way to the stately house of ill repute that they encountered the smiling young neophyte, pilot-wanna-be as he made his way to his airplane and hopefully Reno.

Inside the place was a fabulously breathtaking sight. There were eight gorgeous, well-stacked young maidens milling around the parlor. They were mostly nude, clad in nothing but panties and see-through bras. The only thing lacking as far as Billy was concerned was their virginity. He would have liked to believe that they were virgins. It excited him. He imagined himself wading through the room full of unsoiled young maidens like a tornado. But coming down to earth he new better.

Billy had no intention of indulging. It was not because he was afraid of the social consequences. He was informed that it was impossible to contact the familiar diseases, as the girls were professionals, and were inspected each week by a bona fide doctor. Was it because he was too cheap? Hardly, the fee for a quickie was only twenty dollars. It was simply because he was too used up, having had the encounter with Nancy at 5,000 feet the day before, and was up half the night pounding on her until she "cried uncle." She finally admitted that she had enough and let him doze off to blissful oblivion.

Walter wasted no time. He'd been there before and knew what he wanted. He immediately got with the program by selecting what was undisputedly

For All The Wrong Reasons

the best looking fox of the bunch. That wasn't to say that the others were dogs. All it meant was that Billy happened to agree with his choice. Walter was actually salivating like Pavlov's dog when it was offered a piece of meat. Smiling like the cat who ate the canary and without so much as a "see ya' later" to his pal, Walter disappeared through the doorway with his right arm draped over the shoulder of his prize trophy and his left hand crossing over to ply her left breast. She was all smiles too. For the moment Walter was the only one who meant anything to her, and she intended to let him know it.

Billy nosed around the lounge, eyeballing the remaining stock, and perusing the dirty magazines and equally dirty wall hangings. Before too long it was an offer of a cup of coffee or something stronger, from one of the juicy looking, big breasted morsels that got him involved in an upper level discussion with the fair maiden. It was either the close proximity or the high level conversation that jump-started his genitals.

When she suspected that he was leery because of the questionable safety, she told him that she had just started doing it for a living, and had undergone a complete physical. After much cajoling on her part, he was getting to the point of being convinced. He pondered the prospects and irrational judgment took over. How could someone so sweet, innocent and dainty looking be a risk for anything? Furthermore, she would show him the best time of his life. How could that be so bad? And to cap it off she would even reduce the fee from $20 to $15; better yet.

She still sensed reluctance. She started to wonder if maybe it was his first time in a whorehouse, and accordingly he was shy and reluctant to do it with a stranger. She got graphic, talked a lot about what she was going to do to him and began to fondle his already hardened tool. That did it. If he had doubts they were gone. From that point on, for the next hour and a half he let his dick do his thinking and make the decisions. So the dick put Billy completely in her charge.

She thought it wouldn't take long, but much to her regret, he was still going strong after an hour. She did everything to get him off, and was about to scream foul when he finally got his jollies. She was thoroughly pissed off. All that work for a mere $15. The real reason it took him so long to get his ashes hauled was simply because he was all used up, thanks to Nancy. Even at that he didn't keep Walter waiting.

Chapter 18

    Walter having finished in fifteen minutes, retired to the parlor, inquired as to the whereabouts of his friend, and when Billy didn't show in a reasonable length of time, repeated the process with a fresh girl. Eventually they both walked out of the joint, with their respective joints all screwed out, vowing in a boisterous way, for anyone within earshot, that their newfound lovers were in for a first class buzz job. With that, they departed the facility and headed for the airplane.

    Sitting out in the Nevada sun, the inside of the airplane was very hot. The control wheel was too hot to hold. They opened both doors and waited until the temperature inside the airplane was at least tolerable. Getting in the airplane, Walter inadvertently kicked the near empty bottle with his foot. He hastily retrieved it realizing that it too was very hot, but he could use the drink. He took the final swig, started the engine, headed for the end of the runway, and without the benefit of a run-up, poured on the coal, and headed down the dirt strip, followed by a cloud of dust.

    On breaking ground, he immediately started a steep, nose high, right turn. Billy, for as far back as he could remember, began to sweat for the first time in his flying career, not only because of the hot cockpit, but also for his life. Walter continued the maneuver until reaching about 300 feet and rolled the airplane level in the direction of the whorehouse. Then without hesitation, he pointed the nose down toward his target, building up speed to beyond the red line. Billy was not only sweating bullets, but was on the verge of pissing his pants at this point. He knew that this was the end.

    As the airplane approached the building, Walter fumbled with the window on his side, managing to get it open and control the airplane at the same time, picked up the empty bottle and held it close to the opening. At thirty feet (actually Billy thought they were going to hit the building and accordingly resigned himself to his fate) he leveled off, the airplane screaming as they approached the whorehouse. When he thought the time was right, he chucked the bottle over the side. Billy hoped to Christ that in his drunken stupor, Walter's poor judgment in not anticipating the trajectory of the missile would send it beyond the intended target. As near as he could tell, the bottle did overshoot, harmlessly splattering itself on the desert. Walter recognized his error. He cursed himself, mumbling that he scored a direct hit on his previous visit.

    They flew back to Las Vegas, moored the airplane, and returned to Walter's house to discover that the women were formulating big plans for

For All The Wrong Reasons

the evening. But it was not to be. While watching TV from a prone position on the carpet, both of the intrepid flyers crashed in a drunken stupor. Flying an airplane can be a trying and exhausting experience.

The next conscious thought that Billy was aware of was Monique kicking Walter in the ribs while verbalizing in a few "X" rated epithets that made Billy think that the ugly truth of their exploits had been found out. Instead Monique was carrying on that they were going out on the town, one way or another. With that determination and a few more shoves, the two delinquents still groggy and thoroughly hung over, piled in the back seat of the car, and with the girls at the helm took off for parts unknown. The two reprobates immediately went back to sleep and didn't wake up until 11:30 in a lonely parking lot of one of the casinos. It was all over for them. They had finally pushed the limit of their endurance. All there was to look forward to now was the trip back to Phoenix.

Back at Deer Valley, for a while anyway, Billy continued to bang Nancy. She started to pester him with the notion that she wanted to learn how to fly and eventually own her own airplane, preferably one with a large back seat. Billy tried to ignore that prospect because he knew that if it became a reality, he would be obliged to teach her for free.

As hard as they tried to fix Walter up with one of Nancy's friends, he resisted. He preferred prostitutes instead. They were cheaper in the long run. He didn't have to wine and dine them or let them take flying lessons in his prize possession of an airplane. So when they met at Crazy Ed's, or the airport restaurant, it was always a threesome.

Chapter 19

Billy was sitting at his desk scrutinizing a drawing when the secretary announced that there was an emergency call. In a panic-stricken way, he scrolled through all of the possible scenarios, including some disaster that may have fallen upon his mother or father. He was having trouble controlling his emotions when he picked up the phone, and was equally relieved when he discovered that it was only Walter on the other end.

Billy may have been relieved, but Walter was panic-stricken. His voice was breaking, indicating he was close to tears. It was too involved to discuss over the phone, so would Billy come right out and meet him at the airport? By all means he would. Without hesitation, and thinking that something bad had happened to his family in Las Vegas, Billy dropped everything and rushed out to meet his friend at the airport restaurant.

Sipping a cup of coffee, Walter blurted out that he had just scuttled his prize possession, his airplane. The revelation explained why he wanted to meet at the restaurant and not Crazy Ed's, and why he was drinking coffee and not something stronger. He was just plain scared. The drinking phase would come later.

Walter had all sorts of excuses. No, he assured his friend, he was not drunk. Had he been drinking? He said, "only a couple, for lunch." Like most wrecks that the occupants walk away from, it was a landing accident. When Walt blamed it on the wind, Billy glanced out the window at the windsock and confirmed a strong ninety-degree crosswind. Also the movement of the windsock indicated that it was not only strong but gusty as well. A continued stare showed the wind direction to be variable by as much as forty-five degrees. Walter must have been asleep at the controls to let the elements turn him from airplane driver to passenger.

Enough of this bullshit, an inspection was called for. So out to the airplane they sauntered, Walter sniveling all the way with his lame excuses.

For All The Wrong Reasons

Billy had no sympathy for stupid, whiny pilots who couldn't fly, and was repelled by Walter's display of weakness, until he saw the airplane.

What Billy saw took his breath away, and made him feel awfully lucky that it was Walter that caused it and not him. The wreck was a classic case of a severe ground loop. He was lucky that Deer Valley was not a controlled airport, and was able, with the help of a line-boy, to get the airplane off the runway and back to the tie-down without drawing too much attention. It might have been a different story if the accident had happened on a weekend when the place was bustling with activity. What he didn't need was for some busybody to call the FAA.

As far as Billy could tell this wasn't an incident. It was a major accident. Damages could well exceed $5,000. To add insult to injury, Walter didn't have one thin dime's worth of insurance coverage. When pressed for a reason, he claimed that it was too expensive. Every time he was reminded that the insurance would have cost less than what faced him now, he would choke up and start crying. This was more than Billy could stand. A show of weakness was not exactly what Billy expected from the people with whom he chose to associate.

Walter had the same feeble excuse that all inept pilots use when an airplane gets away from them on landing. It's either the elements or a stuck brake that's to blame. In Walter's case it was both. His right brake failed, he was going too fast, and he had a tailwind component.

According to his story, he was too fast on short final. The airplane began to float unduly in ground effect, so he decided to plunk it down on the mains (wheel landing) to hurry the landing, instead of three pointing it, as was his custom. Then he tried to brake the airplane when he realized he was using too much runway. The right brake failed in the process, and he didn't have sense enough to relax the left one. To compound his problem, the air was gustier than shit as he wiggled his way down the runway. He did eventually manage to get the tail down for steerage, but it was too late. The airplane took off to the left and completed a full turn-and-a-half before coming to rest along the edge of the runway without messing up one runway light.

There it sat listing slightly to the right with the engine stopped until someone from the office came out to meet the guy who had just put on a first class airshow. Walter wasn't about to start it up and taxi to the tie-

Chapter 19

down. He was too rattled. Besides he didn't think it would be safe to do so with the broken brake and gusty conditions. So with the help of the lineboy, they pushed the crippled airplane all the way to the ramp, and into the tie-down space.

On inspecting the damage, the first thing Billy looked at was the right wheel. Yes, the brake was destroyed. If it wasn't busted before the landing, the ground loop managed to trash it completely. The brakes on this vintage Cessna were of the style that used many clips around the perimeter of the assembly to hold the brake disk in place. These were sheared off, leaving the disc to float loosely and worthlessly in the housing. The sides of the tire were scuffed with dirt and scratch marks indicating the wheel had actually tucked under during the side stresses imposed by the ground loop. It was this action that took out the clips leading to a complete brake failure. Billy surmised that the brake failure did not occur on the initial landing roll as Walter had stated; but after the ground loop was well underway.

The airplane was listing, slightly down on the right side. This led Billy to the gear leg. Comparing it with the one on the other side, it didn't seem to be bent, which meant the damage was in the gearbox (the area under the skin where the gear leg attaches to the structure.) He would confirm this by grabbing the wing tip and rocking the airplane. When he reached up to grab hold of the wing tip, he recoiled. It too was a mess of bent and torn aluminum. The outboard eight inches of the aileron and wing from that point on out had contacted the ground on the way around Walter's ride from hell.

That wasn't all. The underside of the right-hand horizontal stabilizer and its associated elevator had also been dragged through the turn. These were not only scraped and torn but were left with a freshly induced dihedral. This bent up configuration meant that either the spar or the attach structure or both were broken and/or stressed to the point of permanent deformation.

Billy looked back at the wing from that vantage point to determine if the same could be concluded for it. Yes, the last couple of feet of the outboard portion of the wing was definitely bent upward. It had to be either a bent or broken spar outboard of the wing strut.

From what he observed of the damage, Billy tried to visualize in his mind the sequence of events leading up to the pile of junk in front of him. It was obvious that the airplane had not only spun around, but was also vigorously sliding sideways on the pavement and adjacent gravel, probably more

For All The Wrong Reasons

sideways than around. In the process, it not only dug the right wing in but seemed to have squatted in a nose high attitude such that the right side tail feathers were not only scraped on the underside, but the spar on the horizontal stabilizer for that side was torqued at the attach points bending the unit up at least twenty degrees. The sideways sliding was also the contributor to the broken landing gear box, the rolling under of the tire, and the trashing of the brake assembly.

Not only was he feeling fortunate that he wasn't involved in the fiasco, Billy was starting to enjoy the misery and predicament of his friend. It was like the good old days at Phoenix Union High School and Phoenix College when the boys actually reveled in seeing their buddies squirm their way out of a bad situation. But seeing the distress that Walter was in, he decided not to exhibit his real feelings. Instead, Billy was outwardly sympathetic and condescending, but he made up his mind in advance that his attitude was definitely not going to extend to financial aid, no matter how hard Walter sniveled that he could not afford to fix his airplane.

His immediate recommendations called for a meeting at Crazy Ed's over boilermakers and draft beer appropriately served in Mason jars, along with the usual highly salted peanuts. This way they could think this thing through with a clear mind. At that suggestion, Walter knew he had done the right thing by calling on his problem-solving friend. After the first drink his concerns for the airplane seemed to melt away. The big conclusion derived from the meeting was to turn their back on the immediate problem, go out on a pussy hunting expedition, and return to the problem after they both had a chance to sleep on it.

Walter was in a slightly cheerier mood when he called Billy at his office two days later. His mood was manifested by the slurring of his words. Billy was also in a cheery mood but for reasons that didn't concern airplanes. He had actually forgotten about Walter's situation. His up-beat mood was attributed to being successful in cornering his petite morsel of a secretary in the stationary closet and obtaining a commitment for some extra-curricular activities which for the time being would be honorable in nature.

Her name was Betty Stone. She was a glamorous five foot-six inches with what he estimated to be a thirty-six inch firmly established set of boobs and a twenty-four inch waistline to go along with her tender age of twenty-four. She gave the appearance of being very innocent, which for reasons

Chapter 19

obvious only to him, turned him on.

Billy's thoughts were interrupted by the problem at hand, Walter's pleadings for attention. Could Billy meet him at Crazy Ed's after work to discuss the wreck of an airplane? For a moment Walter had to refresh Billy's memory. No, not really, he had a hard-on to deal with, but would call him just as soon as his libido was satisfied. Walter was getting desperate, but so was Billy as he glanced out the door of his office at his newfound treasure. Since he hired her two weeks before, he had undressed her in his mind countless times and this instance was one of those times. Walter had to take a "back seat."

His thoughts took him back a couple of weeks to when and how she happened to come on board with the firm. Normally the senior partner interviewed and selected the help. In this instance Jack Long was on a business trip. So he left it up to Billy to interview and hire the replacement secretary for the middle-aged spinster who could no longer stand his foul mouth and sarcastically abusive nature.

Betty Stone by contrast was the vision of loveliness, single and as far as he was concerned, highly qualified. He hired her immediately over several other candidates who were obviously more experienced. When Jack returned from his trip and got a look at what Billy had done, he merely shrugged his shoulders in resignation and regretted having left town, leaving Billy in charge of such a serious undertaking. The simile of the dog in a butcher shop immediately came to mind.

For the last week she had become infatuated with her boss. His infatuation for her was otherwise referred to as lust. He considered her untouchable, pure, and only obtainable through marriage. That wouldn't stop him. He would attempt to soften her up by first indulging her into participating in the famous libation known as the "Scorpion" as only the renowned Trader Vic's could conjure up. He could hardly wait. It was the famous cocktail that served as the prime mover in getting him and his friend Adam Thomas, laid from time to time at minimal expense.

Trader Vic's was a high class dining and drinking place architecturally appointed in the decor and motif typical of the Polynesian Islands. Conveniently, it was located across the street from the offices of Long Staple Cotton, Architectural Associates.

The Scorpion was a concoction formulated as a four-person drink served in what was referred to as a "wash basin bowl" which was an indication of

For All The Wrong Reasons

its mammoth size. The object was to locate the huge container in the center of the table so that all participants could partake in the beverage by drawing the liquid poison through straws, one furnished for each individual. The drink was very potent, formulated with five different liquors, mostly made up with rum. For decor, there was a sizable lily-pad floating on top. This gave one the impression that anything with such an attractive crown couldn't be so potent.

Billy and his buddy Adam would take their honeys to the place and tête-à-tête over the bowl and indulge in small talk while sucking incessantly on the straws. The big difference was that Billy and Adam would pinch their straws to restrict the flow, making gurgling sounds, only pretending to suck in the quantities of the lethal blend, while their counterparts would get the full measure, because as good sports they wanted to go along with the program.

After one drink Billy would invite his date to his office, where if all went according to the script, would retrieve the blanket he had stashed in the closet, and adjourn arm in arm to his office. It was generally downhill (more like down on the carpet) from there.

With his newfound treasure, otherwise known as his secretary, the plan went off as scripted. Before the drink was half consumed she was giddy and spilled out her whole life history. When the mixture was all gone, so was she. Billy suggested they return to the office before continuing on to dinner. At this point, all she wanted to do was get along, so she agreed, an indication of her innocence to the methods of the cruel corporate ways. It took him less time than he thought it would to get the blanket out of the closet, onto the floor of his office, and the victim on the blanket.

She seemed to be all right through the experience and through dinner but before the evening was over and as Billy was opting for seconds at his apartment, she became very ill. So the last half of the program had to be postponed for a better day. For safety's sake he took her home instead of back to her car, saw that she was appropriately tucked in and departed for his own pad feeling less than satisfied.

It was the next morning when he arrived at the office, late as usual, that he found out she had cleaned out her desk, resigned and hurriedly left the premises. In his best show of innocence, Billy wanted to know why. From one of the other girls who had given her a ride to work, he was told that

Chapter 19

immediately after arriving at the office, she went to the lunch room, sat down with a cup of coffee, and began to relate the events of the previous night before an audience of the firm's female contingent. Except, she left out the part that took place on the blanket in his office.

Being matronly, one of the more seasoned of the group responded by cautioning her of the ways of her boss. She elaborated by recounting the rumors that persisted wherein the Scorpion drink was an old trick of Billy and his friends to lure the opposite sex to a position on a blanket on his office floor. She went on to advise that the next time he tried it, she might fall victim and end up like all of the others. Up until that time Betty, was in love. Now she was devastated. The illness she endured up to that moment was minor compared to how she felt when confronted with his true motives. With a sweep of her hand, she knocked over her coffee, burst into tears and left the room leaving her friend wondering what she had said that was wrong.

From there, she went straight to Jack Long's office, tearfully blurted out that she was leaving, where he could stuff his company, and where he could send her final paycheck. Beyond that, she said nothing to explain her sudden resignation. While Jack sat there, mouth wide-open in bewilderment, Betty, as suddenly as she entered his office, departed, cleaned out her desk and made for the door.

Thirty minutes later, Billy Cotton entered. The place was in an uproar. Jack Long, suspecting his partner and protégée had been up to no good, tried in vain to ferret out the truth. But Billy, the pillar of innocence said he was just as interested and would do his best to find out. For as hard as he tried, she would not talk to him ever again. The Scorpion had struck again.

Billy was slightly depressed over the event of losing his secretary when he met with Walter later that day. But a few Mason jars of cold brew seemed to take the edge off of his mood. Walter on the other hand appeared uncharacteristically chipper compared to his state of mind of two days earlier when the two pondered his screw-up and the mess of the piece of shit of an airplane that Walter once considered his jewel. It was different now. He told Billy that he had a plan.

Walter related the fantastic tale of a sergeant friend of his who was in charge of the sheet metal shop at Nellis Air Force Base. The Base was located just outside of Las Vegas. According to Walter, his friend claimed to

For All The Wrong Reasons

be capable enough to repair the damage to his airplane. It was remarkable that the sergeant was able to make the assessment without so much as looking at the airplane. The only catch, or as Billy put it, "fly in the ointment," was that Walter had to deliver the mess to him. Even more remarkable, he would effect the repairs for next to nothing, because he was in control of a couple of flunkies who were not only qualified but thought they were in tall cotton if they had enough in their pocket to buy a couple of beers.

Billy queried Walter as to whether he accurately imparted to his friend the true extent of the required repairs. "Yes, and no sweat. No job was too big for the sergeant." And what about the paperwork required by the FAA, such as logbook entries, and the form 337, which was a must when completing major repairs. Was he qualified to sign these off? "No, but that didn't matter, because he was so good that when he was through with the airplane, nobody would be able to detect the previous damage and subsequent repairs. So it would be like the accident never happened. It would be in as good as, or in better condition than before. Now would Billy fly the airplane to Las Vegas for him?"

Billy contemplated the question for a moment while swigging on the beer in his hand. He wondered if this would be the trick that would finally do him in. On the other hand, if he pulled it off, it would be a great story he could share with the rest of his warped friends over peanuts and drink. He would have to think about it. It never occurred to either one of these bozos that it would be safer and more practical to dismantle the airplane and truck it to the sergeant. If either one of them would have thought the situation through, it would have occurred to them that even if Billy flew the airplane to Las Vegas, it would still have to be dismantled to get it to the sergeant's shop.

Thirty minutes and two beers later Billy had a plan. Why thirty minutes? It took that long to relate the story of the night before to the reprobate sitting before him. Walter had seen the girl before when he occasioned a visit to Billy's office for some nondescript reason, and the prospect of Betty stretched out in her birthday suit on a blanket excited him to no end. He wouldn't be satisfied with the sketchy details that were presented. He wanted a blow by blow (literally) description of the minutest details in the most graphic way possible. Billy suggested that he go out and buy a porno flick instead and for the moment concentrate on getting the airplane to Las Vegas.

Chapter 19

Back to his plan, Billy suggested that he wear a parachute and remove the door on the pilot's side for easy exit in the event he had to part company with the airplane before he got to his destination. He had been told that it was next to impossible to open the door against the slip-stream, at least enough to get man and chute through it. He further suggested that the feat would have a better chance to succeed if he undertook the mission in the early evening when the wind was normally calm and the air was stabilized, i.e. free from thermally induced bumps. And if those precautions weren't enough and something went wrong, like a wing or stabilizer taking a short cut to the ground, he would merely go his separate way using the chute for a soft landing. Would Walter agree to the risk?

Yes, Walter readily approved the plan. He not only threw holy water on it, but he wanted to go along, sharing the adventure with his hero. But it was not in the cards. Somebody would have to drive the vehicle, if for no other reason than to return the fearless aviator and his parachute back to the starting point.

Obtaining the chute was much more of an undertaking than he had anticipated. It took much wrangling with the head of the local skydivers' organization to pull it off. The man's uppity position seemed to be that if one was not a member of their exalted club, they had no business dabbling in the art of casting one's self out of a perfectly good airplane and floating down to earth underneath a canopy of silk or some semblance of the material more typical of modern technology.

Billy always tired easily of the ramblings of these self-righteous, and pompous shit-heads. He had no patience with them and wanted to get right down to business and out of there. Was he going to get the chute or not? Only if he bought it. There just happened to be an old dilapidated WWII surplus seat pack available for $150.00 that one of the members discarded in lieu of a more modern high-performance backpack. It needed repacking, but that could be taken care of for an addition $15.00. If the boys brought it back in the condition that they took it, the exalted one would buy it back for the paltry sum of $100.00. Why not just rent it for a few days? The obvious and expected answer was liability. Billy made Walter cough up the money, and they left, grumbling under their breath about what a shit-head the guy was, and a final instruction to pick it up in a few days fully inspected and repacked.

For All The Wrong Reasons

When they returned to pick up their prize, they left the place with another gem in the form of valuable information. It was a suggestion that the boys remove the right side door instead of the door on the pilot's side. This would make for a less drafty situation for the driver. It would also mean that the right seat would need to come out as well to make the exit easier if the occasion called for it. Climbing over the seat in a desperate move to exit the airplane might prove too cumbersome, resulting in the ultimate marriage between pilot and his ship, 'till death do us part.

Now all they had to do was wait for the following Friday afternoon. In the meantime they would remove the seat and door, adjust the parachute to Billy's dimensions, and fuel the airplane.

Chapter 20

Friday afternoon rolled around with the usual pre-flight briefing at Crazy Ed's watering hole. After a few stiff drinks, last minute plans, and a six-pack in tow, the two gladiators made off for the airplane. Walter helped Billy don his parachute, situate the six-pack in the appropriate spot next to the seat, and untie the airplane. Billy was noticeably nervous at this point. This bothered him because he couldn't remember anytime involving airplanes that he had this reaction. He rationalized that it must be due to the new challenge. Maybe it was because he had never worn a parachute in an airplane before, and it represented a possible disaster. He was having difficulty in getting the prospect out of his mind, so to mask the manifestations he cavalierly reached for a beer.

This time Walter managed to release all three tie-down chains. Billy clambered aboard, situated himself firmly in the pilot's seat, buckled the crotch straps of the parachute, and fastened his seatbelt over the whole conglomeration. It was a tight and confining fit, and he thought if he needed an excuse to back out, this was it. But not Billy, nobody was going to call him chicken. He took another swig of courage.

Then for the first time since entering the airplane, he looked around the cockpit and out the front over the top of the cowling. He was sitting too high in the seat. His head was pressed against the headliner, and to avoid this he had to lean uncomfortably forward. The whole thing felt strange, especially when he found that he had to reach down to grasp the control wheel and throttle.

Then when he looked to the right and saw the gapping hole that at one time was a door, and the blank spot on the floor that once contained a seat, he started to freak out. The wave of adrenaline was surging through his body and he was having second thoughts again, but drawing from the expe-

For All The Wrong Reasons

rience of a few minutes before, it was nothing that a swig of beer couldn't cure.

He shut the door on his side, started the engine and very loudly admonished Walter to get moving so as not to keep him waiting too long at the airport in Las Vegas. As he added power and began to roll, he glanced at his watch and noted that he was getting a much later start than he planned. The second to the last thing he wanted was to arrive at the North Las Vegas Airport after dark. The landing would be difficult enough in the daylight.

The last thing he wanted was to confront the ultimate test of having to leave the airplane before it was time, only to spend the night cuddled up in a silk canopy nursing a broken leg. The prospect once again sent chills up his spine, triggering a reflex action that sent his right hand down to retrieve the can of courage. He decided right then and there that he would not think of that alternative anymore, but instead entertain more pleasant fantasies of getting screwed in Vegas as Walter had promised.

The surface wind at Deer Valley Airport was out of the northwest at an estimated 10 mph. So leaving the parking space, he pointed the airplane eastward down the taxiway for an anticipated departure on runway 25. Taxiing in a tailwind with a left component, Billy immediately encountered difficulty in keeping the airplane headed east on the taxiway. The wind was strong enough to cause it to weather-vane to the left with more force than he could counter with right rudder and the steerable tail wheel. He would need right brake to offset the tendency. But right brake he did not have, thanks to Walter.

When the nose eased northward by about 15 degrees, the steerable feature of the tailwheel disengaged as it was designed to do. As soon as that happened, the nose would swing farther to the left increasing in rate until it reached a northwest heading, into the wind, then stop. The first time it did that, it caught Billy by surprise. But he reacted by merely adding power to continue the turn to the left until he was aligned once again with the taxiway. The ground loop was slow enough to be inconsequential, but it did present a problem. If this shit kept up, how was he going to get the damn thing to the end of the runway?

With somewhat of a struggle he managed to get the airplane rolling once again down the taxiway, but not for long. In less than 200 feet the process repeated itself, very slowly at first but as he ran out of rudder travel and

Chapter 20

tailwheel control, the rate of turn speeded up again until it swung through 180 degrees. But this time with power and left brake carefully coordinated, Billy managed to keep the turn going back to an eastward direction. He was hoping that nobody was watching his flying farmer routine.

On the next cycle, Billy thought he could outsmart the gods by stopping the turn on a southeast direction slightly to the right of the intended track. As it turned out, he ended up in a direction of about thirty degrees to the right of the taxiway heading, and if he continued in that direction for very long it would take him out into the desert. "No matter" he thought, "the desert was smooth and if he wanted, he could actually taxi as far as necessary on the dirt surface." By using this new direction, he had more of a direct tailwind resulting in less left turn tendency.

He went a little farther this time before the elements won out. The airplane once again gradually came around swinging through east then north and with the technique previously tried, he brought it around to the southeast with the right wheel hanging over the edge of the pavement. As irritating as the process of getting the airplane to the run up area was, this new technique proved worthwhile as he gained several hundred feet more progress than he did with the first two ground loops.

Eventually, after several more of these machinations, he ended up at the approach end of runway 25, wondering why in the hell he hadn't taken the easy and shorter way by using runway 7. He had started out from that end of the airport in the first place and a downwind take-off in an airplane with as much power as the Cessna 180 had, would be no problem, especially since he was not carrying a load. He felt beat up, like he had already done a days work, and the trip wasn't even started. With a sigh of resignation and thoughts about something to do with water under the bridge, he downed the remnants of the beer can, tossed it out the "no door" side of the airplane and took to the runway.

As soon as he poured the coal to it and built up a head of steam, he realized the one factor that he failed to take into consideration with all of the planning and preparation that went into the mission was ear protection. The noise generated by the engine and wind blasting through the opening on the right side was deafening.

Walter, as with most pilots of that era, did not believe in using headsets. They relied instead on the speaker and a hand-held microphone. They also

For All The Wrong Reasons

believed that this lash-up was more convenient and actually much safer inasmuch as it allowed the pilot to listen for engine idiosyncrasies that would not be possible with the use of earphones.

When Billy embarked on this half-assed mission, he didn't take into consideration that the existing set-up would not work in the noisy environment. He realized he would not be able to communicate with anyone during the trip and would probably hurt his ears in the process. It was a good thing that North Las Vegas Airport wasn't a controlled facility. There was no way that under the circumstances he would be able to communicate with any tower or enroute facility. It was especially bad considering he might need the radio for emergency purposes.

He considered chopping the throttle and aborting the take-off, but by the time that option registered, he was going too fast. And judging from the trouble he had taxiing the airplane, a landing, or more like a fast rollout, might prove to be disastrous. All of that flashed through his mind until he broke ground and experienced the severe shaking that reverberated throughout the airplane. The deafening noise was inconsequential compared to what was going on and would continue for the rest of the trip.

It reminded him of a recent WWII movie that he saw and liked, where the hero limps back from a bombing run over Germany in a B-17, with half of his airplane shot away, and the whole thing including the control yoke was shaking like crazy. While munching popcorn in the theater and taking in the glamour of the story, he fantasized that if only he had been born ten years earlier, he could have been that pilot. He had always maintained the WWII was the last of the fun wars. Except in this case it was different. He was now experiencing reality. All of the sudden, he saw no glory in what he was doing.

The situation was unbearable, and he was only five minutes into the flight. He considered going back, but thought more of the loss of face than his dumb ass. He tried throttling back to slow the airplane, but to no avail. It still shook and was just as noisy. He looked out at the right wing to see if all of the pieces were still intact, and seeing that they were, chose to add full throttle, go like hell and drink another beer.

The trip would be far from easy. It was a long way to Las Vegas, over 250 miles. Billy would have to muscle the airplane all of the way. The noise was unbearable to say the least. He knew that when this was over, he would

Chapter 20

suffer from irreversible hearing loss. He kept drinking and looking out at the wing for missing parts. It was an exercise stemming more from nervousness than concern. It made no difference to the performance of the airplane whether he slowed it down or added full throttle. It shook severely in both conditions, all the way through to the control wheel. The only grace-saving factor was the calm air in the stillness of the late afternoon.

After what seemed to be an eternity, Kingman finally appeared over the nose of the airplane. Billy figured he was about half way there. There was no telling for sure because in his usual way he neglected to take along a chart. Judging from the time it took to cover the distance from Phoenix to the vicinity of Kingman, he wondered if he could make it to his destination before dark. It was just another item to worry about, another cog in his wheel of injustice, he thought.

For no apparent reason, he looked down at the floor. There were still three cans of beer to consume. If the airplane went down, would that be enough to sustain him in the hot desert until help arrived? Probably not. Besides who would care enough to go out and search for him. These apprehensions and his insecurity and loneliness were indicative of the depression that was setting in. Billy was beginning to see the folly of his planning, with the shortening supply of beer, the lack of ear protection, no chart, and a bladder that was beginning to send signals.

Two more items confronted Billy. How would he get past the main Las Vegas airport, McCarran, on the way to North Las Vegas Airport without communicating with them? McCarran was a controlled airport requiring permission to invade their airspace. He adamantly resisted the thought of taking the alternative of climbing above their sacred airspace. That would take too much time. Going around to the east would take him over Lake Mead. That wouldn't do either. He was afraid of death by drowning. Giving way to the west added too many miles to the already long trip.

The decision was made. He would bust through their sacred airspace. Maybe they wouldn't notice. These air traffic controllers have been known to gather around the coffee pot swapping dirty stories, especially on a slow day. And on a busy day they would be preoccupied harassing some other poor slug of a pilot. And if they did see him, how would they get his number? Somehow he concluded that invading their territory was worth the risk. At the time his logic came into play, Billy would have been willing to

For All The Wrong Reasons

go to jail just to get out of that shitty airplane.

Billy was just barely past Kingman, hanging on to the yoke with both hands, when the beer began to act violently on his bladder. He had no container in which to relieve himself, because as he finished each beer, he would throw the empty can out the space that at better times contained a door. He had trashed the desert along the edge of the run-up area at Deer Valley, now he was doing his best to leave a trail of beer cans between Phoenix and Las Vegas.

He looked around the cockpit for something that he might substitute for a toilet, and finding nothing in the form of a container except the cabin itself, he elected to direct the flow of his urine onto the floor of the airplane instead. Then he looked down in anticipation of the task at hand only to discover that whipping it out to do the job might not be that easy.

First there was the seat belt, and then the parachute crotch straps would have to be unfastened. These would require the use of both hands in an already unstable airplane, and might be impossible to refasten because they were very tight, a necessity so as not to experience castration when one needed the parachute canopy to blossom.

The only other option was for him to pee in his pants. That thought repulsed him. His mother and the nuns raised him better than that. What would the boys say if they found out? He would be laughed out of Crazy Ed's.

In the end, because when nature calls it brings out the best in an individual, he managed to unbuckle all of the fasteners while the airplane bobbled and bucked through the air in response to his reflex actions on the yoke. These machinations were due to the undivided attention and focused concentration on the more important project at hand.

Billy unbuttoned his fly, wriggled his Levis and shorts down to just above his knees, only to realize that without a container, he would still dribble all over his clothing and seat. By this time his bladder was about to burst. In desperation, Billy rolled his body over as far as he could to the right, while still trying to control the airplane with his left hand, and steering his appendage with his right hand, he let go.

And let go it did - another miscalculation. In his desperation he forgot about the severe drafty conditions in the airplane. The phrase "when the shit hit the fan" appropriately illustrates the results incurred when the piss hit

Chapter 20

the drafty cabin. It sprayed all over the place, everywhere except the floor, and either Billy couldn't or wouldn't shut it off. It was too late. He was committed to finishing the job. At the time, if one could have heard over the noisy cabin, the sound would have been a long sigh of relief. It was the sound of unconcern for anything except finishing the job.

The airplane was in an ever-tightening right turn throughout the mess, with Billy flying by sole reference to his dong, and the ragged right wing tip to the ground. It was a disgusting episode. Billy vowed that the best thing he could do when it was all over and he was safely on the ground, would be to jump into a vat of boiling water with a Scotch in one hand and a wire brush in the other.

When he was through coating the inside of the airplane and himself with the contents of his bladder, he sat upright, straightened the airplane back to course, and thought about what a filthy mess he made. He decided that for the rest of the trip he would leave his underwear and pants down across his thighs, and continue on with the parachute buckles as they were, fastening only the seat belt. This was just in case he had to do it all over again. To hell with the prospect of crashing and being found in that condition.

Then it occurred to him that all he would have had to do to avoid most of the mess, was to empty the contents of one of his remaining can's of beer, take out his pocket knife, cut out the top of the container, and use it in stages by throwing out the piss ridden contents each time he filled the can, until his bladder was empty. He would do it this way next time with one exception. He would first drink the beer instead of throwing it overboard. With that resolve, he reached down for another, popped the top with his faithful "church key" and took a long gratifying swig.

The thought of the more rational solution made Billy realize he was not operating with all of his available mental faculties. As they put it in Las Vegas, "he was not operating with a full deck." Being aware of his deficiencies he resolved to try to think more clearly for the remainder of the trip, especially focusing his concentration on the final approach and landing at his destination airport. His worst fears revolved around the possibility of a strong crosswind for his landing. In that case he would certainly have his work cut out for him, if the taxiing experience at Deer Valley Airport was an indication. There was no way he could call ahead on the radio for a report. He could kick himself in the ass for the stupid mistake of not taking along a headset. He now realized that he was inebriated by all he had to drink, even

For All The Wrong Reasons

though he didn't feel impaired, unless feeling dirty all over was the same thing. The drunken condition was in all probability masked by the noisy, drafty, and rough flying airplane.

With his underwear and pants down to his knees, his parachute rendered useless by the unbuckled crotch straps, Billy paddled by McCarran Field at 1,000 feet above the ground, in the setting sun, on his way to the small airport northwest of Las Vegas. As he flew by, he strained for the sight of a windsock to give him an indication of what was in store for him. To his surprise, the windsock and other indications in the valley led him to believe that conditions on the ground were calm.

He continued on, gradually letting down to 500 feet AGL (above ground level) and crossed directly over the top of his destination airport. So far so good. The airplane was still in one piece if one could consider the frazzled end of a wing panel to be one piece. But at least the wing had not separated itself from the rest of that piece-of-shit; at least to this point. It would be a shame, with all the trouble Billy had during the trip, to have the whole godamn thing break up on him now.

The windsock at North Las Vegas Airport also indicated calm conditions, showing no runway preference, and just about the time he was to select a runway, he noticed a Twin Beech Model 18 setting up a left downwind leg for a landing to the east, runway 7. This was great, he would follow the big bird all the way down, but cautioned himself to give the twin a lot of room so as to avoid any propwash.

He was a half-mile on final approach as the sun disappeared below the horizon, and at the same time, the Twin Beech was rolling out toward the far end of the runway. He figured his timing was just about right, so that by the time he touched down, the twin would be well past him on the parallel taxiway, on the way to the terminal. This was important because if his airplane got away from him, and went skedaddling across the infield, there would be no possibility of a collision.

He was a sight to behold, cruising down final in a torn up airplane with no door, sitting extremely high in the cockpit, his drawers pulled down to his knees exposing his private parts for only God and the Angels to see, and his hair sticking out in every direction from being exposed to what could be considered a wind tunnel. It was hardly Hollywood's concept of what a hero should look like.

Chapter 20

He was a picture of concentration, wrestling the shaking mess in a slow-as-possible let down, in effort to plunk it down as close to the end of the runway as possible. He crossed over the fence, chopped the power as the end of the runway flashed by, and mustering all of his faculties needed for the challenge, greased the stupid machine on with nary a bump. Because of the calm and still conditions, he managed to roll straight ahead needing only rudder to control his direction.

For lack of a right brake, Billy was taking no chances, and used the entire length or the runway to bring the airplane to a stop. This was accomplished by gingerly tapping the left brake and as the nose yawed accordingly to the left, he would counter with right rudder. The exercise was repeated with left brake, right rudder application until the airplane was slowed to a crawl. He exited at the end and taxied to the tie-down.

When the airplane came to a stop, reasonably centered in the parking spot, Billy shut it down, unbuckled his seat belt and parachute harness, and literally crawled out the right side, with his drawers still down in a compromising position. When he hit the ground, the first thing he did was to yank his underwear and pants back to their original position lest anyone in the area take notice. The fear was unfounded. The place was as devoid of the living as a potter's field. He passed his hand over his head in a futile attempt at grooming his hair, tended the airplane by tying it down, removed the parachute and proceeded to the terminal building.

It would be a long wait for Walter to catch up. He felt like shit, actually more like a urine and sweat soaked sponge. He kept sniffing at his clothing and finally determined that he felt worse than he looked. After entering the terminal building and plopping the parachute on the floor, he made a beeline for the restroom without so much as a glance at the surroundings. He was very self-conscious of his appearance and eye contact with anybody was the last thing Billy wanted.

He cleaned up as well as he could under the circumstances, and then exited to meet his audience, the crew of the Beech 18. After some indulgence, mostly small talk, they offered him a ride to town. He had no choice but to accept. The office was about to close. A ride out of there would be better than sitting under the wing for several hours.

They were driving a van. It was much more convenient than a car. Billy and his parachute could spread out in the back seat where he thought it wouldn't be so obvious that he stunk. Either his two hosts had lost their

For All The Wrong Reasons

sense of smell or they were being exceptionally polite, for not only did they not show any indication that he was stinking up their vehicle, but they seemed sincerely interested in Billy's adventure. He asked them to first drive him out to the airplane so he could leave Walter a note.

The note that he prepared for Walter would direct him to a nearby topless joint which was a place where his newfound benefactors highly recommended. As a final gesture, Billy took the key out of his pocket and locked the door on the pilot's side, the only door on the airplane. It was an indication of what a dumb-ass he was. He would like to have thought he was so tired that he had lost all sense of reason. While he was doing all this, his newfound friends carefully scrutinized the airplane and were genuinely impressed with Billy's accomplishment in bringing that pile of crap up from Phoenix. They both expressed several times as they went over the airplane, that neither one of them would so much as taxi the thing.

On the ride to the topless joint, Billy felt that he had to exonerate himself so as to leave the two with a more favorable impression of him than he suspected they had. So he told the whole gruesome story. Up until then Billy got the idea that they suspected he had just scuttled the airplane on landing at the North Las Vegas Airport. But when they heard the straight scoop, they all had a jolly good laugh.

The bar was dark and comfortable. The topless waitresses all had flat tits, referred to as "fried eggs." The first thing he did was to snuggle up to the bar, throw his parachute on top, and order a Scotch, straight up. The first thing the bartender did was to order Billy to remove the parachute from the bar. He didn't seem at all impressed that Billy might be a big time aviator or maybe even a stunt pilot. It hurt Billy's feelings. The man didn't even say please.

Maybe the bartender didn't impress easily, but the nice-looking girl sitting a few stools to his right seemed to be. The parachute now resting comfortably on the floor was the "ice breaker." She immediately struck up a conversation using the parachute as the opener. So they could hear each other better, she moved over two seats in his direction, his being one seat the other way, while ordering another round for the both of them. He told her his life story. She told him her's. Her name was Shelly.

She came from Los Angeles to the gambling capital of the world to seek a spot on a chorus line. Instead she had to settle for a position as a hostess in one of the better eating places in town. It just happened to be located less

Chapter 20

than a block away and because of that, she frequented the bar on a regular basis after getting off work, and before going home to her apartment. She confessed to him that compared to the dogs that waited tables in this establishment, she was a "center fold" and had been offered a position many times. It was just not her piece of cake and she was getting tired of turning them down.

After a few drinks and quite a bit of conversation, she began to like him. She had to confess that at first she thought he was a bullshitter, with the parachute and the hair-raising story of his trip. To make it up to him, she suggested that they adjourn to her place of employment where they both could pig out on the best prime rib in Las Vegas. Billy had to refuse as much as the offer was enticing. He was after all hungry but he felt too dirty and disheveled to be patronizing a first-class establishment. What he needed more than anything else was a good hot shower and a Laundromat. She had just what the doctor ordered. So with parachute slung over his shoulder WWII style, they left the place, leaving a sizable tip for the ladies with the fried eggs, got in her car and made off for her apartment.

"Should we stop at a convenience store for some hard stuff and groceries?"

"No I've got everything we need at the pad."

It looked to Billy that this might turn out to be a cheap date. After they arrived at her apartment and he had a chance to scrutinize the place he was sure that in the end he had truly landed on his feet. It was ironic that just several hours before his life hung in the balance, and now he was comfortably established in Utopia with one of the more gorgeous woman he had ever had the pleasure to be with.

What to do next? She poured him a drink. Then she instructed him to remove his clothes so she could launder them, and install himself in the shower. After a few minutes he was shocked in a pleasurable way when she opened the shower door and joined him. It was more than he could stand. If he thought she beautiful before, she was gorgeous now. He could see why they wanted her to wait tables in a topless fashion. She was a real winner. For the first time in his life he was afraid to touch anyone, particularly her. She took the lead by beginning to lather his body. He followed suit, and they began to enjoy each other in ways that one could only fantasize.

It was a fantastic two hours, interrupted only when she had to get up to transfer his clothes from the washer to the dryer. When they were finished

For All The Wrong Reasons

they mutually agreed that they were both spent and famished. It was out to a casino for sustenance and table gaming.

In the meantime, Walter who was in possession of Billy's overnight bag, had arrived at the airplane, read the note, and went off to retrieve his friend and savior. He felt satisfied that his airplane had made it in one piece, if one could consider a stack of trash held together by faith alone a whole item.

When Walter entered the bar to retrieve his friend, the first thing he did was to eyeball all of the tits that were running around serving drinks, snacks, and whatever else they could provide to keep the clients from leaving. Then he searched the area for Billy. Not finding him, he inquired the bartender for information, taking the trouble to describe his friend, emphasizing the parachute. No, the bartender could not help him. But that didn't mean that Billy had not been there. The bartender informed Walter that he had just come on duty, and it was possible that Billy had been there and gone during the previous shift. So thinking that Billy had called Monique for a ride to his house, Walter went home.

Billy and Shelly worked the casinos until three in the morning. He spent three hundred dollars so they could win two hundred. He let her pocket the winnings. They went home, played around for an hour, slept until ten the next morning, played around for another hour, shared her toothbrush, showered and went out for some breakfast.

Walter was beside himself. Billy was nowhere to be found. He resisted panic but he knew that he must do something. He hardly slept worrying about it, and because of his preoccupation with the status of his friend's whereabouts, he once again failed to get laid.

The first thing Walter did when he got up the next morning was to gorge himself. Then he began to retrace the steps that Billy took, starting with the people at the airport terminal. They weren't much help. All they knew was that he took off with a couple of guys who arrived in a Twin Beech. If he left with his ride, and didn't arrive at the topless bar, where could he be? There was only one conclusion as far as Walter's logic was concerned. Billy was floating face down in Lake Mead. That's where all of the misfits ended up when they exposed themselves to the bad elements of Las Vegas. It was time to bring in the police.

The man on the desk was courteous if not patronizing. He said it was too early to be reporting a lost soul, and showed Walter a stack of com-

Chapter 20

pleted forms to indicate that lost in Las Vegas was a way of life and not a condition. "Walking around the city and through the casinos with a parachute slung across one's back is not an unusual sight, especially in this town." Dejected, Walter went home thinking seriously that it might be time to call Billy's partners and his parents in Phoenix.

After breakfast the two lovebirds had a ball. Their day included a host of things, none of which was the exercise of picking up the phone and calling Walter. Lounging around the pool at her apartment house was part of the agenda, as well as more gaming exercises, the proceeds of which again went in her handbag. Eating like the world was going to run out of food was also a major item. In between all of these activities, when his batteries recharged, they bedded down, ferociously engaging in a mutual sexual envelopment as though there was no tomorrow. If nothing else, they agreed that they shared at least two things in common; a fierce sexual appetite and good food.

It was five o'clock Sunday afternoon. Walter was dejectedly sitting at the kitchen table wondering what he could do next to move ahead the process of finding Billy Cotton. It was bad enough that he had this enormous problem, but he had to listen to his nagging wife who was taking pleasure in reminding him that it was entirely his fault. Her indictment included all of his past sins, including the fact that he was a piss-poor lover who couldn't cut the mustard anymore, or even lick the jar, and once again she had to go without.

Walter spent the day on the phone. The worst part of it was calling Billy's parents. His mother was hysterical, and his father at once began making preparations to go to Las Vegas in search for his beloved son. Billy's partner Dave was more cynical. He really knew his long time friend, and didn't appreciate Walter bothering him on Sunday about such a trivial matter. In his closing comments, Dave admonished Walter not to call Billy's folks or their mutual partner Jack. When Dave was told that it was too late, at least part of the deed had been done, Dave hung up and called Billy's parents to undo any damage that Walter may have created.

In the midst of Walter's despair as he sat at the kitchen table, staring out the window while sipping on a beer, listening to Monique nag him to no end, and wondering if Billy's partners would kill him, up drives the man of the hour, sporting the most gorgeous creature that Walter had ever seen. Billy had no explanation, just last minute necking and a resolve to his

For All The Wrong Reasons

newfound love to continue their relationship. In between feeling her tits and swapping spit, Billy pushed Walter to get off his ass and get going. It was late and he wanted to get back at a decent hour.

They hit the road to the tune of country music and Walter's ranting and raving in competition with the radio. In spite of all the noise, Billy dozed off, sleeping most of the way to Phoenix. It had been an extremely good weekend for him, and a very profitable one for Shelly. If she could just do that every weekend, she thought, she wouldn't have to work.

Chapter 21

Dave Staple fell in love immediately after graduating from the ball-busting curriculum of the University of Arizona's College of Architecture. It was with a girl he had met in the Nurse's office just before he achieved what he considered the brass ring, the prize he had been reaching for during the past four or so years. She had treated him for flu-like symptoms, which she thought was more like the final exam syndrome that many in his position experienced at that time of the year. For her, Dave was just another hypochondriac. For him, it was love at first sight and he didn't intend to let her slip away.

Her name was Marsha. In addition to her pleasant personality and extraordinarily good looks, he liked her name. For Dave this was it. He was determined, in his own clumsy way to entice her into agreeing to a date with him, damn the possibility that she might be seeing somebody else. So after a couple more visits to the infirmary for unnecessary follow up treatments and a phone call later, he was pleasantly surprised when she agreed to a cup of coffee at the Student Union coffee shop.

That first meeting was a nervous two hours for the both of them, but highly productive in the exchange of personal information. Like Dave, Marsha was from Phoenix. She was a devout Catholic, and let him know right off the bat that she had never been screwed. She actually put it more eloquently, but later as Dave was reporting the meeting to Billy, he did the rephrasing for his friend's benefit, in terms that Billy could understand.

She was soon to be a registered nurse having graduated from Phoenix's Good Samaritan Hospital School of Nursing. She took the job at the U of A's infirmary as a filler until she could complete the State's required exams to become a full-fledged registered nurse. She had failed the first two times around. Then it would be back to her beloved Phoenix where she hoped to

For All The Wrong Reasons

practice her profession. And no, she didn't have a boyfriend.

These revelations sent Dave into a euphoric state, only to be let down slightly, when as a result of her further chronological narratives, and through a simple calculation, he deduced that she was four years his senior. There was a time when such a discrepancy mattered, but not so much during these modern times, he rationalized. Besides, he was in love. The age difference made no difference. Together they could make it work. They just wouldn't let anybody know. It was none of their damn business anyway.

In short order, Dave and Billy successfully completed their final exams, graduated with the bestowed title of Architect, and moved to Phoenix to start their respective required internships. Marsha also labored through the parts of her exams that she had failed on the two previous attempts and moved to the big city where she took a floor position at Good Samaritan which provided her training.

Whereas Dave and Billy were eager and diligent in their endeavors, Marsha immediately took a dislike to her's. The floor routine was hard on her back, feet, and mind. The patients were demanding, the doctor's were first class assholes, and the political infighting between her and the other nurse bitches were more than she had bargained for. Eight hours a day of that bullshit was four more than she could endure. Dave was her only escape.

When they all settled into their routine and Dave could see the "horn of plenty" at the end of his architectural rainbow, he proposed. Having had a taste of the real world as seen through the eyes of a registered nurse, Marsha readily accepted, trying her damnedest not to appear too anxious. When told of the forthcoming event, Billy thought Dave was crazy, tying himself to one bed partner when there was a virtual cornucopia of voluptuous maidens out there just waiting to have their sexuality harvested by up and coming Frank Lloyd Wright "wannabes."

He conceded that she was voluptuous, but he also opined that as a result, the bride-to-be would lead Dave around by his penis. He was slightly bitter about the prospect of Marsha standing between Dave's and his friendship because of what he considered to be their diverse attitudes, goals and lifestyles. But the opposite was true. She admired Billy for everything he stood for and represented, a carefree attitude, a perverse philosophical outlook, a disdain for authority, and the apparent lack of fear. If she had studied

Chapter 21

psychology instead of nursing, she would have concluded that these manifestations represented a gross sense of insecurity and a subconscious urge for self-destruction.

Partly because she was genuinely fond of Billy for what he represented, but mostly because she didn't want to screw up her deal with Dave, Marsha extended her hand and invited Billy into her future family. Billy, still skeptical, graciously accepted the overture because he too didn't want to queer his deal with his long time friend. In winning Billy over, she professed that all she wanted was a secure life in a monogamous relationship that didn't include a bunch of rug rats scurrying around and getting into things. She confessed to Billy that she discussed a family with Dave and the prospect of raising kids was repulsive to him also. This was one of the reasons she said attracted her to him.

In a further attempt to patronize Dave's best friend, Marsha even declared that she might want to learn how to fly some day and thought Billy should be the one to teach her. But discretion prevailing, Billy immediately begged out as the instructor of choice, not because he thought she didn't possess the aptitude for the challenge, but because so far there wasn't a student of the opposite sex that he didn't end up banging, and while he wasn't about to screw up his most cherished friendship with Dave, he still wanted to keep his record intact.

It was in this revelation that the lower level of his morality was finally discovered. Later on in life, he bragged that by turning this challenge and opportunity down, there appeared to be a slim ray of hope for his shabby character after all.

When all the preliminaries necessary for the mutual understanding of what piece of Dave each one would get, they ultimately became genuinely good friends, a close but strictly platonic relationship. Marsha, Dave and Billy became a threesome, enjoying activities of mutual interest, mostly drinking and telling bullshit stories.

The threesome thing and a platonic relationship with one of the opposite sex, as attractive as Marsha, was another first for Billy. Reviewing the situation one day in his cubby-hole of an office, when there was nothing better to do than to conjure up schemes for getting his next conquest in the sack, he concluded that as far back as he could remember, he never had a female friend that didn't end up in an intimate entanglement of a sexual nature in

For All The Wrong Reasons

some cheap motel, or if she happened to be a really good friend, his place. This bothered him, but he wrote the whole thing off as his getting old.

The length of Dave and Marsha's courtship was traditional considering the backgrounds of the individuals. This meant that by any other standards it was too long. Then they married. Billy was the best man.

Within the first year Marsha discovered, much to her chagrin that she was with child. It was during an era that birth control pills had not gained wide acceptance. Her upbringing and loyalty to the Catholic Church ran counter to any birth control methods anyway, except the so-called rhythm method. She was well familiar with rhythm method because her local parish priest had gone over the entire sexual thing with her and Dave as a prerequisite to marrying them in the Church. It was a credit to this Church sanctioned method that she didn't get pregnant sooner than she did.

By this time, Billy was not only her good friend, but a big brother as well. When they were alone she unloaded on him all the particulars of her problems in the minutest details. Some of these conversations excited him very much, but he resolved to take the high road maintaining a professional decorum, as much as possible. Most of these so-called counseling sessions took place over drinks. The more she drank the more she talked and the more Billy wanted to hear. Sometimes he actually egged her on.

About the pregnancy, Billy queried as to how, due to the long courtship, she managed to avoid being knocked up sooner, in fact before they were married. He wanted all of the juicy details, and she didn't disappoint him. She gave him all of the sordid details as they indulged in their favorite beverage in a dark corner of Crazy Ed's. It was a good thing that they were sitting at a table and the lighting was subdued, because as she unfolded the intimacies of her activities with Dave, his member was fast growing large and hard, and he found himself squirming in his seat in effort to accommodate the tightly confined appendage. It was also a good thing that she was pregnant, because otherwise it was certain that in spite of his self-imposed pledge, he would have made a move on her.

In answer to his question as to how she managed to avoid getting pregnant during the long courtship, she confessed that she was technically a virgin until the night of their marriage vows. It was due in part to the times, but mostly to the strict Catholic dogma that forbade sexual intercourse outside of marriage. Knowing his buddy Dave, Billy thought it was preposterous that Dave could endure such a long term of celibacy. He was judging

Chapter 21

Dave by his own behavior. He pressed her for more details.

Feeling that she should tell all, because he was a very close friend and confidant, the only person she could unload on more and more as their friendship endured, and like all women, it was her subconscious drive to relate to someone the most intimate facts of her life. She confided that virtually every evening before he dropped her off at her house, they would masturbate each other, she stroking his hardened tool, he massaging her clitoris in a gentle circular motion, until they both stiffened in an explosive climax. They got real good at it to the point where they would invariably go off at the same time. Later on, their pleasurable activities progressed to where instead of a hand job they would use their mouths to complete the act. After all, Dave didn't want to risk injuring his hand which he needed to draw great depiction's of future award winning buildings, and she was afraid that the nightly massaging he was administering would cause calluses to form on the most tender part of her body.

They were expecting Dave to join them at any time. He had been delayed in a meeting with a prospective client and asked Billy to keep Marsha company until he could break loose. Billy tried to hurry her along with her story fearing that his friend would walk in and discover his nervous manner and flushed face, not to mention the oversized bulge in his pants. She went on to detail her intimacies with her husband from the first night until the time she discovered she was pregnant. Then according to her, depression set in and she became cold to Dave's advances.

The booze, her detailed descriptions of her lovemaking episodes, and the possibility of Dave entering the place before she finished was almost more than he could endure. He was trying his damnedest to be clinical in his probing for more information, but the images of scenes that floated on the wide screen of his brain caused him to squirm more nervously than ever to accommodate an oversized, rock-hard tool that in addition to all else, was causing an embarrassing wet spot in his Levi's. He hoped that it wouldn't be apparent on the outside of his pants. He was actually grateful, in a perverse sense, when Dave actually showed up. Naturally, he didn't stand up to greet him.

It was a tortuous pregnancy. For the health of his future heir, Dave took her off the booze. Now that she couldn't indulge in the spirits with the boys, she became a bore when they got together in some serious cavorting at their favorite watering hole. She chided Dave about the fact that she never smoked,

For All The Wrong Reasons

depriving him of one more thing he could take from her. And to add insult to injury, she couldn't cope with the unavoidable stretch marks that invaded her body, a lot around her middle, but worst of all, along the sides of her previously attractive breasts.

She made Dave's life miserable by cutting him off, claiming that having sex during pregnancy would harm the baby. And the thought of reverting back to the good old days of oral copulation in the front seat of their car repulsed her. To her, his penis represented something evil, a thing that got her in this miserable condition. She couldn't bear to massage it, or hold it, or touch it, or worse yet, even look at it.

The entire experience confused Dave, but worst of all it drove him away to seek aid and comfort in the beds of other women. The trysts were infrequent, and he took all measures possible to make sure she would not find out. He did, after all, love her and for that reason among others, didn't want to give her any cause to blow him off. The other reasons were of course the sanctity of their marriage, and the child they were about to have.

In the meantime, Billy was sort of the catalyst in the chemistry of their survival. It was no easy task, but it provided the necessary challenge that he constantly needed to feed his ego. She trusted him and felt that she could confide in him. She would use him as a sounding board on the occasions when Dave was out of town doing his thing under the guise of architectural business.

Conversations with Marsha always proved interesting. It was like reading the most intimate details of one's diary without that person's knowledge. During those times, they met at Crazy Ed's where she seemed content to be sipping coke while Billy fortified himself with boilermakers and peanuts. Under normal circumstances in this setting, Billy would have succumbed to the weakness of his loins, but he was truly fond of her, and for reasons he previously rationalized, he was satisfied to assume the role of big brother.

It was toward the end of her pregnancy that Marsha and Dave finally undertook the task of seeking out a name for their future offspring. She confided in Billy, at one of her counseling sessions with him, that Dave wanted to name the baby after his good friend Billy, but she had previously promised her two brothers, each on separate occasions that they would become the child's namesake if by chance it was a boy. Torn between three alternatives, the only way she thought she could escape was that if it turned

Chapter 21

out to be a girl.

Billy, in his infinite wisdom and two boilermakers later, had the answer. First she should not consider naming the kid after him. It would draw suspicion from the more cynical element. He would fix that with Dave as soon as his partner returned from the important meeting he was attending in San Diego. Then as far as her brothers were concerned, she could satisfy them both by using the second name of one as the first name of the baby and the first name of the other as the baby's second name. The brother's full names were Norman Alfred and David Phillip. After much discussion and haggling over the possible combinations and the ugliness of the names Alfred and Norman, they finally settled on Phillip Norman. This way Alfred would be out completely and Norman would be inconspicuous in the chain of names. Now if the baby turned out to be a girl, then by a simple conversion of the name, she could be called Phyllis Norma.

So with that problem solved, all that remained was to sell the idea to Dave. It was a much easier job than Marsha expected because what she didn't know was Dave's easy going, relaxed, and very cooperative attitude was the result of his getting laid on more than one occasion by several partners on the so-called business trip to San Diego. So in due course and many more business trips to San Diego, a normal delivery of an eight pound-ten ounce Phillip Norman Staple came into the world. Billy Cotton was the proud God Father.

Immediately thereafter Marsha went into a deep depression. Her doctor said it was a normal condition for a large percentage of new mothers. He attributed it to the behavior of those around her. Apparently they were devoting all of their attention and love to the baby instead of her.

To add to Marsha's distress, over her vociferous objections, Dave gave the newborn the nickname "Philly." It was his way of showing Marsha and her stupid brothers that if he couldn't name the baby with one of his choosing, more specifically after his friend Billy, then he would do the next best thing, coin a moniker that closely resembled the name Billy. Now there was really trouble in paradise.

The atmosphere was so thick with dissension around the Staple household that Billy felt it was his duty to put in his two cents worth. His opinion still mattered. But not making much headway on his own, he took the initiative and sought out the help of the much respected parish Priest, the same one who provided the premarital counseling which included the prohibition

For All The Wrong Reasons

of birth control devices so the newly weds could fill the world up with Catholic babies; the same one who officiated at the Baptismal ceremony, and the very same one who professed shock at hearing Dave's confessed extra marital proclivities. For those infractions, Dave was given the arduous task of reciting three "Our Father's" and three "Hail Mary's" for his penance.

The kindly Father, responding to Billy's plea for help, and seeing his "calling" finally coming to fruition, rose to the challenge making regular visits to the Staple house for the purpose of counseling the troubled lady, and as a side bar, by way of impressing her and gaining her confidence, he devoted more than the obligatory time to making over the baby. Recalling Dave's confession, the Priest focused more than he should have on the need for Marsha to jump Dave's bones as often as she could. It was the good Catholic thing to do, but just as important, it would keep Dave away from San Diego, where the devils disciples were at work, to spend more time at home.

When the customary six weeks passed since the birth of little Philly, and the significant parts of her body had properly mended, the Doctor gave her the green light to resume "putting out" to her husband. Her negative attitude toward the sex act had not changed, but taking heed to what the Padre mandated, she gritted her teeth and set out to screw his brains out more often than he needed. This caused Dave to stop his extra-curricular activities, stating on more than one occasion when it was thrown up in his face, "I've got more at home than I can handle." His trips to San Diego all but ceased.

Besides gritting her teeth, their lovemaking was very different from the first two times around. The first time being the pre-marital activities, and the second being the pre-birth of their son. This time instead of being a passionate lover, she was passive during the act, doing "it" only because she had to, and being equally relieved when he was finished. She came to resent even the suggestion of having sex and what the act represented, the hated the ugly stretch marks, the added twenty pounds, and worst of all the baby. For Marsha it was an all time low.

The doctor was as concerned for Marsha's mental state as were the rest of her loved ones. He assured Dave that with time, the situation would change for the better. He was right. Within three months, things for the

Chapter 21

most part, were back to normal. She was starting to screw Dave's brains out, a la pre-baby era. In fact she was engaging him with such intensity that one would think that it was the last screw she was going to get and should therefore make the most of it.

Her spirits were high and she began to wonder how and why she had sunk to such depths. She was feeling good about everything except the baby, and to solve that problem, began to relegate the care of the baby more and more to her willing mother. That way she could spend her spare time back with the group talking dirty, drinking Margaritas, and throwing peanut hulls on the floor.

In that state of being, it was only natural that she was once again with child. So the cycle with all of the elements of obesity, depression, frigidity, more stretch marks repeated itself, and shortly after a year since little Philly entered the world, William Joseph Staple followed. Over Marsha's strenuous objections, they immediately hung him with the contracted form of his formal name, Willy. Once again Billy Cotton became the God Father, only this time to his namesake.

Between Dave and Marsha, Dave was the only one who thought it was humorous that his three best friends were called Billy, Philly, and Willy in that order of descending age. What was not so funny to Marsha, was Dave not including her as one of his best friends, otherwise she couldn't have cared less what he called the little shits since he paid little heed to her wishes immediately after the birth anyway.

The truth of the matter was, that not only was Marsha no longer his friend, but he was not in love with her anymore. He resigned himself to the fate of relieving his sexual tensions to others outside of his marriage, and he was at a stage where discretion was no longer a factor. Trips to San Diego for that purpose were not necessary anymore. He got all he needed right there in the big city, Phoenix.

The strain on their marriage by his infidelity and her eccentricities was spiraling exponentially out of control. Her mental condition was many times worse than during the time of her first offspring. She was again depressed, fat and obsessed with booze. The latter was her refuge. She left it up to Dave and her parents to raise the kids.

Between work and chasing pussy, Dave had little time to devote to his boys, but where Dave failed, Billy was more than willing to take up the slack. As Billy professed on several occasions when asked about his interest

For All The Wrong Reasons

in the two kids, he would reply that they were after all his Godsons with one of them his namesake. So early on in their young lives, he began to mold their character and personality in his image.

It was about a year after Willy was born that things came to a "head" in the Staple household. Dave's respect for Marsha was non-existent and his attitude toward their relationship and marriage couldn't have been lower. No amount of counseling by any professional, the priest or even the Pope himself would make a difference. Her good friend Billy, even gave up on her as a cause. Marsha was at the stage of regression of a first class slob on the way to becoming an alcoholic. The only reason Dave didn't try to dissolve the marriage was out of duty and compassion for his sons. Just about the time he had more than he could take and was about to pull the plug, she did it for him.

One afternoon after a particularly hard day over his drafting table and conferences with disgruntled clients, who for the meager fee they were paying, thought that they owned the architect as well as his services, Dave came home to find the house particularly stark and empty. He was exhausted after the trying day and slightly depressed over the outcome of one of the meetings. The aura surrounding the emptiness, quiet, and stale air of the house were causing him concern, a symptom he mostly attributed to his state of mind, but he cautiously stalked the place anyway starting with the bedrooms. He was hoping to see Marsha stretched out in a drunken slumber, even though he knew better, because when he parked his car he casually noted that hers was gone. Not seeing anything out of order, he proceeded to the kitchen for a stiff drink and to contemplate his next move. On entering the kitchen, there in the middle of the table the hand written letter caught his eye.

It read:

> David,
>
> I've had it. I can't take it anymore. The children are at mother's. I've drawn out the $80,000 from our savings account and I'm taking my car, clothes, and some personal possessions to seek a fresh start. Don't try to find me. Good luck with the boys and your career.
>
> Marsha.

He set the note back on the table, and as if in a hypnotic state, methodically went through the steps to verify her claims. The first place he looked was the garage. Sure enough the car was gone. He had noticed it missing

Chapter 21

when he arrived home but thought nothing of it, assuming she was off visiting her mother or on some shopping spree. But now in disbelief he had to be sure. It was as though he expected her car to reappear and everything would be all right. But it wasn't so.

Next he re-inspected their bedroom, this time checking the closet and drawers. All of her clothes were gone, as were her jewelry and some pictures. All of a sudden the closet looked larger in the absence of her things. Otherwise nothing else was out of order.

Dave sat down at the kitchen table and indulged himself with straight swigs from a half-empty bottle of Scotch. He re-read the note over and over again with the expectation that the words would disappear and she would walk in the door looking like she did in the first months of their marriage.

Then coming to his senses, he picked up the phone and called his best friend, relating the whole story in gory detail, sobbing almost hysterically as he did. Billy cynically misconstrued Dave's distress. He thought Dave was more upset over the loss of the $80,000 than his wife, and counseled him accordingly. He assured Dave that the way the company was going, the $80,000 would eventually seem like peanuts. This made Dave sob even harder. So Billy in his overwhelming wisdom quit talking, jumped in his car and proceeded as fast as he could over to his friend's house. Loyalty was calling.

His advice would be short and to the point. File for divorce before she could do any more damage, or worse yet, change her mind.

Chapter 22

To the interested observer, Billy's new role as adopted surrogate father to the young boys was admirable. For Billy they represented nothing more than two additional play toys thrust on him for the purpose of self-amusement. He spent a lot of time with them, attempting to mold them into what he thought growing boys should be. But the time he was devoting to these ends, from the standpoint of an outside observer as being an admirable trait, was no more than occasions to teach his "little monkeys" tricks to be played out in front of others when the occasion permitted, in the same vein that one would do with a dog.

"Roll over" was not part of the program, not because he didn't try, but because they would just not respond to the command no matter how much time he devoted to the exercise. Maybe it was because no one thought it was funny and through body language let the entertainers know that there was no reward for making a fool out of oneself. More often than not, people were referring to them as brats, a term that Billy considered a compliment and a tribute to his efforts.

At first, because he was not yet a partner, Billy hesitated to encourage Dave to introduce the brats to the office. But as soon after he and Dave were made full partners with equal say, and when the kids learned to piss and shit on their own with the benefit of a toilet instead of an oversized liquid absorbing handkerchief, he not only encouraged Dave to include the boys in the daily activities of Long Staple Cotton, but took it upon himself to gather them up them up from wherever they might be; their grandmother's, Dave's or school.

The office became their playpen, as did Crazy Ed's when the occasion permitted, that is, anytime Billy didn't have an agenda involving dirty things with some equally dirty fox. Flight instruction was another matter. He would

For All The Wrong Reasons

bring his boys along. He thought that early exposure to the airplane and its associated benefits was good for them.

Long, the senior partner, wasn't crazy about the rug rats scurrying around the office, playing havoc with the fixtures. It would have been disastrous if not for the women employees. True to their maternal instincts, they literally took charge and were the catalyst for good harmony between the boss and the instigators. There just happened to be two vacant drafting stations in the office where the women parked the boys, one at each table along with enough paper and drafting tools to keep them entertained. For the most part it worked, but when they got bored with that routine there was always the break room where they found good sport in eating out the contents of the refrigerator, drinking pop and throwing the uneaten portions at each other.

Arizona law allowed minors in places of drink as long as they weren't imbibing in anything stronger than a "Shirley Temple." Eating peanuts, being in another category, was certainly allowed. Billy thought it was funny that the kids didn't properly chew the peanuts, sometimes swallowing them whole. The practice on quite a few occasions resulted in severe stomach cramps, and in all cases the material came out of the opposite end in large undigested chunks. It was a wonder that with the care and supervision given the two boys, they survived their childhood.

During the times that Billy socialized at Crazy Ed's with his charges, he found that the scene attracted many of the opposite sex. The children were the common denominator between the parties, allowing for a mutually interesting opening topic, which in most cases for the uninitiated, allowed Billy to advance his cause, namely getting screwed.

As to how he happened to be with the two young boys, he had many versions of the real story all of which he told many times, and being well rehearsed, were down pat. He favored the one where the kids were deserted by their alcoholic and irresponsible mother who ran off with a door-to-door salesman to join up with a religious cult. This move on the mother's part was supposed to be the salvation for all of her ills.

Billy further maintained that being their Godfather he was the only one with the decency and compassion to assume the responsibility and burden of rearing his beloved and true Godsons. Would she like to see the boys do a couple of well-rehearsed tricks or sing a song? Any trick except "roll over." Most of the time this bullshit story worked like a charm. The spiel along with a few drinks brought out the maternal instinct in his prey, espe-

Chapter 22

cially when he got one or both of them to call her "mommy."

Having the kids with him did not conflict with his commitments as a flight instructor. He would merely load them up in the back of the Cessna 150. The airplane had a large baggage platform behind the seats that was separated from the pilot and passenger only by the back of the seats. The area was large enough that the boys could romp around, stretch out to sleep, fight with each other, or lean over the seats and play havoc with the student and her instructor.

It was Billy's intention to ingrain in his two wards the art of flying, and all the advantages both good and nefarious the game had to offer. The younger the better he professed. So as an additional thrill he would retrieve them, one at a time from the baggage area, sitting them on his lap so they could manipulate the control wheel. It made no difference whether he was solo or in the process of attempting to teach someone else to fly. In the later case it was unnerving to the candidate, and if not, it was at least very disruptive. When solo, he would have them both up front, the one in the right seat sitting up on an enormous pile of cushions.

The boys liked the games they played in the airplane, especially when he was giving instructions on stalls. Philly, the older of the two made it a habit of upchucking his peanuts, which distressed the student, especially the ones with weak stomachs. Otherwise, it was a fun thing to do. To the boys stalling the airplane was like a roller coaster ride, and they couldn't get enough of it. Even when the lesson called for low-level maneuvers as in "turns about a point" or "S-turns across the road" the boys would nag him demanding that he stall the airplane. In spite of the low level of 800 feet where the maneuvers were performed, Billy would manage to oblige them, terrifying his student in the process. He bragged before his contingent at Crazy Ed's, that more often than not he would perform for his protégés in the traffic pattern much to the distress of his students. As for the students, he made it up to them in bed, if they were of the right gender.

Even though Philly got the same thrill out of these machinations that his younger brother experienced, his stomach couldn't agree. His vomiting wasn't limited to the violent maneuvers of stalls. Like clockwork he would throw up within thirty minutes from the time they took to the air. In fact, thirty minutes was the outside time limit that he could hold off no matter what they did in the airplane. This anomaly did not deter Billy in the least.

After the first few times of cleaning up after the kid, Billy merely kept a

For All The Wrong Reasons

sick sack in the ready mode and when the urge became a reality, Philly would dispose of his stomach contents, peanuts and all, into the container, hand it with the contents to Billy, who would in turn fasten the top with the built-in tie-wrap, slow the airplane to the edge of a stall, open the window and throw the whole mess overboard. This took place no matter where they were over the ground. Billy often wondered how the people below felt when they would wander out of their houses to discover a sack containing someone's undigested meals on their lawns, or worse yet, on the roofs of their houses. He often joked about it to his friends when they convened at their favorite watering hole.

When Philly wasn't puking his guts out, it never failed that one or the other of the brothers had to relieve himself. The procedure was still the same. Sick sacks were still the solution of choice. When joking about his dilemma, in a flippant sort of way he would also complain that if the situation didn't improve where the boys would outgrow their uncontrollable urge to discharge their body fluids, the whole landscape in the area of the airport would eventually be covered in white plastic sacks. Then the landscape surrounding the run-up area littered with empty beer cans would have to take second place to this more recent phenomenon.

In the beginning, Billy purchased the sick sacks from the local pilot shop, not without first complaining that the cost was driving him to the poor house. The complaining part was duly received by his mechanic friends who were full time with the Arizona National Guard. They rented the same airplane, on occasion, as he was using for flight instruction, and sometimes in lieu of paying the operator, swapped valuable maintenance service for flying time. Through their work they had an unlimited supply of the cherished containers and would be more than happy to oblige him at no charge, except perhaps to the taxpayer.

This worked well until he connected (literally) with a stewardess from a locally based airline that he befriended, first at Crazy Ed's, then in her apartment. She also had access to an unlimited supply of the coveted containers. Now his cup runneth over. He had more sick sacks than he could possibly use, so he took a bunch of them back to the pilot shop under the guise of returning the ones he had purchased, as unused, for his money back. Needless to say his con job didn't work.

The stewardess' name was Jane, plain Jane. They met at Crazy Ed's where Billy was imbibing with a group of friends, including his two charges

Chapter 22

who were consuming peanuts as though they hadn't eaten in a week. She was more taken in by the two kids than she was with Billy or his coterie of bullshitters. The scene was a cue for the others to pick up and leave, each sensing that Billy was positioning himself for the "kill."

Billy and his new target quickly warmed up to each other, thanks to his conversation pieces, and the sad tale that went along with them. Over drink, which he graciously had the waitress add to his tab, he recounted the well-oiled story as to how the boys had been neglected by their mother, and by process of elimination, how he fell heir to their care and upbringing.

It was the usual ploy. By playing on her God-given maternal instinct, he proceeded to reel her in. On her part, exercising the same emotional instinct, and obviously moved by his sad tale, she extended her utmost sympathy; even helping the boys shell their peanuts. Billy, seeing to it that there was no lack of beverage before them, ordered another round for the both of them, while he continued to impress her with stories of his various flying exploits. Naturally it all went on his tab. It wasn't long before she took him and the boys home with her to feast on something more substantial than peanuts.

Her apartment was marvelously appointed. It was decorated in everything that she could procure from her place of employment. These included blankets, pillows, dishes and silverware, most emblazoned with the company logo. Somehow she acquired fabric from the airline to make her bedspread and windows dressing. The company logo was also prominently displayed on these items. Best of all, as far as Billy was concerned, was the seemingly unlimited supply of miniature bottles of various brands of alcohol both premixed or straight.

Incredibly, there was no obvious effort to conceal any of the booty, causing Billy to react with a raised eyebrow. How could she possibly get away with this minor form of embezzlement seeing as to how another employee could see the same thing he did, and blow the whistle on her. "No problem" she replied to his inquiry, "everybody does it."

Under his breath and to his friends, he didn't refer to her as "plain Jane" for nothing. The best thing that could be said for her was that all dressed up she was marginally beautiful, most of it attributed to the intensive training she underwent while in hostess school, to keep herself made up and glamorous for the patrons. Much to Billy's chagrin, that was all gone when she first got out of bed in the morning and stayed that way until she spent an inordi-

For All The Wrong Reasons

nate amount of time on the stool in front of the vanity dresser, putty knife in hand.

When asked by his drunken and crude buddies to explain what he meant by the term "coyote ugly" to characterize his early morning impressions of Jane, he explained that it had to do with the actions of a coyote whose paw was caught in a trap. Rather than die of starvation or get caught, the coyote chewed his paw off in order to escape.

So as the story relates to the human species, there was a fable floating around of an individual who after a drunken spree, woke up one morning next to something that was ugly beyond description. He had picked her up in a bar the night before. He would have slithered off without waking her except for the fact that one of his arms was trapped underneath her neck. After one look at her, and rather than wake her to retrieve his arm, he elected to chew it off and escape.

Jane's sexual appetite and performance were equally marginal, but Billy was an enthusiastic supporter of a philosophy that "there ain't none bad, just some what's better than others." To him, her pad, unlimited supply of drink, and her affinity to his boys were more than redeeming qualities. At least this was how he rationalized their relationship to his drunken friends.

Is was the nature of Jane's job as a stewardess that her trips took her out of town overnight, and sometimes two nights. To maintain the integrity of their relationship, she ceremoniously presented Billy with a key to the pad as a prelude to having him move in. She liked him and had definite designs on him for bigger and greater things. Marriage was not out of the question. He likewise had designs on her, but only because of her inexhaustible supply of booze. As much as he drank, the stash remained relatively the same size, because Jane religiously replenished the inventory every time she came home from a trip. He would drink it down, and she would restock it to its original size. As far as he was concerned, it was a deal that couldn't be beat.

Billy spent a lot of his spare time at Jane's place. It was much more comfortable than his. Besides being well furnished and supplied with his favorite product, it contained the female touch, whereas his place was cold and bland, causing him to mostly just sleep there and get out as soon after waking and showering, as he could. When there was no other action or commitment to occupy his time, he looked forward to adjourning to her apartment, pouring himself a double, and kicking back to watch the tube.

He even found that he could bring his friends along to enjoy his newfound

Chapter 22

and hospitable clubhouse. It made no difference to him that some of these friends were of the opposite sex. He liked to live on the edge anyway. After he and his other female companions were through with the challenge of diminishing the size of Jane's liquor supply, they would top the evening off by cavorting in the very same sack that Jane considered exclusive property, only to be shared by her and Billy.

To the outsider, Billy's situation was very attractive. To Billy, the relationship with Jane including all of the amenities was headed in the downward direction almost from the start. Their lovemaking was mediocre at best and became old and stagnate. He had experienced better. In fact he was getting better, during their relationship, even in Jane's bed. To compound their difficulties, her attraction to the kids waned, as they grew familiar with her, lost their respect for her, and subsequently became outwardly abusive to her. Billy shrugged it off as part of growing up and did nothing to discipline the boys when they got out of line.

To make matters even worse, he was walking a real tight rope when he undertook to romp with another in her bed. He couldn't just get up and leave after his sexual escapades with others. He was also faced with the chore of cleaning up after desecrating their love nest. This in itself became a project subject to possible mistakes. He had to make sure everything was pristine, not a hair out of place, literally. And then there was the occasional problem with "pecker tracks." The sheets had to be spot cleaned to do away with this tell-tale evidence.

One time he performed the act with one of his cuties who was experiencing "those days." The stain left behind presented a real scary problem. It was a good thing that Jane was out of town for two days instead of the normal one day, because it took some doing to remove the "mark of Cain" and sufficient time for the sheet to dry.

Jane's infatuation with Billy waned as well. She eventually took up with one of her Captains, screwing his brains out as frequently as their out of town trips occurred. He was married at the time, but promised her he would eventually divorce if she would only wait for him. To him, she was the best lay he had in twenty years of marriage. What she didn't tell him was he could thank Billy Cotton for her improved performance. If she could be considered in the fair category when she first took up with Billy, she was now, as far as the Captain was concerned, great.

Their lovemaking at first took place in the hotel at the other end of their

For All The Wrong Reasons

flight. Then, as soon as she shed herself of Billy, it progressed to her place with all of the airline company's furnishing included. The Captain never did divorce his wife, as after a while, he found out he had a better deal at home, everything considered, especially the cost of alimony.

Jane's break-up with Billy wasn't sudden. It evolved. They just saw each other less frequently. She never inquired as to why he wasn't waiting for her when she got back from her trips, or why he wasn't driven for the use of her body anymore. She was actually relieved most of the time because those overnight trips actually used up her body to the point where sex was the farthest thing from her mind. All of her sexual appetite was being taken care of by the Captain. Her goal had shifted from being Mrs. Cotton to Mrs. Captain in wedded bliss.

She didn't even bother to ask Billy for the key to her apartment. She wasn't concerned that eventually he might happen on the scene to discover her and her new found friend in something more than a friendly embrace. Subconsciously, Jane would have welcomed the opportunity. She figured that if the occasion did happen, it would happily be the end of her relationship with Billy once and for all.

Chapter 23

The operator who owned the airplane that Billy was using for flight instruction was fast becoming disgruntled with him. He didn't like the way Billy treated the Cessna 150, his drinking, and the unnecessary risks involved when the kids tagged along. They had "words." Billy lost the argument, as he knew he would, but promised in the end that he would clean up his act. It was a false promise used as a stall tactic until he could work something out.

As far as Billy was concerned, he brushed the owner off as an individual with no sense of humor. He'd be damned if he would ever design a house for him or anybody else with the same bad attitude. Billy would show him. He had a saying that "Life was like a shit sandwich. The more bread you had, the less shit you had to eat. If you had enough bread, you didn't have to eat any shit." And Billy was getting to the point in his career that he was accumulating a lot of bread.

Because of the fallout with the operator and others on the airport who were less than sympathetic with his situation, Billy decided that it was time to acquire his own trainer. The good old boys at the Air National Guard were with him, pledging to keep the maintenance up on the airplane in exchange for free flying time. That was all he had to hear. Now it was time to act.

He rightfully concluded that a Cessna 150 was the most practical airplane on which he should concentrate his search. The airplane was a classic. It was efficient, easy to fly and maintain, and since Cessna was cranking them out at such a rapid rate, the price for a good used one was well within reason. Besides, it was configured in a way that his kids could romp around in the back like they had been doing in the rental airplane. And further more, the demand for his services was beginning to exceed his ability to produce.

For All The Wrong Reasons

By using trainers belonging to others, it was tantamount to putting money in the wrong pockets.

Aspiring young pilots sought him out, not necessarily because he was good, but because he was cheaper than his competitors and more efficient. He was able to crank them out in record time. Not only did he solo them in less than the average time, six hours or less, he latched on to a designated examiner who was known to be a real "Santa Claus." He was so designated because he passed virtually every candidate for a private pilot's license that Billy recommended, whether they could fly or not.

Billy's cup runneth over with more students than he was willing to accommodate. Had it not been for his youth and remarkable energy, he would not have been able to meet the demands of his hobby and professional responsibilities.

The workload evolved to the point that in order to accomplish the demands thrust on him, it was necessary that he start his day at sun-up and fly his students until 8 AM. Then it was off to his architectural endeavors in effort to placate the voracious beasts of the expansion industry. There he would indulge his clients and partners until he could reasonably get away as early in the afternoon as possible, doing flight instruction until the sun set below the horizon, and even later when the schedule called for night flying.

These responsibilities he juggled with his self-delegated commitments to the two little monsters he called his protégés, and his social life that included drink, bullshit sessions, and sexual escapades. He often said, "A lesser man would have caved by now."

To justify his decision of becoming an airplane entrepreneur, he rationalized that with his own airplane he could not only make money for the instructional part, but could realize an additional portion. That is the part that normally went to the operator - the airplane rental part. Therefore, it was for all of these reasons, and possibly many more that he hadn't thought of yet, that he embarked on a concerted effort to find his own Cessna 150.

On a daily basis, he carefully perused the "520" column of the Arizona Republic "want ads" for possibilities. Almost immediately he found one that interested him. It was exactly what he was looking for, a Cessna 150.

Three employees of a local piano company owned the airplane. They had purchased the airplane for the sole purpose of learning to fly. It had been their intention to unload it as soon as all three had obtained their pilot's licenses. Having completed their goal, they intended to cash in their equity,

Chapter 23

using the proceeds to upgrade to a larger four-place airplane on the order of a Cessna 172 or the more expensive 182, depending on the size of their pocket book.

The ad didn't show a price. So he placed a call only to find that the initial asking price was $6,000. He thought they were out of their minds. Everything considered Billy estimated that if the airplane was an average buy, it was way overpriced. Was it gold-plated or something? Haggling with the sellers, he was unsuccessful in having them lower the price. As far as they were concerned, he was out for "a free lunch." So much to Billy's disappointment, the deal fell through.

From Billy's standpoint, it was "back to the drawing board" only in the figurative sense. He would continue to search the "want ads" and stomp around the local airports looking for the lonesome airplanes with the telltale "for sale" sign in the window. It was a couple of months later with haggling and tire kicking with other prospects that Billy noticed the same airplane owned by the musical trio reappearing in the paper. This time the price was reduced to $4,000. Now he was interested.

The musical three agreed to meet with him at the airplane, log-books and all. It was parked on the south ramp at Sky Harbor airport. Billy immediately recognized the airplane as one that he had seen before, during his sojourns to the various airports in search for his elusive prize.

The first thing Billy did was to inspect the logbooks. One of the things that stood out was that it was out of license. The airplane's "annual" had expired. Every U.S. certified airplane must be inspected at least every twelve calendar months by an FAA designated inspector, and if deemed airworthy, will be approved for return to service by the inspector, who indicates his approval by an appropriate logbook entry. This logbook showed no such endorsement at any time during the preceding twelve months.

Another item that stood out and caught Billy's interest was the name of the mechanic/inspector who maintained and re-licensed the airplane. He was Mike Bradley, a rickety old fart, local to the airport, whose brain was in the latter stages of closing down, and whose work was beginning to reflect it. The only thing that kept him in business was his long standing in the community, coupled by the loyalties of the old-timers who knew him in his sharper days. Loyalty notwithstanding, they all knew, old cronies and new clients as in the music men, that he worked for fifty cents on the dollar. It wasn't by design. It was more like his feeble mind was estimating the cost of

For All The Wrong Reasons

work by the standards that existed when a dollar was worth exactly that and not fifty cents.

Puffing up like the cat that ate the canary, and in the "gotcha" mode, Billy acting as a neophyte, and in the pretense of looking like an ignoramus, asked in a shrewd non-challenging way, why the partners let the airplane's license expire. Without the annual inspection, in other words no license, the airplane was not airworthy and as such it was impossible for the partners to allow a potential buyer to demonstrate it much like a customer drives an automobile before making the final decision. This handicap makes the possibility of selling the airplane many more times difficult than it would be if the owner flew a prospect around the patch a couple of times to demonstrate the handling and flying condition of the machine.

This technicality might be a handicap to others, but it didn't phase Billy one bit. As far as he was concerned, he was all set to go flying. But the boys from the music shop wouldn't let him, claiming everything from lack of insurance to lack of confidence in Billy Cotton's ability. Well, at least they should let him run the engine. They even protested that, but there was no logical reason for not allowing it.

Even though the engine had not been run for over two months, it started immediately. This was an encouraging sign to Billy. He was starting to get jazzed up about the airplane. He slowly warmed up the engine, checking all vitals like oil pressure and temperature. When the gages indicated that the engine was adequately up to temperature, he performed a power check at full RPM. So far his impression of the way the thing ran was favorable. That is, until he brought the power back to idle by reducing the throttle more rapidly than maybe he should have. The action was instantaneously followed by a loud "bang." He immediately shut the whole operation down. Now Billy was beginning to understand why the logbooks were void of a recent annual inspection, and an endorsement returning it to service as a licensed airplane.

He exited the airplane, faced his sellers, brought the meeting to an abrupt halt, and retreated to his car after telling them that he would let them know. As far as Billy was concerned, this prospect was going down in failure just as the many other Cessna 150's he scrutinized over the last two months, but not necessarily for the same reason.

Strictly on a hunch, which had no logical basis to justify the action he was about to take, he glanced in the direction of the musical three who

Chapter 23

appeared to be in serious debate, and instinctively headed for the repair facility where Mike Bradley hung his shingle. He needed to know a few things that could provide some insight into the uncertainties that caused the engine to react in the abnormal way it did when he powered down. That was the way he put it to Mike. He was afraid to be blunt, because of the mechanics reputation for being cantankerous toward anyone he disliked. Ordinarily Billy would have come directly to the point, "What the fuck is wrong with that piece of shit airplane that you won't re-license?" But he had a feeling that in this case the direct approach wouldn't work, so he relied on "icky" sweet diplomacy.

Mike was well past 70 years old. The quiver in his voice, the slight trembling of his hands, his stooped posture, as well as other manifestations, gave credence to Billy's opinion that this man should be home in a rocking chair, or better yet a nursing home, instead of scratching a living as a mechanic and authorized inspector.

Billy took it real easy with him, bringing the conversation up to comfortable warmth in the same way he treated the engine before he ran it through its paces. They went through a lot of idle conversation that ranged from the weather, to mutual acquaintances, mostly those that were affiliated with the Maddux Flying School. Mike quickly warmed up to Billy as Billy had intended, more probably because he was lonely, not having anybody to visit with most of the time, than he was with Billy's genuine personality.

Then the conversation switched to the Cessna and the particulars that stood in the way of making it air-worthy. Mike blurted it out without hesitation, making Billy wonder if he hadn't been wasting his time patronizing the old fart, when he could have approached him in the direct way that was more his style.

"The engine was shot." There were serious problems that caused it to make that god-awful noise during its operation. "Yes," the engine would need to be overhauled. "No," Mike would not be interested in undertaking the task. But he did allow that the job could probably be done for about $2,000. "With a fresh engine the airplane might be worth $6,000."

Billy thanked Mike and departed to his office where he immediately called his sellers, engaging them in some serious negotiations. He mustered up all of his mental reserves, the same process he normally called on when conning a potential client out of that extra fee. His offer which he declared as final was $2,500 "as is where is." He tried to convince them that in the

For All The Wrong Reasons

condition their airplane was, and not being able to fly it, if they didn't take his offer, with a shot engine and all, the airplane would sit there on the ramp rotting away in the sun, until it eventually would be worth nothing but scrap value. The best thing they could do would be to let him take it off of their hands, take the money and buy the airplane of their choice.

To them, the offer was still unacceptable. They didn't entirely buy his argument, but he could tell that they were softening. "Would you (Billy) entertain $3,500?" "No, but $3,000 might be in the cards." The sellers were a hard sell. After more haggling they eventually settled for $3,150, if the musical trio would top the fuel tanks. The latter bonus was a face-saving concession where each party thought it was squeezing that last dollar out of the other to maximize their position. With both sides feeling they got the better of the other, it was a done deal.

The next day, they met again at the airplane to close the deal. Billy handed the sellers a cashier's check for the agreed amount. A fuel truck was ordered, and the group hammered out a duly executed bill-of-sale, while the gas boy completed his part by topping the tanks. The sellers wanted to know what Billy intended to do with the airplane, "not that we care" or, "it's none of our business." Instead of explaining it to them, he did the next thing better. He showed them.

He locked his car, climbed in the airplane, started the engine, called the control tower for taxi clearance and proceeded to the end of the active runway for the short trip to Deer Valley, all the while assuring himself that the piece of shit was good for at least one more trip. Retrieving his car was the least of his worries. From the time he locked his car until the airplane was out of sight, the former owners silently observed the operation in awe, wondering if they had been "taken" in the deal.

The flight to Deer Valley was uneventful. Everything on the airplane seemed to work fine. It was only when he chopped the power on short final (a quarter of a mile off the approach end of the runway) at Deer Valley that the dreaded noise reared its ugly head. Oh well, he had the runway made anyway. He wasn't concerned about the landing, but the engine thing was a problem he would have to deal with later.

He would consult with his buds at the Air National Guard. They would know what to do, and they did. Their advice was short and to the point, see Lloyd City. The symptoms were above and beyond their knowledge and experience. After all, they worked on large military equipment; KC-97's to

Chapter 23

be exact. It wasn't exactly what Billy wanted to hear. He wondered if he hadn't jumped in bed with the wrong people.

Lloyd City was also a friend of his. They had known each other for over five years, meeting and drinking occasionally at Crazy Ed's. Billy sometimes used him on the company's Beech Bonanza. As far as he was concerned, Lloyd was reasonably qualified, and his prices were in line. He was what was commonly known as a freelance mechanic or in other parlance, a "back-yard" or "tailgate" mechanic. He didn't have to support a large facility to perform his job, but instead worked out of the trunk of his car. In this way, he was able to keep his overhead to a minimum, passing part of the savings on to his clientele.

What Billy really liked about Lloyd was that he was as big a whore as he was a good mechanic, and therefore shared most of Billy's philosophy and integrity. And better yet, he carried the FAA Inspection Authorization certificate that among other things enabled him to annually re-license airplanes.

Besides his reputation as a whore, Lloyd was notorious for his "galloping horse" inspections. He proudly claimed that he was the innovator. It went like this. During an airplane inspection, whatever discrepancy couldn't be seen from a galloping horse wasn't a discrepancy at all. It suited the clientele he attracted to a tee.

Lloyd went over the airplane. He took it around the patch. Like Billy, he noticed that the "bang" only occurred when the throttle was closed. His diagnosis was immediate, precise, and as was later proved, accurate. In his opinion, the engine had a blown (defective) exhaust gasket. He went on to explain that each time the throttle is closed, a negative pressure occurs in the exhaust manifold, allowing outside air to be sucked past the broken gasket into the manifold, where the freshly introduced oxygen reacts with the unburned fuel causing an explosion. The result, he continued, sounds worse that it actually is.

A new gasket plus $50 for an annual inspection, and the airplane would be good for at least another year. The appropriate logbook entries would take place over sauce and peanuts, all on Billy's tab, in a dark corner of Crazy Ed's. Billy was thrilled at the outcome. It was his first experience at screwing someone out of a perfectly good airplane. He toasted himself to many more.

Chapter 24

Phillip Staple, Dave's oldest son, was determined to become an architect from the time he was able to hold a pencil. Both Philly and Willy had their own stations in the sea of drafting tables. As their work became reasonably acceptable, they were relegated to copy standard details that were common to most design documents, and were necessary to amplify the building designs. An example of these, concrete footings or window details would be included.

In addition to keep them out of trouble, they participated in various clerical assignments, mostly those that were considered busy work by the secretarial staff. For this, they were paid the minimum allowed by law.

Even though Willy's proficiency was on a par with his older brother's, his true affinity was the attraction to airplanes with all of the fringe benefits accorded his mentor. When Willy was a mere nine years old, he was capable of flying the Cessna 150 from a platform of several cushions, that when in place allowed him to see over the glare shield, and thus over the nose of the airplane.

Philly was not at all enamored with the prospects of soaring with the birds. In response to his preference of architecture over flying, he stated that it was more important for him to hold his last food intake in its intended place instead of a sick sack, and working in the office afforded that possibility. Besides, contributing to the design of large buildings, to him, was more rewarding in the long run.

Feeling the pressure exerted by the exploits of his younger sibling, Philly reluctantly agreed to accede to the persuasion of his mentor, and attempt to conquer the elements as his brother did, notwithstanding his revulsion to regurgitating his innards.

When he was sixteen, after three hours of concentrated dual instruction,

For All The Wrong Reasons

mostly take-offs and landings, he accomplished what he felt obligated to do, and soloed the airplane. After a few hours of solo flight, he retired as an aviator, having accomplished what he considered his manly duty to Billy, and focused his energies in his other areas of endeavors, mostly school, work in the office, and chasing broads, the latter in the same vein and vigor as Billy did.

As for his academics, Philly wasn't particularly studious, but in spite of his lack of studiousness and his interest in extracurricular activities, Philly still managed to graduate from high school in the top 10% of his class, a distinction so recognized by the specially gold-colored tassel hanging from the mortar board hat worn during the graduation ceremonies, and a gold border with the words "High Honors" emblazoned on the diploma. They were also recognized by the order in which they received their diplomas, the student with the highest grade point first, and so on, with the dumbest in the class taking up the rear.

At the beginning of his senior year, he was well entrenched in the middle of the exalted 10% group, but elected to coast during the remaining two semesters, yielding instead to the weakness of the flesh. He would have finished one short of the coveted group had it not been for the fact that another student in the top 10% transferred out because of his father's military obligations.

Both Dave and Billy knew in advance that their boy was in the group with the top ten percenters, but were taken back somewhat when they noticed during the commencement exercises that he was the last one in the line of those with the gold tassels. It was only after the ceremonies when talking with the principal that they discovered how close he came to be just another also-ran. Besides the transfer of the army brat, they were told that, but for one less point in the third place of his grade average, it would have placed him one student back with a mere black tassel like the other 223 graduating seniors.

Now it was time for Philly to enroll in a school of higher learning. Philly didn't want to move out of town. He liked the firm and wanted to stay on, at least in a part time capacity. The senior partners insisted that in order to work for them, Philly had to go to college and pursue a degree in Architecture. So to accede to his bosses'/mentors' wishes, he enrolled at Arizona State University, which was located in Tempe, twenty miles from the office.

If Philly neglected his studies, in lieu of questionable extra-curricular

Chapter 24

activities, during his last year in high school, he was a full-fledged playboy by the time he completed his first week at Arizona State. He was beginning to have too much fun to take his academic pursuits seriously. He didn't need to work hard because of his background and experience in the office, he already had a jump start on his career and his fellow students, with his wide knowledge of the fundamentals of architecture and drafting techniques. As far as he was concerned he could tell his professors a thing or two. His assignments, especially the more challenging, were completed in the offices of Long Staple Cotton Associates with the help of bona fide professionals.

Shortly into his freshman year, he and three others from the University rented a small house within walking distance from the campus. One of the three was his English teacher, a young, good-looking female, fresh on the scene with a recently acquired college degree and a big set of boobs.

Afraid of disapproval, Philly glossed over the particulars concerning his roommates and the sleeping arrangements when the subject came up at the office. Little did he realize that if Billy knew that his protégé was not only sharing a house with his teacher but was actually sleeping with her, he would have been proud. Billy would have figured that such a situation was a guaranteed "A" in the course.

One day, not long after the sleeping arrangements were initiated, Billy, in dire need of Philly's help at the office to meet an important deadline, called the den of inequity, otherwise referred to as the residence. He was informed by one of the roomies who answered the phone that Philly was out of touch. When asked to elaborate, the roomy went on to explain that Philly was rafting down the Verde River on an inner tube in the company of the big-breasted English teacher.

Billy thought nothing of it, assuming that it was a school function, and after all school functions, in the order of priorities, came first. It was some time later at an office party that Billy met the tubing companion/English teacher for the first time. He almost swallowed an ice cube. All he could think of, when introduced, was how young and gorgeous she was. If only some of his teachers had looked that good. Later, when he described his reaction to their first meeting, all he could say was that his tongue got hard.

At the first opportunity, Billy pulled his protégé aside and began pumping him for details. Philly playing down the situation, went on to explain that he and his buddies took her in to their house because of an acute shortage of places near the school, and because their place had only three bed-

For All The Wrong Reasons

rooms, he graciously offered to share his bed with her. And yes, it was a strictly platonic relationship.

To Billy it was all bullshit, but it helped explain why Philly got his "A" in English when in reality he had trouble putting together a complete sentence around the office. Nevertheless, Billy was proud. If you couldn't get through on academic achievements alone, then by all means screw the right people. And a better choice would be hard to find. Perhaps next semester, Philly could latch on to another who taught an equally formidable subject.

True to his breeding and upbringing, Philly's order of priorities put his studies and office commitments behind carousing around, depleting the world's supply of beer and hard liquor, and screwing his way through life. The longer he stayed at Arizona State, the more corrupt he became. He was going downhill fast. He blamed it all on his friends. They were leading him astray. Recognizing the problem, Billy decided that it was time for a long and earnest counseling session before it was too late. So they sat down to hash it out, leaving no gory details untouched.

The upshot of the meeting was Philly's yearning to get out of town, away from his corrupting influences, for a fresh start. If he could relocate to Tucson or El Paso, he figured he could work for a firm local to the new area, transfer his school records, and resume his studies at a new University. It all sounded nice, but it amounted to running away from his problems instead of meeting them head-on. Billy went along with the solution.

Much more discussion ensued, worthless discussion, because they both knew at the outset what had to be done. The exercise reminded Billy of a famous quote that was attributed to Winston Churchill:

> "We conferred futilely and endlessly until we arrived at the place where we started. Then we did what we knew we had to do in the first place and failed as we knew we would."

The phrase so impressed Billy that he had it framed and mounted on the wall of his office. It served as an aid, in some of those seemingly long meetings, to call a halt to the futility, and prod the attendees into decision-making modes. This session with Philly was very similar. He had to take the bull by the horns. El Paso it was.

El Paso was more suited to the situation. For some time Billy had a yearning to expand the business into other cities of potential growth. Tuc-

Chapter 24

son already had more architects running out of its ass than the growth could support. And from his own experience, the University of Arizona located in Tucson was more of a party school than the University that Philly was attending and having trouble staying focused. If he couldn't succeed at Arizona State, what chance did he have at the U of A?

On the other hand, El Paso was a quiet little cow town on the Mexican border with a small University of less than 5,000 students. There was little architectural competition in the area because growth was slow. But with a little foresight, one could visualize an eventual expansion of industry, mostly because of the twin city feature of the geography: Juarez, with a population of over a million on the Mexican side, El Paso, with about 250,000 on the other.

The plan as presented to the partners was simple. Philly would move to El Paso, manage the branch office, and continue with his education. Billy would spend most of his time there as the Architect of record, doing what architects are supposed to do: obtain work, bullshit the clients, supervise the designs, and chase pussy.

He would use the Bonanza to commute back and forth between offices, generally flying out to El Paso early on each Tuesday morning, spend the next three days in the El Paso office, and return to Phoenix on Thursday after work; that is unless something more urgent interrupted his scheduled like getting his ashes hauled, for example. This scenario would continue until Philly completed his requirements and obtained certification.

Philly was barely nineteen when all of this was taking place. At that age, no matter how much experience he had accumulated, it would be hard to pass him off as a professional with adequate experience, to gain the confidence of potential clients. To the clients, it wasn't a matter of experience, but one of impression. From the experience standpoint, from the time he was nine years old, he was gaining it in all aspects of the trade, but who would believe him when he told the clients he came equipped with ten years in the profession, but was only nineteen.

The answer was for Philly to grow a beard and pass himself off as twenty-eight, a young looking twenty-eight. Then as the years went on, he could drop a year every so often, until eventually his true age would merge with the fictitious one. Oddly enough the charade worked.

John Long and Dave Staple agreed with the plan. Long went along, because at that stage of events he was becoming a passenger to his partners,

For All The Wrong Reasons

willingly letting them run the show, and enjoying the money he was accumulating in amounts that he never euphorically envisioned in his wildest dreams. But subconsciously he was probably happy to rid the office of a couple of degenerates. Dave also went along because as far as he was concerned, Billy could do no wrong, and he too wanted the best for his wayward son.

So with those formalities taken care of, Billy and Philly headed for El Paso with a cashier's check in the amount of $3,500 and a truckload of office furniture. They opened a checking account, rented a small office, and found a two-bedroom apartment less than a block from the office. Having accomplished the above, they felt they had done enough for one day, and should channel their energies to scouting the local watering holes in search for the fairer sex.

The office they leased was unique to them. It came with a steno/secretary that was included in the cost of the office. She served five other offices that, like theirs, were situated in a cluster that could only be accessed by walking passed the secretary. Her duties included typing, taking their calls, and keeping the unwanted from intruding into the offices unannounced. This type of office arrangement was designed mostly for sales representatives who spent most of the time in the field selling the wares and didn't need full time help, except for telephone answering services and the occasional letter or quotation that needed to be typed.

The first day on the job greeted the two with a six-inch accumulation of snow. To Billy, who wasn't accustomed to snow, and who had heard that many bad things can happen to you when driving in the stuff, suffered more than from the hangover from which he was trying to recover.

The two were sitting in the local Hobo Joe's' restaurant next to the window at ten o'clock in the morning, scarfing down the remnants of their breakfast, contemplating their next move while watching the large snowflakes float down and settle on the surface of the cars in the parking lot. To Billy the moment was solemn. After a bit, he finally wondered out loud what the hell he was doing at that far away outpost, suffering the inconveniences to which he was not accustomed? Philly was euphoric. He was thoroughly enjoying the view and his new adventure.

To add to Billy's woes, he hardly slept the night before in the strange place he referred to as his second home. Of all the things they brought with them, the essentials for living comfortably in the new dwelling were left out.

Chapter 24

As a result, instead of drinking up a storm the evening before, they should have been shopping for bedclothes, pillows and towels. Other than those personal effects, the apartment was furnished. They would have to buy these items before the day was out, even though it might mean driving in the snow and killing themselves in the process.

For the first few days they both operated on autopilot. That is to say they did the necessary things without thinking about or analyzing their decisions or methods. Billy just wanted to get the hell out of there. Their time was spent fixing the office, making the apartment livable, and negotiating an eight-inch snowfall.

Before they were fully settled, two jobs came in. Both had to do with the remodel of certain facilities at the El Paso International Airport. From that point on the El Paso branch office was self-supporting. Better yet, it actually generated a profit, small at first but nevertheless a profit. The boys in Phoenix were elated.

More work was commissioned. It came in at a rate that was more than the two could produce. So at first some of it had to be sent to Phoenix to be completed by that staff. Then when it became apparent that the workload would not let up, they moved to a larger office, hired more people, including a secretary. Philly was becoming very successful and well adjusted to his new venture. He was also very proud, mostly for his selection of the new secretary.

Billy's new routine called for him to fly the company's Bonanza to El Paso on Mondays, after first spending some time in the Phoenix office, and return to Phoenix late Thursday afternoon, relegating at least part of Fridays again in the Phoenix office.

Although he would never admit it, the time he spent in the home office was mostly to protect his interest. Admittedly he professed to be only fifty percent paranoid. He always joked that just because he was paranoid, it didn't mean that they were not out to get him. The remainder of the weekend was devoted to flight instruction at Deer Valley Airport, logging time at Crazy Ed's, and rounding up his harem.

Back in El Paso, the two heroes immersed themselves in the community, and were soon getting their "share." Once in a while, when Billy wanted to impress one of his new found Phoenix conquests, he would import her to El Paso on one of his routine trips, introducing her finer aspects of Juarez, El Paso's Mexican sister city.

For All The Wrong Reasons

Philly once again took up his academic goals at the local university, keeping his class load to a minimum. It would eventually take several more years to complete his degree than it would have if he had taken a full load of courses. In the meantime he would have to rely on Billy's architectural stamp to certify the drawings before they were released for construction. It was Philly's intention that his schooling and professional responsibilities not interfere with his sex life. Even though he had it in the wrong order of priorities, he steadfastly maintained that there was room in his life for all three.

A new player on the scene was a young and able surgeon by the name of Dr. Duane Robertson. Dr. Robertson had a local reputation of being very skillful in his profession with a bright future in the community. He skated through his pre-med undergraduate requirements, medical school, internship, and residency in record time. At twenty-eight he had established himself in a solid and successful practice. To match his success and brilliance, he was also very handsome and single. He became a good friend of Philly's. They met early on, in the establishment of the El Paso office, during happy hours at one of the local hot spots. Their mutual interest was picking up on the opposite sex.

If the good doctor could be stereotyped, it would be in the likeness of the character Hawkeye of the famous M*A*S*H series. Like Hawkeye, he was tall and lanky in stature, flippant, often exhibiting his disdain and lack of respect for the medical profession, or the other doctors thus engaged.

The only interaction he maintained with his fellow physicians was that which was necessary to obtain referrals. Socializing with them disgusted him to the extent that he kept that activity to a minimum. The only interaction he strived for with the nurses was strictly of a sexual nature. He bragged that on several occasions he was caught fornicating with one of the ladies in white on a gurney or in one of the unoccupied rooms. For some reason he discouraged being addressed by his title in lieu of being just one of the boys.

Like the others in his profession, he kept a medical bag in the trunk of his car. The only reason he gave for its presence was that somehow he got the impression during his schooling that it was expected of him. He very seldom used it, so as it resided in the dust, dirt, and heat of the trunk, the leather bag became deformed, cracked, and dirty, only to be matched by the equally dirty and beat up car that the kindest thing that could be said for it would be to refer to it as a jalopy.

One bright sunny afternoon, when Philly and the good doctor were bel-

Chapter 24

lied up to the bar taking in a football game when they should have instead been outside participating in some more wholesome activity, Philly in the heat of the occasion inflicted a serious cut on his hand from the sharp edge of broken glass.

The glass in this case was the real victim of a bad call by an obviously biased umpire. It was, in Philly's opinion, such an egregious act on behalf of the official, that it caused him to slam his fist down on the bar. The sad part of the reaction was that Philly was clenching the glass at the time. Still sadder according to Doc was that the glass was still half full, or depending how one looked at it, half empty at the time. In any case, it was time for some real medical attention, the kind that came out of the medical bag from the hot and dusty trunk of Doc's car.

The inside of the bag looked every bit as bad as the outside. It resembled the contents of a back yard mechanic's toolbox. Philly's first reaction as he assessed his chances from getting infected, favored the use of the bartender's offer of a bar towel. As much as he favored the bar towel, he didn't want to hurt Duane's feelings, so with much apprehension, as they continued to watch the dirty ump administer his equally dirty calls, he submitted to Doc's zealous attack on his wounded hand. But in spite of his doubts, he was pleasantly surprised with the end result. It was for this reason when Philly got into some real trouble that he called his faithful buddy to save his good ass, or more like his other unmentionable appendage.

It happened after a long and arduous evening of partying and indulging in the fruit of the vines, when he and his recently acquired squeeze were deeply and vigorously involved in rough sex. He otherwise described it as the orgy to end all orgies. As it materialized, it was almost that, the end literally.

Her name was Candice, Candy for short. She often bragged that she always approached the act as though it was to be the last she was going to get, and with each stroke would thrust her body hard against his, at the same time that he did in kind. The result could only be described as the ultimate clashing of the pelvises.

In this scenario she happened to be on top. For some reason she was driving extra hard, harder than she had ever done before. Philly was on his back, a passive passenger in her performance, literally taking it all in, while at the same time studying the stretch marks on her stomach that resembled a road map of some of the busier sections of the country. He wondered how

For All The Wrong Reasons

many babies it took to produce such a conglomeration of lines. As the sexual escapade heated up, Candy was raising her body higher and higher, and driving each stroke down as hard as she could.

Then it happened, the ultimate in sexual accidents, the orgy to end all orgies. Well almost, as it ultimately played out, thanks to Doc Robertson. On her upstroke, the thing slipped out. But before it could fall back to its natural repose, and still pointing at the stars, she came down extra hard. She struck it squarely on the tip with another part of her anatomy, a firm and non-yielding part, close to the place of the intended target. But unlike the games horseshoes and hand grenades, close in this case, didn't count. Philly's poor tool was, in an instant, bent completely in half, mashed with the same result that would befall an insect after being stepped on by a size twelve.

If his former pride and joy had been equipped with a bone it would have fractured, but instead it was the several engorged blood vessels that let go. Philly was at first stunned, then shock set in as it swelled to what he later described as a basketball full of blood. From his perspective that was probably a fair description. In reality, it took on the size of a regulation "soft ball." Did it hurt? Not according to the victim.

To his surprise, there was no pain, just a popping sound as the arteries let go. Then because the penis could no longer contain the contents, blood started to squirt out the end. Under pressure it squirted all over him, Candy, and the bed. Candy ran for a towel. Philly screamed for ice. They called 911. Philly was understandably scared. He thought he was going to bleed to death. Worse yet, they might have to amputate his tool, his pride and joy. How could he live without it?

The five minutes it took for the ambulance to arrive seemed like hours. They didn't come alone. They brought a firetruck with them. Did they think he was also on fire? When help arrived, Candy still in her birthday suit, scurried around like a chicken with its head cut off. The EMT boys, in their infinite wisdom, ordered her out of the room.

As they wheeled him out of the apartment on a gurney, the last thing Philly did was to order his now former sexmate to call his good friend and savior, Doctor Duane Robertson, to meet them at the hospital. The good Doctor would know what to do.

When they arrived at the hospital, and took the towel away, Philly was aghast. The thing resembled an oversized Christmas tree ornament. Blood was leaking out of a wound in the side as well as the orifice inherent with his

Chapter 24

tool. He was more convinced than ever that he was doomed to the hereafter. To add insult to injury, the EMT heroes, not able to contain normal decorum, spread the word of their first experience of the kind, around to their counterparts on duty. Before long, the curious, including nurses and bedpan jockeys alike, maneuvered for position to observe the phenomenon.

No one in attendance had ever seen anything like it in their careers. They were more than willing to defer the problem to Doctor Robertson, if only he would show up before they had to haul poor Philly off in a body bag. In the true spirit of a fast acting medical facility, it took nearly three hours to muster up the Doctor and a surgical team to do the job. The unusually long time lapse was mostly due to the trouble in rounding up the good Doctor and personal friend, who finally made his appearance stinking like he had just come off the night shift at a whiskey distillation plant.

In the meantime, Philly just lay on his back on a bed in the emergency ward fretting for his future, a bag of ice covering his private parts, and a male nurse's aide gleefully holding his hand. The attending physician thought it advisable for the aide to attend him in this manner because in Philly's frame of mind there was no predicting what he might do. Occasionally, a fresh face in hospital attire, who picked up the word through the grapevine, would drop by to inspect the oddity, shake their head in solemn resignation, and depart, only to further spread the word.

The nurse's aide also contributed to Philly's distress. He too would occasionally inspect the disaster area, ensuring that there was still an ample supply of ice and blood absorbing material at the site, and then excuse himself for what he called a five minute break. On these occasions, he would reappear with a friend or co-worker and ask his patient if the third party could inspect the scene. This novelty was undoubtedly a record-breaking event for the hospital staff.

Dr. Duane Robertson knew no fear, especially when it involved a risk to others. In his overconfident air, he completed his greetings to his associates, being especially indulgent with the nurses he'd screwed, and those he intended to screw, pulled back the sheet, and exposed the area in question. When the ice pack and towel came off, he emitted a shocking gasp, choking on his own saliva and stale booze in the process, and when sufficiently composed, started to laugh.

The staff, those who had gathered around, some merely out of curiosity, in concert with the good Doctor came forth with their own laughter, a ner-

For All The Wrong Reasons

vous one, but one necessary to show respect for the esteemed surgeon, and to indicate their concurrence as if his initial reaction was some form of diagnosis.

The surgery was a very big deal to everyone in attendance except the main man. During the process he conducted himself as though the procedure was strictly routine, something that he had performed a thousand times. The final result could only be described as successful, even though he declared that Philly's penis would have a slight crook in it. But on the plus side, Philly's member ended up a good two inches longer. That was because, according to the good doctor, he had to extend the part that is normally hidden up into the pelvic area, to better expose the damaged veins.

When they finally wheeled the patient out, he came equipped with four drain tubes, three of which were taped into the penis, and the fourth inserted directly into the bladder through an incision on the front of his body. They all drained into a common plastic bag.

The incision was a matter all of its own. Because the operation was mostly exploratory, the final stitching was crooked and erratic. The doctor's first impression was that Philly would have one bodacious French tickler in addition to the added length. Then after suturing the mess, he noticed an amazing coincidence in the irregular pattern of the cuts that he had stitched. It was the outline of one-half of an apparition. His reaction was one of a lightbulb going off in his booze-ridden head. He immediately dismissed everyone except his faithful and trusted nurse. Faithful because she was one who could be counted on for his insatiable quickies he required from time to time, and trusted because she didn't blab about their frequent trysts.

When the room cleared, he called her attention to the pattern. What they were both amazed at was the Doc had inadvertently scribed the outline of half of an image of the Virgin of Guadalupe, the Madonna in the often shown pose so familiar to the Mexican faithful.

Not even trying to resist temptation, in his finest artistic acumen, he once again picked up his scalpel and deftly scribed the other half of the image, so when he was done the finished product was an uncanny duplicate of the "Our Lady of Guadalupe" image that is enshrined just outside of Mexico city. Then he stitched up the new addition to his masterpiece, and retreated slightly as one who was far sighted would do, to admire his work of art.

He was still troubled. Thinking that the scar would eventually disappear,

Chapter 24

he yielded to another irresistible impulse and ordered the nurse to fetch some dark surgical die. When she presented the product, he rubbed some of it thoroughly into the stitched area. There, he was now satisfied that the image would forever remain indelibly prominent, as though a tattoo artist had completed the job.

As an afterthought, he looked at his nurse, and realizing the gravity of his prank, swore her to secrecy. "This must not go further than the operating room." She agreed, promised, but before the week was out, so was the secret. In defense of her lack of ability to maintain the confidence, she didn't tell of the prank, only of the image that she said resulted from the operation. And then she only told a couple of her closest co-workers, who in turn were also sworn to secrecy.

Philly's recuperative powers were amazing. After the initial trauma wore off, his libido returned, stronger than ever. It was all of those nurses hanging around, tending to his needs. It was for this contingency that the doctor equipped him with a small sack of a strong smelling substance, that when the urge to get a "hard on" gripped him he was to take a good whiff, and supposedly the erection would either not happen or immediately go away before any damage could occur. Philly called on the device more times than he wanted to admit.

If the shift nurses knew about the image, they never let on. It was more probable that the massive scabs encompassing the wound, masked the Doctor's handy work.

Shortly before his discharge, when everything seemed to be healing in good order, a young nurse by the name of Rosetta happened on the scene to check on the progress of the healing, and to ensure that the several tubes were still in place. She was very curious about the condition of the penis, the rumor of the extra length that was provided as a by-product of the surgery, but most of all, of the talk of the image of the Madonna that miraculously appeared on Philly's tool. She was taken back. There it was, a bold outline of the apparition.

She stood there and stared for what her patient thought was an unusually long time. He noted a strange expression on her face and wondered if she might become a future prospect. He thought she was marveling over his manhood, or the extension thereof, so he took the incident in stride, picked up the sack of smelling salts, and thinking in graphic detail about their possible future encounters, took several extra long whiffs.

For All The Wrong Reasons

He was about to start a conversation with her, pointed in the direction of a future affair, when in disbelief he saw her genuflect and cross herself. Her face was flush, and the expression was one of seeing a ghost. She was on the verge of swooning. Without saying anything, she stood up, restored the sheet to its proper place, and backed out of the room as she stared hard at the puzzled look on her patients face as he once again brought the small bag of odoriferous material to his nose.

Soon word got out, thanks in part to Rosetta. But mainly it was Doc Robertson's O.R. nurse who started it. Rosetta's recent encounter merely fueled the flames of the hospital's more superstitious contingent. The result was a virtual pilgrimage by those who had official access to the room, and a lesser amount by some who had no business being there at all. They all wanted to pay homage to the "living shrine." One even succeeded in sneaking a kiss not on Philly's lips, but on the part of the anatomy that contained the blessed image.

It was the nurse on the evening shift. While tending her patient at a time when he had visitors, she seemed to nervously pace about the room looking for something to keep her busy. Philly and his visitors noticed the nurse's unusual behavior, but thought nothing of it after she finally left the room. She didn't go very far, lurking as close as she could without drawing attention. It was as though she was waiting for the right moment, because as soon as his people left the room, she immediately reappeared on the pretext of adjusting his blankets.

Before Philly realized it, she uncovered the area in question, gently grasped the limp member, raised it to the erect position, and planted her lips on the area of the apparition. She rose up, crossed herself, and hastily left the room. It was more than Philly could take. He immediately accessed himself to the smelling salts, which were fastened by a short string to the bed railing. As stated before, this sack of strong odoriferous crystals were provided for just such an occasion, the purpose of nullifying any sexual urge, and the resulting erection.

When the smelling salts were first put in place, it was explained to him the gravity of the situation, and the reason for its use. If an erection were to take place before complete healing had occurred, the doctor's fine work could be undone. Philly had assured his friend that the smelling salts were not necessary because, under the circumstances, sexual excitement was the farthest thing from his mind. After his disastrous experience, he doubted

Chapter 24

that he would ever want to engage in sexual intercourse again. But now he was glad that the remedy was within easy reach. To be extra safe, he took several extra sniffs of the strong smelling stuff. He was gradually wearing the contents out.

Billy spent considerable time at his protégé's bedside. He was amused when Philly recounted several incidents where the nurses and their non-staffed friends appeared to observe the phenomenon and pay homage to the apparition, although at the time he still was not aware of the reason for all of the fuss. All Philly knew, was that he was beginning to like all of the attention, and the fondling and kissing of his tool. The nasal intake of the strong smelling aromatic substance was another matter.

The good doctor had previously clued Billy in on the prank. After listening with interest to Philly's tales, Billy fetched a mirror, pulled back the sheet, and placed it in a strategic position to show Philly what all the fuss was about. Philly was shocked, not only because of the image, but more because of the ghastly site of the extra long, still bruised and red, crooked dong, that before then, he was justifiably proud. He had no way of knowing that when it was completely healed, it would be better than ever, and would be the talk of the town.

Billy's reaction was wholly objective. He went so far as to ask their good friend, Doc Robertson, how he could get one of "these" on his pecker as well.

Recovery for the victim was normal if not fast. Word swiftly spread around the community about the walking shrine of the Madonna. Philly upheld his civic responsibility by sharing his good fortune with any who were interested. His male counterparts merely wanted to inspect it. They marveled at the size and shape. The image was of secondary importance. They knew that with a tool like his, the future would certainly be guaranteed.

For the opposite sex, in particular the faithful, he blessed them all with his apparition to any extent they wanted, any time, or any place. He wasn't particular. Some were satisfied only to look, others wanted to kiss it, and when it grew large they lingered as though in a hypnotic state, until sometimes it went off like a cannon. Then there were those who wanted his baby. There was a time and place for all.

It was a common sight on the public streets of El Paso for a group to surround him to satisfy their curiosity with Philly accommodating them ac-

For All The Wrong Reasons

cordingly, depending on the gender of the parties involved. For the males he would merely whip it out for inspection. For the females, depending on their desires, the transactions would take place anywhere convenient, be it the back seat of a car, an alley, a close motel, or his place, all depending on the level of the activity. Most actually wanted his baby. All recipients considered themselves not only blessed but also saved.

He was truly a walking shrine. Like his friends told him, his future in the community was now guaranteed thanks to his good friend Duane Robertson.

Chapter 25

Willy's life followed a completely different path than his brother's. From his first recollection he was part of an airplane. At first he flew the Cessna 150, Beech Bonanza or whatever airplane they happened to be using, from the lap of his mentor. Then shortly after his ninth birthday, Billy fitted him up in the left seat on an outrageous pile of cushions. They were stacked both behind and underneath him until he could both reach the rudder pedals and see over the nose of the airplane. To say that it was an awkward arrangement would be an understatement.

With enough cushions behind him so he could operate the rudder pedals, he was positioned precariously close to the control wheel. Precarious because if a situation called for an inordinate amount of aft movement of the wheel, as is often the case, Willy's body would be in the way. Nevertheless Billy was not to be denied, safety be damned. As far as he was concerned it was a workable solution. So from that time on, the kid flew the Cessna 150, or in a more awkward fashion the Beech Bonanza, from the left seat, with all of his time logged as dual flight instruction, duly endorsed by his flight instructor, Billy Cotton.

Surprisingly, the kid became quite proficient in a much shorter time than Billy had anticipated. It got to the point that to relieve boredom, they indulged in the same contests that Billy and his friends created during the early years of Billy's flying career. These included chasing range horses, forced landings, spot landings, and even chased an unfurled roll of toilet paper from 1,500 to within 200 feet of the ground. Within a couple of years of these exercises, Willy's proficiency was honed to a degree that it could be said he was as good as his mentor. By the time he was twelve years old, the seat cushion requirement became minimal, so the space between the student and the control wheel was more reasonable.

For All The Wrong Reasons

One week after his twelfth birthday, Billy and his protégée were flying the Cessna 150 on a westerly heading from Deer Valley Airport when they over flew Luke Air Force Base Aux.1. Aux 1 was used during the big war, along with several others situated in the valley, for emergency purposes and for the students at Luke to shoot practice landings. At the time Billy was indulging in his games of flouting authority, the Air Force was using the facility only for the practice of instrument approaches. It was not in use on weekends meaning that it was uncontrolled and even unattended. This particular occasion fell on a Sunday.

As they flew over, Billy looking down, got a wild hair up his ass, chopped the power and declared a forced landing. Adhering to the call, Willy immediately wheeled the airplane around, set up an appropriate pattern, and successfully landed on the first third of the runway. The wild hair wasn't the forced landing, it was an impulse to land and have his student solo the airplane from Aux.1. This idea was of course, the farthest thing from Willy's mind. Just as he was about to follow through, Billy held the throttle in the closed position and ordered his student to pull over to the side of the runway. As soon as they quit rolling, Billy climbed out and ordered Willy to complete one solo trip around the patch, while Billy relieved his bladder, land, and return to the spot to pick him up.

At first, Willy resisted. To him, it was the moment of truth. He had been flying for three years and had more logged time than most private pilots with the same chronological time. But he was still unsure of his ability, mostly attributable to his immaturity. There was no choice. Billy shut the door and waived him off. While Willy taxied to the end of the runway, he walked out into the desert a comfortable distance from the edge of the runway, whipped out his thing and took a piss, hosing down the top of a small prickly pear cactus. The rest of the event was textbook; a perfect take-off, standard pattern, and a classic landing. He taxied back, picked up his instructor, and they departed the strip for Deer Valley where they adjourned to Crazy Ed's for the post event celebration.

Over peanuts and a mason jar of draft beer, Billy recounted the feat to his good buddy and business associate, Kirby. Kirby was the proud owner of a 90 horsepower Luscombe. He not only didn't believe the story but also challenged Billy to do it again in his presence. So the following Sunday, Billy and Willy in their Cessna 150, and Kirby and his wife in the Luscombe, flew off to Aux.1 for an encore. This time using Kirby's radio, they were

Chapter 25

able to communicate with Willy, who, while in their presence shot six touch and go landings. It was back to Crazy Ed's for more celebration. Soon the word got out. Willy was an instant celebrity if not an oddity.

From then on, not only did Willy fly the airplane solo, but took passengers along, most of them non-pilots. The first one being the farmer out of the crop-dusting strip outside of Laveen.

About a month after Willy first took to the air on his own, he and his mentor were out visiting their friend Bill Taylor who ran a crop dusting operation outside of the small community of Laveen. A farmer client of Taylor's who was listening in disbelief to Billy's account of the events of Willy's solo accomplishments, proclaimed his doubts about the story. In fact his comment was summed up in a word of one; "bullshit." Now this man had never been in an airplane, and because he had never flown, couldn't fathom the thought that a twelve year old could accomplish what he had never even experienced. He wanted to see it for himself.

So, it was decided, an on the spot demonstration would take place. To the farmer, who had never been in an airplane, it wasn't good enough that the kid fly the airplane by himself, but the dumb shit wanted to go along for the ride. While everybody else was laughing at the prospect, Billy was strapping both the young pilot and his dumb-shit passenger in the airplane, with last minute instructions to Willy as to how long he should be gone, where he should perform, and in general how he should conduct the flight. These instructions were important, seeing as how Billy not only had a neophyte in the airplane, but this would be the first time Willy went out without Billy in the right seat, not counting his solo flights.

The flight was uneventful. The gang on the ground watched in awe. The farmer exited the airplane raving about his experience. There was a lot of backslapping; the kid was the center of attention. The farmer declared that the drinks were on him. As far as he was concerned, if the kid was old enough to fly an airplane, he was old enough to drink.

So with the intrepid aviators in tow, they all piled into their respective pickups, and adjourned to Laveen's main watering hole, where they spent the rest of the day drinking up a storm and shooting pool.

Billy had many faults, but allowing his charge to drink anything stronger than a "Shirley Temple" was not one of them. But shooting pool was within the realm of allowable activities. As the center of attention, Willy spent the rest of the day taking on all comers, holding his own in the process, and

For All The Wrong Reasons

taking the many compliments from the patrons who were made privy to the story of the day's exploits.

From that day, Willy was granted the privilege of flying the airplane out of Deer Valley Airport solo or with anyone he chose to take with him. He had a ball. By the time he was sixteen, he accumulated over 1200 hours, all duly logged, and all duly illegal. Everybody knew what was going on except the FAA. Like the proverbial husband whose wife steps out on him, they are the last to find out. Thankfully, during the four years of the illegal flying, in spite of all the scuttlebutt surrounding their activities, they were never found out by the powers at large.

When Willy was fourteen, after gorging themselves on airport restaurant fare, and were waiting at the cash register for the hostess to get her act together and take their money, Willy picked up a freebie advertising flyer from the display area. The flyer contained primarily airplane ads, which shouldn't be surprising, seeing as to how they were at an airport.

There was a particular ad that caught his attention. It was for the sale of an almost new Citabria 7KCAB, fully aerobatic. The model in question is a tandem two place, high wing monoplane with a complete fuel and oil inverted system. As far as the kid was concerned, it was just what they needed. More than that, he argued, it was the airplane they couldn't do without. By comparison, the Cessna 150 was an obsolete non-entity that could only fly straight and level. The Citabria was a machine in which they could expand their horizon.

Always willing to go along with the spoiled brat, Billy relented and after haggling with the owner about the price, ended up buying the airplane. It was Willy's new toy. He flew it frequently, and as with the Cessna 150, he almost always took passengers with him. The next step was for the both of them to join the local chapter of the National Aerobatic Club. One of the club members who was as much of a renegade as two, and who was himself a highly qualified aerobatic pilot, took the two under his wing. Before long, under the tutelage of his new instructor Willy became a very proficient aerobatic pilot in his own right.

Six months later a photographer from the Arizona Republic, Phoenix' own news rag picked up the story, contacted Billy at his office and requested a demonstration. Better yet, Billy insisted she go along for a ride. When he met her at the airplane he was very relieved that he didn't extend his offer to booze and bed, something he would normally do in the general

Chapter 25

course of a negotiation with the opposite sex. After the mandatory salutations, he loaded her in the back seat of the airplane, camera and all, and with a pat on the back of his protégée, he slammed the door shut and stood back as Willy cranked on the engine.

On their return she had nothing but good to say about the ride. She was thrilled. From her perch in the back seat, she had snapped a picture of Willy at the top of a Hammer Head Stall. The shot was classic. It showed Willy looking out the left side of the airplane, as the airplane was rotating over the top of the maneuver at zero "g's" evidenced by the floating headset leads. The horizon and terrain in the background of the shot were tilted at ninety degrees to the axis of the picture verifying their precarious attitude. During that maneuver and others producing zero or negative "g" loads, Willy took exceptional interest in her large breasts that literally floated upward. He was more intrigued with her anatomical anomaly than he was with his flying. It spurred him on to do more. His observation was something that he recalled, after the ride, over and over again with his mentor. Billy chided him for as much detail and description as the kid would recall.

The picture made the front page of the newspaper, along with a background story on the young pilot. The FAA still didn't get it. Apparently no one down at their office read the paper.

The following year, the events leading to the purchase of the Citabria were repeated, except this time it was a fully aerobatic single place Pitts S-1 that caught his attention. It belonged to a retired Air Force Colonel out of Lake Placid New York, who for an additional $500.00 would ferry the airplane to Phoenix for them. It took him a full five days of battling the November weather and hangovers to do the job. He complained more about the center of gravity changes of the airplane as he consumed the scotch that he brought along for fortification than he did about the weather.

After landing at Deer Valley, the boys from the National Guard spent the next ten hours dismantling the Pitts for a thorough inspection before signing off on it. It was three a.m. when they completed the task and approved the airplane for purchase. After writing the check, all involved helped the Colonel finish off his Scotch, before putting him up for what remained of the night for a hard earned rest. Now the boys had two aerobatic airplanes.

Since there was no way to provide dual instruction in the single place airplane, Willy gained his proficiency by fast taxiing it on the ramp around the airport. It was the day after Thanksgiving that, believing the kid was

For All The Wrong Reasons

ready, the solo event took place. From that day on, while still fifteen and still very much illegal, Willy regularly flew the Pitts, further sharpening his aerobatic skills.

As Willy's sixteenth birthday approached, the age in which he could legally solo, Billy conjured up a scheme that in his opinion would outdo all previous schemes. He decided that his protégée should attempt a world's record for the most different types of airplanes flown by an individual on the day they could legally solo, their sixteenth birthday. With the cooperation of a local used airplane dealer he managed to gather up eighteen of them. Starting at midnight on the festive day, with Billy checking him out, one at a time and finishing at three o'clock on the same day, Willy managed to get the job done. He would have completed more except eighteen was all that they could manage to gather up. The feat did set the record, but it was short lived. The publicity that it generated spurned the interest of another individual who three months later broke it by soloing his daughter in several more.

On his seventeenth birthday he received his pilot's license. One week later at Falcon Field in Mesa, Arizona, he performed an aerobatic routine at his first air show. Because of his age and apparent inexperience, the FAA required him to fly it at a thousand feet. But the next year with an FAA safety inspector watching, Willy successfully completed a low level routine and was granted by the agency what is called in the industry as a "surface waiver." He was eighteen with a new Commercial license. From then on, in addition to his other duties such as school and work in the office, he flew about six aerobatic routines a year at air shows, mostly in Arizona. At the time he was the youngest air show pilot in the country.

Chapter 26

With one of his protégées building an architectural firm in El Paso, the other palling around with him in Phoenix doing their airplane thing, giving dual instruction, aerobatic flying, or chasing pussy, Billy was very busy. To make time for all of the extraneous activities in his life, he all but abandoned his responsibilities with the Phoenix office. These other activities were more important. He used the Bonanza to commute between Phoenix and El Paso, traveling to El Paso near the first of the week and returning either late the following Thursday, or in some cases Friday, depending on the demands for his time.

Nearly all of the pilots Billy talked to, who traveled in their airplane from Phoenix to El Paso, would first take up a heading for Tucson, turn the corner there for Deming, New Mexico, and then on to El Paso. This was the preferred route, which followed the published airways. Billy favored the more direct way, which on a heading of 100 degrees out of Deer Valley took him over Globe, Safford, Duncan, and Deming, and then on to El Paso. This steered him through the Williams Air Force Base MOA (military operations area) that was thought, by the more conservative pilots, too dangerous because of the military air training traffic in and around the MOA. The prospect of a mid-air collision was the argument, which favored the longer southern route.

Billy maintained that during all of his flights over the more direct and shorter route, he saw only two military airplanes, and hardly any other traffic and none of them were even close to his position. On the other hand he opined, that the area over Tucson was an intersection of several crossing airways, and if the pilot didn't communicate with Tucson Approach Control or Albuquerque Center, who could vector the pilot through the area by radar, he was exposed to the possibility of tangling wings with some other

For All The Wrong Reasons

airplane entering from a different direction. And Billy didn't like to talk to the air traffic control people because as far as he was concerned, all they were capable of doing was creating problems instead of solving them.

On a typical trip, as soon as he could after leaving Deer Valley airport and receiving clearance to cross the Scottsdale airport traffic area, Billy would break open whatever book he was reading at the time, trim the airplane, and settle down for the two-hour flight. The Bonanza was equipped with an autopilot, but the thing broke within months after buying the airplane, and Billy never took the time or made the effort to have it fixed, mainly because he was too cheap to expend the necessary funds. He never did believe he needed an autopilot anyway.

To compensate for the lack of the autopilot and still read, he used an unusual technique that he discovered by accident, that allowed him to maintain his heading while his head was down and locked in the indulgence of a good book. It was a simple method of ensuring whatever shadow was cast over the surface of the page would remain stationary. If it began to wander, a subtle nudge of the proper rudder pedal would bring the shadow back to its original position, and thus the airplane to the proper heading.

It was appropriately pointed out by his tormentors during their ongoing debates concerning the best and safest route to take between the two cities, that with his head down and locked, it was no wonder he never observed other traffic during his flights through the MOA. Billy still shrugged them off using his professed belief that what one didn't know wouldn't hurt him. He was also a subscriber to the "big sky theory," the idea being that the sky was big enough for all comers, so big that one needn't worry about conflicting traffic, except maybe over Tucson.

Aside from the broken autopilot, the airplane's directional gyro (gyrocompass) left a lot to be desired. Before taking off at Deer Valley airport for the flight to El Paso, he would appropriately set the instrument to the runway heading. This was necessary over the conventional method of setting it to correspond to the magnetic compass because like most of the equipment in the airplane, the magnetic compass was defective and couldn't be counted on for accuracy. It was out of fluid, the lifeblood of the instrument.

After taking off, using the gyrocompass, he would take up the heading of 100 degrees, but by the time he reached El Paso, it would have precessed to the reciprocal heading of 280 degrees. To Billy, it was almost comical, because as he pointed out on more than one occasion, in theory, the instru-

Chapter 26

ment was automatic and never had to be reset, having always anticipated the return heading and resetting itself accordingly.

The fuel gauges were also faulty. When the fuel supply in the left tank was exhausted, its gauge indicated one-quarter left. The right one was worse. It would indicate a half-tank when the fuel was exhausted on that side. Contrary to the manufacture's dictum, Billy would maximize his range by running one tank completely dry before switching tanks. This method draws air into the system causing problems with the re-start. One time during the procedure, when scud running in less than desirable weather, he lost most of his altitude before the engine came back to life. This was the prime reason the manufacturer frowned on the practice. The boys from the National Guard wanted to calibrate the gauges for the sake of saving Billy's life, but he wouldn't have anything to do with the gesture. He was afraid to let them mess with the problem lest they make it worse. He didn't think there was anything wrong, and in his best philosophical tone, "If it ain't broke, don't fix it."

Most of the time the trips were completed without incidents, but occasionally there were the harrowing experiences. Weather played a big part in raising his adrenaline, especially in the winter, so Billy found himself scud running when the ceilings and visibility dropped to below minimums. If the situation were grave when he was about to leave Phoenix, he would merely cancel the trip, waiting for better weather. But when he was at the other end of the line, he was too anxious to get to Phoenix and his harem to wait for better weather. It was commonly referred to in flying circles as "get-home-itis."

It was at those times he found refuge in flying very low along I-10 through Tucson and on to Phoenix. He figured that if the cars and trucks could do it, then he should be able to. Whoever heard of an obstruction or tower being constructed over a freeway. He concluded that it was perfectly safe unless the road went through a tunnel.

On one of the El Paso to Phoenix trips, he ran into serious weather just east of Safford. Having passed the point where he should have continued down I-10, instead of going back to intercept I-10, he decided to follow the highway through Safford, on to Globe and then to lower terrain west of Globe where the situation should improve. From Safford to Globe the terrain is very flat, the road is straight and the elevation is around 4,000 feet. Then on the west side of Globe, the terrain winds around the hills to a lower

For All The Wrong Reasons

elevation through Superior to the Valley basin of 1,000 to 1,500 feet high.

He was doing real well, flying within fifty feet above the surface of the road, passing very close to small hills whose tops were in the clouds, and reminding himself once again that unless the road turned into a tunnel, there would be no problem. But no sooner that he ground his way through the congested area of Globe-Miami, a sudden chill gripped him, releasing the usual surge of adrenaline that accompanies a close call. It was the result of the shock of reality in which the scenario that he made light of, in fact joked and laughed about, in the company of his friends, existed. The irony was that the stretch of highway between Globe and Superior passed through the Queen Creek tunnel.

Without a second thought, he cranked the airplane around in a tight turn to his reciprocal heading. But before the turn was completed, he found himself in the clouds and was positive that he was also among the hills. This is what is referred to in the industry as flying in clouds with hard centers. All he could envision was the inevitable mountain in front of him.

He added full power, and went to maximum climb, while continuing his turn in a Chandelle-like maneuver which is a maneuver that was designed for just this situation and resigned himself for what he was certain was the inevitable collision with the cloud with the hard center. It was a mad dash for the top of the overcast before colliding with the terrain. Time was on his side. The longer he survived, the better his chances of clearing the mountainous terrain.

He rolled out on what he thought was an easterly heading, remembering that neither the directional gyro nor the magnetic compass were worth a damn, especially in a situation like the one in which he found himself. He would settle for whatever heading he had and make the necessary heading adjustments later; that is if he survived. For the moment it was more important to keep climbing. This he did, and broke out through the overcast at 10,000 feet or 6,000 feet above the ground, still alive but sweating profusely. Safely on top, he turned the airplane around and resumed his heading for home, figuring it should take him about thirty minutes to get there.

Billy tuned his radio and called the Flight Service Station (Phoenix Radio). They reported that the cloud layer became broken in the vicinity of Luke Air Force Base, about twenty miles west of his destination. Broken by definition means sixty percent or more cloud coverage. In a broken layer he was certain to find a hole large enough to spiral down through. He was

Chapter 26

happy that the clouds were diminishing, but he was unhappy over the prospect of overshooting his destination only to have to fly back to Deer Valley.

In a resigned sort of way, he continued on, and when his thirty minutes were up, he observed a hole in the clouds in front and slightly to his left. He flew over to it and looked down. Lo and behold there sat Deer Valley Airport. He figured that he was either very good or very lucky. He didn't care which. He would take advantage of his dumb luck, land and go over to Crazy Ed's for a little therapy to take the edge off of his frazzled nerves.

He was at 10,000 feet, Deer Valley field elevation was 1,500 feet. So without much forethought he lowered the landing gear and flaps, rolled into a tight left turn, and spiraled down to pattern altitude through a hole in the clouds that was barely large enough to take him. The visit to Crazy Ed's would be longer than usual.

The airport Billy used in El Paso was called Sunland Airpark. It was an uncontrolled airport located on the west side of the city, adjacent to the Sunland Park racetrack. He chose this airport over the El Paso International which was located on the far east side because Sunland Airpark was in close proximity to his office, he didn't have to mess with the air traffic control people, who Billy thought were a real pain in the ass, and it cut at least twenty miles off of his trip. On the down side the runway lights were not left on after hours except by prior arrangement.

It was on a cold January day that another hair-raising experience took control of Billy's life. On this particular occasion, Billy had used the Citabria for his weekly trip because the Bonanza was down for maintenance. He had planned to return to Phoenix on Friday, leaving before noon because a weather system was hanging in over his entire route, and if he had to scud run he would rather do it in the daylight. However, on Wednesday evening he received a call from Dave telling him that he needed to be in the Phoenix office at nine o'clock the next morning for and important presentation. That meant he would have to leave very early in the morning to make it to the office on time.

Considering the speed of the airplane, the time it took to put it to bed at the other end, and the drive from Deer Valley to the office, to be on the safe side, he figured he would have to take-off at five in the morning. If, in the final analysis there was spare time in the program, he would indulge himself with a three-egg omelet at the Deer Valley Restaurant. For a five o'clock departure, he would have to be up and at it by four. One other factor caused

For All The Wrong Reasons

him consternation. The early departure meant that at least one-third of his trip would be in the dark in possibly inclement weather. With his usual cavalier attitude, he shrugged it off.

To save time in the morning, Billy showered the night before. At four sharp the alarm went off, he jumped out of bed, threw on his rags, and before he knew it he was on his way to the airport, Philly at the wheel. It was still drizzling; a remnant of the system that should have passed through. They pulled the airplane out of the hanger he was using and he said his goodbyes to Philly. A glance at his watch indicated that he was ahead of schedule.

All of the sudden it occurred to him that there were no runway or taxi lights, something he should have taken care of with a phone call the night before. The drizzle had stopped but it was still very black because of the low ceilings. So he instructed Philly to lead him out to the departure end of the runway, and when he was in position, to drive down the strip to the far east end and point the headlights toward him so he could use the car as a target during his take-off roll. Billy emphasized that Philly should go to the extreme east end lest the same thing happen to him that took place at the Francisco Grande airport in Mean Dean's airplane.

Philly did as instructed. The trip out to the west end was smooth in spite of the very black night. He turned the airplane in the direction of an easterly take-off and completed his run-up as Philly drove down the strip to the other end. He noticed the puddles of water on the runway that reflected from the car's headlights. Waiting for his guide to get in place, he had about a minute to think about the precarious position in which he had placed himself. "What the hell could be so important to warrant this idiotic scenario?"

As soon as the car turned around to face him, he poured the coal to it, and as an after thought flicked on the switch that energized the turn and bank (needle and ball) instrument, thinking that it might be needed if he got caught in the clouds. Besides the airspeed indicator, it was the only instrument that he could use for the purpose of instrument flying. The technique was called "partial panel" or "needle, ball and airspeed."

A full panel, which gave the pilot a distinct advantage, included an artificial horizon and a gyrocompass. These additional instruments would have been nice to have under the circumstances, but Billy wasn't concerned. He felt he was competent to fly "needle, ball and airspeed" only, a task out of

Chapter 26

reach by most pilots. What he didn't realize because he didn't bother to check, was that the needle and ball instrument was inoperative because of a blown fuse.

As he rolled down the runway gathering the necessary airspeed before lift off, he used the reflection from the car's headlights to discern the hazards of a wet runway, in particular the many puddles that might affect the directional control of the airplane. He zigzagged the best he could to avoid the puddles while at the same time tried his best to lift the airplane off the ground in the shortest possible distance. As soon as the airplane lifted off, he immediately started a 180-degree turn to his 280-degree heading for Deming.

Sunland Airpark was situated in a basin along the Rio Grande, a muddy river that was considered by the locals as "too thin to plow and too thick to drink." To clear the mesa on the west side, he would have to immediately climb to more than 150 feet by the time he reached the west end of the airport perimeter. During his turnout he noticed once again how black it was outside. It seemed like it was more so in the air than when he was on the ground. He considered taking up a heading along I-10 to Las Cruces and beyond toward Lordsburg to a point where it would be light enough to break off and fly direct to Safford and from there through Globe and on to Phoenix.

But when he was high enough to see along the surface of the mesa, he picked up several lights on the ground, emanating from the occasional ranch house that were located more or less on his course to Deming. They weren't much, but just enough to keep him in visual contact with the ground. At least if he fixed on one or more of the lights, he could fly over the desert directly to Deming saving himself about thirty miles over the other option of going by the way of I-10 to Las Cruces. Off to his right, 42 miles away, he could pick out the vast sea of lights that defined his alternate target, Las Cruces. If flying directly to Deming didn't work out, he would change his mind and head directly over the desert platform to Las Cruces, using the lights of that city as a target.

Ten minutes into the flight everything was going along just fine. As he flew very close to the desert floor, he could see that he was skimming very close to the bottom of the cloud deck as well. He estimated that the overcast was no more than 100 to 150 feet above the ground. It was a very small needle he was attempting to thread. But keeping Las Cruces in sight and the

For All The Wrong Reasons

occasional lights in his sights, he plodded along in the lonely dark night.

Occasionally he could pick out a star or two through the small holes in the overcast. To him it was an encouraging sight. To the best of his judgment, he estimated that the cloud deck was about 500 feet thick. Every once in a while a chunk of cloud would pass by the airplane, and when it happened on the right side, he would look over in the direction of Las Cruces to make sure his "security blanket" was still in sight, but as expected those lights would fade and then re-brighten as the cloud passed by. He had better push the nose over slightly and drop down a little, but straining out the nose of the airplane he could see enough to realize that he didn't have that much room to play with.

Then it happened; his worst nightmare. All of the sudden he completely lost forward visibility as well as the lights of Las Cruces. He was in the clouds. Instead of pushing on the stick to get out, he succumbed to an irresistible urge to add full power and climb through the stuff. In no time at all, trying to fly by the gauges, he realized that his turn and bank instrument was not working. The needle part of the instrument, that indicates the rate and direction of a turn was dead and sticking straight up. The enunciator on its face indicated that there was no power getting to the instrument. All he had now was the airspeed indicator. He quickly looked at the switching panel. Sure enough, the switch was on. The instrument had to be broken but there was no time to troubleshoot. The rule was to fly the airplane.

The ball part of the instrument that indicates whether or not a turn is coordinated is a mechanical device very much like a carpenter's level in appearance, principle and operation. The ball was right in the middle, where it should be either during a coordinated turn or straight and level. However Billy noted that the airspeed was building. His immediate reaction was backpressure on the stick. The action did nothing to fix it. That fact registered in his mind as a spiral. Up to that point he failed to observe the indication on the accelerometer (G- meter). If he had, it would have confirmed the beginning of a spiral or a tight turn. Billy's scan went to the magnetic compass. It indicated a turn was in progress. But due to the poor lighting, he was unable to determine the direction. Things were beginning to happen fast, too fast for Billy's own good.

The cockpit's only light was a unique fixture that was mounted high on the left side of the cockpit just over the pilot's shoulder. It came from the Air National Guard, confiscated out of a KC-97 by one of its members and

Chapter 26

Billy's part-time mechanic. Its unique feature was that it could also be used as a flashlight, inasmuch as it could be detached from the holder. This was possible because the electrical lead was a tightly coiled, spring loaded cord attached to the holder by a spring loaded ball that with a sight pull the fixture could be detached and used as a flash light. The only restriction was the length of the cord.

Billy's reaction was quick. He pulled the fixture down and focused it directly on the compass. By this time the compass card was spinning at such a rate that it was impossible for him to tell which way he was spiraling. It was a blur. Without knowing which way the airplane was turning it was next to impossible to execute a correction especially in the time frame available.

He did not panic. He continued to study the situation. He knew he was about to die but was determined to continue on a survival path until the lights went out. The airspeed indicator showed a continued build up, so to control it he applied more backpressure. All this did was to tighten the spiral. Throughout all this, the ball was still in the center. For the first time he glanced at the G-meter. It registered a solid four and a half G's. He was definitely in a graveyard spiral and was about to die. Total elapsed time was less than twenty seconds. It seemed to him like forever.

He wasn't through yet. He would take a guess and apply control pressure in the opposite direction of what he thought the turn might be. If his guess was correct, the turn would stop. If not the airplane would roll over on its back. It never came to that.

Before he could execute the maneuver, the gods once again came to his aid. They threw him out the bottom of the cloud base where in an instant the plate of lights representing Las Cruces flashed in front of the nose of the airplane, giving Billy the illusion that they were standing on edge. In reality it was the airplane that was in a ninety-degree bank. Instantly his aerobatic experience came into play and before the lights of the city could pass by the front of the airplane, he rolled it level, immediately stopping the turn and resolving his perception to where the lights and the horizontal axis of the airplane were on the same plane.

It all happened so fast, and he was so busy, he wasn't even rattled. Under the circumstances, he decided that it would be prudent to alter his course and fly directly to Las Cruces, then follow I-10 to Lordsburg as he thought he should have done in the first place.

After a few minutes of this new routine, he kept looking off to his left

For All The Wrong Reasons

toward Deming. The few lights on the ground along the shorter route became too tempting. So once again he altered his course, taking up a heading along the desert directly to Deming. This time he was successful.

It was in the vicinity of Deming that the blackness of the night started to break. It was sufficiently light enough for him to make out the surroundings, and also light enough to establish his relationship with the ground and the base of the clouds. Billy was awestruck when he discovered that he was barely 100 feet above the ground, with the clouds another 100 feet above him. The realization struck him that if he had not fixed the spiral dive, as immediately as he did, he would have been nothing more than a spot on the desert.

Billy flew on past Deming, on the way to Safford, bucking the usual headwinds. Even with the wind on his nose, he should make Phoenix with fuel to spare, as there was slightly more than four hours worth on board. But just to be on the safe side, Billy decided to lean the engine a bit more.

A little farther on course the cloud deck changed from solid to broken and appeared to be thinner than before. Billy thought he would be more comfortable on top, so once again he attempted to punch his way up through one of the holes. This time he was more successful as he had more light to work with, and there was more room to maneuver between the clouds.

For much of the rest of the trip he was bored and irritated. Bored because of the slow ground speed, and irritated because of the headwind. It seemed that wherever he flew, there was always a headwind. He always maintained during the bull sessions with his buddies that he could never get lost. All he had to do was head into the wind and he would be on course. This time was no different.

As he poked along, he could pick out familiar landmarks on the ground as he passed over the occasional hole in the cloud deck beneath him. Mount Graham loomed up on his left side, most of it poking up through the clouds. The mountain is over ten thousand feet high and is located about ten miles south of Safford. When he was abeam the mountain, over Safford, he checked his time, started to squirm, and leaned the mixture some more.

Between Safford and Globe the clouds all but disappeared. This raised his spirits somewhat. If only he could make better time. Slightly past Globe he began to let down as the lowering ground elevation allowed. He thought that if he hugged the ground all the way down to the valley floor of Phoenix, the lower level might bring relief from the plaguing winds.

Chapter 26

But as he approached the north side of the Superstition Mountains, all Billy could see in front of him was a solid layer of low clouds stretching on the left from the vicinity of Tucson, and thirty miles on the right to where the terrain sloped up through the layer in the direction of Prescott and Flagstaff. He felt that it should start to break up, as he got closer to Phoenix. But it was not to be, as it wasn't just any cloud deck, it was a fog layer, starting at the ground and extending to 500 feet. All of the mountain peaks around the valley were ominously sticking up through the mess.

Billy called the local flight Service Station, Phoenix Radio. They informed him that all of the airports from north of Phoenix to Tucson, and west to Luke Air Force Base were down. The whole Valley was fogged in. He virtually had no options from his present position. Going back to Globe was out because of his remaining fuel supply. He knew of no small strips between his position and Globe, and worst yet he didn't have a chart to look for one. He couldn't believe his bad fortune. The gods were sure testing him on this day.

He continued on desperately looking for a solution. As he approached the small community of Fountain Hills he called the Scottsdale Tower. They replied that they were in a zero-zero condition. "What about Carefree?" They were down also. Then he called Deer Valley Tower. They reported the same thing. Other than his conversations with the two towers, the frequencies were quiet. He crossed over the McDowell Mountains still on his way to Deer Valley and still searching for an inspiration.

The four hours of fuel supply were all but up. He was getting frantic and tired. The ordeal was playing hell on his nerves. If the engine quit, there was no way he could penetrate the fog and land the airplane without getting killed, especially since he didn't have an operable needle and ball instrument.

Shortly after passing Scottsdale, he noticed that the rising terrain to the north eventually penetrated the top of the fog. He knew of no airport or small strip in that area, but if he worked his way over there, to where it was clear, he could at least make a controlled survivable crash, no matter how rough the surface was.

Finally Billy had a plan. He would fly along the terrain on the north edge of the fog until he intercepted I-17, the Black Canyon Freeway. It was the north-south freeway that was routed immediately west of Deer Valley Airport, in the direction of Prescott and Flagstaff. There he would descend to

For All The Wrong Reasons

the surface of the freeway, attempt to fly south on the road surface in the fog to a point abeam the airport, then turn east for a straight-in approach to runway seven. Yes, the tower would allow him to make a special VFR approach, just let them know when he was ready. If he found that this plan wasn't workable, as an alternate, he would fly north along the freeway, hoping to find an airstrip of some sort, and if not would land on the freeway when his fuel ran out.

Three miles before intercepting the freeway, he glanced down through the fringe of the fog bank, and recognized his friend Ray McClain's house. He was ecstatic. He not only knew that he could land on the street in front of Ray's house, but had done it before. He had over a quarter of a mile to work with. If the special VFR didn't work out, he would return to Ray's place and land.

And it didn't work out. The fog was just too thick. After giving up the attempt, Billy advised the tower accordingly and returned to try his last ditch effort at Ray McClain's. Clouds had started to drift over Ray's place, but there was still adequate maneuvering room, only if he would quit screwing around and get the job done. By this time the unnerving experience had Billy very shaky. To compound his difficulties, he had to pee in the worst way.

He was so unnerved that it took three passes at the strip before he was able to slow the airplane enough to make it fit in the short length of the landing area. He was so fast on the first two that the attempts would have surely ended up in a ground loop or running into the obstruction at the far end. On his last try with the fuel gauges on empty, he used a longer than usual final approach and slowed the airplane way down to the edge of a stall, plunking it down on the very end and rolling to a gradual stop in front of Ray's house.

The noise brought Ray out of the house in time to watch the show. He directed Billy to taxi the airplane off the road, up the driveway and onto the grassed area. After exiting the Citabria, instead of receiving applause, Ray showered him with criticism for taking three tries at the landing while Willy had landed there before in a single try. "Well and good, but did Willy have to do it with his bladder pressing against his tonsils?"

The first thing Billy did was to pee all over the side of Ray's house. The second thing was to ask Ray for a ride to Deer Valley Airport to retrieve his car. Before they started to roll, the clouds rolled in enveloping the area. It

Chapter 26

was now zero-zero at Ray's. "Yes," Billy acknowledged to Ray, "I'm one lucky son-of-a-bitch, in more ways than one."

And to top it off, he was late for his meeting. In fact it was all over by the time he arrived at his office. Billy was completely exhausted. He felt that he had done a days work and was in no mood for the shit his partners gave him for not showing up on time. He would spend the rest of the day at Crazy Ed's.

Chapter 27

It wasn't long after the fiasco involving the Citabria and the bad weather, that Billy had another hair-raising experience in the Bonanza. It was on one of his trips from El Paso to Phoenix. He was accompanied by two of his employees, James and Irvin, and Irvin's new wife. Irvin's wife, Luanne, was reluctant. She had never been in a "small" airplane before. As far as she was concerned they were unsafe, "especially small ones. Those big airplanes look a lot safer."

On December 1st, he was taking them back to Phoenix with him to attend the company's Christmas party. It was traditionally one of the first parties of the Christmas season among the many thrown by the various architectural firms for their clients, vendors, and sometime competitors. Usually about 200 people attended. The event was expected to be a gala affair, if past parties were an indication. Starting time was generally 3:00 pm, and lasted until the last person was standing sometime after midnight. Getting there on time for the first drink was the reason they departed Sunland Airpark early on the day in question.

It didn't take too much convincing to get Luanne to go along. She was more afraid of Irvin being without chaperon in the big city with the likes of Billy Cotton than she was of small airplanes.

They broke ground at 9:00 am sharp. It was a beautiful morning – not a cloud in the sky. The only downside was a 20-knot wind, right on his nose. This only reinforced his contention that wherever he flew he had a headwind; velocity was the only variable. In this case Billy would fly as close to the ground as possible for two reasons. Down low one gets the illusion that he is going faster than he actually is, and thus feels better for it. For the second reason, as a generalization, the higher you fly the stronger the wind. So with a headwind stay low to minimize the loss of ground speed.

For All The Wrong Reasons

There was another factor Billy always considered under the circumstances. Flying west in the morning with the sun at your back, one generally experiences a surface breeze from the east caused by the convective forces from the heat generated by the sun as the ground warms up. This phenomenon occurs more often than not, no matter the direction of the winds aloft. It was this anomaly from which Billy wanted to take advantage. To benefit from this effect, he would have to stay under 300 feet AGL (above ground level) – no problem.

As soon as practical after breaking ground, he took up his heading of 280 degrees, leveled off at 300 feet above the surface of the desert, broke out his book, and settled down for a two hour flight. Everybody in the airplane was in a festive mood, looking forward to the experience.

Even Luanne seemed to shed her initial nervousness. Billy expected her to object to his reading, but he soon realized that due to her ignorance of the ways of the airplane, she probably thought that his conduct was normal.

The route would take them immediately over the north side of the Deming airport. Deming airport was an uncontrolled facility, left over from WWII, with multiple paved runways. Traffic included student training, a commuter airline, and the occasional transient airplane. The FAA chose the airport for the site of a Flight Service Station. They answered to the radio call "Deming Radio."

Transiting close to the airport at 300 feet AGL was not the safest thing to do, especially at or below pattern altitude. There might be other airplanes in the pattern, departing, landing or otherwise shooting touch and go landing practice. One had to look around for this other traffic when "crashing the pattern" as Billy was about to do, and had done on many occasions in the past under similar circumstances.

When he was ten miles east of the Deming, Billy began to make preparations for the approach and crossing of the airport. He stopped reading at a convenient spot in his book, turned it over with it still opened at the spot where he quit reading and set it down inverted and open on the glare shield in front of him; the idea being that after crossing over the airport, he could resume his reading without the undue effort of finding his place. As far as he was concerned, no one could ever accuse him of being inefficient.

No sooner than he set his book down and concentrated his vision for the possible activity in the distance, there was an ungodly noise from engine. It was a spontaneous noise that could only be described as a loud "bang." At

Chapter 27

the same time it felt like he ran into something hard, and the airplane seemed to stop in mid-air as the engine quit. The wind milling propeller caused a vibration and slapping sensation similar to that which occurs when the fan belt of a car suddenly snaps and begins to beat the rest of the car to death with the loose ends.

Billy immediately knew that they were going down. He knew it not because of what was going on in front, but because his asshole was starting to pucker. He was still monitoring Albuquerque Flight Watch on the radio, not having had a chance to change frequency to the Deming Flight Service Station for traffic advisories necessary for safe transit over the airport. He picked up the mike and in his best Chuck Yeager modulated tone, called "Mayday-Mayday" followed by his predicament and the fact that he was "going in." There was a woman on the other end. She replied "Good luck." As much as he wanted to, he didn't have time to indulge in flattering small talk with her in hopes of getting in her pants. That would have to wait.

At the same time this was going on, and his dirty mind was working, he was looking for a place to land. The only place practical was a cow pasture on his right. Yes, it really had cows in it. Considering his altitude and position relative to the field, he was already on base leg. That's what he liked about these precarious situations, decision-making choices were eliminated. A ninety-degree turn to the right would put him on final.

He intended to land with the landing gear up, but as his approach shortened, he found that he was high enough to lower the wheels. Immediately after throwing the gear switch, his hand subconsciously moved over to the left side of the panel, and he threw the flap switch. His only thought at that point was, "I had better make this good or my students will make me their laughing stock."

The airplane crossed over the fence in good shape, but the gear light was still red indicating that it had still not fully extended. Billy flared. He held the airplane off as long as possible, one eye on the gear light, the other on the field in front of him. Then the gear light went green and the airplane hit the ground, in that order, but almost simultaneously. But the flaps were still in transit, indicated by the familiar grinding sound that is produced when they're lowering.

The surface of the field was hard, dry and sterile – certainly not inviting to some grass hungry cow. It was moderately rough, because sometime back when it was wet and muddy, the cattle had evidently churned it up,

For All The Wrong Reasons

leaving their footprints to form hard pockets. Patches of brush were growing in randomly isolated places – some of these were directly in Billy's way. There was no way Billy could negotiate them. Driving through the clusters caused an unnerving thrashing sound as the branches slapped at the airplane.

To add insult to injury, the cattle in the field were spooked by the intruder and were running from left to right across the front of the airplane. In an attempt to avoid them, Billy steered the airplane about thirty degrees to the left. All of the cows escaped the monster except the last one in the herd. He or she, as the case may be, almost made it. The right wing tip barely grazed the rump of the animal. Other than knocking off the position light and collecting hair where the fixture once lived, there was no damage.

When the airplane finally came to a stop, it was a mere eight feet short of the edge of a twelve-foot high flood control dyke. The silence was deafening – especially from the passengers. They were just sitting there staring straight ahead. It occurred to Billy that sometime during the fiasco he should have clued them in on what was going on and what was to be expected. Instead he had been oblivious to their presence during the entire time. When he reached over to unlock the door, it also occurred to him that according to the "book" it was a function that he should have completed before the landing.

Billy picked up the mike and attempted to call Flight Watch. No luck – everything was dead. He shut off all switches, opened the door, and told his passengers to get out. While they were unloading their baggage, Billy strolled around the airplane assessing whatever damage he expected to find. The biggest thing was all of the oil dripping from the engine compartment. The farmer who owned the property, and who witnessed the whole thing, helped gather up their belongings and drove them to the airport.

The man let them out at the Flight Service Station where Billy completed a hand written narrative outlining the details of the forced landing. He only did it to satisfy the attendant who insisted that he had to file a report since he declared an emergency. She envisioned Billy composing a lengthy formal document sometime later, and she wondered what he had in mind when he requested a paper bag or a segment of toilet paper. Instead, when she grasped his sarcasm, handed him a ruled sheet of paper. In the following five minutes, in his worst handwriting, he scribbled a rough dissertation, handing the completed work back with a verbal footnote that

Chapter 27

insinuated that if her bosses didn't like his report they should see his attorney. Then he walked out duly impressing his employees in the process.

He then contacted the local mechanic as the first step in retrieving the airplane. He was surprised when the mechanic told him that he was married to the agent in the Flight Service Station. Billy thinking back at his indiscretion hoped that there wouldn't be any repercussions as a result.

He strolled into the FBO to rent an airplane. He had to settle for a Cessna 172. It was better than nothing. Billy loaded James, Irvin and Irvin's rattled wife in the Cessna and flew them back to El Paso. Their enthusiasm for the adventure had evaporated with the engine failure. After dumping them out, he proceeded to Phoenix in the Cessna in time for the party, and proceeded to get good and drunk.

The mechanic later reported that the cause of the failure was the departure of the crankshaft counter-weights exiting the case at the top and rear of the engine – one weight on each side of the seam. These are flat devices, made of steel, several inches long, weighing less than a pound each, and are shaped in the image of a partial moon – that is one edge is flat while the other is elliptical. Their exact location is directly underneath the two magnetos.

The force was such that they not only penetrated the case but also succeeded in knocking the magnetos off their mounts. It was actually the dislodging of the magnetos from their drives that caused the failure. If not for that he may have had enough power, albeit rough, to get to Deming before all of his oil would have left via the holes.

On the other side of the argument, it could be said that had not the magnetos absorbed the energy of the flying missiles, the weights might have continued on through the cowling, then the windshield leaving a permanent moon shaped impression on Billy's face.

It took longer than expected to settle with the insurance company. When this bureaucratic exercise was finally settled, the mechanic had to order a new engine from the factory - more delays – hang the engine, then ferry the airplane to Phoenix to complete the necessary cosmetic repairs.

There were quite a few places on the airplane that needed attending to because of the damage incurred when the airplane traveled through the brush on the landing roll, and when the mechanic loaded the airplane on the flat bed trailer for the trip to Deming. When all of this had taken place, and the new engine hardly broken in, another incident took place that if not so seri-

For All The Wrong Reasons

ous would have been funny.

Bill Simon was not only the company's highly capable attorney, but he was also a long time loyal friend of Billy's, dating back to just before the Francisco Grande incident involving Mean Dean's Cessna 182. He was fresh out of law school at the time, and since then had handled all of Billy's corporate and personal legal affairs. He was mature beyond his years, becoming one of the finer minds in the legal profession. In Billy's mind, Simon could do no wrong.

Billy drove cars with the same attitude he flew airplanes. Therefore on many occasions, Simon was called upon to save Billy's bacon in traffic court - as many as nine times in one year alone. All of the traffic citations were dismissed.

Occasionally they played golf together. Bill Simon was not an enthusiastic flyer, mostly due to the bad experience with the Francisco Grande thing, but when it involved using the airplane for a day of golfing, he would grit his teeth and go along. On this occasion it was a short trip to Prescott. They invited their stockbroker, Charlie Henderson, and Bill Simon's brother-in-law to join the mix.

They were to play at Prescott's Antelope Hills municipal golf course. The course was actually located on the airport property, accessed from one of the paved taxi strips. From the taxiway there was a decomposed granite strip wide enough to accommodate an airplane, and leading to a large parking area immediately next to the pro-shop.

Unlike other fly-in golf courses where it is still necessary to obtain a ride from the airport to the clubhouse, this one was made to order for pilots who liked to play golf. The walk from the airplane parking area to the clubhouse was actually shorter than it was from the automobile parking lot.

The flight up was pleasant an uneventful. After landing Simon re-iterated his distaste for that mode of transportation, recounting to the others the fiasco at Francisco Grande. He did concede that his love of golf overshadowed his fear of flying, not the trust he put in his friend's flying ability. After all there were Billy's driving habits to consider in the overall theme of safety.

Equally pleasant was the day on the links – all but the last two holes. It was then that one of those horrendous mountain thunderheads moved over the airport and dumped a copious amount of water on the foursome. In spite of that setback they stayed out to finish the round, and drenched to the

Chapter 27

bone, waddled into the clubhouse to dry off, drink, and indulge in heated arguments over equally heated topics.

Their stay in the lounge wasn't determined by their capacity for drink, but instead on the amount of time it took to dry out. Billy would not allow anybody draped in wet attire to grace the interior of his pristine airplane. The wet clothes won out. The time it took to dry out exceeded the group's capacity for liquor – albeit beer.

For the two hours while they swilled their beer in the warm lounge, they argued the law – at times using Billy as an example – and the financial market; topics of mutual interest that were represented by experts at the table. All this time, they stacked the empty beer cans in the middle of the table, in the shape of a three-dimensional pyramid, that when it was all over produced a sizable structure as well as an indication of the amount of alcohol consumed.

Then at the same time they dried out, the clouds parted, and they decided it was time to head back to Phoenix. Billy took one for the road. On the way out, the waitress expressed her incredulity at the prospect of one of them flying the airplane. She directed her comments at Charlie Henderson, who immediately pointed Billy out as the pilot. Billy who was taking it all in was certain that once again he would need Bill Simon's services at the resulting FAA hearing.

The loaded four loaded their clubs and clambered aboard. Billy set his half full (half empty?) beer can on the glare shield in front of him and started the engine. Being new with less than fifty hours on it, the engine – all 260 hp – roared to life. Billy liked the sound of it and appreciated the fact that it was new.

From the tie-down spot, the route required a sharp right turn across the parking area to access the narrow, decomposed granite taxi strip. Then it was another sharp right turn onto the strip. All around the parking area and on both sides of the taxi strip weeds and grass had grown to about three feet – maybe a little higher.

About ten feet off to the left side near the entrance to the taxi strip was a prominent sign about four feet high indicating the direction to the parking area. It was secured to a "T" post such that the upper end of the post extended six inches above the sign. If one stayed reasonably close to the center of the strip, negotiating the sign would be no problem, evidence the fact that they had no trouble with it when they taxied in.

For All The Wrong Reasons

But the two sharp turns and his state of inebriation did our hero in. He was more concerned over spilling his beer than he was with the safety of the operation. His turn from the ramp to the strip was erratic. He was focusing his attention on the beer, his right hand clutching it so it would not slide across the glare shield, or worse yet, tip over. As a result his turn was wide, so wide that the airplane's left wheel ran off the left side into the growth. Billy attempted to correct it, still trying to do two things at once, but before he could complete the turning arc necessary to get the airplane back onto the strip, he felt a jolt along with as sudden yaw to the left. The airplane came to an abrupt stop with the left wing impaled on the "T" post.

He shut the engine down and ordered everyone out. Beer still in hand, he strolled around the left side of the airplane to assess the damage. It was hideous! The top of the post had started to eat the wing with a prominent scratch on the bottom side of the forward wing spar, then proceeded to split open or gouge the aluminum skin aft of the spar, for about another foot.

The damage was more complete than one could have accomplished with an axe or at least a can opener. The reason the spar was vulnerable is because on a Bonanza the bottom of the front spar is flush with the undersurface of the wing. It appeared that the spar took the brunt of the hit, and after it passed over the top of the post, the post snapped back to the vertical, tearing the underside of the wing.

It took all of their combined effort to lift the wing high enough and then bend the "T" post over far enough for the airplane to clear it. Then they pushed the Bonanza back onto the graveled area and proceeded to inspect the damage and cogitate their next move. Billy was sobering real fast. The whole episode sickened him. He swore, on the spot, that if he succeeded in getting out of this mess, he would quit drinking.

The airplane was not airworthy, but Billy was hell bent on flying it home. He assured the others that the damage was purely cosmetic and that it was safe to go. They were too drunk to know the difference. And so away they went.

Back at Deer Valley Airport they looked it over again, thinking that maybe it wasn't as bad as it first appeared. Billy wanted to cry. The others wanted to cheer him up. So away they went to Crazy Ed's for a strategy meeting, and of course, more booze. At first, things seemed to be going downhill for Billy, but as the meeting progressed and the booze flowed, his spirits picked up.

Chapter 27

The human mind is a wonderful thing when it comes to rationalizing a bad and stupid thing into something more palatable. In this case the incident revolved from negligence on the part of Billy to unavoidable. The more they talked, the more they twisted the facts. It wasn't the beer that was the cause; it was the location of the sign. The logic of Bill Simon's legal mind came into play. The sign was too close to the taxiway. It shouldn't have been there. And then there were the weeds hiding the sign. The city should have been more prudent in keeping the landscape more closely cropped. The sign and the overgrown field were definite safety hazards. The city should be made to pay. They would sue. This called for another rounds of drinks - the reason given - to toast Bill Simon's ingenious legal mind.

Two days later, after obtaining bids for the repair, for an amount that more than covered the damage, Bill Simon in his most legalistic form sent a demand letter with all of the particulars to the mayor of Prescott. The mayor then forwarded it to the city attorney, who in turn passed it on to their insurance company.

There didn't appear to be any investigation on the part of the insurance company, unless all they did was to go to the site and observe the condition of the sign and the overgrowth surrounding it. It was obvious that they failed to interview the people in the clubhouse; otherwise they would have known what actually took place. Nor did they examine the airplane or ask for competitive bids. They merely paid the claim – in full.

The check came with a letter of apology from the city attorney. He implored them not to use the unfortunate incident as a reason for not returning to use their golf course.

Chapter 28

Billy Cotton was tired. There were too many close calls. It was getting to the point where he was beginning to confront his own mortality. Flying on the edge was no longer appealing, in fact it was getting downright scary. Besides, he was in love. It was time to settle down, get married and have children. His parents were beginning to nag the hell out of him because they wanted grandchildren.

It was during the time that the airplane was under repair for damage to the left wing panel, that he took stock of his situation. For the month that the Bonanza was down, he took the airlines back and forth from El Paso to Phoenix.

The Citabria was too slow. Besides he still had a bad taste in his mouth stemming from the bad experience with the Citabria and the weather on the early morning trip to Phoenix. So spending time waiting for his commercial flights that were seldom on time gave him plenty of opportunity to think things out.

It was the latest two scud running events that finally tipped the scales in the decision to change his life. The first one occurred on an early trip from El Paso to Phoenix. The wet, dismal weather had been hanging in for a couple days producing low ceilings, and equally low visibility. When he left Sunland Airpark in the Bonanza there was a slight drizzle.

Flight Service reported during his briefing that the weather he was observing around El Paso was destined to hang in along his route until he approached the vicinity of Phoenix. In Phoenix they were reporting slightly better ceilings and improved visibility.

It was then that he resolved to follow the southern route. Since it was light outside, in spite of the bad experience in the Citabria, he still decided to fly low over the desert to Deming then follow I-10 though Tucson and up

For All The Wrong Reasons

the valley to Phoenix.

The trip to Deming went without a hitch. But as expected, from there, the weather worsened. He continued on, staying extremely low on the interstate to Lordsburg. It was there that conditions became close to intolerable. It was also at Lordsburg that he would normally make the decision to either continue down I-10 to Tucson, or break off and head for Duncan and Safford.

Looking off to his right, he could see that he had little chance through the Safford area. All of the hills and mountains were obscured. So resigning himself to the additional thirty minutes of flying time, he continued on to Tucson, flying extremely close to the interstate. This time he knew the road didn't pass through a tunnel.

Between Lordsburg and Wilcox the weather got worse if that was possible. The elevation and thus the highway sloped up, gradually at first to Wilcox, and then more steeply to the pass at Dragoon. It was the rising terrain that was the cause for the degrading conditions. It sloped up and into the clouds.

The airport at Wilcox was located close to the freeway. He decided that when he got there he would land and wait for improving conditions instead of trying to follow the road through the Dragoon Mountains, and the Dragoon Pass that was located just east of Benson. But the visibility was so bad that he flew right by the airport without seeing it. It was only when the terrain started its increasing grade elevation, and the highway twisted around the hills that he realized his mistake.

He also concluded that due to the conditions of next to zero visibility and the proximity to the hills there was no turning room for a 180-degree turn back to Wilcox. The other alternative was to add power and climb out through the overcast to clear weather. This was out of the question because of the mountainous area around his position.

Not only was he as low as he could get on the highway, he was now in the clouds. The only ground reference that he had was a small circular area out the windshield in front of the airplane showing the right half of I-10. He overtook and passed over cars and semi-trucks, so close that he marveled at the sight of the plumes of water the trucks were throwing behind them. It was as though he was in the traffic and driving down the highway with them, only faster.

He was completely enveloped in focus and concentration. He knew that

Chapter 28

he dare not take his eyes or concentration off the small circular tunnel in front of him lest he lose his reference altogether. Then he would be gone. He was experiencing the urge to add power and climb out of there. But down deep he knew that this too would spell his demise.

The small area at the Dragoon Pass consisted of a tourist center, restaurant, service station, etc. on the south side of the highway, and a sheer rising cliff on the right. The cliff was the result of earthmovers that chopped off the side of a hill to make room for the right-of-way that defines the roadbed. Directly in front of the tourist center, just off of the right-of-way, was a tall antenna tower. The pass was over 5,000 feet high the highest on his route.

Billy couldn't have clenched his teeth any harder as he paddled his way along the freeway on the way to Dragoon. He had no idea how far ahead it was. It was impossible to tell, given his absolute concentration on the small area of visibility in front of him and his position relative to the freeway. As the road twisted and turned so did he. He needed to slow the airplane down, but he dare not. He might need the excess speed as well as the remaining power to climb out of a situation where the road might slope sharply upward. He was in deep doo-doo and he knew it.

When he finally couldn't resist the urge to give up, throw in the towel, and try to climb out of the mess, the restaurant and antenna flashed by uncomfortably close on the left. At the same time, on his right, he could actually make out the graffiti splattered all over the sheer face of the cliff that was also so close he was certain he would scrape his wing tip.

Then the road started downhill and so did Billy. To say it was a relief would have been an understatement. As he descended, out of the bottom of the clouds he went. From there it was a Sunday drive in the park. Visibility improved dramatically compared to what he had been through, and the ceilings relative to his perspective also improved.

He had the urge to land at Benson to settle his nerves, but as he approached the city, the urge passed. He felt better about the situation, so he decided to press on, resolving never to let that happen to him again. When he arrived at his destination, Crazy Ed's, he took an oath to himself that he would never attempt end-runs around weather as long as he was able to fly. He decided he wanted to live. The beer and peanuts even lost their appeal.

But before his resolve lost its appeal, he was once again called upon to pull his chestnuts out of the fire in the form of a serious encounter with a local thunderstorm east of Safford. It was once again on a trip from El Paso

For All The Wrong Reasons

to Phoenix. The weather briefing indicated nothing but clear sailing all of the way.

Just as he was passing over Duncan he observed a local thunderstorm in front of him dumping its load of rain from a black formation of clouds. He could have skirted it on either side, but he decided on an end-run around the north side to avoid playing footsies with Mount Graham. Besides, the terrain on the north side of the valley consisted only of small hills which he thought he could negotiate with ease. Little did he know at that moment, the system was moving from south to north, directly into his intended path.

It was only when he was deeply engrossed in his end-run that he realized that either new weather was forming up in front of him or the thunderstorm was moving north or both. In any case he was once again running out of maneuvering room, and he was in too deep to turn around. He was low in the hills threading his way between them, noting that their tops were obscured by clouds, and no road to follow. He wanted to stay as close to the valley floor as possible, so as he approached each small mountain he would alternate the way it was negotiated, altering his course to the left on one occasion and to the right the next time. He was always following gullies.

He kept pressing on, staying as close to the surface of the gullies and washes as he could. A driving rain obscured the forward visibility. Every time he decided on the proper course around one of the hills, it occurred to him that his decision might lead to a blind alley (box canyon.) The urge to alter his course to the north in a further attempt to skirt the weather was tempting, but common sense told Billy that there might be bigger hills in that direction, and staying as close to his original course was the best thing to do.

The situation couldn't have been worse. It was against every rule he set for himself in the art of scud running. For one thing there were no roads to follow, just washes or gullies. He knew he was in deep shit waiting for the next turn to lead him into a box canyon. Billy was getting to the point of giving up, throwing in the towel. Another urge to add full power and climb like hell out of there gripped him, but he resisted that as well, swearing to continue as long as he could.

In the course of his dilemma, Billy began to think of the consequences of straying too far to the north, especially in the dense hilly terrain. He was certain that this, his worse nightmare, would be the end. So in his convoluted reasoning, he repeated to himself, "How would they know to look for

Chapter 28

the wreckage this far off course in these remote hills?"

Suddenly it was over. He was dumped out on the west side of the system. Still in the hills, Billy immediately altered his course to the valley floor where he once again took up a heading to Phoenix. In front of him the weather was clear all the way. It was hard to believe the drastic contrast between what he had been through and what lay ahead.

He looked back at the storm and saw that if he had negotiated it around the south side, there would have been no trouble. There was a wide area of clear between his course and Mount Graham. The system had been moving north and in front of him all of the time.

He was pissed off, frustrated, and tired. The gods had pushed him too far. This had to be the final straw. He wanted to go straight but they wouldn't let him. He was for sure going to turn over a new leaf both in the way he flew airplanes and in his personal conduct as well.

Wanting to live took on several twists to the way Billy ran his life. For one thing he quit whoring around. To the chagrin of his asshole buddies, he gave up combining alcohol and airplanes. They soon declared that he was no longer any fun. Then he flew only when the cards of fate were stacked in his favor. Billy rightfully figured that there was no place he had to be that couldn't wait for him to travel on his terms. After all, he was successful financially, and the work and money continued to pour in whether he participated or not. Then there was this girl. He was for the first time in his life in love.

Her name was Susan. She was a project manager for one of the commercial developers with whom he did business. The relationship started out simple enough from business meetings to lunch at the Mesa Street Bar and Grill. As far as Billy was concerned, she was just a future lay. But as he soon learned, she was different. Unlike most of the other women with whom he surrounded himself, she had morals. The more she resisted him the more he wanted her. He was gradually becoming hooked.

Susan was young, classy looking if not downright beautiful, and above all smart and self-sufficient. She didn't need him. She always had more than enough suitors pounding at her door. In fact he needed her more than she needed him. If he had to write a specification for the woman with whom he could spend the rest of his life, and whom he thought should bear his children, she was it.

He still wanted to get in her pants. His sex drive and his desires for her

For All The Wrong Reasons

body had nothing to do with her other distracting qualities. He wined and dined her to weaken her resolve, but to no avail. She imbibed only in moderation. She had been through it all, and from experience knew how to cope with the likes of Billy Cotton.

She was of the Catholic persuasion. Unlike Billy she was devout. They compared their younger more impressionable years especially where it concerned the parochial schools they both attended. He recounted his experiences during his grammar school education in particular where it concerned his exposure to the nuns and how they inflicted corporal punishment on him every time he got cross-wise with them or the ridiculous rules they imposed.

The method of choice was a strap a left over segment of a used conveyor belt that when applied to the palms of the hands left indelible marks not only on the hands, but on the individual's psyche for a long time, if not for the rest of his life, as in the case of Billy Cotton. To give an idea of the severity of the punishment, he explained that fighting with a classmate warranted five cracks on each palm.

He went on to explain the nun's idea concerning venial and mortal sins and how the best one could expect, was a term in the fiery place called purgatory, but more like hell if you committed a mortal sin by missing church on Sunday. He explained that it was this early upbringing under the influence of the nuns that caused his separation from the Church.

Her early upbringing was more favorable. She was born and raised in El Paso and attended St. Mary's Academy. The nun's treatment of her was diametrically opposite to that which Billy described. There was no corporal punishment only tender loving care. They were taught that if you were good you went to heaven. The way heaven was described was motivation enough for Susan to conduct herself in a stellar way. One of the "good" ways the good Sisters professed was to save "it" until marriage. And she stressed to Billy, this is exactly what she was going to do.

If he thought by telling her of his early experience with the nuns would culminate in drawing out her maternal instincts, and thus sympathy, he was wrong. Her only reaction was to try convincing him to take up the religious route with her and experience the changes in the Church. If he wanted her, then this was the price he would have to pay as one step in the process of proving himself worthy.

Because of Susan, he spent more of his weekends in El Paso. They con-

Chapter 28

tinued to date as frequently as possible, and lunched on the occasions when their mutual business interests coincided. Since she made her views on sex known from the outset, he made no outward attempt to get her into bed. Then as he grew fonder of her, he was more motivated in treating her with the respect she deserved, not because he was forewarned but because he didn't want to hurt her.

Then they got downright serious. It was only after she was convinced that he had shed all of his vices and promised his undivided devotion to her that she allowed him to get intimate. He found out for the first time that sex with somebody you loved and cared about was many times better than doing it for fun with somebody with whom he had little or no respect. It was more than an exercise in fun to satisfy a conquest, it was more like a ritual to be shared with the special person, and designed to reinforce the love each has for the other. He was for the first time in his adult life sincere, deeply in love, faithful, and concerned about his future, a future that included the rest of his life with her and the children they would have.

Even with his devotion to her, he was still reluctant to participate in the church thing. Susan, being a devout Catholic, set the requirement as an ultimatum, a mild one, but still an ultimatum. They had many discussions concerning his distaste for the Church, and even included the pastor of her church in on the discussions. He reiterated to the good padre his grammar school experiences with the good sisters, and how when he went out on his own to taste the good life, pooh-poohed their ideas once and for all.

The good padre assured him that the dogma that caused his childhood aberrations no longer held with the Church. One wasn't automatically doomed to purgatory if they died in their sleep. Nor were any of the other restrictions that he was held to, in effect. He might even find the tenants of the Church appealing if he would only give them a chance.

Billy would settle for nothing short of an apology, something that the padre was more than willing to give if it meant another notch in his record of conversions. The deal was struck. The padre gave himself credit for saving a lost sheep, and Billy knew down deep that he was only going along for Susan's sake. For her he would do anything. From the padre's standpoint, now with that chore behind him, he could once again concentrate his efforts on the altar boys.

They made plans for a trip to Phoenix to visit his family. He was sure that they would approve of her, especially if they all attended mass together.

For All The Wrong Reasons

Better yet, they should spend Christmas with them and attend midnight mass together. Of course they would have to sleep in separate rooms given the traditional attitude of his parents. So he set it up with his folks who wholeheartedly agreed and began immediately to make plans for it. Susan and Billy were also making their plans by vigorously shopping for lavish gifts. The lavishness was on the part of Susan who was naturally insecure, so was making an additional effort for acceptance into the family.

Chapter 29

On December 23rd, the day they were to leave, events affecting Susan, delayed their departure. They had planned to leave immediately after work, but last minute decisions involving one of her projects and the resulting extended meetings kept her at the office until after six. It was already dark. Originally they argued about whether to use the Bonanza or make the trip via airlines. Billy opted for the air carrier, but Susan thought their schedule would be more flexible by using the company airplane. Besides, she thought it would be more exiting if Billy was the pilot. Furthermore there were too many packages to make airline service practical. Now because of her disrupted schedule, Susan was glad that they had decided to use the Bonanza.

At seven o'clock they were in the airplane and ready to go. The weather in Phoenix was good but there was a system between Deming and Globe. Billy thought that he could go the regular route if he flew high enough in the weather to clear Mount Graham. In any case, there would be no more scud running. It would take 11,000 feet to be safely over the mountain.

He would just maintain his heading of 280 degrees and stay on the instruments. He had to do it this way if he wanted to fly the shorter route because there were no navigational aids along the route except for the Deming and Phoenix VOR's. He would home in on the Deming VOR and after passing over the top would track out on the 280 degree radial until he lost the signal, which would be around the continental divide north of Lordsburg.

He planned to maintain that heading until he came within striking distance of Phoenix. Then he would pick up the Phoenix VOR and complete his trip. Hopefully, by that time the weather would have cleared, and he would be able to let down visually into Deer Valley. It was simple and much better than scud running.

He didn't feel the need to file an instrument flight plan (IFR) as most of

For All The Wrong Reasons

the route was in uncontrolled airspace. Besides, he was too much in a hurry to mess with the Flight Service Station. It was against his religion to do so anyway.

They took-off and climbed out without incident. He chose a lower altitude to Deming because none of the terrain was above 5,000 feet. After leaving the Deming VOR he started a cruise climb at 200 feet per minute on his way to 11,000 feet. He had thirty minutes to get there so he was in no hurry. What he didn't realize was that he had an unexpected and substantial tailwind as he climbed out of the Deming area. That and the high airspeed he was maintaining during his climb would put him over Safford earlier than he estimated. Under normal circumstances this situation would be inconsequential, but in this case it was important that Billy knew where he was at all times. And without a VOR to navigate by, he could only estimate.

Ordinarily it was boring flying in the clouds. But Billy's workload under these conditions in the Bonanza was inordinately high. For one thing the autopilot hadn't worked since right after he bought the airplane. Then there was the directional gyro. He had to reset it frequently to the magnetic compass because of its higher than normal precession rate. While resetting it he had to be sure that the airplane was level and steady as the magnetic compass was out of fluid and would drag in the case giving erroneous readings, when in any attitude but level and smooth flight. Expecting reliability in the instrument in turbulent conditions was out of the question.

It was only a two-hour flight, one and a half hours in the clouds under instrument conditions. So with a little patience he could endure. Not being a frequent flyer, Susan took it all in good faith that Billy knew what he was doing and that everything was normal. He explained to her, "It was strictly routine." She took his word for it. She was just happy to be going to Phoenix to meet her future family.

Then twenty-five minutes out of Deming, when Billy thought he was in the vicinity of Duncan, he ran head-on into severe icing conditions, something he wouldn't have encountered if he was scud running. In reality, his position was over Safford if not slightly beyond. This misestimate was due to the unexpected tailwind. The sudden surge of ice felt and sounded like a gravel truck had suddenly dumped its load on the front of the airplane, including the windshield.

The ice kept building. Before long he found he was unable to hold 11,000 feet. He desperately needed something to home in on. He reached over to

Chapter 29

the side pocket and pulled out an out-of-date regional chart which was the only chart he had. The closest VOR that could be picked up from that location was San Simon, a navigational aid located just east of Wilcox along Interstate 10.

Thinking that Mount Graham was ahead and to his left, he tuned his radio to the San Simon VOR, turned the airplane to the appropriate heading, and started to home in on that station. He was certain that at a lower altitude, he could shed the ice and either land at Wilcox or continue on to Tucson depending on the cloud ceilings. Another scan of the chart indicated that there was no terrain of significance in his way. But he was actually over Safford and not Duncan, with Mount Graham directly between his position and Wilcox.

In one regard he was right. At 10,000 feet the airplane began to shed the ice. He could actually see out of the windshield, for what little comfort it gave him, because all there was to see was a black sea of fog. But in spite of still being in the soup, he was beginning to feel better about his situation. He glanced over at Susan and was pleased that she appeared in a relaxed state, unconcerned and oblivious to the dilemma that Billy got her into.

Although still in the clouds, he was still in control. The frequency of the San Simon VOR was dialed into the radio, the omni-bearing selector (OBS) was adjusted so its needle hung in the center where it should be, and the airplane appeared stable at 9,500 feet. He was unconcerned about the accuracy of the direction gyro or the magnetic compass, for as long as he kept the OBS needle in the center of the instrument he would eventually end up over the top of the San Simon VOR, where he planned on spiraling down until he broke out of the clouds. Then he could decide whether to fly I-10 to Tucson or land at Wilcox, check into a motel, get laid, and a good night's rest, not necessarily in that order, and continue on the next day in more favorable conditions. He felt good about his plan.

Once again he glanced over in Susan's direction and was happy that she was unaware of the grave situation he had just put them through. As he looked at her, a surge of warmth overtook him when he realized more than ever how much he cared for her. At that moment he vowed to himself that he would never again put her life in jeopardy.

It was when he shifted his gaze away from her and back to the business at hand that he saw it. It was a huge extra black shape that loomed up in front of the airplane. He sensed immediately what it was and accordingly

For All The Wrong Reasons

jerked back on the control wheel with favorable results. As fast as it appeared, it likewise vanished. But no sooner than he gave a sigh of relief the mountain once again reared its ugly head.

This time when he horsed back on the wheel the stall-warning horn sounded. He could literally see trees rushing up in front of the airplane as it mushed forward in a full stall. The next thing Billy became aware of was a snapping sound as the airplane took out the top of one of the pine trees, yawing slightly in the process. Like an animal groaning in its final death throws, the Bonanza slowed and settled, clobbering two more trees on its way to the ground. Control of the airplane had gone with the first impact.

During the process of destroying the airplane, Billy's mind instinctively raced with the events. It was all happening very fast, but to Billy it was in slow motion. In his thoughts he was surprised that the jolts weren't as hard and sudden as he would have expected. In fact the trip to the ground from the first impact appeared to Billy to be reasonably soft, not much worse than a bad landing. The difference between the reality of the events and his perception was nature's way of shielding the poor ignorant fool from the severity of crash.

Then everything was dark and eerily quiet. He sniffed the air for tell tale signs of smoke. There was none, which meant no fire. For that he was grateful. He stared down at the instrument panel as if to obtain an inspiration or an idea. There was nothing, no panel lights or noises indicating gyros unwinding. This struck him as odd. He concluded that he must have been sitting there longer than he thought; perhaps he was stunned by the impact or momentarily knocked out. Groping around Billy cycled the master switch for some sign of life. Then he went for the radio to see if it worked. Nothing; everything was dead.

He then reached across Susan to unlatch the door and became alarmed when he noticed she was slumped over and moaning. He lifted her head and asked her if she was all right. She nodded in the affirmative. There was this urgency to get them both out of the airplane, so he scurried over the top of her, opened the door and scrambled out onto the wing panel. Once out there, he turned around, unbuckled her seat belt, and pulled her out. Her right leg was either broken or badly sprained at the knee. As gently as he could he maneuvered her out on the wing and lay her down. It was then that Billy realized just how cold it really was.

Cold, dark, and foggy was all he could make out when he surveyed the

Chapter 29

area from his perch, except a blanket of snow that surrounded them, and the broken hulk of what used to be an airplane. Despair set in. He had to do something, so he decided to scrutinize the area, but when he stepped off the wing, it was into snow three feet deep. It surprised him, and as a result he stumbled and fell head long into the stuff. At least it was dry and powdery and not the wet variety, so getting wet from the experience was not a factor.

Walking in the snow in the dark was next to impossible, so he climbed back onto the wing panel to be with and to attend to Susan. There they both rested, he in a sitting position, she lying down, while they collected their thoughts and assessed their fate.

Susan wondered out loud how long it would be before help arrived. Billy ignored the question, too embarrassed to admit that he didn't file a flight plan, and therefore it could be two days before his folks reported them missing and a search initiated. How about a signal fire? They had plenty of fuel to keep it going. But once again it occurred to him that he came unprepared. He had no matches.

As he considered other options, the extreme cold gripped him. He checked Susan. She was lying there in a passive state. Billy wondered if she was going into shock. He had to do something, and it had better be quick.

Then he hit on an idea at last. As gently as he could he helped her climb into the back seat of the Bonanza and closed the door. To keep them both warm as possible they huddled together. But it was still very cold. Billy then realized that if he could retrieve the suitcases from the baggage compartment, they could both add layers of clothing to their bodies.

He took the key from the ignition switch and climbed out of the airplane and off the trailing edge of the wing to the baggage compartment door. He was having a lot of trouble getting to and opening the door in the dark. As he fumbled with the key, Billy confronted another goof. There was no flashlight on board. Here he was stripped of the essentials for survival with the only woman he truly cared for.

"Was this poetic justice?" He asked another question that began to haunt him. "Is it time to start praying?" He continued to struggle in the dark until he finally got the door opened, and threw everything that was inside out onto the wing, Christmas presents and all. By then his hands were so cold they were numb. Finally a positive turn of events, the boxes contained sweaters and bathrobes.

Back on the wing Billy emptied the boxes and suitcases throwing the

For All The Wrong Reasons

contents onto the front seat. From there he sorted through the garments, passing most of the effective ones back to Susan. Cold to the bone, exhausted and breathless from his effort at the high altitude, he crawled into the back seat with her, and covered them both the best he could. Then he advised that they should try to get as much sleep as possible. There wasn't much they could do in the dark anyway, and the dawn of the next day would produce the light necessary to engage in some lifesaving strategy.

It was a bad night. Cramped as they were, sleep was next to impossible. Billy was troubled by the condition Susan was in. Since the accident she had communicated with him hardly at all. He wasn't able to draw her out even when it concerned her injuries. He wondered if she wasn't hurt worse than the knee injury. There was no way to tell.

Before dawn the clouds went away and a partial moon lit up the area somewhat. Billy decided to climb out of the airplane, survey the area and take stock of their situation. The first thing he noticed as he peered around was the sea of lights in the valley on the north side from what he deduced as the lights of Safford. They looked so close, but in reality he estimated them to be twenty or thirty miles away, and 6,000 feet below them. From his position he thought it would be an easy hike out of there for help. But first things first, he had to pee.

Then as it got lighter, he began to feel more optimistic about their situation and climbed back into the airplane to report his findings to his fiancée and further assess her injuries. He thought that his favorable report would open her up to talking. And it did somewhat. What she finally disclosed was that other than her knee she was in good shape. She did confide that she thought they were going to die. He recommended that she get out of the airplane and move around a bit. She agreed.

He helped her out and onto the wing. She couldn't put weight on her right leg, let alone walk on it. He helped her off the wing and into the snow bank. For her, maneuvering in that much snow in her condition was next to impossible. He asked her if she had to relieve herself and when she nodded he cleared a three-foot wide area next to the airplane. Vigorously stomping around and packing the snow down accomplished this.

Then he had a plan. He would start a fire using the wrapping paper soaked in gasoline, and a spark generated from the battery terminals. But once again the fickle finger of fate dealt him a bad hand. He had no screwdriver to unlatch the cowling that contained the battery. And even if he had

Chapter 29

one, there were no wrenches available to remove the cables from the battery posts. He could even get around that obstacle if he could find a lead wire to short circuit the terminals. This might be possible by ripping out existing wire from one of the systems.

Now, the immediate problem was how to twist the Dzus fasteners that secured the cowling. In lieu of a screwdriver, he could use a knife or a small coin. A coin he had. Again his spirits soared. Using a dime accomplished the feat. Once the fasteners were twisted, Billy pried and pulled on the cowling doors until he managed to expose the battery box. But what he found discouraged him again. The engine was twisted in the motor mount to the extent that the right rear cylinder impacted the battery box smashing the battery and leaking its fluid all over the ground. There would be no spark today. This he rationalized, explained why the electrical system was dead when he first tried to activate the radio.

He could try the old boy scout method of rubbing two sticks together. But there were no visible signs of any firewood in the area. Everything combustible, except the airplane, was buried in the thick blanket of snow. By now Billy was depressed. It was worse than that, his clothes had gotten wet and were beginning to freeze. He started to wonder if this was the way it was all going to end. Then he looked over at Susan and swore to save her life.

They spent the rest of the day trying to figure out how to get out of the mess in which Billy put them. By the end of the day the lower part of their bodies were wet. They both agreed that their wet lower extremities, under the circumstances, posed a dangerous condition. They would have to take special precautions to stay as dry as possible. On the positive side, the weather had cleared and the sun was out. But even this fact wasn't all that encouraging, because they were on the North Slope and in the shade all of the time.

By nightfall Billy discussed the possibility of walking out to Safford for help, leaving Susan behind with the airplane. He wasn't going to wait for the possibility of being found and rescued. They retreated to the back seat of the Bonanza, covered their huddled bodies with as much fabric as they could for warmth, and discussed a plan Billy was formulating for their survival. Susan would go along with anything he decided as long it was a plan that would get her out of there. It was another long and restless night. They were both extremely cramped and cold, and her knee was throbbing

For All The Wrong Reasons

with pain.

By early the next morning, Billy was preparing to embark on the long journey to Safford. He would leave behind every piece of fabric or clothing, except his light jacket, for Susan to use against the cold. As a last minute thought, Susan asked Billy to retrieve a note pad and pen from his briefcase so she could maintain a diary of the events. It would be more of an exercise to keep her occupied than it was for a historical record. She was still confident that he would return with help within a couple of days.

As Billy started down the mountain, he realized that the loafers he was wearing were a poor substitute for hiking boots. His feet and legs were wet and to some extent ice had formed on his pant leg. His feet were so wet and cold that soon after he started out he lost all feeling in them

He was trying to move as quickly as possible, wanting to get to Safford before nightfall and as a consequence stumbled or fell in the deep snowdrifts that hampered his way. In spite of all his efforts, progress was very slow. By the end of the day, as daylight diminished, he concluded by sighting on Safford, that he had traveled only a short part of the way. Due to the extra hazard of moving in the dark, he considered stopping and resting for the night, but thought that if he was careful he could still continue on. He further concluded that resting for even a short time, his members might seize preventing him from getting back up, and as a result could freeze to death on the spot.

But traveling in the dark was more difficult than he imagined. There were more hidden hazards with which he was unable to cope. With almost every step he slipped and fell in the deep snow. On one occasion he sprained his ankle. But as able as he could, he continued on. After traveling half the night, focusing on the light of Safford, he was so exhausted and cold that he had no choice but to lie down and rest. Opportunity presented itself in the form of a spot underneath an overhang that was relatively free of snow, so he took it.

As he lay in the meager shelter of the overhang, taking stock of the situation, he reached down to remove his shoes for the purpose of massaging his feet. He thought that this might bring the much-needed feeling back to them. But what he saw alarmed him. He had lost one of his shoes. It must have happened when he fell in one of the extra-deep snowdrifts. Should he retrace his tracks in an attempt to retrieve it? No, he must get up and continue down the mountain at any cost. He had Susan to consider. But he

Chapter 29

was too tired to go on.

Now his thoughts were directed more and more toward Susan and her welfare. It was the only thing that could keep him going. He didn't care anymore about his predicament. His only concern was with saving her life. He was tempted to try to return to the airplane to be with her, "Till death do us part." But now, even getting up was an insurmountable feat. He was finally in the throws of confronting his fate, the fickle finger of fate.

Billy was now unaware of how long he lay there under the overhang. He only knew that he was no longer cold. In fact for the first time since the crash he felt warm, comfortable, and even sleepy. Maybe if he did sleep a bit, he could regain enough of his strength to continue on. But down deep he knew better. This was to be the place where he would die, his final resting place. He knew that if he did go to sleep he would not wake up, so he resisted the urge as long as he could, waiting for the sun to come up.

It has been said that in your final hours, your whole life flashes before your eyes. In Billy's case it was the philosophical portion of his life that was in his thoughts. He finally understood what the "good sisters" were trying to tell him. This, and not the often-described fiery place, was purgatory.

The mental anguish was more than he could endure. The physical pain was now nonexistent. But knowing that the only person in his life that he most cared for was alone, and like him, slowly freezing to death, gave meaning to his suffering. God was going to punish him for his passed indiscretions by taking her away from him. He screamed out to God, using his name in vain, and even cursing obscenities in his frustration for relief, and when that didn't bring satisfaction, turned to Satan himself, offering to sell his soul to save his Susan. He was serious. He would do anything to guarantee her survival.

It wasn't fair. All his life he lived on the edge, dangerously and carefree, but now, just when he had reformed and straightened his life out, the fickle finger of fate was about to do him in. Was this what they called poetic justice?

In this situation Susan would have discouraged him from being so cynical. She would have counseled him to instead make peace with their Lord and ask forgiveness for the sins of his past, instead of making demands and cursing Him. But at this time survival was not a consideration for him as it was for Susan. He didn't care for his own well-being. If he could only get through the ordeal facing them and get help back to her, he would gladly end his life. So asking for absolution was not an option. It would be hypocritical. He journeyed through his entire life on his own, without prayer or divine help; he certainly was not going to be a hypocrite now for his own salvation. His only motive for surviving was for Susan.

Billy carried on in his delirious state until the light of dawn broke in the east. He mustered all of his remaining strength and stood up one more time to start the remainder of his trek down the mountain. He still had absolutely no sensation in his legs and feet, his hands were numb. He was surviving and continuing on sheer determination and willpower. He was walking on what felt like wooden stumps.

He went on, one small step at a time for almost an hour. The temperature was well below zero, but that meant nothing to Billy. Then he fell for the last time, not to get up again. He was too exhausted and sleepy. In his mind, he would stay down and rest some more.

Billy closed his eyes and decided to sleep. It came immediately after he resigned himself. He was peaceful and finally comfortable. In a semi-state he dreamed of his family, friends, and Susan. These images became distant as he drifted deeper into unconsciousness. Billy was on his way to meeting his maker.

Epilogue

The following June a logger was driving his truck along the rough gravel road that traveled along the top of Mount Graham. He felt the urge to relieve himself so he stopped the truck and walked to the edge that coincidentally overlooked the valley to the north, in particular toward Safford.

As his bladder emptied, he scanned the area down the slope to the north marveling at the view when he observed the glitter of a metallic object reflecting the sunlight. It appeared to be about 200 feet from where he stood and slightly downhill. He was intrigued and curious enough about the strange sighting that he was motivated to take the short hike down to investigate. He mumbled to himself, as he zipped up his pants, something to the effect that nothing exciting ever happens to him and he would give just about anything to stumble on the wreckage of a flying saucer.

As he progressed down the rough terrain, he could make out the shape of an airplane. His first impression was that it didn't appear to be badly damaged. For this reason he felt compelled to call out, half expecting someone to appear from the surrounding trees or from the inside of the airplane. There was no reply. The scene was very still and quiet.

As the logger approached the airplane, he noticed that the cabin door was open, so he climbed onto the wing and poked his head inside. All he could make out was scattered clothing, shredded upholstery, and several suitcases randomly situated in and about the fuselage.

Then he discovered the dreaded gruesome sight of a skull, bones and bone fragments scattered about the area. He panicked, scurried back up the slope to his truck, and drove off as fast as he could for help.

They all came, the Sheriff, Highway Patrol, and Park Rangers and not to be denied, the CAP (Civil Air Patrol). They did their thing which was mostly interfering with each other. The most valuable find was a detailed diary of Susan's final days, written out on eight and a half by eleven-note pad. The final entry was dated January 14. There was no telling how much longer she lived. The officials determined that after she succumbed, the animals got to her, devoured her remains, and scattered her bones around the area in the process.

In her narrative, Susan described, as well as she was able, the trip, the crash, and the short time she and Billy stayed with the airplane, and his decision to hike out in the direction of Safford. After he left for help, she mentioned that she spent most of her time in the airplane because of the difficulty moving about on her bad leg, and the extremely cold conditions she had to endure. She went on to describe three snowstorms, each of which blanketed the airplane, and her frustrations to keep a path cleared for her to exit the airplane from time to time.

The troops, after studying her narrative, sent out a search party to find Billy's remains. It was only 500 feet down the side of the mountain that they discovered his lost shoe. From there a week of fruitless searching failed to find what remained of Billy Cotton. To this day he still rests somewhere on the north slope of Mount Graham, perhaps half way down.

It was a sad thing to behold. They speculated that if only he had ventured in the opposite direction, up the hill instead of down, he might have chanced on the logging road and walked out on a better surface. Billy had more than once conjectured to his friends that if he ever "bought the farm" it would be the Fickle Finger of Fate that would do him in.

ORDER FORM

Clip and send bottom of form with check or money order to:

Billville Press
87130 Muirland Dr.
Veneta, OR 97487

(541) 935-3223
(541) 935-1832 fax

Hardbound books are $29.95 plus $3.95 shipping and handling.
Soft bound books are $21.95 plus $3.95 shipping and handling.

ORDERED BY: Name_____

Address: _____

City, State, Zip:_____

Phone:_____

Shipping address if different from above:

Name:_____

Address:_____

City, State, Zip:_____

Please allow 2 weeks for delivery.

Thank you

ORDER FORM

Clip and send bottom of form with check or money order to:

Billville Press
87130 Muirland Dr.
Veneta, OR 97487

(541) 935-3223
(541) 935-1832 fax

Hardbound books are $29.95 plus $3.95 shipping and handling.
Soft bound books are $21.95 plus $3.95 shipping and handling.

ORDERED BY: Name_____

Address: _____

City, State, Zip:_____

Phone:_____

Shipping address if different from above:

Name:_____

Address:_____

City, State, Zip:_____

Please allow 2 weeks for delivery.

Thank you

Bill Robinet started flying in 1948 and has remained an active pilot for more than 50 years. He is a Registered Professional Engineer, Certified Flight Instructor, Aircraft Mechanic and holds an Inspection Authorization. He is also the author of ***By The Skin Of My Teeth, A Cropduster's Story.***